MEN AND POWER
1917-1918

The heights by great men reached and kept
Were not attained by sudden flight,
But they, while their companions slept,
Were toiling upward in the night.

LLOYD GEORGE, pictured here with Haig and Joffre. "Were these glittering commands to be entrusted to mediocrities, bred with obsolete tactics, and mouldering in military routine?"

LORD BEAVERBROOK

MEN

and

POWER

1917   1918

DUELL, SLOAN and PEARCE
NEW YORK

CONTENTS

v

CONTENTS

Appendices

ILLUSTRATIONS

ILLUSTRATIONS

BIOGRAPHIES

I remember—

ADDISON, Rt. Hon. Christopher

M.P. for Hoxton Division, Shoreditch, since 1910, in 1917 Addison was forty-eight years of age. He was married and had two young sons and two daughters.

Educated at Trinity College, Harrogate, and St. Bartholomew's Hospital, he was a doctor of medicine.

He was attractive in conversation, but not generally popular, though he grew in public favour through the years. His achievements in politics far outstripped his performance in medicine. Several doctors have received peerages, but only Addison could claim the Garter, an honour usually reserved for Members of the Royal Family, acquiescent aristocrats, and retiring Prime Ministers.

In 1917 he was one of Lloyd George's principal supporters. He fell out with Lloyd George soon after the war, and resigned from his Ministry. He joined the Socialist Party, becoming in time Leader of the House of Lords.

AMERY, Leopold Stennett

M.P. for South Birmingham and forty-four years of age in 1917, Amery was married to a sister of Sir Hamar Greenwood, M.P., and had one young son.

He had been educated at Harrow and Balliol College, Oxford, where he obtained a first-class degree. He was a Fellow of All Souls. He did not get a place in the Government until after the war.

A member of Lloyd George's Secretariat, although a militant Conservative, he was a warm supporter of the Prime Minister during the war. He held strong views, especially on Empire affairs.

He was a good writer, though dull. Earnest in conversation, he was active in expressing his opinions and always sincere and sure of himself. Short in stature and pugnacious by temperament, he was given to making long speeches. He was generally trusted, but never reached public popularity.

In 1917 he was Assistant Secretary to the War Cabinet.

BIOGRAPHIES

ASQUITH, Rt. Hon. Herbert Henry

M.P. for East Fife, Asquith was sixty-five years of age in 1917. He had been married twice. His first marriage was at the age of twenty-four to Helen Melland of Manchester, a match within his own social class; then he married into the fashionable world. His second wife was Margaret (Margot), the youngest daughter of Sir Charles Tennant's first marriage. In 1917 he had six children, his eldest having been killed in action. Three other sons also served in the war.

Educated at the City of London School, he won a scholarship at the age of seventeen to Balliol College, Oxford. There he had a distinguished record; he obtained first classes in classical moderations and in literae humaniores, and was awarded the Craven scholarship. And in 1874 he was elected a Fellow of Balliol.

Aloof in the House, yet recognised as its greatest Member, he venerated the Sovereign and received Royal attentions with gratitude.

His friends were devoted to him. In his leisure hours he was at his best in mixed company. He gave much time to conversation, companionship and social pursuits. For recreation he played bridge, chess and golf. He wrote letters in his own hand, with vivid accounts of his colleagues.

He repeated at intervals certain cycles of stories. If his attention was directed to a portrait of Charles James Fox he made the same remarks.

Asquith resigned as Prime Minister and First Lord of the Treasury in 1916, when the second Coalition Government was formed under Lloyd George. He never held office again.

BALDWIN, Stanley

M.P. for the Bewdley Division of Worcestershire since 1908 and fifty years of age in 1917, Stanley Baldwin was married, with two sons and four daughters. He had been educated at Harrow and Trinity College, Cambridge. His eldest son was serving in the war; his second son was too young.

He was stout and sturdy, pipe-smoking frequently, and then rubbing the bowl of his pipe on his nose, possibly to polish it (the pipe).

His home life was happy, and he had a passion for a mechanical piano-player. A contented middle-class millionaire, he was not widely read, but he had literary associations and would stroll round his library, picking up a volume at random and reading out those passages which caught his eye. His simple jokes endeared him to his friends, and he was much liked and greatly respected.

Up to the outbreak of war he showed not the slightest trace of political push or ambition. He had given no sign of his great oratorical talents and immense political prescience. He was busy with the directorships of various important companies. His contemporaries regarded him as a man of affairs who had all the characteristics of a country squire. His conversation turned on the beauty of the mountain rose, and the splendour of hawthorn buds in spring.

In 1917 he began to ascend the political ladder; he had placed a foot on the first rung when he became Bonar Law's Joint Financial Secretary to the Treasury. His appointment was due to no past performance, but to the fact that he was rich enough to entertain among Members of Parliament, and popular enough to win friends for himself and for his chief.

On attaining to Junior office his character changed. Ambition marked him. Thereafter came a steady development of growing powers.

BALFOUR, Rt. Hon. Arthur James

M.P. for the City of London in 1917, Balfour was a bachelor of sixty-nine years of age. He had been educated at Eton and Trinity College, Cambridge.

Tall, slim and good-looking, like Asquith he was much admired. His intimate friends were few in number, and it is just possible that he didn't believe in anything or anybody. Asquith described him as a man of "superficial charm". Others considered that his outstanding quality was his political cunning. He was, in fact, a crafty man. During the peace conference in Paris in 1919 Clemenceau used to speak of him as 'cette vieille fille'.

Dominating the House of Commons, although an indifferent speaker, he would often hesitate as though searching for a word or phrase—but he was not really doing so. He addressed his colleagues in familiar terms, but in correspondence and conversation they frequently addressed him as Mr. Balfour.

Deposed from the leadership of the Conservative Party in November 1911, he retained membership of the Committee of Imperial Defence. He worked with Asquith's Government from the outbreak of the war, although never separating himself from his Conservative colleagues. In Asquith's First Coalition Government of May, 1915, Balfour became First Lord of the Admiralty. He was Secretary of State for Foreign Affairs in Lloyd George's Ministry in 1916, until after the war ended.

BEAVERBROOK, 1st Baron (William Maxwell Aitken)

M.P. for Ashton-under-Lyne until his *relegation* to the peerage in 1916, Lord Beaverbrook was thirty-eight years of age in 1917. He was married, with two young sons and one daughter, and was living at the Hyde Park Hotel.

He had been educated at the Government School, Newcastle, New Brunswick.

In 1915 he was a Lieutenant-Colonel in the Canadian Army and in charge of Canadian War Records. Next year he was Canadian Government Representative to the Army Overseas.

In 1918 he became Chancellor of the Duchy of Lancaster and Minister of Information in Lloyd George's Government. He was the youngest and most inexperienced member of the Administration.

BRADE, Sir Reginald Herbert

Fifty-three years of age in 1917, Sir Reginald Brade was married with no children.

Educated at St. Andrews College, Bradfield, he was Secretary of the War Office.

See page 44.

CARSON, Rt. Hon. Sir Edward Henry

M.P. for Dublin University since 1892 and sixty-three years of age in 1917, Carson had been married twice. He had by his first marriage two sons serving in the war, and two daughters.

A graduate of Trinity College, Dublin, he was a loyal Ulster leader. He was a clever lawyer and a rebellious politician. His admirers believed to be clever is good, but to be rebellious is splendid.

He had an intensely emotional nature, which was nurtured by the vast crowds attending on his public appearances.

Carson spoke slowly and he had a melodious voice. His speeches were easy to hear, but difficult to read.

For nearly four years he held the issues of civil peace or civil war in his hands. He was First Lord of the Admiralty until July, 1917, when he became a member of the War Cabinet.

CECIL, Rt. Hon. Lord (Edgar Algernon) Robert (Gascoyne-)

M.P. for Hitchin, Lord Robert Cecil was fifty-three years of age in 1917. The third son of the third Marquis of Salisbury, he was married, but had no children.

Educated at Eton and University College, Oxford, he had studied law.

Highly respected and greatly admired for sturdy qualities of character, his habits were all good. He was a Free Trade member of a Tariff Party. His chief political interest was the Church.

Minister of Blockade and Under Secretary of State for Foreign Affairs in 1917, he was appointed Assistant Secretary of State for Foreign Affairs in July, 1918.

CHAMBERLAIN, Sir (Joseph) Austen

M.P. for Birmingham since 1914 and fifty-four years of age in 1917, Austen Chamberlain was married, with two young sons and one daughter. He had been educated at Rugby and Trinity College, Cambridge.

About him gathered glowing affections; there were no hatreds. He was trusted and respected and he always told the truth, rare gifts for a man born to public affairs. Lord Birkenhead said of him: "Austen always played the game, and he always lost it."

Since 1915 Chamberlain had held the appointment of Secretary of State for India. He resigned in July, 1917, returning again to the War Cabinet in 1918.

BIOGRAPHIES

CHURCHILL, Rt. Hon. Winston (Leonard Spencer)

M.P. for Dundee and forty-three years of age in 1917, Winston Churchill was married, with three young children, and living at 41 Cromwell Road, S.W.

He had been educated at Harrow and Sandhurst. By 1917 he had won for himself a considerable reputation as a writer. His biography of Lord Randolph Churchill was acclaimed as a masterpiece. Although he had begun to paint, he had not yet received recognition as an artist. He was in this year of decision the most astonishing and the most remarkable of all the Ministers.

His conversation was pleasing, his companionship was exciting. He had no rancour and few hatreds.

He was in every sense a professional politician, having trained himself for his vocation. Impetuous in action, he was determined when resisting opposition.

He sang the popular music-hall melodies in a raucous voice, and without any instinct for tune. His bridge, which he played occasionally, was exceedingly careless, and his card sense almost non-existent.

He lived well, and ate everything. He exaggerated his drinking habits by his own remarks in praise of wine and brandy. He appeared to smoke cigars incessantly. Not at all. He smoked very little, although relighting a cigar frequently. His use of matches outstripped his consumption of cigars.

Throughout the war of 1914–18 he was involved in political storms and tempests. He tried only to do the right thing, but occasionally in the wrong way. Critics frequently found fault with him through prejudice and without reason. He had no friends in the Tory Party. Many Liberals believed that he had betrayed Asquith, and therefore they were displeased with him. The Lloyd George Liberals were none too friendly. Churchill at that time had no intimate contacts with the Labour Party.

Driven out of the Admiralty in May, 1915, he held for a short time the Chancellorship of the Duchy of Lancaster. On the issue of the evacuation of Gallipoli he resigned in November, 1915, and in the following year commanded a battalion in France. In 1916 he returned to his Parliamentary duties, and joined Lloyd George's Government as Minister of Munitions in July, 1917.

In 1917 and 1918 Churchill was a Liberal. Nobody believed that he would be a Conservative Prime Minister in years to come. If such a prediction had been made, it would have been ridiculed, although he was regarded by many as a possible future Liberal Prime Minister.

CUNLIFFE, 1st Baron of Headley (Walter Cunliffe)

Lord Cunliffe was sixty-two years of age in 1917. He had been married twice, and had two sons and three daughters. One of his sons served in the war.

He had been educated at Harrow and Trinity College, Cambridge.

Governor of the Bank of England, in 1917 he was created a G.B.E.

CURZON, 1st Earl (George Nathaniel Curzon)

Fifty-eight years' of age in 1917, Curzon was married for the second time during that year. He had three daughters by his first marriage, but no sons.

Educated at Eton and Balliol College, Oxford, he was elected a Fellow of All Souls. He was a polished orator.

In 1898 he was created Viceroy of India, an office filled with pomp and ceremony, at the youthful age of thirty-nine. In his train followed long strings of elephants and retinues of gaily colourful servants. But his years of semi-kingship came to an end in 1905, when at forty-six years of age he left India an angry and embittered man.

For all the rest of his life Curzon was influenced by his sudden journey to heaven at the age of thirty-nine, and then by his return seven years later to earth, for the remainder of his mortal existence.

Lloyd George treated him roughly but gave him compensation in the form of a Marquisate, in which he took pride.

Curzon changed sides on almost every issue during his long career. Often undecided whether to desert a sinking ship for one that might not float, he would make up his mind to sit on the wharf for a day.

He had many intimates, but none of them deplored his reverses in public life.

From 1915 to 1916 Curzon held office as Lord Privy Seal, and in 1916 became Lord President and Leader of the House of Lords.

DERBY, 17th Earl of (Edward George Villiers Stanley)

In 1917 Lord Derby reached the age of fifty-two. He was married, with two sons and one daughter. One of his sons was wounded in the war, and his son-in-law was killed in action.

Derby was a tiresome speaker but a good letter-writer, often in his own hand. He ate heartily and was over-stout. But he lived to the age of eighty-three, disproving the adage that the fat die early, the thin die late.

Educated at Wellington College, Derby had been Secretary of State for War since 1916.

Popular and holding the affectionate respect of the public, he was never a heavyweight contender in Cabinet Councils. Supported by his Town Properties and his Broad Acres and the Hereditary Virtue of his House, he was the Champion in Lancashire Party organisations. He took infinite trouble to please the Press, and reaped his reward in high praise from Government and Opposition newspapers.

He was an incessant smoker of cigarettes. He pretended to confine himself to nineteen a day. In fact he deceived himself.

Always threatening resignation, he never signed off. Derby was the godfather of Haig's child, yet of him Haig wrote "like the feather pillow [he] bears the mark of the last person who sat on him."

GEDDES, Rt. Hon. Sir Eric (Campbell)

Sir Eric Geddes was forty-two years of age in 1917. He was married and had three sons, who were too young for service.

The ten years of his schooldays were spent at seven schools; six of these claim him as a distinguished old boy. At the age of seventeen he went to the U.S.A., where he worked in the Carnegie Steel Works and on the Baltimore and Ohio Railways.

He was General Manager designate of the North Eastern Railway.

In July, 1917, he took office as First Lord of the Admiralty, and in the following year became a member of the War Cabinet.

Punctuality was his passion, and routine his practice. He lived at Hassocks, near Brighton. Leaving by motor at exactly 8 a.m., returning again at 7 p.m., he spent three hours daily in these journeys. At 7.30 p.m. he sat down to dinner. At 8.15 he rose up again.

His way of life conformed to the teachings of the Shorter Catechism. He was looked on as the strong silent man of real power and influence.

In his home a telephone was on a pay-box system.

Created a Privy Councillor in 1917, he was also awarded the K.C.B. and G.B.E. in that year.

GEORGE, Rt. Hon. David Lloyd

M.P. for Carnavon since 1890 and fifty-four years of age in 1917, Lloyd George was married, with two sons and two daughters. His sons both served in the war.

He had been educated at Llanystumdwy Church of England School but never attended University.

In politics he attempted to straddle all parties. The inevitable consequence was to confuse the issues, and this led him to adopt a series of inconsistent policies.

To Lloyd George no policy was permanent, no pledge final. He became like a trick rider at the circus, as he was compelled to leap from one back to another in his party-coloured team. Thus in the middle of a great and glorious career he was faced with failure and disaster.

In 1916 with the formation of the second Coalition Government Lloyd George became Prime Minister and First Lord of the Treasury. In 1922 he was driven out of Downing Street and never held office again.

He was the only Minister who served from the outbreak of war on 4th August, 1914, to the end of it in 1918.

GUEST, Capt. Hon. Frederick Edward

M.P. for East Dorset since 1910, Guest was forty-two years of age in 1917. The third son of the 1st Baron Wimborne, he was married, with two sons and one daughter. His sons were too young for service.

BIOGRAPHIES

Educated at Winchester, he became an officer in the East Surrey Regiment. He had served in the South African War.

He was Winston Churchill's first cousin and intimate friend and political disciple.

He served in East Africa. In 1917 he was awarded a D.S.O. He also became chief Liberal whip of the Coalition Government in the same year.

HAIG, Field-Marshal Sir Douglas

Fifty-six years of age in 1917, Haig was married, with one son and two daughters. He had been educated at Clifton and Brasenose College, Oxford, from which he went on to Sandhurst.

His war diary is a self-revealing document: frank, truthful, egotistical, self-confident and malicious. His spear knew no brother.

Careful of his health, he ate sparingly and drank with moderation, yet he died in 1928 at the age of sixty-six. With the publication of his Private Papers in 1952, he committed suicide 25 years after his death.

Throughout the war Haig held high command in France. He was Commander-in-Chief of the Expeditionary Forces in France and Flanders. In 1917 he was raised to the rank of Field-Marshal.

In 1918 he received the American Cross of Honour and the American Distinguished Service Medal. In 1918 he was offered and refused a Viscountcy. In 1919 he was offered and accepted an Earldom. The same year brought him £100,000 from Parliament and the Order of Merit. In 1920 public subscriptions provided a fund for the purchase of Bermersyde Mansion and estate.

Thereafter Lloyd George's "War Memoirs" and Haig's own Private Papers redressed the balance of public favour.

HANKEY, Lieut.-Col. Sir Maurice Pascal Alers

Forty years of age in 1917, Sir Maurice Hankey was married and had three sons too young for war service, and one daughter. Educated at Rugby, he joined the Royal Marine Artillery.

He was Secretary to the War Cabinet, to the Imperial War Cabinet and to the Committee of Imperial Defence.

He received from Parliament a gift of £25,000, his name,

BONAR LAW. "Unselfish in public affairs, he always took the best chair in the room."

BALDWIN. Mrs. Baldwin called him "Tiger."

BIOGRAPHIES

Lieut.-Col. Sir Maurice Hankey, being included in a list of fighting Naval, Army and Air Force officers.

Protest was raised at the inclusion of officials among the fighting men. The Prime Minister explained that while he took no part in battle he was as essential to our success as any name in the list.

HOUSE, Colonel Edward Mandell

Fifty-nine years of age in 1917, Colonel House was married but had no family.

He had been educated at Cornell University, which he left without taking a degree.

Formerly a planter and farmer in Texas, he had acted as Personal Representative of President Wilson to European Governments. In 1917, he was appointed by the President to gather together material for the Peace Conference. He attended the Inter-Allied Conference at Paris as Special Representative of the U.S.A., and was designated by the President to represent the U.S.A. at Versailles in the Supreme War Council.

House walked delicately. Everything was done softly. He had a rare capacity for gaining confidences, which he always passed on to the President.

LAW, Rt. Hon. Andrew Bonar

An M.P. since 1900, Bonar Law was fifty-nine years of age in 1917. A widower, with a family of four sons and two daughters, 1917 was a tragic year for him. His two elder sons were both killed on active service, one in Palestine and the other in the air.

Educated at Glasgow High School, he left school at the age of sixteen, and did not go on to University.

Lonely and austere by nature, spare of stature but of sound constitution and good health, he smoked incessantly but never drank. Almost every idle moment he passed in playing bridge and chess. His meals—which consisted generally of vegetables, rice pudding and a glass of milk—were swallowed swiftly. Possessing a prodigious memory, he read the newspapers regularly and also light romantic novels. Upright and straightforward in conduct, he was well liked by opponents and beloved by friends. He rejected all offers of honours and decorations.

BIOGRAPHIES

In the second Coalition Government he was Chancellor of the Exchequer and Leader of the House of Commons.

LONG, Rt. Hon. Walter Hume

M.P. for the Strand Division of Middlesex and aged sixty-three in 1917, Walter Long was married, with three children, his eldest son having been killed in January, 1917.

In his youth he attended Harrow and Christ Church, Oxford, which he left without obtaining a degree.

Generally popular, he was modest by temperament. Although of strong character, his objectives were often confused. Under medium height, but of pleasing countenance, his bald head would grow red with anger or excitement. Certainly seeking popularity, he was quick to take offence. He carried on a feud against Austen Chamberlain.

Leader of the Agricultural Section of the Conservative Party, he was not too closely tied to the Home Rule or Welsh Church Groups. Since 1916 he had held the post of Secretary of State for the Colonies.

MACLAY, Rt. Hon. Sir Joseph Paton

In 1917 Sir Joseph Maclay was sixty years of age. He was married, with four sons and two daughters. One son had been killed in action at Gallipoli. Two other sons fought in the war.

Educated in Glasgow, he had gone into business at an early age, and made a vast fortune in shipping.

While holding his ministerial office as Shipping Controller he refused to appear in the House of Commons.

MILNER, 1st Viscount (Alfred Milner)

Sixty-three years of age in 1917, Lord Milner was still a bachelor. He was born in Germany, and his father, although descended from an English family, was a German by nationality. Milner's claim to British nationality was derived from his grandfather, a native of Manchester, who settled in Germany in 1805.

He was educated in Germany and at King's College, London, and Balliol College, Oxford. His academic record was distinguished and he obtained a first-class degree, later becoming a Fellow of New College, Oxford.

Milner was a Freemason. He was a member of Brooks, and liked his club. He took little interest in food or drink. He was impressive but not attractive. Efficiency was his aim, and the unity of the Empire, political and economic, was his goal. That Britain was no part of Europe was his conviction.

He admired Bismarck's Zollverein of Central Europe, a land empire. He strove for a union of Britain and British territory, extending over lands and seas.

He was a Tory Radical, calling himself a Liberal Unionist, frowning on reductions of taxation, and favouring extensions of social welfare.

He was a Member of the War Cabinet without portfolio, and Secretary of State for War in April, 1918.

NORTHCLIFFE, 1st Viscount (Alfred Charles William Harmsworth)

Fifty-two years of age in 1917, Northcliffe was the son of a barrister practising in Ireland. Born at Chapelizod in 1865, his father moved to London two years later to take up practice there. He was married, with no children.

Self-educated, he was confused and sometimes incoherent in conversation, and had no patience with argument. His occasional speeches were badly delivered. During sixteen years of membership of the Lords he only spoke 968 words in the House.

He influenced politics, but always from the outside, priding himself on having no social relations with Ministers.

A man of brilliant creative talents, touched by the hand of genius, he was on the whole democratic in opinion, and was never carried away by royalty or aristocracy, yet he liked his titles. In the presence of men of high educational attainment he was not at ease. His intimate circle was small. He believed a newspaper proprietor should have no friends; yet he was a Freemason, although not an energetic member of that order.

He made violent attacks on public men; yet he was hurt by criticism, and would refuse to print unfavourable comments on himself.

BIOGRAPHIES

His power was so considerable that it was of the utmost importance in all matters of public interest to secure his assistance or at any rate his neutrality.

In 1917 Northcliffe was Chairman of the British War Mission to the U.S.A. In 1918 he was Director of Propaganda in Enemy Countries.

READING, 1st Earl (Rufus Daniel Isaacs)

Fifty-seven years of age in 1917, Lord Reading was the second son of a Jewish fruit merchant. He was married and had one son serving in the war. He was created a Baron in 1914, a Viscount in 1916, and an Earl in 1917.

He had been educated in London, Brussels and Hanover. His regular schooling came to an end when he was under fourteen years of age.

Reading had a pleasing countenance. In conversation he had little to say, but when he spoke it was with authority. He did most of his talking and much of his public speaking with his hands on the lapels of his coat. He smoked cigarettes frequently and used a cigarette holder. He could sleep anywhere at any time.

Lord Chief Justice of England since 1913, he was appointed President of the Anglo-French Loan Mission to the U.S.A. in 1917.

RIDDELL, Sir George Allardice

Fifty-two years of age in 1917, Riddell had been married twice, but had no family. He began his career as a boy clerk in a solicitor's office.

On acquiring an interest in the *News of the World*, he devoted himself entirely to newspaper work. He wrote a column called "Gossip of the Day", which carried much exclusive news.

A good conversationalist, he was presentable in appearance and pleasing in manner.

His diaries, which were published in 1933, are important.

For many years he was Lloyd George's familiar companion. After Lloyd George's defeat Riddell deserted him. In the election of 1922 he turned swiftly to the support of Lloyd

George's opponents. This was described by George's friends as an act of treachery. Although the separation is shrouded in mystery, the view widely held is that Lloyd George was responsible for the parting of their ways.

ROBERTSON, General Sir William Robert

Fifty-seven years of age in 1917, Robertson was married, with two sons and two daughters. One of his sons was serving in the war.

His father was a tailor and he had been educated at the village school. After leaving school he became a domestic servant. Then in 1877, at the age of seventeen, he enlisted in the 16th Lancers as a trooper.

He dined well and drank moderately. He was fond of shooting over the fields. A frequent visitor with the Duke of Portland, his great friend, he often stayed at Langwell, the Duke's country house in Caithness-shire.

When the king dined with Lord Derby, the Chiefs of Staff and others, the drink was limited to cider because of the King's pledge that had been given when Lloyd George at the outset of the war asked for total abstinence. Derby passed the word that after the king left the party drinks would be served upstairs The king stayed late. General Robertson asked impatiently, "When do we get our pop?"

Since 1915 Robertson had been Chief of the Imperial General Staff. He was known to the French Generals by the nickname 'General Non'.

In 1919 he got a Baronetcy from the Sovereign and £10,000 from Parliament. The money reward was inadequate considering the payments to other soldiers. Jellicoe, his opposite number at the Admiralty, dismissed in 1917, was given a Viscountcy and £50,000. But after all Robertson had taken a pot-shot at Santa Claus, and missed.

ROTHERMERE, 1st Baron of Hemsted (Harold Sidney Harmsworth)

In 1917 Rothermere was forty-nine years of age. The younger brother of Northcliffe, he had married in 1893 and had three sons. One son was killed in action in November, 1916, and another, Harold, died of wounds in February, 1918. Although

Rothermere lived entirely in hotel rooms, moving occasionally from one leading establishment to another, his sons lived with him on intimate terms, ānd their family relationships were close and attractive.

Rothermere had been educated at St. Marylebone Grammar School.

In 1914 he received a peerage on the nomination of Asquith, as a reward for press support, both in his own newspapers and also in the Northcliffe journals, for the Liberal measure limiting the powers of the House of Lords.

Before the outbreak of the war in the same year he had switched his newspaper support to Bonar Law and the Conservative Party, on account of the Home Rule for Ireland Bill, which he bitterly opposed.

Generous, kindly and companionable by nature, his conversation was vivacious. He had a highly developed sense of humour, which at times might be described as a sense of fun.

From 1916 to 1917 Rothermere was Director-General of the Royal Army Clothing Department. In 1917 he was appointed Air Minister.

SMITH, Rt. Hon. Sir Frederick Edwin

M.P. for the Walton Division of Liverpool and forty-five years of age in 1917, F. E. Smith was married, with one son and two daughters.

He had been educated at Birkenhead School and Wadham College, Oxford, and had obtained a first-class Final Honours in the School of Jurisprudence in 1894.

For further and fuller particulars see Chapter I.

Since 1915 he had been Attorney General.

SMUTS, Lieut.-Gen. Rt. Hon. Jan Christian

Forty-seven years of age in 1917, Smuts was married, with two sons and four daughters. He was living at the Savoy Hotel.

He had been educated at Riebeeck West School and at Victoria College, Stellenbosch. He won a scholarship to Christ's College, Cambridge, where he had a distinguished record, and was awarded a Double First in Law.

He fought against Britain in the Boer War. In 1916 he commanded the forces in British East Africa. In 1917 he held the offices of Minister of Defence and Minister of Finance in the South African Government. He was known by his opponents in South Africa as "Slim Jannie".

He joined Lloyd George in 1917, sitting with the War Cabinet although not a member until June. He was appointed to the Privy Council and to the role of Member of the Order of Companions of Honour all in the same year. In 1917 and 1918 he sat as the South African Representative on the Imperial War Cabinet.

SPRING-RICE, Sir Cecil Arthur

Fifty-eight years of age in 1917, Sir Cecil Spring-Rice was married, with one son and one daughter. His son was too young to serve in the war.

Educated at Eton and Balliol College, Oxford, where he attained first-class rank in both moderations and finals in the classical school, in 1917 he was Ambassador to the U.S.A.

He died in Canada on 14th February, 1918.

TRENCHARD, Major-Gen. Hugh Montague

Forty-four years of age in 1917, Trenchard was as yet unmarried. He failed to pass examinations for Dartmouth and Woolwich. It was through the Militia that he began his career in the Army, joining the Royal Scots Fusiliers in 1893. He served in the South African War.

A tall spare man, his loud penetrating voice won him the nickname "Boom". Endowed with a strong sense of duty and a singleness of purpose, he kept his mind firmly fixed upon his goal. A visionary by nature, he was self-centred and inarticulate. He read out his speeches from a vast bundle of manuscript written in a large sprawling hand, and very badly. He had common sense, but limited ability. In political circles he had no friends, but elsewhere he had many strong friendships and he enjoyed bitter hatreds.

Trenchard, who was Chief of the Air Staff for three months, received a Baronetcy from the monarch and £10,000 from Parliament. Sir Frederick Sykes, who was Chief of the Air Staff for over a year, got a G.B.E. "He sendeth the rain on the just and on the unjust!"

When he retired from service he acquired a number of directorships (Goodyear Tyre and Rubber Co. and United Africa Co.) which he held to the day of his death in February, 1956, at the age of eighty-three.

WILSON, Lieut.-Gen. Sir Henry Hughes

Fifty-three years of age in 1917, Sir Henry Wilson was married, with no children.

He had entered Marlborough College in 1877. Having failed to gain admission into Woolwich twice, and into Sandhurst three times, he finally obtained a commission in the Longford Militia, without examination.

He served in the South African War, and in 1914 was appointed sub-chief of the general staff of the British Expeditionary Force in France.

In March, 1917, he returned from a supply mission to Russia. In September he was appointed to the Eastern Command. In February, 1918, Wilson replaced Sir William Robertson as Chief of the Imperial General Staff.

Wilson had bitter enemies and devoted friends. Most of his colleagues in the army were opposed to him. His intellectual gifts outshone those of every other soldier. Asquith hated him; Bonar Law was his friend.

At the end of the war Wilson was given a Baronetcy and a grant of £10,000. He was a member of the House of Commons when an assassin's bullet ended his career.

WISEMAN, Sir William George Eden

Thirty-two years of age in 1917, Sir William Wiseman was married, with two daughters.

He had been educated at Winchester and Jesus College, Cambridge.

He served in the European War in 1914 and was gassed at Ypres. In 1917 he was Chief of the British Intelligence Service in the U.S.A.

Colonel House fell under his spell, declaring him to be "one of the most efficient men of his age I (had) ever met."

In 1918 he was appointed Chief Adviser on American Affairs to the British Delegation in Paris.

THE PRIVATE PAPERS OF MANY PUBLIC MEN

THIS narrative has been fortified by an immense accumulation of private and personal correspondence and various documents which are accessible to me.

Possibly my resources are more extensive than any other private collection of political papers and records of the years of the First World War.

The Lloyd George Papers comprise more than one thousand boxes and most of this material is as yet untapped. These were available for Frank Owen's brilliant book *Tempestuous Journey*.

The Bonar Law Papers, which are in excellent order, will shortly be shipped to the University of New Brunswick. These papers were left to me by Bonar Law in his will. And I hope I have made good use of them.

The diaries and letters of Lady Lloyd George extending over twenty-five years are now in New Brunswick.

The records of Lord Bennett, who was Prime Minister of Canada for many years, are in my keeping. They are deposited in the Bennett room at the Bonar Law-Bennett Library in the University of New Brunswick.

And my own private papers have been drawn on for my narrative in no small measure.

Other manuscript collections, in Britain and in Canada and America, have been made available to me.

Lord Wargrave took a prominent and important part in the affairs of the Conservative Party over the critical years culminating in the war of 1914–1918. His papers were placed at my disposal by his great-nephew, Sir Basil Goulding.

Sir Reginald Brade, Under-Secretary at the War Office, gave me several extracts from his diaries relating to the war.

Sir John Elliot has allowed me to take a letter from the papers of his father, Mr. R. D. Blumenfeld, one-time distinguished and beloved editor of the *Daily Express*.

The papers of Sir Robert Borden, Canada's Prime Minister during the First World War, are of course in the National Archives of Canada, but I was permitted to examine the complete photographic copy at the Library of the University of Toronto. Mr. Henry Borden, Q.C., most generously made them available to me.

Extensive research has been carried out on the papers of Colonel E. M. House and of Sir William Wiseman which are held by Yale University. The library gave facilities to my colleagues and I am grateful.

Detailed research has also been performed on my

behalf covering the papers of Walter Hines Page, American Ambassador to Britain during the First War. These papers and correspondence are deposited at the Houghton Library, Harvard University and I am obliged for permission to examine them.

Fredericton,
New Brunswick,
Canada.

ACKNOWLEDGMENTS

I HAVE to acknowledge the gracious permission of Her Majesty the Queen to make use of material from the Royal Archives, Windsor Castle. Sir Owen Morshead has given me guidance in the use of this material.

I wish also to thank the Earl of Balfour; Margaret, Countess of Birkenhead; Collin Brooks, literary executor for Lord Rothermere; Lady Carson; the Public Trustee on behalf of the Northcliffe Estate; the Chamberlain Trustees; the Rt. Hon. Sir Winston Churchill, K.G.; the Marchioness of Crewe; Grace, Lady Curzon; the Earl of Derby; Henrietta, Lady Henderson; Viscount Long of Wraxall; Lord Maclay, K.B.E.; Lady Milner; the Rt. Hon. the Marquess of Reading; General Sir Brian Robertson, Bt., K.C.V.O.; Captain J. C. Smuts; Viscount Stonehaven; and Viscount Younger of Leckie for permission to publish correspondence of importance and in many instances essential to the form of my narrative.

To Sir William Wiseman I am grateful, not only for permission to publish correspondence but also for advice and material of value to my story.

ACKNOWLEDGMENTS

I acknowledge with thanks permission for the use of copyright material from:

Sir Harold Nicolson for consent to publish material from *King George V, His Life and Times*.

Dr. Charles Seymour for extracts from *The Intimate Papers of Colonel House*.

Eyre and Spottiswoode Ltd. for extracts from *The Private Papers of Douglas Haig, 1914–1919*, edited by Robert Blake; *The Unknown Prime Minister* by Robert Blake; *Reginald McKenna* by Stephen McKenna; *The World Crisis, 1916–1918* by Winston Churchill.

Ernest Benn and A. P. Watt & Son for extracts from *The Intimate Papers of Colonel House*, arranged by Charles Seymour, and from *The Life of Lord Curzon* by Lord Ronaldshay.

Constable & Co. Ltd. for extracts from *The First World War, 1914–1918* by Colonel Repington.

John Murray Ltd. for extracts from *George V. A Personal Memoir* by John Gore.

The Times Publishing Company for extracts from *The History of The Times*.

William Heinemann Ltd. for extracts from *Woodrow Wilson's Life and Letters* by R. S. Baker.

Hutchinson and Co. Ltd. for extracts from *Tempestuous Journey* by Frank Owen; *Four and a Half Years* by Christopher Addison; *The Life of Lord Oxford and Asquith* by Stephen Spender and Cyril Asquith; *My War Memories, 1914–1918* by Ludendorff; and *My Political Life* by L. S. Amery.

ACKNOWLEDGMENTS

The following literary agents have also given their consent, and I am grateful:

Messrs. Curtis Brown for extracts from *The Life of Lord Oxford and Asquith*, and *My War Memories, 1914–1918* by Ludendorff; Messrs. Albert Bonnier Forlag, Stockholm, also for extracts from *My War Memories, 1914–1918* by Ludendorff; Messrs. Pearn, Pollinger and Higham for extracts from *My Political Life* by L. S. Amery; and A. D. Peters for extracts from the *Life of Lord Carson* by Ian Colvin.

I am indebted to Mrs. Ann Cousins for research at Harvard, Yale, Toronto and New Brunswick Universities and for extensive assistance and much hard labour.

Mr. George Malcolm Thomson has been reading my proofs and at the same time making corrections.

I have relied too upon invaluable help from Mrs. Elton, the custodian of the Lloyd George and the Bonar Law records.

I owe them all my grateful thanks.

INTRODUCTION

THE year 1917 opened up in disaster for Britain. Germany was the military master of Europe. The French nation was exhausted. Russia was staggering to her doom. The British people were dispirited and a food shortage threatened the very existence of the nation.

The Army was stalemated in France, and the Navy was unable any longer to provide protection for the Mercantile Marine. The sea communications to east and west had been interrupted. Even the freedom of the Channel was challenged.

The public at large were certainly not aware of the dreadful danger, and even important Ministers were incapable of grasping the terrible truth. A few of the leading politicians spoke to each other in alarming terms and some newspapers gave repeated warnings which were almost disregarded.

Thus it was when the reins of office fell from the nerveless grasp of Asquith. Britain was in the shadows.

Lloyd George occupied the seat of power, the chair at No. 10 Downing Street where Asquith had sat for seven years, and where eminent predecessors in peace and war had dispensed patronage and exercised authority.

He was flattered and praised by his intimate circle, adored by his secretaries and courted by society—courted all the more because he rejected the overtures of the social leaders and the social climbers in the West End of London.

Bonar Law was his colleague in a coalition Government, the leader of the Tory Party which gave the Government its majority in Parliament. The Tories were at that time a cohesive party, save only for their Right Wing which accepted their leader for the time being but could not be counted on to give him unswerving allegiance in the years that lay ahead.

There were also more than a hundred Liberals willing to lend support to the Coalition. But of these many were associated personally with Lloyd George, while others had their eyes on office and employment. A few of his followers sought only recommendations for honours.

When the year 1917 opened there were forces pleading for peace in the allied countries.

In France there was a great deal of conversation and some intrigue aimed at making peace before an outright military decision had been reached on the battlefield. The lobbies of the French Chamber echoed with discussions which had peace and the advocacy of peace as their theme. Defeatism was rampant.

In London, powerful elements argued that a negotiated peace was inevitable. Lord Lansdowne, an immensely respected and influential Tory magnate, member of Asquith's Coalition Cabinet and Tory leader in the House of Lords until Lloyd George became Prime Minister, had already submitted a Peace Plan as a Cabinet paper to the Asquith Government in 1916. This document had been roughly and effectively dealt with by Lord Robert Cecil who rejected the Lansdowne plan insisting that any such peace would bring final disaster to Britain.

The Lansdowne Peace Plan was widely circulated in the early days of 1917 and fully discussed in political circles throughout the year. Finally publication in the newspapers was launched in November, 1917.

Many voices were raised in support of Lord Lansdowne. Even Colonel House, envoy extraordinary and travelling representative of the President of the United States, saw Lansdowne and discussed the terms of the "Peace Letter". He wrote to the President: "We scarcely disagreed at all."[a]

More important, however, at the outset of Lloyd George's administration, was the attitude of McKenna, who had been First Lord of the Admiralty in Asquith's government and who was the most formidable and important Liberal spokesman of the peace programme. He got support from Runciman, another influential Liberal.

Where did Asquith stand? He had been the all-powerful First Minister. He had the confidence of the King. His immediate followers were loyal to him. His political character was good; there was no blemish on his party consistency. He was trusted by the Liberal leaders, agents, managers, and in a lesser measure, by their Press.

Would he join the Lansdowne peace movement? Many predicted that he would become the leader of such a party on a convenient occasion.

Walter Page was the American Ambassador in London. He was fanatically attached to the British cause and favourable to Lloyd George's administration. He had entry to every section of political opinion in the community. When the Lansdowne letter was the subject of discussion and dispute in the private parlours and the dining-rooms of London, he reported to the President:

> Lord Lansdowne and his friends (how numerous they are nobody knows) are the loudest spokesmen of such a peace as might be made now, especially if Belgium can be restored and an agreement reached about Alsace-Lorraine. But it is talked much of in Asquith's circle that the time may come when this policy (its baldness somewhat modified) may be led by Mr. Asquith. He has up to this time patriotically supported the Government. But he is very generally suspected of intrigue, and his friends openly predict that at what they regard as a favourable moment he will take this cue.[b]

Fortunately for Britain, at the beginning of the fateful year of 1917 the men of little faith had been expelled The men of war were in complete control of the administration. Lloyd George and Bonar Law were supported by colleagues who thought as they did and who believed in a fight until victory came. There was no room for doubters in the Ministry.

There had been in the past a great controversy between Eastern and Western schools of military strategy—a dispute whether troops should be sent to the Middle East to attempt the conquest of the Balkans, or whether all military resources should be concentrated on the battle of the Western Front.

Nearly all of the generals were the exponents of the Western strategy. Lloyd George and a few politicians expounded the plan for "victory in the East". Even after he became Prime Minister, he continued to dwell upon the benefits of an Eastern venture, but he could not carry with him the majority of his own Cabinet colleagues.

Indeed the expedition to Gallipoli, and the disaster that overtook it, had given the opponents of war in the East an argument so powerful that the issue, though frequently raised, never assumed any reality.

It had become obvious that the West was the principal theatre of war and it was impossible to contemplate any substantial diversion of the troops from that theatre.

Thus although the controversy was carried on with every appearance of a genuine struggle, the movement had really lost its force and strength. The opponents of any more Eastern escapades had little difficulty in vanquishing the arguments of the Eastern schools.

The victory of the generals over Lloyd George's Eastern yearnings gave them courage and confidence to persist in another and much more dangerous division of opinion.

The generals claimed the right to deal with the various campaigns free from political interference.

The politicians declared that, with the whole male population engaged in the war, political direction and civilian control was essential.

The generals maintained that the politicians, by their muddling, were responsible for the various defeats in the field. The politicians, for their part, blamed the generals for the military misfortunes and for the large and horrifying casualty lists.

Such was the domestic atmosphere at the beginning of the third year of war when I take up my story. This conflict between soldiers and politicians was the dominating element in the political crises which followed one after the other, almost to the day of victory.

The underlying issues of all these events may be summarised as follows:

The politicians gave little credit to the generals.

The generals denounced the politicians.

The soldiers and sailors serving in the forces had little confidence in either.

The public had no heroes.

Now it has been my intention in this work to describe these disputes and the personalities involved. I have attempted to give an account of the conduct and dispositions of many public men responsible for the higher direction of the war.

It is not my purpose to write a chronological record of the political events.

Two volumes of *Politicians and the War*, written and published by me many years ago, were an earnest attempt to provide an impartial political history from the outbreak of war to the end of the Asquith administration.*

The present work is not a continuation or a sequel to that historical record. In this book I make no attempt to deal with the general course of political events; I tell only of the crises which emerged from the general trend. They are the highlights of political history, the moments when the politicians take the centre of the stage. Certainly these politicians live and thrive in crises and on them. And it is then that public men can be studied to the best advantage.

A chance remark, a single story, a characteristic gesture may give us the man himself, as a sudden flickering flame lights up the twilight room and shows the cold or coloured face and figure set in some imperishable pose against the sombre background of history.

My labours must not be judged by literary merit. But I am in a position to give an account

---

* It is my intention some day to bring out a political history already in form which will be entitled *The Age of Baldwin*. And my hopes are centred on another work on the Second World War. For this task I have gathered an immense mass of material.

of vital moments in the course of great events from personal knowledge and experience.

It may be asked: "Were you there?" I was there!

I have known and worked with all the principal characters in this narrative.

My intimate knowledge of events and persons may justify me in the belief that this record might prove to be of real value to the historians of another generation.

With this brief introduction, I launch my chapters with the confidence that I have written with complete impartiality and entirely independent of party or personal affiliations.

CHAPTER I

THE CLEVEREST MAN IN THE KINGDOM

IN 1917 my position in public life was that of a frustrated and disappointed seeker after employment. I had hoped to get office in the Lloyd George administration; I had failed. The best I was offered was a tiny office of no importance. This I had refused. I had stumbled into the House of Lords. But I had no intention whatever of being relegated to a dying House and I could not take very seriously a hereditary chamber in which I had no faith.

No sooner had I fallen into a place in the hereditary system than the absurdity and futility of the political structure of the House of Lords became clear to me. Certainly I had no respect for the aristocracy as such, and no lingering admiration for the doings of the squire and his family.

I was, of course, happy in the honour that had been conferred on me, and the title gave me real pleasure. Since then I have come to take a different view, believing myself to have lacked sound judgement when I accepted the peerage.

I still kept a room at the War Office.* And for three of the leaders there I had great respect. Sir William Robertson was Chief of the Imperial General Staff. His deputy was Sir Robert Whigham. Sir Reginald Brade was Permanent Under-Secretary.

I was on good terms with Robertson, friendly with Whigham and intimate with Brade.

Robertson appealed to me because of his sturdy independence. He was a man whose origin was humble and who had forged steadily ahead in the army, from Private to General and at last Chief of the Imperial General Staff.† His advancement was the outcome of character, ability and determination. They are rare qualities.

Whigham, too, was a man with whom I found it easy to deal on agreeable terms. He came from the same stock as I did—a stout, sturdy Scottish family. We often talked and there were many occasions when he gave me sound advice and good direction. I was to see much of him in the future.

Brade was my friend. He was well educated, a good conversationalist, a real wit, loyal to his friends, and devoted to his task. He was a good companion and much sought after in political circles. He was short of stature, and had a pleasing countenance with a big head which gave him an appearance of importance. I was devoted to him.

---

* I was Canadian Government Representative for affairs concerning the Canadian Army and dealing with personnel and supply problems.

† The Chief of the Imperial General Staff was responsible for overall strategy and policy and was the Military Adviser to the Secretary of State for War and to the War Cabinet.

These three were destined to play dominating and important parts in the events of this era.

With the appearance of Lloyd George as Secretary of State for War in the summer of 1916, friction prevailed between these Army Chiefs and their civilian Minister. The reasons are easily explained. When Lord Kitchener, the former Secretary of State, was to be removed, Asquith wanted to take over the War Office while retaining the Premiership. He was willing to leave the War Administration entirely in the keeping of Robertson.

Lloyd George also wanted the War Office. He was determined to have it. He intended to deprive Robertson of some of the power already possessed by him as C.I.G.S. I quote an extract from Sir Reginald Brade's Diary, dated 13th June, 1916.

> I told him (Lloyd George) of the suggestion that I had made to the Prime Minister [Asquith], viz: that the Prime Minister should retain the seals and Lord Derby* should be President of the Army Council. He said he thought this was impracticable. It would never do.

The last two sentences are written in block capitals and underlined. There is a marginal note in Brade's handwriting, as follows:

> I did not mention Lord D. by name. I said some Provincial man not a member of the Cabinet.

In the struggle that followed, Robertson and his colleagues at the War Office stoutly opposed the appointment of Lloyd George. None the less, Lloyd George became Secretary of State for War

* Lord Derby was Under-Secretary at the War Office.

on 6th July, 1916. Bitter hostilities flared up at once, and the quarrels between Lloyd George and Robertson increased in violence up to the very day that Asquith fell from power.

But now that Lloyd George was Prime Minister it seemed likely the strife would die down. Lloyd George with his increased authority, immense public popularity and freedom from intrigue and frustration from above would be strong and sure in action, thus establishing complete leadership of politicians and generals, too.

These hopes were disappointed. The generals were to claim a freedom from restraint. They demanded the sole right to determine all military issues even though their decisions would have repercussions for the whole population of Britain, soldier and civilian, man and woman, shopkeeper and banker, financial and commercial, every section of the community.

Lloyd George found himself exposed, too, at the very outset of his Ministry to pressure from newspapers. Word had been passed to Lord Northcliffe* and others that the new administration sought to send troops to the East in defiance of military advice. The Generals claimed that all available resources should be directed to the Western Front.

A threat was spoken to the new Prime Minister by Lord Northcliffe in the early days of January, 1917. Sir Reginald Brade wrote to me on the 6th, one month after the new government was formed:

---

* Proprietor of *The Times*, the *Daily Mail*, the *Evening News* and the *Weekly Dispatch*.

46

You ought to know, but not from me, that L.G. and Northcliffe quarrelled in Paris when they met during this week and the latter threatened to break the former. Salonika was the matter in dispute. L.G. and Derby* are quite friendly.

Northcliffe was the most powerful and vigorous of the newspaper proprietors. In the rivalry between politicians and generals his attitude was not in doubt. He had "favoured the removal of Asquith because he considered that greater power should be given to Haig† and Robertson. . . . At times he used language suggesting that he almost favoured a military dictatorship."[a] In the opinion of Mr. Stanley Morison, the historian of *The Times*, "To the right soldiers he would have given almost unlimited power."[b]

But it was one thing for vague aspirations towards military rule to exist in Northcliffe's mind and among members of the public in general. It was quite another when a clash was threatened between soldiers and politicians which promised to become a struggle for power. Then the support of Northcliffe's newspapers, and most of the Conservative journals (*Morning Post, Globe*) on the side of the generals would be critical indeed.

An entry in Brade's diary gives a clear indication of the intense hostility directed against Lloyd George and the civilian Administration by the Military High Command.

* Lord Derby was by this time Secretary of State for War and Lloyd George was Prime Minister.

† Sir Douglas Haig's official title was Commander-in-Chief of the British Forces in France. He made immediate decisions there, though responsible for his conduct to the Chief of the Imperial General Staff.

I suggested to Lord Derby that I should try to see Rufus Isaacs (Lord Reading) and impress upon him the difficulties, and especially the certainty that L.G. would find himself up against the soldiers and *might not* get the best of it. Derby agreed and I accordingly wrote the letter.

It was my habit at that time to talk over my political problems with F. E. Smith, the Attorney-General. Early in January, 1917, I went to ask the advice of this wise counsellor. What would be the outcome of frictions between Lloyd George and the Military? What would be the immediate effect of traffic between the War Office and Fleet Street attributed to emissaries believed to be close to Sir William Robertson?

F. E. Smith was a man of supreme intellectual ability with an amazing power of making mistakes in the minor affairs of life. He was always the worst judge of his own affairs and the best judge of other people's affairs. His story was a tale of unbroken success in his public career. There was at that time no height to which his talent might not carry him.

He held a far bigger position than that of the usual political lawyer who becomes Attorney-General. In the Conservative Party, which was weak in public appeal and platform ability, he almost alone had only to put up a notice that he would speak in order to fill any meeting place in Britain. But the war had deprived him of his foremost weapon, since the guns abolished the mass meeting as the last word in politics.

He had been a member of the Privy Council for five years, a distinction that had come to him in the Coronation Honours when George V ascended the throne. The story of how it came to him illustrates F. E. Smith's strength and also demonstrates a certain weakness in the man.

Two Privy Councillorships in the Coronation Honours were designated for the Conservative Party. One honour was certainly destined for Bonar Law. F. E. Smith deserved the other but was not likely to get it. Balfour, who was then leader of the Conservatives, intended that it should be given to Hayes Fisher, a regular party hack.

Smith was indignant and Balfour endeavoured to assuage his wrath with a letter of explanation expressing strong personal appreciation. F. E. Smith regarded it as a bear might look on a bun at feeding time.

"Ah!" said Bonar Law, in an honest attempt to pour oil on the troubled waters, "but what a letter, F.E., to be able to show your son in future years!"

"Well," Smith retorted, "I do not know if my son has any brains, but if he has and thought I was put off with this letter he would say—'My father was a mug!' "*

F.E.'s friend, Winston Churchill, then took a hand. He persuaded the Prime Minister (Asquith) to declare that, in offering two Privy Councillorships to the Opposition, he was not giving Balfour a blank cheque, but one

* See *Appendix* IV, No. 1.

specifically made out in favour of Bonar Law
and F. E. Smith. This, however, did not settle
the issue. Balfour insisted on his own candidate,
Hayes Fisher, so Asquith, who had now committed himself to Smith, was compelled to hand
over to the Opposition three Privy Councillorships instead of two. Both F. E. Smith and Hayes
Fisher came under the wire.

When F. E. Smith heard the good news of the
impending honour he was jubilant. He said to
me, "The Conservative Party is the one for us.
What have the Liberals got to offer us? We are
sought out by Dukes; we are flattered by Mar-
chionesses; Countesses give us dinner parties.
What have the Liberals to offer us? Nothing but
the society of Knight's ladies!"

Alas, I had in my pocket a letter informing me
that I was to be in the Conservative list of Coronation knights. I had intended to tell him of my
good fortune. I was silent.

Yet only a few days after the announcement of
the new list of honours, F. E. Smith met Bonar
Law at a social party of a political character.
"Ah! Bonar," he exclaimed, "they don't want us
there for ourselves but simply for our brains."

This attitude in F. E. Smith was quite inconsistent with his social conduct. He really held to
the belief that he was sought after for himself, for
his own qualities of personality. And he had good
reason to think so. For he was brilliant and
witty. His conversation was like a flashing display
of fork lightning.

F. E. SMITH. A biting and witty tongue that spared no man and every woman. He had a soft heart.

MILNER. He led the "Don't Hang the Kaiser" Party.

RIDDELL. He controlled the *News of the World* and the *Church Family Newspaper*. He scattered his mercies.

READING. The go-between.

He was a man without nerves, physically brave to a point of recklessness; willing at any time to put his limbs on the board as cheerfully as a smaller stake.

Before the year was over, the Government sent him out upon an oratorical tour throughout the United States. His labours there have been recorded by him in a small book[c] which is a living embodiment of his Tory democratic principles, for after telling in the opening passage of his hurried departure from a Christmas party at Blenheim Palace it goes on to say that when he reached New York he dined with Miss Maxine Elliott (a popular Shakespearean actress) and sealed his departure by a tennis party with Miss Elsie Janis (a well-known entertainer of the Danny Kaye type).

Throughout the war he adhered always in the end to Bonar Law. Yet he never swerved in devoted and sacrificing friendship for Winston Churchill. In many ways he was in accord with Lloyd George, although he never put too much trust in the new Prime Minister.

He was throughout his career a consistent Tory, faithful to a version of the party philosophy that was not harsh or unfeeling but was full of light and sentiment and sympathy for the problems of his fellow-countrymen. In council he was sensible and prescient; in argument he was persuasive, while his methods in debate gave additional proof of his superior ability.

He was a good friend. I always thought of him as the cleverest man in the kingdom. He did not dissemble. He did not suffer fools. And of him Bonar Law said, "It would be easier for him to keep a live coal in his mouth than a witty saying."

F. E. Smith was not the man to conjure up out of nothing a menace to Lloyd George's government from generals or any other quarter. I was impressed, therefore, when he advised me to talk with Bonar Law. He believed there was a real threat to the Government. He put forward a plan for dealing with it. He recommended an immediate reorganisation of the high offices in the military command at the War Office. Why not act now? Get rid of Robertson and Haig,* too, for that matter. Both were survivors from the Asquith regime, standing in the way of the new direction. Robertson had always sought and found in Asquith protection from the fury of Lloyd George, who tried at one time to send him to Russia for the purpose of getting him out of the way.

I told F. E. Smith that Curzon, Chamberlain, Cecil and Long† had exacted a pledge from Lloyd George that he would not dismiss Haig. But there was no promise to retain Robertson. Then, "Sack him now," said F.E. in effect.

I then went off to see Bonar Law, to whom I gave my information about the developing struggle between the generals and the Prime Minister. But Bonar Law was not disposed to attach serious importance to this picture of events. He was

---

* Robertson was Chief of the Imperial General Staff, and Haig Commander-in-Chief in France.

† Curzon, Chamberlain, Cecil and Long were all Conservative members of Asquith's Coalition Government, holding high office.

decidedly favourable to Sir William Robertson*
and supported him in his post, expressing confidence that there would be good relations in
future between Lloyd George, now that he was
Prime Minister, and the Chief of the Imperial
General Staff. The prescience and political judgement of F. E. Smith did not move him. He spoke
of F. E. Smith as a man with the vision of an eagle
but with a blind spot in his eye.

Lloyd George shared F. E. Smith's apprehension. He was at this time nervous, perhaps unduly
nervous, about the possibility of attempts to overthrow the Government with the help of the
military and set up a new government which
would be the tool of the generals. The German
Government in 1916 had been overthrown and
replaced by Hindenburg and Ludendorff. Could
not a similar change be brought about in Britain
with Robertson playing the part of Hindenberg?

In his *War Memoirs*[e] Lloyd George wrote, at a
later date: "We were about to witness a very
determined effort—not the first nor the last—
made by this party to form a cabal which would
overthrow the existing War Cabinet and especially
its Chief, and enthrone a Government which
would be practically the nominee and menial of
this military party."

Lloyd George believed that Robertson was the
leader of the cabal. Asquith and others would
give support. Therefore the activities of the
Chief of the Imperial General Staff must be

---

* Bonar Law in 1916 had written to Sir Robert Borden, the Prime Minister
of Canada, saying: "in Robertson we have I believe as good a man as we could
get for the purpose."[d]

watched with anxiety. What began with obstruction would swiftly develop into a challenge to the Government which must result in the fall of the Administration or the dismissal of Robertson.

The conflict was confined at the moment to claims of prescience in military matters. Soon there would be attacks on civilian administration. Swiftly, Lloyd George believed, the military leaders might attain to a power and authority with the public excelling that of Cabinet Ministers. Then, and then only, the country would be willing to substitute what would be in effect a military dictatorship for democratic forms of government.

Lloyd George knew himself to be surrounded by political enemies, Liberals he had worsted and driven from office, Conservatives whom he could never hope to placate. A combination of ambitious generals willing to take over control of the Administration in association with political figures who were in opposition to Lloyd George's Ministry would certainly be able to turn him out in a crisis of the war.

Asquith might be a party to such a coalition, although Lloyd George did not believe that the House of Commons would turn him out of office in order to put Asquith back in power. Asquith had been given a chance and had muffed it. But Churchill was a formidable figure and Sir Edward Carson* was most dangerous.

* Carson was, of course, a member of Lloyd George's Administration. But he could not be described as a colleague. He was disgruntled and dissatisfied. The day before Lloyd George became Prime Minister, Carson was consulted about everything. The day after, nothing. Lloyd George made use of the Ulster leader when necessary and tried to push him as far out of sight as possible when no longer required.

Although there was always a great deal of newspaper support for the conception of military control of war-time policy, Lloyd George firmly believed that the Press campaign flowed from War Office sources.

Here again is an illuminative extract selected by me from an earlier entry in the diary of Sir Reginald Brade:

> Met L.G. at the office door. He suggested that I should tell W.R. [Sir William Robertson] to stop the press campaign—See D.C.* Two could play at that game and he, L.G., could do it better than most. So far he had not started.

There were many indications in the Press of the gathering storm which developed over the next year.

It is expedient to quote now from newspapers even though criticism developed slowly. It is often a practice in newspaper offices to give a new Administration a spell of repose from opposition.

The loudest and most consistent voice in the future "press campaign" was not the *Daily Chronicle* but the *Globe* newspaper. It spoke wistfully of the advantages which Germany enjoyed through the military dictatorship of Hindenburg and Ludendorff. At first the *Globe* said that only the direst necessity should induce Britain to follow the German example. The newspaper in course of time overcame its own reluctance and asked the rhetorical question, "Is there any other means of bringing this war to a swift and successful end

* The *Daily Chronicle*.

than by committing the conduct of it, and all that implies, without reserve to the greatest soldier we can find?"*f* It was not long before the *Globe* declared flatly, "Democracy has proved a failure under the stress of war. . . . In fact to be successful we must have a clean cut from democracy to autocracy 'for the period.' "*g*

The case that the *Globe* put bluntly the *Morning Post* argued with greater subtlety. It suggested that there should be two Cabinets, one for War and one for Civil Affairs, each under the leadership of whatever Prime Minister might be chosen, but the War Cabinet to consist of the Service Chiefs with the Secretary of State for War and the First Lord of the Admiralty.*h* The proposal fell short of military dictatorship but it would have increased enormously the power and authority of the generals. A government shared between generals and civilians would, in due course, have become a generals' government.

Such were the views of two important Conservative newspapers though the timing of their hostile outburst was delayed. There could be no doubt where the Northcliffe Press would stand if the movement for military control over policy gathered force.

As for the generals themselves, the men on whom the burden of power would fall should civilian administration be discredited, there was talk and there were expectations. General Sir Frederick Maurice, writing before the debate to which he has given his name, found it necessary to make a disavowal: "I am by descent and conviction as sincere a democrat as the Prime Minister, and the last thing I desire is to see the government of our country in the hands of the soldiers."[i] The declaration in support of democracy did credit to General Maurice, even though he failed to name the colleagues at the War Office who sought to place the government of the country in the hands of soldiers.

Ministers and others were well aware of the propaganda which threatened to undermine the Government. The effects of the Press campaign have been sardonically summed up by a great historian, Winston Churchill:

> The foolish doctrine was preached to the public through innumerable agencies that Generals and Admirals must be right on war matters, and civilians of all kinds must be wrong. These erroneous conceptions were inculcated billion-fold by the newspapers under the crudest forms. The feeble or presumptuous politician is portrayed cowering in his office, intent in the crash of the world on Party intrigues or personal glorification, fearful of responsibility, incapable of aught save shallow phrase-making. To him enters the calm, noble, resolute figure of the great Commander by land or sea, resplendent in uniform, glittering with decorations, irradiated with the lustre of the hero, shod with the science and armed with the panoply of war. This stately figure, devoid of the slightest thought of self, offers his clear far-sighted guidance and counsel for vehement action or artifice or wise delay. But his advice is rejected; his sound plans put aside; his courageous initiative baffled by political chatterboxes and incompetents. As well, it was suggested, might a great surgeon, about to operate with sure science and the study of a lifetime upon a desperate case, have his

arm jogged or his hand impeded, or even his lancet snatched from him, by some agitated relation of the patient. Such was the picture presented to the public, and such was the mood which ruled.[j]

Given a sufficiently grave turn in Britain's military fortunes, the "bumbling politicians" might be set aside and the god-like generals elevated to the summit of power. The process would probably be accomplished in two stages. First a new government would be set up dependent on military support but with civilian ministers in the home departments. And in due course this would be followed by military rule, pure and simple.

Against the background of fluctuating war, of newspaper agitation, of a precarious government and nervous ministers, the quarrel between soldiers and politicians raged, a furious struggle marked by many complex manœuvres and claiming distinguished victims.

Where would the dissensions end? Could the Prime Minister stand before the storm? Would his government go the way of the Asquith Administration?

Many political prophets predicted ruin. Few were the stalwarts who gave complete faith and undeviating confidence to the new administration.

CHAPTER II

THE FALL OF A GIANT

WHEN Churchill denounced in resounding terms "the foolish doctrine" of military control as opposed to civilian domination he was, of course, delivering an attack on Lord Northcliffe and his newspaper publications, *The Times* and the *Daily Mail*, the *Evening News* and the *Weekly Dispatch*.

And, indeed, Lord Northcliffe's position in British public life, in December 1916, when Lloyd George became Prime Minister, was a formidable one. He was fifty-one years of age and had built up a newspaper empire of enormous power and influence over which he was the undisputed ruler. Not only did he own *The Times*, politically of high importance, but he also controlled half the daily newspapers sold in London.*

To-day no parallel exists to Northcliffe's domination of newspaper sales in the metropolis. The circulation of my newspapers is the nearest approach to it. Beaverbrook Newspapers hold one-fifth of the London newspaper market. But Northcliffe held one-half.†

* Writing to H. W. Wilson, Lord Northcliffe declared that his Press was the sole source of his power. He boasted that his position was new to the world of affairs, but that he preferred it to any other as a means of getting things done.

† Beaverbrook overall circulation is now three times as great as that of Lord Northcliffe in 1917.

It conferred on him a power over the public mind and over war-time Government which he had already exerted with effect. At the outbreak of hostilities, he had defeated an attempt by Asquith to place Lord Haldane at the War Office. He had forced the Government to take in Lord Kitchener. Then, within eighteen months, he had carried out a press campaign against Kitchener which led to his being sent on a mission to Russia in 1916 on which he was drowned. Again, it was Lord Northcliffe's agitation over the Shell Shortage that had ensured the creation of a Ministry of Munitions with Lloyd George at its head.

In effecting these major changes in the administration, Northcliffe made use of a style of journalism which was highly distinctive and belonged to his character. In private conversation he never conducted an argument; in journalism, he used the same method. I once entertained him to lunch with Bonar Law and the talk turned to a discussion of the "Stomach Tax" and the election prospects. "You will lose the Election," Northcliffe said to Bonar Law. On being asked his reasons for holding this opinion, he simply repeated, "You will lose the Election."

He hammered and reiterated his themes until the point was firmly driven home.

Northcliffe may have been wrong. No one can tell. War put an end to the impending election.

For all that Lord Northcliffe's was an attractive personality; and he was capable of sudden flashes of humour that relieved the strain of his dictatorial manner. On one occasion, he instructed his newspapers to offer a substantial money reward for the discovery of a motorist who had killed a pedestrian and driven on. By an unlucky chance it turned out that the car belonged to one of his brothers, though at the time of the accident it was being driven by a chauffeur. Northcliffe never failed to remind his brother about this incident. Years later, when it was suggested that a reward should be offered for the apprehension of a train murderer, Northcliffe replied, "Better see where my brother was that day."

Northcliffe was an immensely likeable and generous man with spectacular achievements to his credit. He raised the standard of living in Fleet Street. He set up a new system of journalism. *The Times* was dying when he took charge of it and living when Northcliffe died. The man was great.

Lord Northcliffe's home was at Sutton Place, a historic and magnificent Elizabethan residence near Guildford. He spent much of his time at Broadstairs. More and more, he chose to supervise his papers from this retreat, enjoying the delights of a country villa, and retiring to bed, as was his custom, at 9.30 every evening. He avoided the social intercourse customary to a man of his position; little was known of his private life. His immediate associates may have known of his mysterious social relations. But political circles were uninformed.

In politics, Northcliffe's position was a nebulous one; he had once stood as a Tory candidate but he never had more than a very loose foothold in the Conservative camp.

His influence, however, particularly when he was assaulting the public reputations of ministers, was something which had constantly to be reckoned with. Politicians, therefore, feared and hated him. Northcliffe, for his part, never attempted to understand them or to cultivate relations of amity with them.

In the political crisis of December 1916, Northcliffe came down strongly on the side of the anti-Asquith faction. He did this because he sincerely believed that the Asquith government was a government of weak men and, as such, a peril to the country. He used his papers to urge that they should be replaced and to prepare public opinion for the reception of a new and determined administration.

His attitude was thus of the greatest value to Lloyd George; but it was given independently of that statesman and not by pre-arrangement with him.[a]

In fact, Lloyd George's relationship with Northcliffe was not a close one and there was little confidence between them. Northcliffe's sympathies lay not with the politicians but with the generals. Shortly before the fall of the Asquith Government he had declared in favour of something approaching a military dictatorship under Haig and Robertson.[b] Lloyd George later disparagingly declared that, ever since 1916, Northcliffe had become "the mere kettledrum of Sir Douglas Haig, and the mouth-organ of Sir William Robertson"[c]—the one Commander-in-Chief, the other Chief of the General Staff.

Lloyd George's distrust of Northcliffe was shared by his supporters in the Government. Four important Conservative ministers, in fact, so strongly resented the activities of the powerful Press Lord that they made it a condition of their acceptance of office under Lloyd George that Northcliffe should be given no part in the new administration.[d]

Thus, at the beginning of 1917, despite the power and influence he had built up in Fleet Street, Lord Northcliffe was hated and rejected by the political leaders. The Government had been manned at the price of his exclusion from it, and the Prime Minister had made plain his unwillingness to work with him. An attempt which I had made to secure a reconciliation between them, soon after Lloyd George moved to Downing Street, had come to nothing.[e]

In the middle of 1917, however, Lord Northcliffe's political fortunes entered a new phase. At the end of May, he was invited by the British War Cabinet to head a British Mission to the United States of America.

It was a surprising development and behind it there were complex motives.

At this time, Lloyd George was contemplating bringing Churchill into the Government, appointing the most unpopular political figure in England to be his colleague. It was a step fraught with difficulties, one of which was the fact that Lord Northcliffe's criticism of Churchill had been most bitter. Hence it was of definite concern to Lloyd George that the powerful force of Northcliffe's opposition should, on this occasion, be out of the way.

Now the idea was a splendid one. But how might it be received in the inner government circles? It was certain to provoke a considerable resistance, as events were to show.

The difficulty of bringing Churchill into the Government was serious indeed, but the difficulty of winning approval for the appointment of Northcliffe to an important American Mission was also immense. Trouble would be the portion of the Prime Minister; and well he knew it. Thus it was that Lloyd George decided to go about his business with considerable caution.

First he persuaded Bonar Law to endorse the Northcliffe appointment. He said nothing to the Conservative leader about Churchill.

Then he called together the Heads of Departments concerned with American purchases including the Admiralty, War Office, Munitions, Food, etc. Putting the question by the system adopted by the Scottish Divines who prepared the Shorter Catechism, the Prime Minister asked: Should Northcliffe represent us in America? Answer: Yes, Northcliffe.

Thereafter the Cabinet colleagues were consulted and on 25th May, 1917, approval was given to the choice of his Lordship, subject to the views

ASQUITH. Uniformed indolence, gentle indifference.

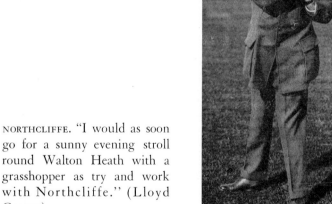

NORTHCLIFFE. "I would as soon go for a sunny evening stroll round Walton Heath with a grasshopper as try and work with Northcliffe." (Lloyd George)

THE FALL OF A GIANT

and opinions of Balfour, the Foreign Secretary—then completing a wartime mission in America—and also of the British Ambassador in Washington, Sir Cecil Spring-Rice.

Balfour had already requested that the question of representation on a permanent mission should be postponed until his return. He wished to present his considered view to the Government. A worthy representative must be chosen to take up a task of such importance. He did not look on Northcliffe as that "worthy representative". He cabled his earnest opposition from Ottawa. Spring-Rice, the Ambassador, was frankly and outspokenly hostile to the Northcliffe appointment.

Lloyd George, faced with this response, which in effect amounted to the rejection of his candidate, determined to find another way round the problem.

The American Ambassador in London, Mr. Walter Page, was consulted. He gave enthusiastic approval of Lord Northcliffe, transmitting his glowing message of support through the British Foreign Office.

The Cabinet met on Wednesday, 30th May. After hearing the message of Mr. Page, the Prime Minister was given the necessary authority to invite Lord Northcliffe to head a British Mission to the United States for the purpose of co-ordinating the machinery of the various branches of the administration there. Evidently the Ministers who had been consulted forgot all about the decision to seek the opinion of Balfour and Spring-Rice whose hostile views were not re-

65   E

ported. The Cabinet agreed without further debate to the appointment of Lord Northcliffe and the offer was made to him that same day.

Northcliffe responded with enthusiasm. Indeed the invitation to represent his country in this important capacity was most attractive to him. For here was an opportunity he had long awaited. It was the first public task he had been asked to undertake and it marked a starting-point in his political office-holding career. Northcliffe accepted with joy; his role as critic and spokesman discarded in a moment. He was off without a backward glance. Within thirty-six hours he had boarded a liner for America.

From the ship he addressed a pencilled note to his brother:

Adieu, my dear Cecil. I was unable to find you ere I made my sudden and very unwilling exit.[8]

Northcliffe was on the high seas before the political pundits had observed his departure.

There was about his flight that characteristic of the flamboyant and the dramatic that always marked the major gestures in Northcliffe's life. He set off alone, without waiting for his staff, and he took elaborate precautions to veil his departure in secrecy. Before sailing, he arranged with the newspapers that his appointment should be released to the British and American Press just before his arrival in New York. Thus he made certain of balking opposition that was sure to come. He showed prescience.

There was indeed a big resistance movement.
The tempest raged for many days, developing into
a whirlwind of trouble. There were three separate
storm centres: Northcliffe's unpopularity in political circles which stood high; the large group of
enemies he had smitten who had been for long
patiently lying low; and also the opposition to the
Northcliffe appointment by Balfour, Secretary of
State for Foreign Affairs.

In his *War Memoirs*, the Prime Minister gives
the following account of the selection of Lord
Northcliffe. The War Cabinet, writes Lloyd
George, met on 25th May to discuss the appointment.

"Those Heads of Departments concerned who
were present were of opinion that Lord Northcliffe might be a very suitable person for this
appointment, and the War Cabinet decided that
a telegram should be transmitted to the British
Ambassador at Washington as well as to Mr.
Balfour, asking them for an early expression of
their views on the proposed appointment. A
satisfactory response was cabled by Mr. Balfour
on 28th May."

But other evidence refutes this story of the satisfactory response of Balfour. Lloyd George had
forgotten that the very contrary was the case.

R. S. Baker, in his book *Woodrow Wilson
Life and Letters*, quotes a letter written to Wilson,
dated 31st May, from his political adviser Colonel
House reporting that the British Ambassador
had been to see him very much perturbed over a

message Balfour had received from his Government about the Northcliffe appointment and had shown House Balfour's reply, which "was a very earnest argument against sending any such representative here at this time."[1]

An examination of the diaries of Colonel House confirms this statement. It gives conclusive testimony to Balfour's very great hostility to Northcliffe's appointment to America.

Lloyd George's own papers disclose another facet of this extraordinary story.

Asquith had come into possession of a detailed account of Balfour's unfavourable reply to the telegram of 25th May. The Prime Minister at once assumed that the Foreign Office had circulated the Balfour reply to Asquith. An enquiry drew from Lord Robert Cecil, the Minister in charge during Balfour's absence, a curt and formal denial. I quote it here in full:

> Prime Minister,
>   I find that Balfour's telegrams about Northcliffe did *not* go to Mr. Asquith. So the leakage must be elsewhere.
>
>   R.C.[1]

Lloyd George was in fact furious about this leakage of information which could have been used most dangerously against him by his political opponents. Suspicion fell heavily on various members of the Government.

Edwin Montagu, who was serving at that time on the Committee of Reconstruction, was suspected of making disclosures to Asquith. But Montagu had no access to Cabinet Minutes and he was therefore exonerated from the charge.

Sir Maurice Hankey was Secretary of the War Cabinet. There was no reason for his intervention except that he had been a close friend of the Asquiths and was still on good terms with them. Certainly he was aware of everything that was going on.

He wrote Lloyd George a full disclaimer of any indiscretion.* He denied that there was any possibility of his having let slip a hint of Balfour's telegram to anyone in the Asquith entourage. Indeed, he was at such pains to dispel any possibility of doubt in Lloyd George that he accounted for his social activities since the telegram had been received.

There was no reason for anxiety about the "leakage" so far as Asquith was concerned. He made no public reference to the Balfour message. But others were to exploit the opportunity, and with good results for themselves.

Now while Lord Northcliffe was crossing the Atlantic in one direction, Balfour was crossing it in the other. When he arrived in England on 9th June, Lord Northcliffe's appointment had already been announced.

For it was on 7th June, 1917, that news of the Northcliffe Mission was released in the British and American papers. A Press Bureau statement published by the majority of London newspapers declared:

The War Cabinet have invited Lord Northcliffe to go to America to co-ordinate the work of the several British Missions that are already established there and to continue the task so successfully initiated in that respect by Mr. Balfour. Lord Northcliffe has accepted this invitation and has already sailed for the United States.

The Times carried arresting and exciting headlines. "Lord Northcliffe's Task. Successor to Mr. Balfour." Fury was let loose. Successor to Mr. Balfour indeed! Balfour's bitter enemy appointed to a diplomatic post in Washington. Indignation and denunciation in and out of Parliament flowed from Opposition, Government supporters, Press and public, and particularly from the personal friends of Balfour.

Bonar Law, Leader in the House of Commons, was deluged with hostile questions. Had Mr. Balfour been consulted and was it upon his advice that Northcliffe went to America? Bonar Law replied that Northcliffe's appointment had been confirmed before Balfour's return and that there had been no opportunity for consultation.'

In the House of Lords, Curzon's answers increased the state of confusion and added to the growing crisis. The *Daily News* reported that, asked whether Balfour had been consulted, Lord Curzon, "displaying considerable uneasiness, remained silent but was pressed for a reply. Rising, with marked reluctance, he said: 'I cannot possibly give an answer to that question without consulting Mr. Balfour.' ''" The critics, comparing Bonar Law and Curzon, swiftly seized upon the confusion. There was a field day in Parliament. The war was forgotten while the critics of the Administration tried to trip up the Government.

Lord Curzon, indeed, found himself in a position of some difficulty in the House of Lords where attacks came from several noblemen who were familiar with the substance of Balfour's disapproval to the appointment. Curzon disclaimed all Government responsibility for the announcement in *The Times*, assuring the House that there was no analogy whatsoever between the appointment of Lord Northcliffe and that of Mr. Balfour.

Criticism broke loose in the Press. The *Daily Chronicle* seized upon the inconsistencies in the Ministers' explanations." The *Daily News* considered the choice of representative a "humiliation" to the country.º The voice of the *Morning Post* too was raised in loud astonishment and alarm.ᵖ

Growing public opinion hostile to Northcliffe, with censure upon the Prime Minister, was widespread. David Davies, M.P., faithful and devoted follower and unpaid secretary, wrote to Lloyd George:

> If Northcliffe is to go to U.S.A. as head of the British Mission you will be making a damn bad appointment and you will raise a devil of a storm in the liberal party, which is just what you want to avoid just now. Northcliffe is one of the biggest intriguers and most unscrupulous people in this country. It is a gratuitous insult to the Americans to send him there —he will do more harm in a week than Balfour has done good in a month. He is not a business man—in

the sense that you want for this job. If you are sending him there to be rid of him, you are making a huge mistake. The restless devil will be back here in less than two months, having in the meantime played hell all round and injured your reputation. Here it will be said that you are afraid of the Harmsworth Press. Rothermere at the War Office; Cecil (Harmsworth) in the Garden City;* Northcliffe in New York. . . . We shall soon have a Government of the Harmsworths, thro' the Harmsworths, and for the Harmsworth Press.[1]

So much had been said and such furious attacks were being made, that Lloyd George gave a sharp and devastating answer to his old friend and supporter. Davies was dismissed from the Secretariat, and with contempt and derision.

While Northcliffe's appointment upset both Parliament and the Press in England, the intimation was to prove distressing to the administration on the other side of the Atlantic.

Although warm approval for the Northcliffe Mission had been secured from the American Ambassador in London, no attempt had been made to seek the President's consent, and no overtures were made to the State Department in Washington. Instead, on 31st May, Sir William Wiseman, chief of the British Intelligence Service in Washington, submitted a memorandum on the War Mission to Colonel House. Wiseman, a young man of thirty-two, had served in France before taking up his post. He had got on to good terms with Colonel House, and through

* Garden City was the name given to the yard of 10 Downing Street, where huts were set up for the overflow of secretaries.

him had influenced the President. Their relations developed into intimacy, and House in his memoirs speaks of Wiseman with admiration and affection. Wiseman's memorandum outlined the nature of the work to be undertaken and announced that the British War Cabinet proposed to appoint Lord Northcliffe.'

The proposal was received with genuine dismay in America. Frederick Dixon, the editor of the *Christian Science Monitor*, wrote to Balfour:

> ... Whatever induced the Government to send Lord Northcliffe here? May I explain hastily that this is not a question to which I expect an answer. It is merely a horrified note of exclamation. I thought everybody knew that the gentleman was regarded here as the British Mr. Hearst. ... The fact is, if I may so say, that I should think a man less a persona grata it would have been difficult to find, nor is it very wise surely to have as a government representative, in any way, a man with a journalistic claque always rubbing the skin off its hands, in its exertions.'

In official circles there was stout resistance. The appointment was particularly unacceptable to the President.

Northcliffe, self-educated and unruly, was the man least calculated to appeal to President Wilson. Hence, when the news came to him from Colonel House, the President sent an immediate rejoinder:

> Action mentioned in your letter of yesterday would be most unwise and still more unwise the choice of the person named.'

The appointment was equally unwelcome to Colonel House. He wrote to Wilson:

> I am sorry Northcliffe is coming, I thought Balfour's cable had headed him off . . . I am afraid his visit may stir up the anti-British feeling that at present is lying dormant."

The opinion of the State Department was so strong that the Secretary of State, Robert Lansing, sought to prevent the dispatch of the Mission.

In the event, Lansing's intervention was answered by the arrival of Northcliffe in New York.

President Wilson was thus confronted with a *fait accompli*. His hand was forced. And he was obliged to accept the appointment. Northcliffe's swift departure from Great Britain had clinched the job.

But recognition was most grudgingly given. As Northcliffe came ashore Colonel House advised the President that, as the British Government had given Northcliffe the widest possible powers, "it would therefore seem necessary to give him proper consideration".

But he added that, at his suggestion, Wiseman was advising Northcliffe not to talk through the Press and not to attempt to force his opinion upon the American people."

In fact, Northcliffe took the initiative. On the morning of his arrival in New York he telephoned to Wiseman, who was at that moment in the office of an American official.

"Is that you, Sir William Wiseman? The Prime Minister told me to get in touch with you as soon as I landed. I have been disgracefully treated. There was no one from the Embassy to meet me and no arrangements have been made for my staff, not even a secretary. I am cabling the Prime Minister to say that after this disgraceful treatment I am returning at once."

Wiseman, thinking the conversation unsuited to a public telephone, proposed to go and see North-cliffe.

"By all means," Northcliffe replied, "come and lunch with me at the St. Regis Hotel."

Arriving there, Wiseman found himself one of about ten guests, among whom were T. P. O'Connor, William Randolph Hearst and Pader-ewski, the Polish pianist and patriot. Pader-ewski was seated on Northcliffe's right and Hearst on his left. The atmosphere was strained, although Northcliffe seemed to be quite uncon-scious of this. For Hearst's newspapers were violently anti-British and Paderewski's sympathies were, of course, passionately on the side of Britain. He would not speak a word to Hearst, and Wise-man almost imagined that he was fingering his knife.

Northcliffe—now completely restored in temper —turned to the guest on his left, and said: "Hearst, I have known you for a long time, you are a poor journalist, you know."

In British official circles the chatter was not directed to Hearst. Everybody concentrated on criticism of Northcliffe. His appointment was particularly disagreeable to Sir Cecil Spring-Rice, the British Ambassador, who imagined he had suffered during the war from direct attacks in the Northcliffe Press.

Lord Northcliffe's reception at the Embassy was therefore a dramatic one. Later he wrote a lively description of it to Lloyd George's secretary, J. T. Davies.

My reception at the hands of the British Ambassador could not have been worse [he recorded].

I was not received on my arrival here even by the British Consul, who excused himself by telling me that, although he knew I was coming, he had not been formally notified by the Embassy. The Embassy excused themselves by saying that they were told from London to keep the matter entirely secret.

It was not secret because I was met by the usual gang of reporters, photographers, and cinematographers. That didn't matter, but it necessitated my reading to the members of the Commission my agreement with the Government, to prove my authority.

Sir Cecil Spring-Rice is an odd person. He is under the obsession that anybody who comes here is a reflection on himself. He was rude to Sir Hardman Lever and ruder to me.

Here is an account of an amazing scene which took place in his room at the Embassy, which I dictated immediately after my return . . .

"In the evening—after introducing me all day to a number of the Ministers—Sir Cecil gave a dinner to me at the Embassy. He asked me in the afternoon to come a little beforehand as he wished to go into a few private matters. I went.

"He was sitting at a table before his red boxes, and, suddenly looking up, produced a cutting from the pro-German *Evening Post* which had appeared prior to my arrival and which said, as far as I can remember, that it was odd that a man who had criticised the Ambassador in scareheads and articles (a concoction) should be coming to this appointment.

"He then suddenly rose, looked at me in a very queer way, and pointing his finger at me, said: 'You are my enemy. Apart from these criticisms, you inserted four years ago an anonymous attack in *The Times* which nearly killed me; *and Lady Spring-Rice declines to receive you on that account.*'—(There are, fortunately, other charming ladies in Washington!)

"I replied that I had never criticised him. He rejoined that he was criticised in a letter to *The Times* for his prolonged absence from the Embassy and for travelling on German ships; that his absence was due to his health, and to diplomatic circumstances which he could not publicly explain.

"I observed that, as this was his view of my visit, I proposed to leave the house, and I walked towards the door with the intention of so doing, when he rushed after me, put out his hand, and said: 'We have to work together whatever we may feel about each other.'

"I accepted his hand, and the incident was fortunately closed at that moment by the announcement of the French Ambassador.'"[w]

Spring-Rice gave an account of the Northcliffe incident to his chief, the Foreign Secretary, Balfour, on 13th July. It does not convey an identical record of the interview. It may be described in the words of the Scottish Psalter as "Another version of the same".

When Lord Northcliffe arrived, he sent for Gaunt*
and Wiseman and complained very bitterly that the
Embassy had not sent to meet him at the Dock. He
said it was an intentional insult and that he felt inclined
to go home again. They explained to him that strict
orders had been given to keep his movements secret. . .

On the day of his arrival, Tom Spring-Rice† and
Gaunt met him at the station with a message from me
that I was attending an entertainment in honour of the
French Scientific mission but would go at once to his
lodging if he wished to see me that night. He
preferred according to his habit to go early to bed.
The next morning he called at the Embassy and I
arranged to take him to the State Department. . . . In
the evening, he dined with me to meet the Italian
and French ambassadors. . . .

. . . He asked me how it was that the opinion
seemed to prevail that there was hostility between
himself and the Embassy. I told him that, as far as I
knew, no one in the Embassy was responsible for this
impression which certainly prevailed in the press.

The cause of it was no doubt the attacks made in
his papers on several occasions against the Embassy.
Before the war he had made in *The Times* an anonymous
and libellous attack on myself which, being an official,
I was unable to resent in the manner which my
solicitors had informed me was open to me if I
desired. During the War, his paper, in conjunction
with the *Tribune*, had attacked the Embassy for not
having imitated Count Bernstorff's policy as regards
the press. This also we had not resented and had made
no reply, but of course the impression prevailed that
his attitude towards the Embassy was as hostile now
as it had been before. I said that under present
circumstances it would be childish and wicked to allow

* Captain Guy Reginald Gaunt (later Admiral Gaunt), Naval Attaché for the
United States.
† Hon. Thomas Spring-Rice, Second Secretary at the British Embassy in
Washington.

personal antagonisms to prevail over the public advantage. He entirely agreed and our relations have been very pleasant and friendly.*

After this opening storm, Lord Northcliffe settled down to his tasks. His responsibilities raised him up. He showed traits and qualities which surprised his critics and comforted his friends. Certainly at this time his mentality was not fashioned out of marble. His character was not graven in stone. He listened to advice but not always with understanding. He was a charming and interesting companion with a gay humour. Occasionally he had entirely different manners and attitudes. Sometimes he would scold the journalists and the politicians and almost everybody about him.

He always saw a situation with truth but he invariably painted it in bright colours. Reiteration and over-emphasis, a part of his newspaper technique, still broke out in crisis. Yet he was adaptable to his surroundings and he possessed brilliant talents for improvisation. His immense prestige served him well. With swift and certain touch, he gained influence and authority in both British and Allied circles. Steadily his power developed and his prestige extended until in the early autumn of that fateful year of 1917 his administration had won the approval and praise of the staffs of British missions and even of American Government officials of high rank.

True there were occasional outbursts and now and then examples of vain and self-centred diversions. Such an incident is recorded in the Page Papers.

It was on 13th August, 1917, that Northcliffe informed the United States Ambassador in London' that the British Fleet had been in danger of being put out of action for the want of fuel oil. Balfour, he declared, had put on him the "enormous responsibility" of remedying this "shortage of oil".

So, Northcliffe told Page, he got up bright and early thus protecting his countrymen from "a jump in the oil market." That day he devoted to "cautious pussyfooting". Then he got on the telephone to the Standard Oil Company and all was well. The British Navy was in action again with oil and at a "less price than we would have averaged over here."

There is no record in the Page Papers of any reply to this account of Northcliffe's pussyfooting activities. But Page might have asked: "Since the British Fleet is conveying American soldiers to the battlefront why not ask the President or the Procurement Agency for fuel oil?"

Northcliffe's enthusiasm and his powers of improvisation swiftly won for him the admiration and even the approval of his enemies. Sir Cecil Spring-Rice, writing to the Foreign Secretary not long after Northcliffe's arrival, declared:

Lord Northcliffe is making an excellent impression and is seeing a great number of prominent persons here. He must be collecting a great deal of valuable information. There is no objection to him on the part

of any official and the President has given him a very
favourable reception. . . . He is on very good terms
with M. Tardieu [head of French Mission], who is an
old friend, and this is a very important matter at the
present moment.¹

Colonel House, with whom Northcliffe worked
in close co-operation, was glowing in his praise,
and references in his private papers reflect an
increasing admiration and even affection for
Northcliffe. In August, House cabled to England
that Lord Northcliffe was accomplishing wonderful work and was getting on well with everyone.
Later he recorded: "He was tireless in his en-
deavours to stimulate the courage and energy of
the Allies, and he succeeded in bringing them to a
realisation of the mighty task they had on their
hands."ᵃᵃ

Was there any discordant note? Yes, the voice
of Lord Reading who was in America on a special
mission. It is written in House's Diary. Said
Reading when leaving House one day to make
room for Northcliffe: "I will now turn you over to
Northcliffe in order that he may tell you the things
he told you the last time you met."ᵃᵇ

Northcliffe's long association with Americans
stood him in good stead. He wisely acknowledged
that "nothing can be gained here by threats, much
by flattery and self-abnegation."ᵃᶜ He worked
incessantly to bring home to the American people
the measure of Britain's war effort.

He never once put a foot wrong. He moved
from triumph to triumph. And he wrung a tribute
from the President.

Northcliffe had climbed out of the Valley. Now he stood upon the Summit of the Mountain.

At the end of September, Northcliffe decided to return to England and Lloyd George was not unwilling to welcome him home again. "I have never worked so hard before"[ad] wrote the founder of the greatest newspaper power of his time. Northcliffe invited his brother, Lord Rothermere, to take on the American job and received an acceptance of the offer. He then recommended the appointment to Lloyd George. There is no trace of any answer. Certainly Lord Rothermere did not go to New York.

In November, Northcliffe's mission came to an end. By that time he had reached the ranks of successful political administrators. He returned to England to receive from the War Cabinet its thanks and congratulations, and from the Monarch a viscountcy in recognition of his work. * He stood in such favour with the public and had made such a good impression on the politicians that high office stood open to him. It was almost like Napoleon returning from Elba.

And it was in just such terms that the gossips chattered in the clubs and luncheon rooms and at dinner tables. "Northcliffe is coming! What will he say? How will he be received by Lloyd George? Will he be in the Government?" Both political parties talked of this man. His name was echoing through the corridors and the meeting places of Whitehall.

* See Chapter VII, The Birth of the Royal Air Force, p. 217.

82

Three days after his arrival, the answer to all these puzzles that excited the pundits was given by Northcliffe himself.

On 15th November he lunched with Lloyd George at Downing Street. In the course of their conversation Lloyd George sounded him on the subject of the Air Ministry, a new department of State.

Lord Northcliffe left the Prime Minister under the impression that, if an offer of this post was made to him, it would be accepted.

Bonar Law had been persuaded to approve of Lord Northcliffe's appointment to the Ministry. His presence in office would obviously be of considerable advantage, and his support for the Government in the gathering struggle between Soldiers and Civilians could not be underestimated.

But before nightfall all the plans and projects crashed and perished. Lord Northcliffe released that evening through the Press Association a public rejection of the Air Ministry, condemning in outrageous terms the very ministers he had been asked to serve with as colleague and co-worker. He attacked the delays of Balfour's Foreign Office and the misuse of Censorship. Praise was given to Haig and his generals, although Northcliffe knew well that the Prime Minister was moving into a crisis on account of the conflict with the Army Chiefs, and the Military threat to the very existence of his Government.

Lord Northcliffe's open letter appeared in the Press the following morning. It opened thus:

Dear Prime Minister,

I have given anxious consideration to your repeated invitation that I should take charge of the new Air Ministry. The reasons that have impelled me to decline that great honour and responsibility are in no way concerned with the office which is rightly to be set up.

From this Northcliffe went on to contrast the "virile atmosphere" on the other side of the Atlantic with the dallying and weakness which he alleged prevailed in Britain. He spoke of obstruction in Government departments, and of men in authority "who should have been punished" but had been elevated.

We have, in my belief, the most efficient army in the world, led by one of the greatest generals, and I am well aware of the fine achievements of many others of our soldiers, sailors and statesmen; but I feel that in present circumstances I can do better work if I maintain my independence and am not gagged by a loyalty that I do not feel towards the whole of your Administration.

Northcliffe's action in publishing this letter was the grossest breach of political etiquette. *

On the day of its publication Colonel House lunched at Buckingham Palace. While he ate, he sat between the Queen and the Prime Minister. He talked mostly with Her Majesty. His diary

---

* Lloyd George described the action as "one of those lapses into blundering brutality to which his passion for the startling gesture sometimes led him".*ae*

records: "She recalled with some amusement my prediction that Northcliffe would begin an attack upon the Ministry, and cited his letter in the morning press declining to accept a Cabinet position as evidence. She seemed to talk without hesitation about matters of state or of personages, which would be embarrassing if repeated."

After eating, House "stood apart" with Lloyd George, he wrote in his diary, "telling jokes and laughing at his (Lloyd George's) predicament with Northcliffe. I told him of Northcliffe's visit and of how perturbed we were when we heard he was coming. He said, 'Of course you know why I sent him'. I gave him an account of the way we took him in hand and of how we had tried to steer him straight. George thought it was a remarkable achievement, but he said towards the end, 'I notice before he left, Northcliffe was doing much more talking, and I expected every day to have to recall him.' I asked if Northcliffe was to return to the United States. He (Lloyd George) replied: 'I hope you will ask for him because I would like to send him. I would even be willing to take Roosevelt* for a while in exchange, although,' he added quickly, 'not permanently.' . . .

"We had a good time and I am afraid the King and Queen, who I know dislike George, wondered how I could be on such friendly terms with him."[af]

Four days after this conversation the King asked House to come to Buckingham Palace.

---

* Former President Theodore Roosevelt—bitter enemy and critic of President Wilson.

House writes in his diary: "The King was full of Northcliffe and his dictatorial assumptions. He asked me to find out quietly, without using his name, if the Prime Minister intended to let Northcliffe go back to the United States. He also wanted to know whether the Prime Minister would take General Sir William Robertson, Chief of Staff, to Paris for the Inter-Allied Conference. I told him I was sure he would, and I was also certain Northcliffe would return to America whether the Prime Minister desired it or not."[ag]

Colonel House saw Lloyd George at dinner that same evening. "We talked of Northcliffe," he reported in his diary. "He (Lloyd George) evidently is afraid of him, and, unfortunately, Northcliffe knows it."[ab]

Five days after Northcliffe's offensive letter appeared in the Press, Sir Edward Carson, who by this time had become a member of the War Cabinet, said in a speech at the Constitutional Club:

> I do not understand this kind of criticism. After all, if a man has a seat in Parliament, and he thinks things are going wrong, why does he not go to his seat in Parliament and tell us what we ought to do to set them right? There he could be answered. I have had a search through the volumes of *Hansard*, and this great man, so far as I can see, has never made one single suggestion since the war from his seat in Parliament, where it can be criticised.[al]

Austen Chamberlain, speaking later in the House of Commons, said of it:

THE FALL OF A GIANT

[Lord Northcliffe] addresses to the Prime Minister a public letter which I should have thought was contrary certainly to practice and perhaps to the honourable traditions of confidence which prevail in public life to have published at all, in which, with an insolent and offensive patronage of my right hon. Friend, he combines an equally insolent and offensive criticism of my right hon. Friend's colleagues.[j]

Not only was the letter a direct affront to the Prime Minister, but it also aimed a humiliating blow at the President of the Air Board, Lord Cowdray. Lord Northcliffe's opening reference to a "repeated" invitation was both at variance with the facts and deliberately misleading. And it was deeply wounding. Lord Cowdray never recovered from this public humiliation; and he never forgave Lloyd George. He submitted his resignation at once. In this way, thanks to Northcliffe's untimely and discourteous act, the ranks of the anti-Lloyd George Liberals received a bitter and influential recruit.

But Northcliffe himself was the real victim of his own rash act. The great newspaper Viscount, by his diplomacy and by unremitting work, had earned at last an elevated place among the politicians. Once he had been wholly rejected by them; now he had returned from a triumphant mission. He could surely take his place as a gladiator in the political arena. There seemed to be no limit to the political power that stood open to him. The Premiership itself was not beyond his grasp. Yet within days of his arrival in the country he chose deliberately to flout the prized con-

ventions of public life and set himself at odds with
the politicians. From that moment he never again
set a foot right in politics.

The rise and fall of Lord Northcliffe was
accomplished in the short space of six months.
And it was a rise and fall unprecedented in political
history. The tragedy of Lord Northcliffe was that,
in his hour of political pre-eminence, he cast himself down. Never again was he invited to take
high office.

Later, in the middle of 1918, he made another
bid for political power. The war was going badly
and Northcliffe was increasingly obsessed with the
belief that he was the Man of Destiny whom public
opinion would call upon to take over the Government. He would become Lord President of the
Council in a Lloyd George-Northcliffe administration. He would, in effect, divide Downing
Street with Lloyd George, and he would keep
Fleet Street for himself. His demand amounted
to that.

In making this overture for place and authority
Lord Northcliffe employed two intermediaries,
Lord Reading and myself. Accompanied by Sir
Campbell Stuart, he then left for Scotland by
motor-car. On the journey Sir Campbell Stuart
telephoned frequently on Northcliffe's instruction
to ask for the Prime Minister's answer. When he
reached Glasgow he was told it was a downright
refusal. The Coalition leader had rejected him.
The Conservative colleagues of Lloyd George
would not receive him.

Northcliffe was to experience a final and a

grievous disappointment. When the composition of the Peace delegation was under discussion in the Press and the lobbies, Lloyd George suggested to Lord Northcliffe that he should take a house in Paris close to the Prime Minister so that consultation between the two men might be facilitated.

Northcliffe regarded this proposal as an invitation to join the Peace delegation and informed his newspaper colleagues accordingly. When, however, Northcliffe asked Lloyd George for his warrant or commission as a Peace delegate, the Prime Minister informed him that he had no intention of including him in the British delegation.

He had now three grievances rankling in his mind continuously and exciting him to bouts of extreme and vitriolic criticism of the Prime Minister: (1) The refusal to give him a place in the Government which Northcliffe foolishly thought could be had for the asking. (2) The conviction that he was entitled to a place on the British Peace delegation. (3) The confused belief that a place had been offered and then withdrawn from him.

His fury consumed him and he made use of his newspapers to pour contempt and ridicule on the author of all his discontents.

When the General Election of December, 1918, returned Lloyd George triumphantly to power, in spite of the vituperative opposition of the Northcliffe Press, he suffered a humiliating defeat.

Night of gloom closed in upon Northcliffe. His gaiety and high spirits were memories of the past. Although he gave much attention to his newspapers, his shadow was no longer lengthening across the land.

In 1922 Lord Northcliffe's life came to a close. Yet even in his dying hours, hatred for Lloyd George dominated him. Sir Thomas Horder (later Lord Horder), that most famous of physicians, was attending him.

Horder had been recently knighted, on the recommendation of Lloyd George. He was called to Northcliffe's bedside as he lay desperately ill. As he entered the room, Lord Northcliffe brandished a revolver which had been hidden under his pillow. Pointing it at Horder he cried, "One of Lloyd George's bloody knights."* The male nurse struck at Northcliffe's hand. Lord Horder lived.

Northcliffe died.

* See *Appendix IV*, No. 2.

CHAPTER III

NABOBS AND TYRANTS

DURING the summer of 1917 one episode occurred which was destined to have a far-reaching importance. It concerned the relationship between the Chancellor of the Exchequer and the Governor of the Bank of England. It began with the firmness of Bonar Law, who, slow to anger, was finally roused to assert his principles and thus establish the authority of the Treasury over the Bank of England. And it ended, some thirty years later, with nationalization, when the strong hand of the Government was laid upon the nation's banking operations.

The Bank was the property of private investors. The Board of Directors was elected at annual meetings of shareholders. The Governor in turn was chosen by the Board. In selecting him, the Treasury was not consulted. In all financial concerns the Bank exercised coequal authority with the Government. Currency notes of five pounds and over were issued under the authority of a parliamentary charter. No other Banking house shared the Government accounts and none dared give advice or comment on financial issues at variance with Bank of England decisions.

The Governor of the Bank of England in 1917 was Lord Cunliffe. He had been elected to the post in 1913, and he had the distinction of becoming the first war-time peer created by Asquith, who announced the honour with dramatic incidence at the Guildhall, at the Lord Mayor's Banquet, on 10th November, 1914. Asquith's statement was received by the large City audience of bankers and bill-brokers and barristers with splendid enthusiasm. If the war conferred this titular honour upon him, it also brought to his office a great accession of influence and power. In fact, Lord Cunliffe soon became practically a dictator of finance.

Lloyd George's period at the Treasury * undoubtedly contributed to this result. The two men, though sharing no similarities of disposition or temperament, got on remarkably well. Lloyd George managed to penetrate the gruff, almost surly exterior of the banker and to establish a basis of understanding and respect. More important, he was ready to concede the last word to the Governor in matters of financial policy.

Nor was the financial policy at the outbreak of war at all obscure; it was in fact a stand-still order and a very necessary protection against the wave of mistrust and fear that swept through the Bank Parlours of the City. Exchanges were demoralized. Gold was in demand. Then the ameliorating measures were applied.

No maturing obligation was immediately payable except at the option of the debtor. Bills of

* Lloyd George was Chancellor of the Exchequer 1908 to 1915.

exchange were indefinitely renewed. Banks were given a holiday; thereafter restrictions were placed upon withdrawals of deposits. Cunliffe had the power; Lloyd George got the credit. The politician had saved the City. He had sustained the financial structure, giving peace and tranquillity to all those financial gentlemen who were temporarily seized with panic. Lloyd George was ever grateful to the Governor of the Bank for the credit. The Governor was always pleased and satisfied with the power.

When McKenna came to the office in the Coalition Government of 1915, he found the Exchequer already under the dominance of the Governor of the Bank of England.

But the new Chancellor had views of his own on many matters previously left to Lord Cunliffe, and he was not prepared to follow Lloyd George's methods in dealing with him. Lord Cunliffe clung tenaciously to the belief that all matters of foreign exchange were his exclusive province; McKenna thought otherwise. It was only a matter of time before there was a trial of strength between them.

At the very first encounter, McKenna yielded unwisely to the demand of Lord Cunliffe, who insisted that all meetings between the Chancellor and the Governor should be held in the presence of the Prime Minister. This arrangement considerably undermined McKenna's position. Asquith, striving to achieve a compromise where no compromise was possible, failed to give the Chancellor a proper reinforcement.

His role as negotiator between the two men left him a prey to Cunliffe's determination to assert his authority, as the following correspondence will show.

On 25th July, 1915, two months after McKenna had come to the Exchequer, the Prime Minister wrote to him:

> The Governor of the Bank came to see me again yesterday morning, and I have had the opportunity of talking over the situation with the Chief Justice and Montagu.
>
> The result is that I feel a good deal of disquietude.
>
> Without going into details, there are two or three points which seem to me to be clear:
>
> (1) that it is of primary importance to our credit that none of the American contracts should be dropped through inability to provide exchange for the moment. I understand that provision has now been made for the immediate case;
>
> (2) that the process of acquiring and collecting American securities here for export should be conducted as quietly and unostentatiously as possible;
>
> (3) that every possible effort should be made to withdraw gold from circulation and accumulate it: so that a substantial reserve will always be available for export;
>
> (4) that both Russia and France should have it made clear to them that they must be ready to part with substantial contributions of gold, if they expect us to continue to render them effective financial help.
>
> All these are matters which cannot be put through without delicate handling, and the closest and most cordial co-operation between ourselves and the Bank of England. The Governor has rendered us invaluable service during the past year. He has (like most people) limitations of outlook and faults of temper. But I am

satisfied that, though not nimble either in thought or expression, his deliberate judgment is always well worth taking into account, and that he is perfectly straight.

In regard to Morgans, while I do not doubt that they have made & will continue to make all they can out of us, I see no reason to think that they have been acting unfairly, still less treacherously. The original contract with them may or may not have been wise, but it wd. be bad policy to swop horses now, or to make them suspect that we distrust them.

I have spoken with the frankness which I always use to you, and wh. you never resent.[a]

Now this was by any measure a tough letter. The use of the word "disquietude" gave the message the appearance of a severe reprimand from an angry Prime Minister to an erring subordinate. The letter carried the inference that the Lord Chief Justice and Montagu approved of these strictures on the Chancellor.

But Montagu was Financial Secretary to the Treasury. He was in effect McKenna's Under-Secretary. It was his duty to support and sustain his own chief. Only in serious circumstances could he justify hostile criticism of his Chancellor. Montagu's support for the Prime Minister's letter gave added weight to the reprimand.

Lord Reading, the Lord Chief Justice, was a formidable critic and an important influence in war-time finance. He had financial understanding, a legal training, a career in government and experience in Cabinet. He was well equipped to give good counsel and wise guidance. Holding a non-political post, he had immense advantage in relations with ministers irrespective of Party allegiance.

Reading's outstanding quality was his tact. This gift enabled him to be on intimate terms with Lloyd George, McKenna and Bonar Law, three successive Chancellors of the Exchequer, all of varying natures and diverging temperaments, yet all willing and anxious to avail themselves of Reading's fundamental qualities. Reading kept in with all three, just as he managed to keep on terms with Asquith and Lloyd George throughout the strife between these two Liberal leaders.

As a public speaker and as a parliamentary performer he was a failure. I have heard him in both the Commons and the Lords. His speeches were always dignified and dull. It is acknowledged that at the Bar he was magnificent, yet in private conversation his vocabulary was limited. He never resorted to picturesque phrases. Yet his success as an advocate was immense.

He was cautious, so cautious that he never gave an opinion until he was forced to do so. He was just and a most likeable fellow. Indeed he was a lovable man with an abundance of personal charm.

In the Walter Hines Page Papers at Harvard, there is an account of the character and conduct of Reading. It is not a penetrating analysis though an interesting human document.

London, 16th Jan., 1918.

Dear Mr. President,

You know Lord Reading and have taken measure of him, but the following facts and gossip may interest you. He is one of the ablest Englishmen living—everybody concedes that. But, with that, agreement about him here ends. The very general Conservative view of him is that he cannot be trusted. See and compare the view taken of Disraeli, the other Hebrew Earl, by his political enemies. As between the two, my judgment would be in favor of Reading. He is not so spectacular as old Dizzy was, but he is far sounder. I doubt if Dizzy was honest and I think that Reading is. As Rufus Isaacs he began life as a stockbroker. A high-sporting Jew named Joel caused Isaacs's bankruptcy by some stockbroker's trick. A bankrupt in England is likely to remain a down-and-out for the rest of his life. He suffers a far severer penalty than an American bankrupt. Joel was and is rich and he had much to do with the turf—a common highway whereon brilliant nobodies travel to association with the nobility and sometimes even with royalty. Isaacs forsook the stock exchange and took up the law. Soon after his admission to the bar, Joel became involved in a lawsuit—about something, I don't know what. When the case came to trial, lo! Isaacs appeared in court as the lawyer of the other party to the quarrel; and Joel recalled Isaacs's threat to "get even with him". When that lawsuit ended, Joel had to give up all his social ambitions, and he has lived in retirement ever since. And the event was the making of Rufus Isaacs. It soon became apparent that he was one of the most brilliant and able members of the bar. He has himself told me that for years he worked from early hours to early hours again, day in and day out, for years—a prodigy of industry. When he left the bar gossip has it that his income was not less than $200,000 a year, and his fees were prodigious.

He is, of course, a Liberal, and, under the Asquith Ministry his advancement was most rapid. He was made Solicitor-General 1910, Attorney-General 1910–1913, a Knight in 1910, Privy Councillor 1911,

Baron 1914, Viscount 1916,* Lord Chief Justice in 1913. He is the son of a London merchant and he married a daughter of a merchant named Cohen. The Isaacs and the Cohen are now swallowed up in the Earl and Viscountess, and "Reading" gives no hint of Jewry.[b]

It is necessary to point out that there are several inaccuracies in the letter, not however relevant to the very favourable estimates of Reading's character.

Page did not know that within ten years Lord Reading had paid in full all the debts he contracted when he defaulted on the Stock Exchange. He never was a bankrupt.

With the Prime Minister and McKenna's formidable Under-Secretary Montagu, and also the Chief Justice, banded together in support of the claims of the Governor of the Bank of England, the Chancellor had no choice. He was compelled to resign or give way. His letter to the Prime Minister dated the next day was by no means a fighting reply.

Your letter has caused me not less surprise than pain. I am at a loss to understand what can have been said to you by the Governor of the Bank, the Chief Justice and Montagu to lead you to write it. Nothing that I am conscious of having said or done could make you think it necessary to recommend the course of action suggested in the four propositions in your letter, in the correctness of which I concur so fully as to think that the neglect to adopt them would be most

---

* Lord Reading was created a Marquis in 1926. The Marchioness, his first wife, died in 1930. In August, 1931, he married Stella, the present Dowager Marchioness.

culpable. I should be glad of an opportunity of meeting the Govr.,* the C.J. and Montagu in your presence in order that I may know the precise terms of their complaints.*

Co-operation between Chancellor and Governor practically ceased. At best it could be said that an armed truce existed between the Treasury and the Bank. McKenna at this stage consented to the most amazing encroachment upon his authority. He agreed to a London exchange committee for the regulation of exchange. This committee was given full rights of access to all the gold, assets and securities of the Government. And Lord Cunliffe was appointed chairman. Thus power over Government assets passed from the Treasury to a privately owned banking company in the City—the Bank of England.

Lord Cunliffe was henceforth the financial dictator of Great Britain. Power had passed to him without the knowledge or consent of the House of Commons. Naturally his untrammelled authority went to his head. Like all dictators he acted as a tyrant.

And like many a tyrant his fame did not long outstrip the brief space of time when he strutted through the City like a great Gargantua. A search of the files of the British Museum fails to disclose the name of Lord Cunliffe in the catalogue of the records of the important men of Britain, although he was Governor of the Bank of England for five

* The Governor did not act on the Chancellor's invitation to a meeting.

years—a record term of office at that time. Nor is his career recorded in the Dictionary of National Biography.

Cunliffe was a second-generation hereditary financier—a rare type among successful men of affairs. He inherited from his father a large portion of a fortune of over one million pounds. It was not the fashion of those days for men of wealth to part with their money to escape the death levy. It is interesting to note that his Lordship at his own departure left behind him only £650,000.

And it is indeed a deeper mystery that his name, which was so familiar in political, financial and Fleet Street circles has now been forgotten. It would seem to be lost and gone forever.

But in the days of his glory, and until the fall of the Asquith administration, Cunliffe, the Governor of the Bank of England, dominated and ruled the greatest banking centre in the world—the City of London.

Bonar Law, the new Chancellor of the Exchequer, was no sooner installed at the Treasury than he experienced the full weight of the Governor's opposition. This arose over a £600,000,000 War Loan.

Bonar Law believed that a loan of this scale could be raised in the country at an interest lower than the current rate, which had reached the high level of 6 per cent. He was guided by what he considered the people would do in a spirit of patriotism rather than as a matter of finance. He argued that the country could be made to see the need for money as well as munitions, and would not question the rate of interest.

This was not the opinion of Lord Cunliffe. He firmly maintained that the loan could not succeed at less than a 6 per cent interest rate; the country would not support it. As for the size of the loan, it was impossible to estimate it. The Governor of the Bank of England was convinced that the general public would take little part in the subscriptions, and he declared that the Bank could not co-operate with the Government in launching it. Bonar Law replied that, in that event, he would deal with the Joint Stock banks. This was a warning but Cunliffe was too vain to see it. Bonar Law maintained that there was a limit to the price the Government was justified in paying in loan interest and that it would therefore be better to risk a comparative failure of the loan than to commit the Government to the figure of 6 per cent. From this conviction he refused to budge.*

As I had been advocating a thousand million loan and at the rate of only 5 per cent, with the beating of drums and the blowing of bugles when the subscription lists were opened, I was called on by Bonar Law to attend at his home at Pembroke Lodge in Edwardes Square in order to give testimony to Lord Cunliffe, and possibly make an impression on him. Bonar Law thought I could

---

* Bonar Law described his attitude in an interview with an American correspondent, Mr. Lowell Mellet, reported in *Daily Express*, 5th April, 1917. "The bankers, as was natural, looked at it as a financial problem. I didn't. I considered what the people might do as a matter of patriotism, not as a matter of finance. . . . It was because of this high level of money that many men most competent to judge warned me that the loan could not succeed at less than 6 per cent."

convince most persons, particularly on financial issues. He was wrong about Lord Cunliffe.

It would be unnecessary to say that my representation to his Lordship did not improve his temper or contribute to the general amenities of the discussion. Although I lived next door to him, there was not any evidence of neighbourly sympathy or understanding.

Even though Cunliffe dismissed my arguments with some measure of impatience and displeasure, Bonar Law persisted in his plan.

Events proved him right. The War Loan, announced with a 5 per cent interest rate in January, 1917, was received with great enthusiasm. When the loan closed in February, a total of £700,000,000 had been subscribed.

In this encounter with Lord Cunliffe, Bonar Law had won a resounding success. The real test of authority was yet to come. In one matter, however, Bonar Law took a firm stand from the outset. He would have nothing to do with the condition previously imposed by Cunliffe that the Governor and the Chancellor should meet only in the presence of the Prime Minister. This stand at once consolidated his position.

Matters came to a head in the summer. Lord Cunliffe had lately come home after a three-months' visit to America with the Balfour Mission and it is fair to say that he found things, on his return, far from his liking. He believed that the position of the Exchange Committee had been usurped by the permanent officials at the Treasury and he lost no time in writing in vigorous terms of complaint to the Prime Minister.

Cunliffe contended that all the means of controlling the exchanges had been taken out of the Committee's hands and that the information guaranteed by McKenna, and subsequently by Bonar Law, was being withheld from them. The London Exchange Committee, he said, had therefore become "a mere cypher entirely superseded by Sir Robert Chalmers * and Mr. Keynes". [d] The Governor asserted that the former Chancellor had given him a verbal promise that Keynes "should not meddle again in City matters", a promise that had been kept until McKenna went out of office.

At the same time Cunliffe made representations both in person and in writing to Bonar Law.[e] In fact, he approached the Chancellor with what amounted to a demand for the dismissal of Sir Robert Chalmers.[‡]

Bonar Law replied to these criticisms in a friendly manner, though he considered that Cunliffe had taken an unwarrantable liberty in suggesting the dismissal of Chalmers. He proposed that the Exchange Committee should meet at the Treasury to ensure a closer co-operation and that Stanley Baldwin, the joint Financial Secretary, should become a member of it.

* Permanent Secretary to the Treasury.
† Later Lord Keynes.
‡ In describing this occasion in his letter to Lloyd George on 9th July, 1917, Bonar Law writes: "He did not, of course, put the demand in this form but he told me that it was impossible for him to continue on the Exchange Committee under these conditions. I asked him whether that meant that he was not prepared to go on if Sir Robert Chalmers remained and he replied in the affirmative."[f]

If Cunliffe had confined his disapprobation to
a mere verbal expression, it is possible that some
workable adjustment could have been achieved.
Bonar Law was the most amenable of colleagues,
and the least sensitive about his own dignity and
status, as his fellow politicians were often to dis-
cover to their advantage. But Cunliffe had gone
beyond words and Bonar Law rightly resented
the Governor's attitude. He said to Lloyd George
that Cunliffe's demand for the replacement of
Chalmers was a proof "that he entirely mis-
understands the relations between the Government and the Bank when he ventures to dictate
to me as to the men whom I am to have as my
assistants at the Treasury."[8] Bonar Law was still
anxious to establish a practical co-operation with
the Bank.

At this time, a large quantity of gold was
held for the account of the Bank of England in
Ottawa in the care of the Canadian Government.
The precious metal had been shipped to the
Dominion so that in the event of invasion the
enemy would find at the Bank an empty cupboard.
Now it so happened that on the morning after
Bonar Law had proposed to the Governor that
Stanley Baldwin should deal with Exchange, he
received a letter from Cunliffe informing him
that, without any consultation with the Treasury,
he had instructed the Canadian Government not
to deliver any further amounts of gold when
asked by Sir Hardman Lever, Financial Secretary to the Treasury, and to place the whole
of the gold in Canada at the disposal of the

BALFOUR. Charming and ruth-
less.

CUNLIFFE. The City tyrant.

Banking House of J. P. Morgan and Co. in New York.[h]

Cunliffe, of course, contended that the gold must be held by the Bank of England as security for the note issue. This plea was looked on as so much nonsense by Bonar Law, who demanded from all sources and from every citizen the surrender of assets essential or even desirable for the fulfilment of the needs of an all-out war. All other Banks had been required to surrender their gold; insurance companies, trust companies and private citizens had been directed to give up their various American securities. Some men, Bonar Law would have said, were giving up their lives; why should others be permitted to hold their gold? The Government itself was the real backing for the note issue. There was no possible argument on which Cunliffe could resist the surrender of the gold of the Bank of England.

The instruction, therefore, of the Governor to the Dominion Government not to honour demands for gold made on behalf of the Treasury was fantastic. It was a direct contradiction of the spirit of the nation at war. It could have no precedent in banking history. In effect, Lord Cunliffe had dared to stop the Government's cheque.

I have seldom seen Bonar Law so incensed. His anger was not appeased by a letter from Cunliffe which the Prime Minister passed on to him next day.

Lord Cunliffe was then taking up the attitude, both with Lloyd George and Bonar Law, that he had made an unpardonable mistake in ever allowing anyone outside the Bank to control the Bank's gold. *

Indeed, he went so far as to assert to Bonar Law that he was sure the Court of Directors of the Bank of England would not only never permit it again, but would censure him for having betrayed his trust in ever permitting it at all. At the same time, he disclaimed any idea that the Bank's faith in the Chancellor or Sir Hardman Lever had been impaired.

This moved Bonar Law to action. He communicated his views at length to the Prime Minister. The following letter gives a clear indication of the strength of his feelings in the matter:

9th July, 1917.

My dear Prime Minister,

The letter which you handed to me from Lord Cunliffe is itself an additional proof, though that was not needed, that the present position is impossible and must be brought to an end. In that letter he says—
"I will do anything you can suggest to remove the idea that the Bank's faith in you and Sir Hardman Lever is impaired as such is not the case and never has been."

It is no doubt very kind of him to make this handsome declaration, but I should be sorry to ask for a vote of confidence by the Bank of England in the Chancellor of the Exchequer.

He says also in his letter that I consider the Bank has damaged our credit in Canada. . . . This is not merely a question of damaging credit: it is an act of extraordinary disrespect towards the British Govern-

---

* Cunliffe wrote to Lloyd George on 7th July, 1917, enclosing this letter to Bonar Law and saying to Lloyd George on this point: "I feel you will agree that I did very wrong in ever allowing it."[i]

ment and as I think a direct insult to me who, as Chancellor of the Exchequer, had authorised Sir Hardman Lever to act for the Government. . . .

Bonar Law went on to recount his own interview with the Governor following the news of his action.

I sent for the Governor and pointed out to him that this was a step which ought not to have been taken without consultation with me. He admitted it but said that that was not the principle on which we were now working. In other words, as "reprisals" for what he considered to be a failure on the part of the Treasury to supply the Exchange Committee with the necessary information he took a step of vital importance without consultation with me although he himself admitted that this consultation ought to have taken place. . . .

For these reasons I have, as already discussed with you in conversation, come definitely to the conclusion that the present position cannot continue. There were three possible methods of dealing with it.

One was that I should cease to be Chancellor of the Exchequer and leave the Government, but this you have ruled out: the second is that Lord Cunliffe should cease to be Governor of the Bank of England. There is, however, a third possible alternative, which is that Lord Cunliffe should agree to work with me in a reasonable spirit and with a full knowledge that the Chancellorship of the Exchequer is not in commission and that the views of the British Government, as represented by me, must be carried out.

If you are willing to see him and find out from him whether or not he is ready to continue on these conditions, I should be glad, but I cannot run the risk of a repetition of the friction of the last weeks. . . .

Yours sincerely,
A. BONAR LAW.

Bonar Law was quite unyielding in his determination. He was not fighting to uphold the dignity of his own place in office, but to establish the true relationship between the Government and the Bank of England. The action of the Governor, taken in a spirit of "reprisal", had entirely confounded him. He regarded the Bank of England as the wartime servant of the Government, and the policy it pursued in financial affairs must conform to the Treasury. The Governor's claim that the gold then in Ottawa was to be dealt with entirely by him was contrary to the whole principle of Government.

Bonar Law, moved to a pitch of righteous indignation, was determined to secure a true apportionment of authority once and for all. He now advised Lloyd George that he was willing to allow the present arrangement to continue only on the condition that Lord Cunliffe should send him a written declaration that he would at once resign the Governorship of the Bank on a request from the Chancellor to that effect. Should he decline to do so, Bonar Law would take steps to ensure his immediate replacement at the Bank.

Events now moved with swiftness. Lord Cunliffe soon comprehended the fatal consequences of his action. On 13th July, Bonar Law and Sir John Bradbury, the Joint Permanent Secretary to the Treasury, met the Prime Minister at No. 10 Downing Street. Their meeting produced a statement for Lord Cunliffe's signature clearly defining the Bank's relationship with the Chancellor of the Exchequer. The gist of it was the Bank must act in all things on the direction of the Chancellor for the duration of the war and must consult him in all matters affecting credit. At the same time a draft declaration was prepared to the effect that Lord Cunliffe would be prepared to retire from his position if the public interest required it.*

The documents were forwarded by the Prime Minister to the Governor that evening.

In requiring such an agreement with the Governor of the Bank, Bonar Law was not prompted by any spirit of malice. He had no desire to humiliate Lord Cunliffe. But he believed that without such a commitment the situation would remain open to all the former friction and rivalry which would seriously prejudice the country's war effort.

But Cunliffe was not ready to renounce his authority so easily. He was not prepared to put his signature to such a declaration. His reply to Bonar Law,[j] while expressing his apologies for the action he had taken, contained no acceptance of Bonar Law's demand.†

He asked for support from Lloyd George and Lord Reading. They tried and their intervention was rejected.

Mr. Brien Cokayne,‡ the Deputy-Governor of the Bank of England, now called upon Bonar

* The terms of the draft letter said: "the relationship between the Treasury and the Bank must, during the war, be so intimate that if you felt that there could not be complete and harmonious co-operation between yourself and me, I should not think it compatible with the public interest that I should continue to occupy my position as Governor of the Bank of England."[k]

† Cunliffe, in his reply, covers most of the same points outlined in Bonar Law's draft, but in place of the important phrase (see previous footnote) it says: ". . . the relationships with the Treasury must during the war be so intimate that complete and harmonious co-operation is of paramount importance."

‡ Later Lord Cullen of Ashbourne.

Law. His mission was to intercede on behalf of Lord Cunliffe. He pointed out that the Bank insisted on reserving the right to select its own Governor. This was not, he maintained, a matter for the Treasury. But to this request for consideration Bonar Law returned a firm refusal.

In the City, the repercussions of the quarrel were vast. Lord Revelstoke, a Director of the Bank of England, became identified with those favouring Cunliffe's resistance. He repeated the claim that the selection of Governor was the concern of the Bank alone and not the Treasury.

The Joint Stock banks, under the direction of Sir Edward Holden, were then called together and asked to pass resolutions supporting Lord Cunliffe.

The Times reported that all the great Clearing Banks had joined in the plea for Cunliffe. But *The Times* was in error.

Sir Edward Holden's manœuvre broke down. with Bonar Law's permission I called upon Mr. F. C. Goodenough, then chairman of Barclays Bank, and Sir Herbert Hambling, head of the London and South Western Bank, and put the case to each of them in turn. As a result, they both declared that they would not accept the proposal that the Joint Stock banks should resolve to support Cunliffe.

Bonar Law declined to give in. Thus, in August, Cunliffe fled to the north of Scotland, whence he made a final effort at appeasement. In a letter to Bonar Law on 12th August, 1917, Cunliffe stated that he was sincerely sorry to learn that both he and the Prime Minister were dissatisfied and that they looked for a personal apology. He offered it unreservedly, and he assured Bonar Law that as long as he was Governor of the Bank he would work with him loyally and harmoniously, tendering such advice as he thought necessary to offer. "I fully realize," concluded the Governor, "that I must not attempt to impose my views upon you."[m]

Protestations of loyalty so long as Cunliffe remained Governor of the Bank did not interest Bonar Law because the Chancellor was determined that there must be a change. He would have no more of Cunliffe. He replied that he would be glad to see the Governor when he returned to town. But it made no difference to Bonar Law's determination; never again did he deal with Lord Cunliffe.

When the Court of Directors of the Bank of England met early in November, the decision that Sir Brien Cokayne,* who had been carrying out the duties of Governor since early in August, should succeed Lord Cunliffe as Governor was formally announced.[n]

Even after the decision had been taken, *The Times* and the *Daily Telegraph* carried on an organized campaign to save the Governor from the consequences of his own folly. The *Telegraph* actually described him as "the kindliest and most accessible Governor".[o]

---

* Cokayne had been made a K.B.E. on 24th August, 1917.

There were deep rumblings in the City. Many Bank Directors and others who hoped to attain to high place in financial circles made complaints, but the trumpet gave an uncertain sound.

Such was the termination of the dispute between the Chancellor of the Exchequer and the Governor. But, of course, the significance of the quarrel went deeper. The authority of the Treasury had been explicitly exerted over the Bank of England. That authority was never relinquished. Bonar Law had established a principle on which the final seal was fixed when in 1946 the Socialist Government nationalized the Bank of England.

CHAPTER IV

"IF YOU CAN TRUST YOURSELF WHEN ALL MEN DOUBT YOU"

WINSTON CHURCHILL was the most miserable man in Britain when 1917 ushered in the fourth year of battle.

A great and critical war was unfolding its drama, yet he was playing no part in guiding the struggle—he who felt himself, who knew himself to be equipped by instinct and training for a directing role in war. Quitting Asquith's government after Gallipoli, he had gone to command a battalion in France. On 10th April, 1916, he wrote from Plugstreet (front-line trench) to Sir Edward Carson who had advised him to come home and resume his part in politics. This seemed to hold the prospect of a place in government. He returned to London and, on 20th April, 1916, Lady Carson wrote in her diary:

E. [Sir Edward Carson] and I dined with the Winston Churchills. Who would have thought that could ever have happened? He talks an awful lot and gave me the impression his tongue works faster than his brain, though it goes pretty fast.[a]

But when Lloyd George's government was formed at the close of the year 1916, Churchill was excluded from it. The Conservative Ministers refused to serve with him. Bonar Law opposed office for him. And even Carson, now First Lord of the Admiralty, wrote to the Conservative leader rejecting a proposal to appoint Churchill to a subordinate task as a Member of the Air Board, operating under the authority of the Admiralty and War Office.

Secret   20th December, 1916.

My dear Bonar Law,

I fear this matter creates much difficulty. I do not yet know what the relations between the Admiralty and the Air Board are to be, but certainly it will require great tact and forbearance all round to get any new system into working order. I should greatly fear friction if the appointment is made. I much dislike having to seem opposed to the suggestion as my personal inclination is towards utilizing Churchill's undoubted ability—especially so as he is so down in his luck at present but I hope some other, more suitable opportunity may be found.

Yours sincerely,

E. CARSON.[b]

But exclusion from office would not be regarded by Churchill as either natural or likely to last. And soon events so shaped themselves that opportunity came his way once more.

The over-riding factor in the political situation was the progress of the war. There was every appearance of defeat.

Russia was to all intents and purposes out of

the struggle. Rumania could no longer be counted on as an effective ally. News from the Italian front brought little relief from tension. More disastrous still, the offensive in France, commanded by General Nivelle, was smashed in the Battle of the Aisne in April. On this attack immense hopes were pinned. Its defeat was a correspondingly bitter blow.

If the sky of war was overcast, the scene of domestic politics was troubled and stormy. A gathering combination of forces threatened the administration of Lloyd George.

There was above all the struggle, steadily growing in its intensity, between the Prime Minister and the High Command.

Many civilians and some politicians who had been excluded from office were now talking and writing in support of placing the civil Government in the hands of the generals for the duration of the war.

In this contest, the generals drew more and more comfort and support from influence and affiliations in high places.

Lord Northcliffe persisted in his advocacy of the cause of the generals. He was their valiant champion. He supported them against every challenge from the politicians. So pronounced, indeed, were his sympathies by this time that in May 1917 he made a speech to a newspaper press luncheon at the Mansion House where he declared in favour of something approaching a dictatorship for the High Command.

Lord Northcliffe began with a tribute to the guest of honour, Sir William Robertson, the Chief of the Imperial General Staff, who had spoken in praise of the newspapers. Northcliffe continued: "Our journals felt at liberty, and they thought it their duty, to criticise politicians, because, being very close to the politicians, perhaps not greatly enamoured of them, they knew something of their wiles. [Laughter.] They thought it necessary on occasion to stimulate them to further effort and to ask them, for example, not to interfere with the Army. But there was one thing newspapers did not do. They did not criticise our generals. [Cheers.] They had no need to do so. Each one of them had proved in the last three years that he was a match for the German commander in front of him."[c]

Then there was the King, whose hostility to Lloyd George in this dispute was marked. Frequently he delivered sharp attacks on the Prime Minister urging the soldiers and sailors to defy him while counselling them never to run the risk of a General Election.

In the circumstances, it was natural that Sir Douglas Haig, Commander-in-Chief in France, should be in direct and effective contact with Buckingham Palace. This was no secret. In March, 1917, Haig paid a personal visit to the Palace. He gives this account of the interview in his private papers:

The King . . . stated that he would "support me through thick and thin", but I must be careful not to resign, because Lloyd George would then appeal to the country for support and would probably come back with a great majority. . . . The King's position would then be very difficult. . . . We went over the whole Calais Conference. . . . The King said my account agreed entirely with Robertson's. He was furious with Lloyd George, and said he was to see him tomorrow.[d]

In Parliament the generals found allies against Lloyd George among the ranks of the old administration. "The Asquith-Brass-Hat Alliance" was the name given to a group forming in opposition, slowly—but certainly in considerable strength.

In the month of May 1917 it was plain to the administration that the strength of the Brass Hats and their allies must be tested. Could the generals be detached from their alliance with Asquith? Very soon it was clear that Lloyd George could hope for nothing in that direction. Lloyd George was persisting in his demand for civilian control of strategy. The generals, for their part, were unswerving in their demand for freedom from civilian interference and looked on him as an enemy with whom there could be no truce. And Lloyd George dared not yield to the generals. Their victory would be his defeat in Parliament.

What of Asquith himself? The Prime Minister would gladly have taken him into the Government if Asquith had been willing to serve. But some gulfs are too deep and too wide ever to be bridged. The gulf between Asquith and Lloyd George was one of them. And besides, Asquith's friends were confident that his return to office and power could not be delayed for long.

The front made up of Asquith and the Generals could not therefore be broken. It represented a danger to Lloyd George's government which was formidable enough and might at any moment become fatal.

A more immediate danger than any of these elements confronted the administration in critical and even hostile guise. Winston Churchill. Here was a man of extraordinary abilities, of adroit debating strength, of originality and resourcefulness. At the height of a major war he was out of employment. Yet the greater part of his career had been occupied with problems of a military kind. He had made a thorough study of the arts of war; he had published no fewer than five books on military subjects; he had served actively in Malakand, the Sudan, South Africa and in the trenches in France. And he had held command at the Admiralty at the outbreak of the present disaster. He rightly felt that he had special talents to offer in the crisis of world war.

Instead he was extruded from the centre of action by men of lesser ability and initiative, and his knowledge and his inventiveness of mind— all were wasted. It was a time of grievous frustration for Churchill. Indeed, there were days when he feared that all might be lost if his services were denied to his country.

But for Churchill it was not a time of idleness. He wrote a series of articles for the *Sunday Pictorial*, Lord Rothermere's newspaper, for which, to the envy and admiration of all contributing journal-

CHURCHILL. He smoked matches and ate cigars.

ists, he was paid £250 an article. He talked incessantly about the war and made contacts with journalists and others who helped to form public opinion.

A letter from Churchill to R. D. Blumenfeld of the *Daily Express* shows him at his best.

My dear Mr. Blumenfeld,

I was very glad to get your letter, the more so because I heard from F. E. [Smith] that you felt some compunction about the attacks which the *Daily Express* has made on me during the last year. But really there is no need for this. I am a regular reader of yr. paper and have never seen any criticism wh. I did not think perfectly fair politics. Above all, there has never been anything so far as I am concerned reflecting on private or personal conduct. That after all is the line wh. politicians and political journalists ought to draw. Also I have been greatly amused by many of your cartoons. Therefore pray banish from yr. mind any idea that there has been a breach between us.

Yours vy truly,

WINSTON S. CHURCHILL.*

Churchill was always free from rancour and never treacherous. Unlike the elm tree which gives no warning of falling branches, Churchill gave plenty of notice of changing dispositions; then as now, he was reliable and dependable.

He gave attention to members of Parliament, particularly important back-bench Tories. He took account of the serving soldiers' grievances and spoke in the House in support of their claims. And there were frequent meetings of a dinner club which brought him together with Ministers and other important figures. When Churchill was present at that table, war and war administration were the sole topics of discussion.

In this mood, Churchill became an outspoken critic of the Government. He was constantly formulating criticisms against the offensives in France. Even in the House of Commons he attacked the Government for their conduct in war. Strangely enough, he seldom voted—perhaps in one division out of three—and never against the Government. He sat on the Opposition Front Bench with his old Ministerial colleagues about him. Yet between Churchill and his neighbours there was a failure of sympathy. They saw him as a useful but incalculable ally. They were aware that he was seeking office under Lloyd George. In the meantime his brilliant gifts of oratory were an ever-present menace to the administration. And now that the old dividing lines of party loyalties had melted in the confusion caused by the Lloyd George Coalition, Churchill could sway the House of Commons and win it over with his eloquence.

Lloyd George's position while the war continued to go badly was therefore immensely precarious.

A great speech by Churchill, a cunning move by the generals, a direct thrust by the Asquith group—each of these or all together—might carry the day against the Government.

And there was also Carson, disgruntled and disillusioned, endowed with a mind and a tem-

perament that could prove destructive to the
Government. He had helped to put Lloyd George
in. Would he decide perhaps to help to put him
out again? For it could not be disputed that the
whole force of the man lay in attack. He shone in
opposition, and realized instinctively that his
strength lay there. He had therefore always to
be taken into account in estimating any political
combination against the Government.

But Churchill, although hated by the Tories,
and mistrusted by half the Liberals and all of the
Socialists, would be the linchpin in a coalition
that might and could drive Lloyd George from
the seat of power.

Seeing the whole picture with the eye of a
master of political tactics, Lloyd George was
frightened. Very soon he had still more cogent
reason for alarm.

One day, he passed a message to Bonar Law as
they sat together at a meeting of the War Cabinet.
It read:

My dear Bonar,
   I think you ought to know that Asquith told Win-
ston that, if he came in, he would put him in the
Admiralty.
                                        D.L.G. *

The implication was clear. Churchill would be
tempted to join the Asquith Alliance. Up to this
point his relations with Asquith had been no
more than friendly, neither strained nor intimate.
He had been a powerful independent critic of the

Government. In future, he might be a captain in the hostile forces. The danger was grave indeed. At any risk, the possibility of Churchill joining the Asquith-Brass Hat Alliance must be shattered.

On 10th May, 1917, in a Secret Session, Churchill opened the debate for the Opposition. He reviewed the military position in France and Europe and spoke with intense conviction against a policy that would lead the French and British High Commands to drag each other into fresh and disastrous adventures. It was a speech of considerable power and authority, and Churchill resumed his seat amid the enthusiastic acclaim of the House.

Lloyd George, confronted with a Parliament critical of his administration, knew at once that the crisis could not be far off. He had no doubt of the urgent need for action, and little doubt what form that action should take. Churchill could not be left out of the Government. He must be fenced in, and that forthwith. What could not be squashed must be squared and what could not be squared must be squashed.

Faced with the danger of Parliamentary defeat, Lloyd George displayed his usual intrepid coolness. Indeed, his courage was always more of the moral than of the physical order.

Rising to Churchill's challenge, he delivered a speech which commanded the attention and respect of the House. Frederick Guest, the Chief Liberal Whip, wrote him a letter of congratulation that same evening:

10th May, 1917.

Dear Prime Minister,

The impression in the house, lobby, and smoking room is that you have made a great speech. It has been a good days work in more ways than one.

Winston's speech is also considered to be a fine statesmanlike effort.

Yours sincerely,

FREDDIE GUEST.[g]

This was not, however, the end of the business. After the debate, Lloyd George met Churchill behind the Speaker's Chair. What happened then is recorded by Churchill.

"In his satisfaction at the course the Debate had taken," he writes, "[the Prime Minister] . . . assured me of his determination to have me at his side. From that day, although holding no office, I became to a large extent his colleague. He repeatedly discussed with me every aspect of the war and many of his secret hopes and fears."[h]

Churchill's return to the inner circle is clearly established by two letters which he wrote to Lloyd George later that May. They are now in the Lloyd George collection.

The first is dated 17th May, 1917. It reads thus:

My dear David,

The French Government invited me to go to look at the Front Verdun etc. a fortnight ago, but I had to put this off on account of the secret session. I now think of going next Thursday for a week or so. I should be glad if you would send a personal telegram

to M. Painlevé (who I only know very slightly)
commending me to him and the French Military
authorities. This will ensure their making my visit
pleasant and interesting.

Yours sincerely,
WINSTON CHURCHILL.ⁱ

The second, written two days later, is brief and
jubilant:

My dear David,

A line to remind you to write a letter to Painlevé
and one to Haig about my visit to France.

Do not I beg you however, in writing to the latter
touch on the political matters which we talked of
yesterday.

We had a jolly afternoon and I hope I was not the
only one who liked it.

Yours,
W.^j

The "jolly afternoon" had cemented the new
alliance. Lloyd George had set his sail to catch
the wind. But he could hardly have reckoned
with the buffeting he was to encounter.

The actual task of finding Churchill a place in
the administration was a serious political problem
confronting the Prime Minister. It could only be
achieved with infinite care and preparation. At
best, it must involve him in an open breach with
his Conservative supporters in the Government.

The attitude of the Conservative Ministers to
Churchill had been plainly defined in December,
1916; they were still rigidly opposed to his inclusion in the administration. Bonar Law was no

more disposed to look with favour upon Churchill. There was, in truth, never any real sympathy between the two men. I can recall many occasions when their mutual lack of understanding came to the surface.

Bonar Law had given his opinion of Churchill to Lloyd George when the Prime Minister was pointing out the danger of Churchill as a critic of the Government. "Is he more dangerous," Lloyd George had put it, "when he is FOR you than when he is AGAINST you?" Bonar Law had replied: "I would rather have him against us every time."[k]

Bonar Law's antipathy to Churchill was of long standing, as an extract from his correspondence reveals:

> I agree with the estimate you have formed of Churchill. I think he has very unusual intellectual ability, but at the same time he seems to have an entirely unbalanced mind which is a real danger at a time like this.[l]

In a letter to Bonar Law, Sir Henry Wilson once wrote:

> A man who can plot the Ulster Pogrom,* plan Antwerp and carry out the Dardanelles fiasco is worth watching.[m]

Sir Henry Wilson's criticism would probably have Bonar Law's approval and, in substance, it summed up the whole case for Tory hatred of

* The "Ulster Pogrom" described events when troops and Navy movements took place in 1914 which threatened Ulster. Although the Rt. Hon. J. E. B. Seely, Secretary of State for War, was dismissed over the incident, the Tories believed that Churchill was the moving spirit.

Churchill. Protestant Ulster was the real obstacle to trust and confidence.

Bonar Law always accepted the "Pogrom" theory of the Ulster crisis, blaming Churchill as the real leader. Thus when Bonar Law and Churchill served in the same administration, hostility often broke out in violent controversy even in the presence of many colleagues.

On one occasion, after Churchill joined the Government and in the Prime Minister's absence, when Bonar Law was holding a meeting of Ministers, Churchill uttered prolonged denunciations of the system under which he and also the Service Ministers were excluded from the War Cabinet. These important Chiefs were precluded from exercising any influence on the general policy of the War Cabinet and therefore the Government as a whole. It was wrong, he said, in principle.

Bonar Law listened in silence, and after Churchill had concluded his remarks, said to him: "Mr. Churchill, if the Government is doing something wrong in principle, you have your remedy —why don't you resign?"

Churchill was silenced for a moment. Then he replied: "That is a question you have no right to ask. Only the Prime Minister is entitled to question his subordinate in such terms."

Even when Churchill spoke in jest Bonar Law occasionally gave him a harsh answer. When the War Office was under discussion and Churchill was asked to make up his mind to take the

War Office or the Admiralty, he said jokingly: "What is the use of being War Secretary if there is no war?" Bonar Law made the comment: "If we thought there was going to be a war we wouldn't appoint you War Secretary."

Churchill's opinion of Bonar Law was no less harsh. He attached little weight to Bonar Law's intellectual ability. Writing of him to the Prime Minister, Churchill said: "Most men sink into insignificance when they quit office. Very insignificant men acquire weight when they obtain it."[n]

But while Lloyd George had yielded to Tory antipathy to Churchill as the price of the accession of four Conservative Ministers when he formed his administration,* the situation had now fundamentally altered. The Prime Minister was faced with a mortal threat to his leadership and power. He had to choose between the danger of Conservative resistance over Churchill and the greater hazard of the rising forces of a powerful opposition. He had to choose quickly, and there was no doubt what his choice must be.

So Lloyd George began to test the political atmosphere and to prepare the ground for the return of this contentious figure to Whitehall. At the beginning of June, five weeks before Churchill re-entered the Government, a kite was flown to test the weather. He could be re-admitted to the Government either by way of the Air Board, which was to be reconstituted as a ministry with independent status, or

---

* Curzon, Chamberlain, Cecil and Long had required and received a pledge from Lloyd George that Churchill would be excluded from office.

by the Ministry of Munitions. These were the alternative suggestions Lloyd George put forward.

They won warm support from General Smuts and from Lloyd George's Liberal colleague, Dr. Addison, the Minister of Munitions. General Smuts was anxious that Churchill's initiative and great constructive ability should be used in the Air Department, and he sought to put pressure on Churchill himself to this end. He wrote enthusiastically of the idea to Lloyd George.

Savoy Hotel
London.
6th June, 1917.

Personal
Dear Mr. Lloyd George,

At the request of Capt. Guest I saw Churchill last night and expressed to him my view that if Air was offered to him instead of Munitions (which you had previously mentioned to him) he should accept it. I pointed out that Munitions had become somewhat of a routine department while Air offered great scope to his constructive ability and initiative, and that with effective help from America our aerial effort might yet become of decisive importance not only in the anti-submarine campaign but also on the Western Front in the next twelve months.

The result is that, although he prefers Munitions, he will accept an offer of Air on the assumption that real scope is given him and that he must control the higher patronage in the Air Service.

In spite of the strong party opposition to his appointment, I think you will do the country a real service by appointing a man of his calibre to this department, the vital importance of which will more and more appear.

Yours sincerely,
J. C. SMUTS.[o]

Addison, whose own promotion was under review, was ready to support Churchill's claim either to Air or Munitions, but he counselled Lloyd George to act quickly, since discussion would give opposition time to gather.[p]

Sir Edward Carson's attitude to Churchill's appointment was equivocal. Although he had receded from his opposition as stated in his letter to Bonar Law of 20th December, 1916, he made no effort to help Churchill into the Government. It is true that Churchill had confidence in Carson and believed that the First Lord of the Admiralty would support his return to office. However, there is no evidence of any such activity on Carson's part in the papers of either Lloyd George or Bonar Law. The truth is that Churchill thought more of Carson than Carson thought of Churchill. And Churchill was more friendly to Carson than Carson to Churchill.

Frederick Guest, first cousin of Mr. Churchill and his long-time personal and political friend and follower, entirely under his influence, gave Lloyd George a valuable reinforcement. He wrote encouraging him to press on with his plan to bring Churchill into the administration.

> Your will and influence with your Tory Colleagues [Guest assured Lloyd George] is greater than you have credited yourself with and . . . sooner or later you will have to test it—why not now?
> I have the strongest reasons to believe that the Tories mean to support your leadership even at the expense of their personal feelings.[q]*

* The full text of the letter appears in *Appendix IV*, No. 3.

But the news * of the proposed appointment of Churchill fell like a Big Bertha into the Conservative camp, and such an explosion resounded that the edifice of the Coalition Government trembled, and hovered precariously around Lloyd George's head.

Furious letters poured in upon the Prime Minister.

Lord Curzon expressed the most bitter indignation. He had been the target of Churchill's criticism in a speech in the House of Commons in April. Now he wrote in the most vigorous terms of protest to Lloyd George.

Confidential.

1 Carlton House Terrace,
S.W.
June 8, 1917.

My dear Prime Minister,

May I again and for the last time urge you to think well before you make the appointment (W. Ch.) which we have more than once discussed? It will be an appointment intensely unpopular with many of your chief colleagues—in the opinion of some of whom it will lead to the disruption of the Government at an early date—even if it does not lead as it may well do, to resignations now. Derby, who opened the subject to me of his own accord this evening and who has spoken to you, tells me that it will be intensely unpopular in the army. I have reason to believe the same of the Navy.

Is it worthwhile to incur all these risks and to over-ride some of those who are your most faithful colleagues and allies, merely in order to silence a

---

* The Press Association announced on 8th June, 1917, that Churchill would be appointed to the Air Board. This was a balloon or a kite issued by Downing Street for the purpose of sounding public opinion.

possible tribune of the people whom in my judgement the people will absolutely decline to follow?

He is a potential danger in opposition. In the opinion of all of us he will as a member of the Government be an active danger in our midst.

Yours sincerely,
CURZON.^r

At the same time, Bonar Law received a telling reminder from Lord Curzon of the Tories' December pledge. Curzon wrote:

Confidential.

1 Carlton House Terrace,
S.W.
4th June, 1917.

My dear Bonar,

Possibly there may be no truth in what we read in the papers as to Govt. reconstruction, e.g. Addison in War Cabinet! Churchill at Air Board and so on. I just write a line to say that I hope none of these steps if contemplated will be done behind our backs.

As you know some of us myself included only joined Ll.G. on the distinct understanding that W. Ch. was not to be a member of the Govt.—It is on record and to the pledge I and I think all my colleagues adhere.

Again if it is necessary to remove Addison from Munitions, as to which I know nothing, I can see no reason why he should be lifted up to War Cabinet to which he could add neither [efficiency*] nor strength.

Yours ever,
CURZON.^s

* The letter is written in Curzon's hand and this word is indecipherable.

An urgent warning reached the Prime Minister from the Chairman of the Unionist Party, Sir George Younger, who feared the force of the charge Lloyd George was about to explode. He used the strongest language to dissuade Lloyd George from the course of action he proposed:

8th June, 1917.

Dear Lloyd George,

I do trust there is no foundation for the persistent rumour that Winston is to join the Government. I am seriously afraid that such an appointment would strain to breaking point the Unionist [Conservative] Party's loyalty to you. His unfortunate record, the utter futility of his criticisms of your War Policy at the last Secret Session, and his grave responsibility for two of the greatest disasters in the War have accentuated the distrust of him which has prevailed both in the House and outside it for a long time past, and I feel certain that his inclusion in the Government would prove disastrous to its fortunes. I believe the Unionist Party in the House would unanimously back this opinion and I am certain that our great organisations in the country, of which, as you know, I am Chairman, would strongly assert it.

I have never in my life passed through a time of greater anxiety politically than during the last two or three months. I have been sitting on the safety valve all the time and up to now have succeeded in securing at least an official acceptance of the Government's policy.

The last difficulty was created by the Franchise Bill and Bonar Law will be able to tell you by what a narrow squeak I managed to secure acceptance of the general principles of that measure, with the result that no amendment of any kind against its main principles is being moved by the Unionist organisation.

To test their loyalty so soon again would certainly invite serious trouble, and I cannot be responsible for the result.

It would be an impertinence on my part to interfere in any way with your choice of Ministers, but it is my bounden duty to tell you, as I told Bonar Law last week, that I am satisfied from the present temper of the Unionists in the country that the greatest care is necessary not to put any further strain on their loyalty.

I write you direct as I do not care to trouble Bonar with letters just now.*

Yours sincerely,
GEORGE YOUNGER.†

The anxiety of Lord Derby, Secretary of State for War, was no less acute. Indeed, the prospect of serving at that post with Churchill as head of the Air Board led him to make out a list of stringent conditions which he believed should define Churchill's future relations with the War Office."† By this formula Derby sought to hold down Churchill's appointment to a minor level, to limit his influence. Thus we have the unusual spectacle of a powerful Conservative seeking to prescribe to the Prime Minister the status and authority of a colleague.

Lord Milner also was on the side of the

---

* Bonar Law had at this time received news that his second son Charlie was missing. He was full of anxiety and pinning his faith to a report that Charlie was a prisoner in Turkey. His hopes were soon to be shattered. There was no truth in the rumour.

† Derby's programme proposed that it should be clearly understood that (1) Churchill should not be a member of the War Cabinet or attend any meetings unless specially summoned for business connected with the Air Board: (2) that his duties as Chairman of the Board should be the same as were Lord Cowdray's and that he would have nothing to do with personnel and tactics, and (3) that he should receive no War Office telegrams other than those which were connected with his department. See *Appendix IV*, No. 4, for full text of letter.

discontented politicians who opposed Churchill's introduction into the Government.ᵛ

Criticism in the Press sounded a violent note. In almost every direction comment was unfavourable. There were, however, important and significant exceptions—the newspapers controlled by Lord Northcliffe.

Lord Northcliffe's hostility to Churchill was well known. It had been violently expressed in December when even the fact that Churchill shared with Northcliffe the disappointment of exclusion from the new Government failed to blunt the sharp edge of the newspaper magnate's criticism. Nor had the two men enjoyed at this time any amity in their personal relations to soften the asperities of public antagonism. But, the situation was altered, and in a vital respect. Northcliffe had been "squared" by his appointment in Washington and New York.

"Lord Northcliffe was on a mission to the United States," observed Mr. Churchill, "and appeased."ʷ And indeed, amiable and even friendly cables to and from America passed between them, concluding before long with a message from Northcliffe to Churchill, asking for help and expressing gratitude for what he was about to receive.ˣ

The reaction of the inner council of the Conservatives, expressed as it was in violent terms, came, however, as a serious setback to the Prime Minister. Indeed, the force of their outcry astonished and overwhelmed him and he lacked the

faith in his own influence with the administration
to drive the issue through to a conclusion. He
sought to alter course and to engage Churchill
in another capacity. He sent Frederick Guest to
propose to Churchill that he should accept his
former office of the Duchy of Lancaster, with
"elaborated uses and functions". Churchill, burn-
ingly eager to serve the country in a truly national
capacity, either in the War Cabinet or in charge
of a war department, rejected the offer in a
perfectly friendly manner. He was well aware of
the potential strength of his political position.

Thus Lloyd George wavered in the uncertain
political balance. His fear of Churchill impelled him
onwards, but his concern for the consequences of
Conservative antipathy paralysed his final action.

It was on 17th July in the afternoon that I
was summoned to No. 10 Downing Street. As
I walked through Whitehall my unfailing measure
of optimism prompted me to believe that I
would be offered at last a place in the Government dealing with war issues. My confidence
was strengthened by the veiled sunshine and the
warmth, with dry exhilarating air.

When I was shown into the Cabinet room,
Lloyd George was genial and talkative. But he
did not say the words I expected him to speak.

He reminded me that I had for long urged him
to bring Churchill into the administration. Very
well, the time was at hand. What, he asked,
would Bonar Law say when the Conservative
back-benchers howled in angry unison?

The question could not confidently be answered. Lloyd George would announce to the newspapers the changes in Government bringing into the Ministry of Munitions the much-praised and greatly abused Member for Dundee (Winston Churchill).

It would be my task to go at once to Bonar Law and tell him of this exciting news. A strange method indeed of informing the Leader of the House of Commons; but it was a line of communication which Lloyd George adopted in difficult conditions, and not for the first time.

As I was a warm supporter of Churchill the mission, although difficult and tiresome, was by no means unacceptable to me.

I found Bonar Law in his sitting-room with papers spread about him on the floor. Not newspapers but his departmental and official papers. It was not his habit to stir from his chair if he could avoid it, although he was a polite man. His pipe was lighted. It flashed through my mind, "This will put his pipe out." And it did.

Bonar Law was indignant that the Prime Minister had taken his decision without consulting him. Rufus Isaacs (Lord Reading) wrote a few days later to Lloyd George, to advise him of Bonar Law's feelings in the matter, of which I had already acquainted the Prime Minister.

July 22, 1917.

My dear L.G.,

On quite *reliable* authority I hear that B.L. is sore about the Winston appointment—his point being that

WHERWELL PRIORY,
ANDOVER,
HANTS.

Confidential

July 22/17

My dear L.G.

On quite reliable
authority I hear that B.L.
is sore about the Winston
appointment - his point
being that he wasn't told
it was to be made before
it was actually given to
the Press. - He is not complaining
of it but nevertheless is aggrieved
I thought it might to let you
know.

Yours
Rufus

LORD READING TO LLOYD GEORGE.

he wasn't told it was to be made before it was actually
given to the Press. He is not complaining of it but
nevertheless is aggrieved.

I thought it right to let you know.

Yours always,
RUFUS.[y]

But Bonar Law, in spite of his distrust of
Churchill and his indignation with Lloyd George,
could not allow himself to be guided by these
two considerations alone. Opposed as he was to
Churchill's inclusion in the Government, he had
either to support Lloyd George and his administration or to retire from it. Viewed in this light,
his course of action was straightforward. He
must continue to uphold the Government. He
must give the Prime Minister the support which
was essential over the Churchill case. But he
said, "Lloyd George's throne will shake." And
it did.

The announcement of Mr. Churchill's appointment as Minister of Munitions, together with
other changes in the administration, was published in the Press on 18th July.

At this, the tempest broke with perilous force
over the Prime Minister.

The effect upon the Tory Ministers exceeded
all expectations. Lloyd George, in his *War
Memoirs*, has said: "the insensate fury they displayed . . . surpassed all my apprehensions, and
for some days it swelled to the dimensions of a
grave ministerial crisis which threatened the life of
the Government."[z]

Walter Long sent a letter immediately to the Prime Minister, advising him that the situation made it "extremely difficult for many of my friends to continue their support."[aa] This was tantamount to a threat of resignation; it therefore held the most serious implications for the Coalition. Bonar Law persuaded Long to take no further action.

In the House of Commons, the Unionist [Conservative] Business Committee * was hastily summoned by telegram. At the meeting which followed, members registered their strong dissent from the appointment. That evening a deputation waited on Bonar Law.

A resolution was passed by the 1900 Club (another Tory Committee), profoundly regretting that such "scant regard" had been paid, in appointing Churchill to the Government, to the previously expressed apprehensions and opinions of the Unionist Party, upon whose loyal aid Lloyd George's Ministry so largely depended.[ab]

Churchill's appointment was also assailed in the Conservative Press. The *Morning Post* became the spokesman of the most hostile elements. The newspaper's censure of Churchill knew no bounds: "That dangerous and uncertain quantity, Mr. Winston Churchill—a floating kidney in the body politic—is back again in Westminster."[ac] "By his appointment Mr. Lloyd George loses enormously in prestige, for it proves him to be a

---

* An important and influential group of members of both Houses of Parliament resembling in structure the American Party caucus but exercising no real power or authority.

man who allows private partiality to overcome public duty."[ad]

"The one thing certain," declared the *Morning Post*, "is that the Lloyd George Ministry has been dangerously weakened by what has happened."[ae]

Never before in history had the selection of a Minister of the Crown given rise to such a vehement opposition. A stick had been thrust into the political beehive and the rage of the drones and the workers was terrible to behold.

Lloyd George's throne tottered. But it did not fall.

Bonar Law met the deputation from the Unionist Business Committee with a stiff resistance. He had made up his mind to support the Government and he did so now with all his might.

He assured the deputation that Churchill's appointment had been accepted by the King and would stand.[af]

Nevertheless, Lloyd George was seriously damaged and he sustained prolonged and bitter hostility for his action in forcing the appointment. Walter Long represented the feeling of the Conservative Ministers to Bonar Law. "The real effect," he asserted, "has been to destroy all confidence in Ll.G. It is widely held that for purposes of his own, quite apart from the war, he has deceived and 'jockeyed' us."[ag]

In this atmosphere, Churchill returned to the administration. He was to prove a powerful reinforcement, but it was many years before the ill-feeling and the recriminations died away.

Churchill, rejoicing in the opportunity to serve the nation in an important office directly bearing upon the war, had no illusion about the feelings stirred up by his appointment. He looked round at his new Conservative colleagues with an understanding and humorous eye. As the Prime Minister set off for France a few days after the appointment, the new Minister made an amusing appeal to him.

"Don't get torpedoed;" he enjoined him, "for if I am left alone your colleagues will eat me."[ah] But he knew that he had reason to be grateful to Lloyd George.

The Prime Minister, too, had sound reasons for solid satisfaction. He had removed danger from his seat. He had regained the companionship and association of a man he liked and admired. He had shown gratitude for unflinching support at that black moment some few years before when Marconi was the principal subject of discussion in and out of Parliament. He had cancelled out his later actions.

For in 1915, Lloyd George, partly out of shrewd judgement of what was and what was not possible, partly out of pure self-interest, would not lift a finger to help Churchill when misfortune overwhelmed him over Gallipoli. Lloyd George let him fall without making any effort to save him. Asked to support him for a command in East Africa, which Bonar Law as Colonial Secretary was willing to concede, Lloyd George shook his head and murmured something of the feelings of the widows and orphans of Gallipoli.

He accepted Churchill's help in the crisis which made him Prime Minister, but denied him any reward. He pleaded Tory hostility to making Churchill a Minister, with justice and fair cause. But he added charges on his own which, if true, ought to have meant the permanent exclusion of Churchill from power. "Why," he said, "he brought Turkey into the war. Such men are too dangerous for high office."

Now these events and this indictment had been forgotten and these criticisms did not prevent Lloyd George from making Winston Churchill his Minister of Munitions on 18th July, 1917.

By January, 1919, Lloyd George's confidence in Churchill had risen to higher altitudes. Then the feeling of the widows and orphans of Gallipoli had been forgotten, and the man who was too dangerous for high office was told to choose the War Office or the Admiralty and, said Lloyd George, "whichever you take, you may carry the Air with you."

Churchill replied to Lloyd George accepting the Admiralty:

> My heart is in the Admiralty. There I have long experience, & any claim I may be granted in public goodwill rests on the fact that "the Fleet was ready". In all the circumstances of the present situation I believe I shd. add more weight to yr. Administration at the Admiralty than at the War Office.[ai] *

By the time this communication reached the Prime Minister, the option had expired. Lloyd

* See *Appendix IV*, No. 5, for full text.

George put him at the War Office. It often happened that way.

Churchill was well pleased with his new place in 1919. Colonel Seely at the Air Ministry was peeping out from behind his coat tails.

I have a picture of Churchill in my mind striding up and down in his room at the War Office, tingling with vitality. Bold and imaginative in the sweep of his conceptions, prolific of new ideas, like a machine gun of bullets and expelling his notions in much the same manner. Fertile, resourceful, courageous, he was always tolerant, though in this age occasionally wanting in prudence.

The political front was of course in confusion. These were days of broken lights of political faith. Was he nearer to Asquith's brand of Liberalism or did he freely accept Lloyd George and the Coalition? Was he a Liberal or a Tory?

He did not know himself.

Surely he had a foot in both camps. Not intentionally, but none the less, what he did abroad pleased the Tories and infuriated the Radicals. When he spoke at home, he was cheered by Radicals, and how he annoyed the Tories!

It was not inconvenient to be in a position which permitted him to step off with either foot.

He talked brilliantly and with all the ardour of middle age. Some persons said he talked too much. He never surrounded himself with those who were only good listeners. His conversation was best when he spoke with a trusted companion.

Although he had not attained to his great prestige, he was apt even then to hold sway in a large gathering, acting all the time. He was a fine actor. And occasionally he indulged in mimicry of the speech of certain of his colleagues.

He drew from his well of experience. He differed from many of his political contemporaries who had a stock of stories frequently repeated. He was always truthful. He could keep a secret.

Here I leave him. All the years of the First War may be regarded as a schooling in strategy and in politics equipping Winston Spencer Churchill as the Master Mind of the world war as yet far, far distant.

CHAPTER V

THE ULSTER PIRATE

CARSON never put his trust in Lloyd George. And Lloyd George never could rely upon uncritical support from Carson.

They had worked together in presenting an ultimatum to Asquith demanding that the direction of the war should be handed to the triumvirate of Lloyd George, Bonar Law and Carson. And when it was rejected, the Triumvirate brought Asquith down and destroyed his Government.

Now Lloyd George had climbed to power on the steps of the ladder held in position by Bonar Law and Carson. When he reached the seat of authority he forgot about the ladder. Instead of a war committee of himself, Bonar Law and Carson, the new Prime Minister called into an enlarged and somewhat decorative body, named the War Cabinet, the old cart-horse Curzon who could be relied upon to support his master providing the fodder held out and Lord Milner, a very different type.* He had been a Civil Servant. But he never was a candidate for elected office; he

---

* Milner's name was pressed upon Lloyd George and others by Geoffrey Dawson, Editor of The Times, at that moment a supporter of Lloyd George and also a powerful influence in Cabinet-making circles.

never had taken part in the hurly-burly of political meetings; he never had to defend himself in debate, even in the calm seclusion of the House of Lords, where he sat for many years. Carson was sent to the Admiralty, a post that was not suited to his abilities.

In his *War Memoirs*, Lloyd George has given two reasons for Carson's exclusion from the inner Cabinet circle and the central direction of the war. He was overridden, he says, "by the personal prejudices of the majority of the Conservative leaders against Carson. They all admired but disapproved of him".[a] His inclusion, moreover, would have tipped the balance of membership of a small war council too heavily in favour of the Conservatives.

These explanations are unsound. Lloyd George could have overridden Tory opposition without difficulty. For Carson was quite a different proposition from Churchill or Lord Northcliffe. The Tory Party chiefs had refused to serve with either of them. But no Cabinet denying ordinance fenced Carson in.

What then was the real reason for Carson's exclusion from the Triumvirate which was to have governed Britain for the duration of the war?

The explanation is a simple one. Lloyd George was suspicious and distrustful of Carson. There was no real basis of understanding and confidence between these two Celtic characters.

It is right to record that Lloyd George looked upon Carson as a potential enemy, and with some justification. He was in direct conflict with the

Irish leader over many political issues. And he often spoke of Carson's conduct in derogatory terms. Moreover he was convinced that collaboration with Carson alienated support from Liberals in Parliament and from Liberal newspapers in the country. He would use Carson when necessary. He would avoid close association when convenient. Nor were they suited to each other in social contacts.

When Carson became First Lord of the Admiralty he was in a despondent and indifferent mood. He was discontented and disaffected. "The moment that Asquith's fall was accomplished," I wrote of him in my previous volume, "a kind ot incuriousness seemed to descend upon him. He was like a man whose task is accomplished."[b]

That office of state, moreover, had proved no safe harbour for the politicians appointed to it. Two eminent leaders had already held the post of war-time First Lord and both had walked the plank, Churchill and A. J. Balfour.

Churchill was the first to go overboard. Following upon his dramatic mobilisation of the Fleet on that dark night at the outbreak of war, he did not remain long in the position of responsibility where he believed his talents were used to best advantage. Within eight months he was driven from office by the forceful action of the First Sea Lord, Admiral Fisher, who pulled down the blinds and took the train to Scotland.

It is a matter for regret that Churchill was ever sacrificed. He had the spirit, the drive and the energy. He had the redoubtable Jackie Fisher to help him. But he failed to manage Fisher. This was strange because in the Second War Churchill proved to be a manager of men and a master of his colleagues.

Balfour filled the vacant place. His appointment was unsuitable. His erudition and his powers of reasoning did not equip him for the post of political head of the Admiralty at the height of a Naval war. His career there was not free from storms.

There was, in fact, one important occasion when Balfour wholly forfeited the sympathy of the public. At the end of May, 1916, the Germans engaged the British Fleet at the Battle of Jutland. News of the encounter was depressing in the extreme; Balfour believed that the nation must be given the full facts of the battle and he himself prepared a statement.

It was a catalogue of appalling disaster. Three battle cruisers and three cruisers had been sunk, five destroyers had been lost in action, six others were unaccounted for. "The enemy's losses," said the communiqué, "were serious." *c

The despatch flashed like a message of despair throughout the country.

Balfour had acted in the conviction that the people must be told the unvarnished facts. Later news was to bring brighter tidings of the battle, but in the meantime consternation and alarm had

* In the final score, Britain lost 3 battle cruisers, 3 cruisers and 8 destroyers at the Battle of Jutland. German losses were 1 battleship, 1 battle cruiser, 4 light cruisers and 5 destroyers.

spread throughout the nation and to the allied countries.

So great, indeed, were their feelings first of anxiety, and then of righteous anger when comforting reports were circulated that Churchill was called in, at Balfour's own request, to write an official appreciation of the Battle of Jutland and to allay anxiety among the friendly neutrals. Balfour's prestige suffered heavily over this unhappy lapse of judgement.

In the last months of the Asquith Administration, Balfour became the subject of a vigorous campaign conducted by Lord Northcliffe to remove him from the Government. "BMG" became the popular catch-cry for the second time in one decade. "BMG"—"Balfour Must Go"—was the invention of my political friends when Balfour was pushed out of the leadership of the Tory Party in 1911. His successor was Bonar Law. Now in 1916 it was reiterated by the powerful giant of Fleet Street.

In this campaign Northcliffe was openly encouraged by the critical attitude of Lloyd George, at that time Secretary of State for War, whose views were widely disseminated by the Liberal Press. Balfour, however, was retained by the same Lloyd George when he became Prime Minister and actually promoted to the Foreign Office. Indeed his retention as a prominent member of the Administration was the hinge of the Conservatives' accession to Lloyd George's Coalition.

Now Carson's appointment to the Admiralty

gave satisfaction to the public. It was believed that he would be a stern man of action, silent in a silent service.

He was one of the most interesting personalities of the war. His position in British public life was unique. As the "uncrowned king of Ulster", the unchallenged chieftain of the stern Orangemen of Northern Ireland, and hope of the Protestant diehards of the South, he was more than a political leader. He was almost a feudal lord, commanding allegiance from devoted and ardent followers and treating with the Conservative Party as if he were an independent and equal ally.

He was a man of very high intellectual attainment, his mind possessing a startling clarity, sharpened by many encounters at the Bar; his gifts of advocacy were immense. He had the talent of lighting at once upon the defects and weaknesses in a situation. This made him formidable in counsel, powerful in opposition, but a source of danger and weakness in harness. He saw the flaws in every Administration. He was, by temperament, opposed to every Government. He was admirably adjusted to taking high place in any Administration and at the same time acting as leader of the Opposition.

Yet he took up his work at the Admiralty with a full sense of responsibility. He was eager to make a success of his task. He wrote to a friend, Gibson Bowles, "I feel full of responsibility, but you may be quite sure I will try to get the fullest play for the Navy; and I don't intend to become an amateur in naval strategy or tactics. The submarine peril is a deadly one, and I am turning all attention to it." [d]

The submarine peril was indeed deadly. The year of 1917 opened on a scene of desolation and anxiety. The survival of Britain hung in the balance. On the land, the great forces of German military power massed themselves for an offensive on the Western Front. At sea, the striking power of the U-boat accumulated a terrible intensity. The toll of shipping, with the Channel routes open to constant attack from bases at Zeebrugge, mounted with every month.

It was becoming increasingly apparent that the fate of Great Britain would be settled on the sea. Everything, indeed, turned on our ability to combat the menace of the submarines. The danger that, should we fail to do so, the country would be starved into submission had constantly to be taken into account.

It was a vital and tremendous challenge for the new First Lord.

From the very first days, however, Carson defined his position. He placed himself at once at the disposal of his expert advisers. He became to a marked degree dependent on the advice and guidance of his department. And he resisted staunchly any inclination to develop his own ideas of Naval strategy.

Indeed, he went further. In public pronouncements the First Lord proclaimed his intention to support and to protect the policy of his admirals.

In March, 1917, he made a public declaration of striking frankness which disclosed his attitude to the Administration. He would be the refuge and strength of the admirals and the protector of the generals; he would espouse their cause against the politicians.

At a luncheon gathering at the Aldwych Club, when Lord Northcliffe—that great champion of the generals—was in the chair, Carson closed his speech with these words:

"I advise the country to pay no attention to amateur strategists, who are always impatient and always ready for a gamble. We cannot afford to gamble with our Fleet.

"As long as I am at the Admiralty the sailors will have full scope. They will not be interfered with by me, and I will not let anyone interfere with them."[e]

Carson thus stood in defiant hostility to any pressure from the politicians upon the admirals. When analysed, his attitude was strange and even self-contradictory. He would see that the admirals were allowed to go their own way and pursue their own strategy. And if things went wrong— who were to be criticised? Not, it seemed, the admirals. Criticism could fall only on the politicians.

Lloyd George was, of course, the "amateur strategist". It was an open avowal of Carson's prejudice against the Administration. For the contest between Service or Civilian control of the wartime direction was in full swing. It was the topic of the political clubs, in the lobby, and in the daily newspapers. Carson had come out frankly on behalf of the generals.

It was not long before an open clash flared up between the Prime Minister and his First Lord of the Admiralty.

The question of convoys was the preoccupying problem of those grave days in the late winter of 1917.

Lloyd George at once became the ardent exponent of the convoy principle.

The Admiralty, however, did not support the proposal. Several strong arguments against the system were adduced by the Naval authorities. It was contended that the convoy offered too large a target. "The system of several ships sailing together in a convoy is not recommended in any area where submarine attack is a possibility," stated an official Admiralty publication in January, 1917. "It is evident that the larger the number of ships forming the convoy, the greater is the chance of a submarine being enabled to attack successfully, the greater is the difficulty of the escort in preventing such an attack."

It was also argued that the merchantman, sailing alone, and able to load and turn round swiftly, was a more efficient vessel than it would be as a member of a Fleet compelled to wait for the assembly of its consorts and to sail at the pace of the slowest vessel.

The experts, wrote Lloyd George, were "unanimously and stubbornly opposed" to the adoption of convoys.^f

Carson's position in the continuing dispute was unequivocal. He firmly supported the admirals. He had been ready to concede a trial of the convoy plan, but he had no intention of pushing the project against the opinion of his Naval advisers.*

By April, the figures for losses of British merchant tonnage were four times as great as those of January, 1917.† News of sinkings became from day to day an increasing worry to the War Cabinet. Indeed, at one time, only one week's stock of wheat remained in the country.

It was in this critical emergency that Sir John Jellicoe (the First Sea Lord) submitted a memorandum entitled "The Submarine Menace and the Food Supply". It was a document of ominous character. It could not be disguised that the shipping losses would produce the most serious results for the country.

What then was the solution the First Sea Lord had to offer? Jellicoe's recommendations contained no recognition of the convoy system. Conservation of the existing food supplies and an intensification of the present methods of anti-submarine action were the measure of his remedies.

His report left the Prime Minister profoundly disquieted. Lloyd George was now convinced of the need for decisive action.

Here was his position. At the height of crisis in the war the Prime Minister found himself in

* Lloyd George writes of Carson: "Personally, he favoured a trial being made, but told me he had no official support from any quarter in his department." g
† In January, 153,512 tons of British merchant tonnage was lost by enemy action; in April the figure had reached 545,282 tons.h

direct opposition to his Naval advisers. And the First Lord of the Admiralty (Carson) gave his support and allegiance, not to the Prime Minister, but to the Naval staff. Yet the policy pursued by the admirals was condemned on the evidence of the shipping losses.

The Prime Minister decided the convoy plan must be adopted. This was the programme Lloyd George proposed now to force upon the Naval Board.

On 26th April, 1917, he determined to take action of a most aggressive nature. He informed the Press that fifty-five merchant ships had been sunk in seven days. Then he sent the following letter to Sir Edward Carson.

My Dear First Lord,
  Since we met this morning I have received enclosed. There seems to me to be no doubt that it is vital to this country that we should settle this infernal question. Otherwise we might sink.
Ever yours,
D. LLOYD GEORGE.'

At the same time he told his colleagues of his intention to go down himself to the Admiralty and make peremptory decisions; thus establishing the convoy system of transportation by sea.

Lloyd George wanted a Conservative reinforcement. Bonar Law declined the duty, pleading his difficulties with Carson over the Irish situation. With good reason. Several sections of the Press were saying that criticisms of the Admiralty from some quarters were really attacks on Carson "for quite different reasons". One newspaper gave outspoken expression to the view that the attacks were inspired "not by any knowledge of naval affairs, but by the hope that if he can be driven from the Government Irish Home Rule will be brought appreciably nearer".[1]

Lord Curzon was chosen as the Prime Minister's bodyguard. On the day of the impending visit to Admiralty House, he wrote to the Prime Minister.

My dear Prime Minister,
    Coming up in the train, I have been thinking of the subjects which I understand that you and I are to raise at the Admiralty in the investigation that is to begin at noon today.
    On the accompanying sheet, I have jotted down some of these in some sort of order. Probably you have thought of many more but perhaps this list may be useful.

Yours sincerely,
CURZON.[2]

On 30th April, with the submarine peril at its height, the Prime Minister descended upon the Admiralty and seated himself in the First Lord's chair.

This was possibly an unprecedented action. It was well within the powers and competence of the Prime Minister; yet there may be no parallels in our history. For one afternoon the Prime Minister took over the full reins of Government from the head of a major department of state. It was inevitable that, as a result, Carson's prestige suffered a serious blow.

The meeting was a minor triumph for the Prime Minister. A re-examination of the figures of shipping losses prepared by the Minister of Shipping had brought a frame of mind in which the admirals were at least willing to experiment with a convoy.

"The High Admirals," wrote Lloyd George, "had at last been persuaded by the 'Convoyers' not perhaps to take action, but to try action."[l]

Lloyd George had staged a deliberate encounter with the Naval High Command, and had emerged triumphant. But he had lost faith in Carson, Jellicoe and even his Board of Admiralty.

The main struggle had yet to be faced. There could be but one sequel: the dismissal of Jellicoe and the replacement of Carson.

"So I made up my mind," writes Lloyd George in his *Memoirs*, "to effect a change at the top in the Admiralty . . . I therefore contemplated a change in the First Lord, Lord Carson, and the First Sea Lord, Admiral Jellicoe. They were both men of great influence and authority, and both possessed a formidable following, one political, the other naval."[m]

It was a brave decision. The consequences might be severe and even fatal to Lloyd George himself. Would Carson resist? Would he get extensive support? Would the Board of Admiralty resign in a body? The House of Commons might become a tribunal deciding the issue, where Carson's strength was certainly extensive, though undefined.

Yet there was the terrible toll of losses, mounting every day. The correspondence of Walter Page, U.S. Ambassador to Great Britain, gives a startling account of the Naval balance sheet. I reproduce an extract from an illuminating letter of 4th May, 1917.

London, May 4, 1917.

Dear Mr. President,

The submarines have become a very grave danger. The loss of British and Allied tonnage increases with the longer and brighter days—as I telegraphed you, 237,000 tons last week; and the worst of it is, the British are not destroying them. The Admiralty publishes a weekly report which, though true, is not the whole truth. It is known in official circles here that the Germans are turning out at least two a week—some say three; and the British are not destroying them as fast as new ones are turned out. If merely the present situation continue, the war will pretty soon become a contest of endurance under hunger with an increasing proportion of starvation. Germany is yet much the worse off, but it will be easily possible for Great Britain to suffer to the danger point next winter or earlier unless some decided change be wrought in this situation.

One help—how great it is yet somewhat too soon to know—will come when all merchantmen are armed and properly manned. Arming here is going on, and, of course, all our trans-Atlantic ships are armed.

But the greatest help, I hope, can come from us— our destroyers and similar armed craft,—provided we can send enough of them quickly. The area to be watched is so big that many submarine-hunters are needed. Early in the war the submarines worked near shore. There are very many more of them now and their range is one hundred miles, or even two hundred, at sea.

The public is becoming very restive with its half-information, and it is more and more loudly demanding all the facts. There are already angry threats to change the personnel of the Admiralty: there is even talk of turning out the Government. "We must have results, we must have results." I hear confidentially that Jellicoe has threatened to resign unless the Salonika expedition is brought back: to feed and equip that force requires too many ships.

And there are other troubles impending. Norway has lost so many of her ships that she dare not send what are left to sea. Unarmed they'll all perish. If she arm them, Germany will declare war against her. There is a plan on foot for the British to charter these Norwegian ships and to arm them, taking the risk of German war against Norway. If war come (as it is expected), England must then defend Norway the best she can. She will close the German access to Norway with mines and with such of the Grand Fleet as can be spared. And *then England may ask for our big ships to help in these waters*. All this is yet in the future, but possibly not far in the future.

For the present the only anti-submarine help is the help we may be able to give to patrol the wide area off Ireland. If we had one hundred destroyers to send the job there could, I am told, be quickly done. A third of that number will help mightily. At the present rate of destruction more than four million tons will be sunk before the summer is gone.

Such is this dire submarine danger. The English thought that they controlled the sea; the Germans, that they were invincible on land. Each side is losing where it thought itself strongest."

Carson and his friends now began to show fight. They felt that they were being knocked about. They believed that Carson was to play the role of

CARSON. No one knows to this day whether it was bluff or not.

a scapegoat. They wouldn't have it. Sir Hedworth
Meux, Admiral of the Fleet, spoke out strongly.
At Liverpool on 2nd May he asserted:

> In Sir Edward Carson we have got what the Navy
> considers the right man. I hope you will not allow
> these attacks . . . to drive him out of office.°

Conservative newspapers gave their confidence
and support to their old hero. They had faith in
him. Then Carson's loyal friends in the House of
Commons made up a mighty band of stalwart and
vehement champions.

For Lloyd George the predicament was acute.
He was playing two hands. He was preparing to
bring into the Ministry of Munitions the weak
man Churchill and he was preparing to drive out
of the Admiralty the strong man Carson. Carson
was a formidable and respected figure whose
removal must excite the hostility, not only of the
admirals and the generals and the military faction
but also of a considerable section of Lloyd
George's own following in the country.

Yet the shield that sheltered Jellicoe must be
thrust aside. It was a political tactic requiring skill
and daring, and much preliminary labour.

Another extract from the correspondence of
Walter Page written to President Wilson gives a
vivid picture of the tension between Lloyd George
and Carson.

> A little while ago [writes Page] he [Lloyd George]
> dined with me, and, after dinner, I took him to a corner

of the drawing-room and delivered your message to him about Ireland. "God knows, I'm trying," he replied. "Tell the President that. And tell him to talk to Balfour." Presently he broke out—"Madmen, madmen—I never saw any such task," and he pointed across the room to Sir Edward Carson, his First Lord of the Admiralty—"Madmen." "But the President's right. We've got to settle it and we've got to settle it now." Carson and Jellicoe came across the room and sat down with us. "I've been telling the Ambassador, Carson, that we've got to settle the Irish question now—in spite of you."

"I'll tell you something else we've got to settle now," said Carson. "Else it'll settle us. That's the submarines. The press and public are working up a calculated and concerted attack on Jellicoe and me, and, if they get us, they'll get you. It's an attack on the Government made on the Admiralty, Prime Minister," said this Ulster pirate whose civil war didn't come off only because the big war was begun—"Prime Minister, it may be a fierce attack. Get ready for it."[p]

Now Carson had on this occasion used offensive and even insolent language to his Prime Minister and in the presence of a Foreign Ambassador. It was a measure of their relationship.

There was little or no sympathy between "the little man" (as Carson called Lloyd George) and "the Ulster Pirate" (as Page called Carson).

No doubt Lloyd George feared Carson. Yet it was imperative that he now grapple with the problem. There were dangers too great to be shirked. Should the losses of merchant ships continue at the prevailing rate, then disaster must fall upon Britain within a few weeks.

Carson's administration must be terminated and the Lords of the Admiralty must be brought under control. There was no escape. Lloyd George must act, and act at once.

There were other warnings that could not be neglected with safety—written warnings that might be published. Lloyd George was being bombarded with letters of complaint from the Shipping Controller, Sir Joseph Maclay, himself a wealthy shipping magnate who commanded immense respect on account of his complete integrity and who enjoyed, in addition, the esteem due to one who was the undisputed leader of Britain's shipping industry. Maclay was a deeply religious man who for many years carried on a Christian mission at Marrakesh. He compiled a volume of family prayers, "The Starting Place Of The Day".

At any moment the Shipping Controller's resignation might be tossed on Lloyd George's table. Bad enough. But made worse because Maclay had the reputation of being a "man of God", thus commanding strength and support in Lloyd George's own nonconformist circles.

All these circumstances helped Lloyd George to make up his mind; he was determined that the admirals must be subjected to civilian discipline. Someone of resource and vitality who could, if necessary, carry out a naval strategy independent of the Board, must be made First Lord. And another First Lord must be fortified by a change in his Chief Naval Adviser.

Carson, well aware of the gathering storm, took a strong line of defence. He made public declaration of his confidence in Jellicoe with a subtle suggestion that he despised his own Prime Minister.

At a luncheon gathering on 17th May in honour of the American Navy, he denounced his critics with the burning fervour that distinguished him in attack.

"I am so constituted," he said, "that I cannot get cold feet. I can divide my critics into various categories. There are my political critics. I despise them in the middle of war. Then there are the critics who have been disappointed in the past. Whenever you read criticisms of my colleague Sir John Jellicoe, try to find out what is the origin of them. But after all it does not really matter. . . . Let them grumble and growl and let us get on with our work."[q]

Lloyd George now decided to adopt an audacious method. It was full of skill and daring, and of that talent for the ingenious that put him in the front rank of political tacticians. For in preparing to instal a strong man at the Admiralty and thus reduce the influence of the admirals, Lloyd George enlisted the aid and support of the generals—Carson's natural allies in the struggle.

In the early months of 1917 there was no unified front of Army and Navy against the civilians. Had there been, events would have taken a very different turn. Instead we find the Prime Minister taking the generals into his confidence over the situation at the Admiralty, and receiving their enthusiastic backing for his plan.

At the beginning of the summer, Lloyd George spoke with Sir Douglas Haig, who was himself in danger of being handed the black spot.

In his *War Memoirs*, he records: "A conversation I had with Sir Douglas Haig in the early summer of 1917 finally decided me. The Commander-in-Chief was also alarmed at the dismaying ravages of the submarine. He was apprehensive that the War might be lost at sea before he had an opportunity of winning it on land. He had great admiration for Jellicoe's knowledge as a technical sailor, but he thought him much too rigid, narrow and conservative in his ideas. . . . Sir Douglas Haig had no opinion of his [Carson's] qualities as an administrator. . . . He strongly urged upon me the appointment of Sir Eric Geddes to that post.'"

There has since been a great outcry by the defenders of both Carson and Jellicoe against this claim made by Lloyd George.

Ian Colvin, Lord Carson's biographer,* has rejected Lloyd George's record of his conversation with Haig and Lloyd George's assertion that Haig was responsible for convincing him that he must dismiss both Jellicoe and Carson. "Sir Douglas Haig, had he been alive," declares Colvin, "would no doubt have been flattered to know that a Minister who misprized him on land should have so deferred to him at sea.'"

---

* Colvin wrote a lively biography of Lord Carson. He was, of course, the most powerful leader-writer of his time. His writings had a wide circulation in political circles and much influence.

Sir Reginald Bacon in his biography of Admiral Jellicoe * has also denied Lloyd George's story, and with asperity. Indeed he goes to the extent of declaring that there is nothing in Haig's diary or papers that gives the slightest colour to such a statement. He acquits Haig of being a collaborator.

But the publication of Haig's private papers † destroys completely the position taken up by Colvin and Bacon. Sir Douglas Haig himself discloses that he took a dominating part in driving both Carson and Jellicoe out of Admiralty House.'

Encouraged by Lloyd George, Haig became at once the Prime Minister's battering ram against the gates of Carson's stronghold at the Admiralty.

For ten days in June, 1917, he apparently spent his time in London, carrying out a well-organised, thoroughly considered and widespread campaign to drive the First Lord and also Jellicoe from their posts.

On 20th June, 1917, he visited Temporary Admiral Sir Eric Geddes (a political appointment), at this time Carson's subordinate, but by no means loyal to his chief. He agreed with Geddes that the Admiralty was in the hands of a number of incompetent sailors, Jellicoe feeble to a degree and vacillating in conduct.

Of Carson himself Haig declared: "The First Lord has recently married, he is very tired and

---

* Sir R. H. Bacon: *Life of John Rushworth, Earl Jellicoe* (London, Cassell, 1936), p. 378.
 † *The Private Papers of Douglas Haig*, 1914–1919, edited by Robert Blake who deserves praise for the wisdom and discretion he has shown in his editorship. His book on Bonar Law, *The Unknown Prime Minister*, is one of the best biographies of recent times.

leaves everything to a number of incompetent sailors."

Haig promised Geddes that he would arrange for an interview with Lloyd George, so that the desperate situation at the Admiralty could be put before him. He agreed with Geddes that an audience should be sought from the King, for the same purpose.

Now Haig had immense influence at the Palace. The King relied upon him. Without doubt, he was the Keeper of the Palace gates. This close and trusting relationship is an interesting and absorbing subject, peeping out from time to time in the diaries and letters of His Majesty and his Commander-in-Chief.

Within five days (25th June, 1917) Haig had spoken to Lord Curzon, complaining about the seriously inefficient state of the Admiralty. He then saw Lloyd George and repeated his arguments, which might be summed up as "action this day".

He lunched with Balfour. Then he called on Asquith, Leader of the Opposition in Parliament. He had a talk with the "old man" (Haig's phrase) about the unsatisfactory state in the Admiralty and the ignorance of the high Naval officers.

The next day the promised interview between Geddes and the Prime Minister took place at 10 Downing Street with Haig present. It was at breakfast. When Geddes had made his complaint Lloyd George declared he was much impressed and sent for Milner who was a critic of Carson's administration.

At the breakfast party a proposal was put forward to promote Robertson to Carson's place; a proposal which suited Lloyd George admirably. For Robertson had by this time become the Prime Minister's "turbulent priest", and Lloyd George would pay any price to get rid of his tormentor.

Breakfast over, away went Haig to the War Office, but Robertson refused to become First Lord of the Admiralty, because he said it would mean he would have to become a politician.

On June 28th, 1917, after all these labours, Haig returned to his Headquarters, from which he had taken leave while promoting his intrigues in London.

It is interesting to speculate on Haig's real motives. It may have been that he was moved by genuine anxiety. He had informed Lady Haig as early as May that he looked on Jellicoe as an "old woman". Or again, it is possible that he may have been interested mainly in diverting the lightning from striking at himself, for the dismissal of Haig had been a principal objective of Lloyd George for many months.*

Haig, in fact, had managed to hold his job in defiance of Lloyd George's hostility, only through the intervention of four Tory Ministers and, more important at this time, the interest and support of the King himself.

* Indeed as early as February, 1917, two months after Lloyd George's pledge to his Conservative colleagues to keep Haig in command in France, a letter from Lord Derby discloses an ominous attack on Haig by the Prime Minister. See *Appendix IV*, Nos. 6 and 7. Letters of Lord Derby, 19th and 20th February, 1917.

He needed all the help he could get. For Lloyd George never did give his trust to Haig and never did cease to threaten the Commander-in-Chief with dismissal.

There is, in conclusion, a sad commentary upon the strange character and conduct of the Commander-in-Chief. Within three months Haig and Carson had a happy meeting at Army Headquarters in France. They criticised the Prime Minister, denouncing his meddling practices. "Carson," wrote Haig, "is so straightforward and single-minded."[u]

Even though the proposal at the breakfast party to get rid of Robertson by sending him to the Admiralty had come to nothing, Lloyd George had no hesitation in trying to mobilize Robertson's strength in the attack on Carson and Jellicoe.

But the old General was cautious. He replied in terms that might be described after the words of the Emigrant's Lament, "I am sitting on the stile".

I quote the letter in full.

26.5.17.

Dear Prime Minister,

I hear good accounts of the naval officer—Richmond. He is evidently a keen student of naval history and warfare, and is described to me as "the first naval officer met who seems to have a General Staff mind". I gather that he would be a great asset at the Admiralty—on the War Staff—and probably of far more use there than in a ship.* I am sorry I can hear nothing of the two other naval officers you mentioned. I may warn

* Robertson proved an accurate judge of this man. Richmond became Commandant of the Imperial Defence College. In 1929 he was appointed Professor of Imperial and Naval History at Cambridge where he published valuable works on Naval strategy.

you that it will take a *long* time to get going what you want, there is bound to be much obstruction by the old gang. It was so here, and took us years. We are progressing now because the younger generation have in recent years got into the top places. "General Staff" was anathema to our top generals even as recently as 8 years ago.

Yours sincerely,
W. R. ROBERTSON.'

At the same time the Prime Minister was mobilising the support of his Cabinet colleagues. Here the voice of Lord Milner carried a considerable authority. Milner had been originally considered for the post of First Lord when Lloyd George formed his Administration. The Prime Minister's distrust of Carson, however, had elevated Milner to the War Cabinet.

In counsel Milner's advice was moderate. He desired to carry the soldiers as far as possible with the administration.* But now, after the breakfast party at 10 Downing Street, he devised a plan and at once he wrote to Lloyd George:

26.6.17.

My dear Prime Minister,

It may seem a rather startling proposition, but I think it would be the best plan to bring Carson into the War Cabinet, where he would be excellent, and to make Geddes First Lord. In that case, with a really first-rate administrator at the Head of the Board, the great requisite in the First Sea Lord would be courage and knowledge of men, an intimate acquaintance with

---

* There was as yet no evidence of the preoccupation that caused Milner to use all his efforts at the beginning of 1918 in order to drive General Robertson from office.

the best men in the service and a determination to
bring them on and put them into their right places
regardless of seniority and red tape. Such a First Sea
Lord can be found more easily than a naval man, who
is a great administrator. That quality must be im-
ported from outside.

Yours very sincerely,

MILNER.

I think it should be part of the bargain, that Carson
helped B.L. in the House of Commons, where I think
the Govt. lacks fighting power."

The Prime Minister seized on the Milner Plan.
It brought wonderful relief and a magnificent
escape from the perils of political strife with
Carson.

Bonar Law was in agreement but he was
anxious that the change should be carried out
with the least possible offence to Sir Edward
Carson. He recognised that Lloyd George's plan
was beset with danger.

Curzon, too, was firmly behind the Prime
Minister. His support had been strengthened by
conversation with Haig.

But the most powerful reinforcement came from
Sir Joseph Maclay, Shipping Controller, who
wrote two letters on 28th June, one to Lloyd
George and one to Bonar Law. I give them both
here in full.

28th June 1917.

Dear Prime Minister,

I had not intended in view of your leaving for the
North to trouble you today further about the shipping

169

position, but it has come to my knowledge this morning that private meetings are being held of shipmasters and others, to consider the position and there is a danger that unless something is done in connection with the Admiralty, we shall have these men refusing to go to sea.

Statistics prove that what are called the areas of concentration as now managed, have become veritable death traps for our Mercantile Marine and our men are realising this.

I am led to believe that confidence in the Admiralty has pretty well gone but the coming of a few American destroyers has given them a little heart, which is a melancholy reflection on the position. The confidence of our Mercantile Marine in the Admiralty has been flittered [*sic*] away and does not now exist.

I am only sending you this letter after full consultation with Sir Kenneth Anderson and Sir Norman Hill, who are of opinion it should go.

Yours very truly,

J. P. MACLAY.[x]

Private & Urgent   28th June 1917.
Dear Bonar Law,

I think it right to send you copy of letter which I have sent to the Prime Minister this morning. I will try to see you today but I am convinced that unless something is done promptly relative to the Admiralty, we shall have an exhibition somewhat along the lines of the Mesopotamia report of this morning.—The position is just as bad as it can be and my conviction is that no man or shadow of a man should be allowed to stand in the way of the country at the present juncture while the country is in such dire peril. Changes are wanted right from the top downwards, and the position should be faced.

Yours truly,

J. P. MACLAY.[y]

Now Lloyd George turned to the King—the master move in his devious strategy. At the beginning of July he had an interview with Lord Stamfordham. Their conversation was reported in a Minute to His Majesty.

Humbly submitted.   July 5, 1917.
I have seen the Prime Minister this afternoon. He seriously contemplates making changes at the Admiralty. When he visited the Grand Fleet last week he gathered that there was dissatisfaction with the Admiralty: the Government are of the same opinion. Sir John Jellicoe is too pessimistic: if things do not go quite right he "is apt to get 'cold feet': grouses: says the War can't go on many months more &c &c". Both Sir W. Robertson and Sir Douglas Haig think that things are not right at the Admiralty, and the Prime Minister suggested Your Majesty might perhaps speak to the latter on the subject. He is inclined to put Sir E. Carson into the War Cabinet where he would be very useful and especially in making speeches in the country which the P.M. says ought to be more done just now but unfortunately there are very few in the Government who attract public audiences! I remarked it would be difficult to find the man with "driving power" "resourcefulness" and "of an inspiriting nature" such as he said was necessary as 1st Lord "who would hearten up everyone on the Board". He replied that the man he had in his mind was Sir Eric Geddes. He had got on very well with the soldiers when once they overcame their first antagonism to the introduction of a civilian "outsider"— and he would soon have the Army working amicably with him. . . .[z]

But then it was that Lloyd George hesitated. Would Carson go quietly? Would he be willing to separate himself from Sir John Jellicoe? There was no certainty when Carson was concerned. He conjured up Carson's face on the Opposition Bench. So far, he had only been able to see the profile as they sat side by side on the Treasury Bench. What of that frown? What of those phrases tumbling out in disorder, but influencing many members? Could he really afford to take a chance? Would Carson accept a transfer to the War Cabinet, with all that it implied for the fate of Jellicoe?

He was fearful of the support Carson could command, he was nervous and distrustful of the weight of his own following should an open challenge take place. What about the Press? A sure source of trouble! One good thing, Northcliffe was three thousand miles away and he could rely on Milner to look after Geoffrey Dawson, the Editor of *The Times*. If *The Times* walked in the straight path the *Daily Mail* might come along too.

Thus the Prime Minister walked delicately.

On 6th July, 1917, he addressed the following letter to the First Lord.

My dear Carson,
    This morning I told my colleagues the purport of my conversation with you yesterday as to the desirability of strengthening the War Cabinet with your presence. They all agreed that an additional member was needed in view of the overwhelming character of the work both in mass and in responsibility, and they were also unanimous that you would be the most helpful choice.
    You know my opinion on the subject. I wanted you in the Cabinet from the start. My plans were then thwarted for reasons you know. The time is now ripe

for reverting to my original idea. I hope therefore you will join us as a full member of the War Cabinet. We need your insight, courage and judgment. We have momentous decisions to take in the course of the next few days. I should therefore like to announce the appointment at once. Bonar foreshadowed it today.*

I tried to see you today to get your views about your successor at the Admiralty. I can see you Monday.

Ever sincerely,
D. Lloyd George.

Please let me know your desires by messenger.[aa]

At his home at Birchington, Carson was roused in the middle of the night by the message. The circumstances were not calculated to produce the most favourable reception. On the following morning, Carson despatched the messenger with a reply that left Lloyd George with no doubt of the formidable character of the man he was seeking to displace. Carson would not be hustled unceremoniously from office in order to placate the Prime Minister. He returned an austere answer:

July 7, 1917.

My dear Prime Minister,

Have received your letter by special messenger. Of course I am ready to fall in with your views that a change should be made at the Admiralty if you consider it in the public interest. It is vital that you should have confidence in the administration of so important a department. As regards my entering the Cabinet, I

---

* In the House of Commons, 6th July, 1917, Bonar Law, speaking in the debate on National Expenditure, said that he had not been able to give the time that he should have liked to have given to his duties in the War Cabinet. He said: "I think the result will be that the Prime Minister, with whom I have discussed it within the last few days, will find it necessary to make other arrangements and probably have an addition to the Cabinet to do the work that if I were free I should be able to do."

173

am very grateful for all you say but I should prefer not to have to give an answer today. I am suffering from a bad attack of neuralgia but hope to be all right by Monday.

Yours ever sincerely,
EDWARD CARSON.[ab]

Surprised by the sharpness of Carson's reply, Lloyd George wrote a new letter in conciliatory tones:

July 7, 1917.

My dear Carson,

I am afraid from your letter that you have misunderstood mine. We sincerely want you in the War Cabinet, but if you cannot see your way to join the Cabinet and prefer to remain at the Admiralty then the suggestion falls to the ground. We must have your help in this terrible war. I have all along—and so has Bonar—wanted you here. But it is for you to decide.

The changes I wanted at the Admiralty could be effected under your leadership. You know my views about that. The present Board is unsatisfactory.

I am so sorry you are suffering from neuralgia. It is a plague.

We have just had a Cabinet over the air raid.

Ever sincerely,
D. LLOYD GEORGE.

P.S. We can have a talk on Monday.[ac]

Here was the most astonishing retreat. Carson could remain at the Admiralty. The Prime Minister was showing incredible vacillation and amazing indecision. For the second time Lloyd George drew back. He hesitated and debated with friends and colleagues. Many were consulted and there was much conversation. The theme varied from Carson to Churchill and back again to Carson.

At last, after ten days of vacillation, Lloyd George was driven into action by an urgent warning from Lord Milner.

Very Confidential 16.7.17.
My dear Prime Minister,

Forgive my worrying. I am very anxious about the Admiralty. It is more than a fortnight now since I think you recognised there must be a change and every week is precious. Besides, the longer we wait, the more likely it is that something will get out, and then the papers will begin gossiping and criticising and the whole thing will be blown upon. [*sic*]

It would be best to make all Ministerial changes at once, but if this is not practicable, cannot the Carson-Geddes business in any case be settled right away? It is very urgent.

Yours very sincerely,
MILNER.*ad*

On the following evening the Ministerial changes were announced in the Press.* Milner's sensible letter had precipitated the decision.

Dr. Addison, whose place at the Ministry of Munitions was taken by Churchill, gives the following description of Carson abruptly disinherited of his role as First Lord. Addison recorded in his Diary [Tuesday, 17th July, 1917]:

Carson told me that L.G. had insisted on making the announcements tonight and that he did not intend

* Carson to War Cabinet, Geddes to Admiralty, Churchill to Munitions, and other changes.

to consult his colleagues, except Milner and Bonar, himself and myself. . . .

Carson was rather sick about it. I gathered that he had not discussed it beforehand with L.G. to the same extent as I had and that this apparently needless abruptness was rather a blow to him.[ae]

Carson had been dismissed. He was despatched to the War Cabinet* while Sir Eric Geddes† took his place as First Lord of the Admiralty.

But what of Jellicoe? Geddes asked to be relieved of the First Sea Lord before taking up his duties at the Admiralty. Carson refused with indignation. He went to the War Cabinet in relentless adherence to his belief in Jellicoe.

When Geddes saw that he could not persuade Carson to dismiss Jellicoe, he did not dare to implement the transfer himself. He knew there would be an outburst of opposition if Jellicoe should be dismissed just at the time when Carson was being removed. He could not face the odium of making a change in his professional subordinates before he had the opportunity to dig in at the

---

* Thus another Conservative was in the War Cabinet. Yet Lloyd George claimed that Carson had been rejected in December, 1916, because there were three Conservatives in the War Cabinet. Now there were four.

† Geddes had been in charge of Army Transportation in France. He was an interesting character; the son of a Presbyterian family, with the influence of his upbringing upon him. He could not be called a dutiful son of the Church, but he was quite unable to throw off the effects of his early instruction. He was a man of remarkable ability, though too forceful and determined to make a real success of public life.

He had sustained a tragedy in his domestic affairs which saddened his life. He had a large family of excellent sons who gave him much satisfaction though on account of his own upbringing Geddes was a stern and unbending parent.

Geddes was fond of medals and titles. He aspired to and attained the rank of General while in France in charge of Army transport. When he joined the Admiralty he insisted on being given the rank of Admiral. Sir Philip Sassoon, Geddes's Secretary, a shrewd and competent adviser who afterwards served Sir Douglas Haig and Lloyd George. Sir Philip's collection of Secretaryships was somewhat akin to Geddes's assumption of military and naval titles.

Admiralty. Besides Lloyd George advised his new First Lord to walk with short and cautious steps.

But Jellicoe was not backward in carrying the struggle into Geddes's domain. He claimed that he was the First Lord's colleague and not his subordinate.[af] Geddes was shocked and somewhat alarmed, possibly because he was inexperienced in public affairs.

He consulted with Bonar Law who took him to the Prime Minister. Forthwith an Order in Council dated 23rd October was handed down as from Sinai, defining the subordination of the First Sea Lord (Jellicoe) to the First Lord (Geddes).

Under Geddes's resourceful administration, however, there was a conspicuous improvement in Admiralty results. He was to prove a competent and proficient administrator. Indeed, Geddes's ability to shine in every field to which he was called won him an astonishing and, possibly, an exaggerated reputation.

By November, 1917, figures for Allied shipping losses gave testimony to his success in action. Losses of total Allied shipping had been reduced from the 900,000 tons claimed by the enemy in April, to 200,000. New ships being produced now exceeded the numbers destroyed. Here was reward and recompense. From the disastrous days when Britain's survival hung in the balance on the seas, the position had been wholly retrieved.

But for Carson there was disaffection and discontent. In the War Cabinet, he took little part in the conduct of the war, but continued to nurse his grievance. He remained faithful in his defence of Sir John Jellicoe. There was never any doubt of his allegiance. He was on the side not only of the admirals, but of the professional military advisers of the Government as a whole. As a member of the War Cabinet he extended his front while maintaining his allegiance.*

In September, 1917, Carson paid his visit to G.H.Q. in France. There he talked with Sir Douglas Haig, who three months before had helped to drive him from the Admiralty. Haig gives this account in his papers:

> Sir Edward Carson arrived today and stays two nights. It is quite a rest to deal with him after Winston! He is so straightforward and single minded. He is convinced that the military experts must be given full power, not only to advise, but to carry out their plans. He is all opposed to the meddling now practised by the Prime Minister and other politicians . . .
>
> He considers that Lloyd George has considerable value as P.M. on account of his driving powers, but he recognises his danger. He has no knowledge of strategy or military operations, yet he thinks he is well qualified to direct his Military Advisers! Carson wished me to talk freely with Mr. Asquith because the latter, though in opposition, has very great power.
>
> Sir E. Carson left at 9.30. He said he was delighted with his visit, and he assured me that the War Cabinet would not be allowed to interfere with me or my arrangements. . . . Mr. Asquith and Bonham Carter

---

* Carson's willingness to help Robertson is indicated in an extract from his biography. Robertson, says Colvin, with Carson's support usually got more or less what he wanted. There was thus good reason for Carson to suppose that he could best help Robertson by remaining in the Cabinet.*⁸*

arrived in time for dinner. Afterwards I had a long talk with Mr. A. He said that the present Government is very shaky.*ah*

Here was a truly extraordinary situation, but it was a sure indication of Carson's hostility to Lloyd George and of his bitter prejudice against the Government. In a word, he was urging the Commander-in-Chief to consult with the Leader of the Opposition at a moment when the Government, as Asquith rightly said, was "very shaky".* It was typical of the man, of his intense respect as a professional lawyer for the generals—and of the confusions of purpose that beset Carson at that time.

He returned to London and a few weeks later made what, in effect, was a public declaration of opposition to the Government of which he was a member.

I have met in the course of my work as a member of His Majesty's government three great men—I say that advisedly—Field-Marshal Haig, Sir William Robertson and Sir John Jellicoe, with whom, while I was in the Navy, I was brought into the most intimate relations. They have my absolute confidence.*aj*

It was open defiance of the Prime Minister at a time when Lloyd George had intimated to Carson his determination to dismiss Jellicoe and had shown clearly that he intended to come to grips with the generals.

---

* It was about this time that Sir William Robertson wrote to Haig: "He [Lloyd George] is a real bad 'un. The other members of the War Cabinet seem afraid of him. Milner is a tired, dyspeptic old man. Curzon a gas-bag. Bonar Law equals Bonar Law. Smuts has good instinct but lacks knowledge."*ai*

The *Morning Post*, ever faithful to Carson, gave frantic support to the generals. "If anything could ensure the collapse and disappearance from public life of Mr. Lloyd George, it would be an attempt on his part to upset the Chief of the Imperial General Staff and the Commander-in-Chief of the British Armies in France. If he tried to replace Robertson and Haig with more amenable generals, he could not hold his office for a week."[ak]

Christmas Day dawned before the struggle with the First Sea Lord (Jellicoe) was rounded to its conclusion. On the last day of the year, a year fraught with the gravest consequences for the Navy, Carson wrote in vigorous protest to the Prime Minister.

Confidential. 31.12.17.

My dear Prime Minister,

Can I have a private interview with you today if possible.

I am very much concerned about the dismissal of Sir John Jellicoe and even more so at the appointment of Admiral Wemyss as First Sea Lord and I greatly resent the manner in which my name has been brought into the matter. I am sorry to trouble you but I cannot allow the matter to pass in silence.

Yours sincerely,
EDWARD CARSON.[al]

It was, of course, a letter from a Minister to his Chief giving notice of an intention to resign. The request for an interview carried its own implication.

The meeting followed at once. Carson made his protest, and Lloyd George made an excellent argument in favour of finding other reasons for resignation thus avoiding any possibility of stirring up anxiety and want of confidence in the Higher Command among serving sailors. It is, of course, the stock argument in such circumstances.

In January, 1918, Carson's resignation was announced. He said it was over the condition of Irish affairs. It seemed he was disturbed by the remote possibility that the Government might produce a remedy, but one of which he did not approve. He required a free hand in dealing with the Irish problem.

In any event the pretext for departure was Ireland, as on the last occasion it had been Serbia. Small nationalites could be relied upon to justify Sir Edward Carson's resignations.

But the real reason for his departure must be sought elsewhere. It would seem that Carson, having stayed in the Government to protect Jellicoe, resigned now he could no longer save him.

In March, after he had left the Government, Carson explained in Parliament what had guided his attitude during his period of office. It was a startling pronouncement. "The whole time that I was First Lord of the Admiralty," he declared, "one of the greatest difficulties I had was the constant persecution—for I can call it nothing else—of certain high officials in the Admiralty, who could not speak for themselves—constant persecution which, I have no doubt, I could have traced to reasons and motives of the most malignant character. Over and over again while I was at the Admiralty, . . . I had the most constant pressure put upon me—which I need hardly say I absolutely resisted—to remove officials, and among them Sir John Jellicoe."[am]

Carson in due course became the leader of an Opposition. He gathered round him the dissident elements in Parliament.

Not long after his resignation, he had a skirmish with Bonar Law over Ireland in which for the first time the Conservative leader defied the "King of Ulster". Bonar Law wrote:

11 Downing Street,
28th April, 1918.

My dear Carson,

Your letter, if it is to be published, must be the beginning of conflict between us and my reply, if for publication, must be of the same kind. . . .

That may be inevitable. But I should like to delay it as much as possible.[an]

The tone of this letter showed that already the powers of Carson had waned. He had paid in loss of prestige for his excessive reliance on the judgement of the Naval technicians. He had failed to disclose the strength of mind and independence of judgement that an administrator of the first rank must possess. In fact his political career was really over when he left the Government. What came after was nothing more than the shadow of greatness—the image without the substance.

And Carson's career as a leader of an Opposition was doomed to disappointment. When his chance came at the crisis of the Maurice issue * later in May, he lacked the support to push home his assault upon the Prime Minister, and in the division that followed in the House of Commons on that dramatic day, Carson ended up voting for the Government.

Four months after the Maurice debate, Carson had ceased to be a menace to the Government. He talked with Bonar Law about the position and prospects of his old enemy Lloyd George. The war was drawing swiftly to a conclusion and war-time controversy was dying down. It was then, according to a letter written by Bonar Law to Lloyd George himself, that Carson spoke of his antagonist "very nicely" and "very kindly", telling Bonar Law among other things that "we must not kill the little man".[ao]

At the General Election of December, 1918, Carson was returned to Parliament as a Coalition member from Ulster.

His term of office in the Lloyd George Government had lasted thirteen months; seven at the Admiralty and six in the War Cabinet. It was an inglorious era in a life filled with action and studded with courage—political, moral and physical courage.

Much has been said in criticism of Carson's administration. But the Prime Minister must be given the blame for hesitation and delay in

* Lloyd George was charged by General Maurice with telling lies.

reorganizing the Admiralty. It has been shown that he lost faith in Carson and confidence in Jellicoe, yet he had taken three months to dismiss the politician, and another five to rid the Admiralty of the First Sea Lord.

The charge can be answered. There was much hostility to the Prime Minister. His parliamentary position was weak and dangerous. To take action without a long period of preparation and a wide mobilisation of support might have resulted in the destruction of Lloyd George himself. Believing as he did that he alone could win the war, an argument can be stated in defence of his conduct. In any case, events were fully to justify his course of action in sacking Carson to make Geddes First Lord.

Nor was Sir Edward Carson in any state of rancour against his old enemy when war was over and peace reigned. Speaking in the House of Commons on 3rd July, 1919, he said: "I had the honour of serving in the Cabinet with him [Lloyd George] in the very darkest days of our country's history in this War. His patriotism, his courage, and his genius . . . were the greatest contribution that any man in the whole country has given to the War . . . [and history will say of him] that he did more than any other man to preserve the liberties of the world."[ap]

Lloyd George responded generously. In the summer of 1921, he nominated Carson for the House of Lords, the mausoleum of weary titans. There he carried on sham battles with his former friend Lord Birkenhead over "Home Rule for

Ireland". Plenty of fireworks. That was all. Nothing happened.

On a dark morning in October, 1935, Lord Carson died of old age. Then it was that all men spoke well of him. But throughout his life his intimate colleagues had frequently prefaced their remarks by saying: "If I understand Carson aright."

No man possessed a greater or more overwhelming charm of manner. He appeared to be dour and grim in the eyes of his devoted followers in Ulster and Britain. His "ignorant and hostile" enemies fell into the same error. Yet such a description could only be justified by the expression of gloom which frequently marked his features. He was a rare combination of hypochondriac and man of action. His pleas of ill-health and his oft-repeated claim for sympathy over the pain and misery that oppressed him and the impending abdominal operation were, with Carson, an interesting opening gambit in many a conversation of first-class political importance. His second marriage, late in life and on the eve of war, to a beautiful and clever young woman who had the advantage of many years in age brought him much happiness.

So I leave this figure who bestrides a decade, standing in characteristic attitude of dark yet clear-cut outline against the sky of storm and strife, a hero in the eyes of his devoted young wife and of his faithful followers.

CHAPTER VI

ALL THE KING'S MEN

NOW came the decision in the long-drawn-out conflict for power between Lloyd George and Robertson.

Lloyd George, convinced that Robertson and his military colleagues now aimed at overthrowing the Government and setting up a new administration under Army control, determined that he must get rid of both Robertson, the Chief of the Imperial General Staff, and Haig, the Commander-in-Chief.

Robertson and Haig too were well aware of the Prime Minister's intention to remove them from their posts. They were bent upon holding fast.

Thus it was apparent that compromise or reconciliation became impossible. The political chief and the Army commanders looked out upon one another just as two boxers in training approach the day of trial when one or other must have the decision, even to the extent of a knock-out.

Lloyd George had real reason at this time to complain of Haig's conduct. He had muddled the battle of Cambrai.

For the first time the wonderful war-winning weapon, the tank, was launched en masse against the enemy on 20th November, 1917. The offensive was an immediate and immense triumph. Much territory was taken from the enemy and the newspapers announced the victory in terms of a military decision.

The Infantry, however, was not prepared to consolidate the gains. And when the Germans counter-attacked, within a week their lost ground was regained. After many days, slowly and reluctantly the Press was informed of the failure of Cambrai. The public had been swindled by means of suppression and deception.

The Lloyd George case against Robertson arose out of victory and not as a result of defeat. Allenby, in command of the army in Palestine, had been directed to take Jerusalem. He gave an exaggerated and extravagant estimate of the strength of the Turkish forces opposing him and asked for an extensive reinforcement of his own army. Lloyd George believed that these false claims of Turkish strength and British weakness were promoted by Robertson for the purpose of destroying the plan for the attack on Jerusalem lest the operations should interfere with the flow of manpower to the Western Front. The Lloyd George Papers and documents do not establish the charge against Robertson. Nor does Lloyd George allude to it in writing of the event in his *War Memoirs*. However, Jerusalem fell to Allenby two weeks before Christmas 1917 without the aid of reinforcements.*

* Balfour, the Foreign Secretary, sent Allenby a vast quantity of pamphlets publicising the Balfour Declaration, with its promise of a National Home for the

It was on the basis of these complaints that the
Prime Minister called upon the Secretary of State
for War, Lord Derby, on 11th December, 1917,
asking him, in effect, to dismiss his Chief of the
Imperial General Staff and also his Commander-
in-Chief. He invited Derby to appoint both Sir
Douglas Haig and General Robertson to sinecure
posts which would remove them from Lloyd
George's path. The sinecures would take the form
of consolation prizes.

Lord Derby refused. He replied with a carefully reasoned and cogent statement of his own
position, which is indeed a brilliant document.

It was a determined and well-argued case in
support of both Haig and Robertson. Indeed it
carried with it a clear indication that if Lloyd
George's programme was to be carried out, Lord
Derby would not remain in the Administration.

Derby's letter* was in fact the first information
that he was prepared to support Haig and Robertson, even to the extent of resigning if they were
dismissed.

Derby was emphatic that the Cambrai affair
(the Lloyd George case against Haig) was not a
just cause for hanging Haig, and he reiterated his
faith in the Commander-in-Chief.

Derby then dealt with the charge made by
Lloyd George that Robertson had been deliberately trying to deceive the Government. "I

Jews. These were to be distributed in Jerusalem in advance of the entry of
Allenby and his triumphant army. But at this time the population of Jerusalem
was made up mostly of Arabs. Allenby took the decision to reject the order
from the Foreign Office and Balfour's pamphlets were consigned to other uses.

* The full text of the letter is printed in *Appendix* IV, No. 8.

ROBERTSON. Frequently answering the arguments of his opponents by saying, "I've heard different."

confess that what you told me with regard to your suspicions today," he wrote, "has shaken my confidence but I cannot believe that he [Robertson] would deliberately ask Allenby to send in a false telegram in order to deceive the Government. I agree with you that read in the light of subsequent events Allenby's telegram asking for the enormous increase of force in order to do what he has done with the existing forces seems very ridiculous but that his former proposal should be put forward with a deliberate attempt to deceive the Government and that at the instance of Robertson, is almost beyond belief." If Robertson had deliberately deceived the Government, and it could be proved, said Derby, "I could have no further faith in him but I cannot believe it and assuming therefore that is not the case I take Robertson as I have found him and that is a very honest man endeavouring to give the Government the best advice that it is in his power to give."

As to the position of the War Cabinet, they had, said Derby, every right to change a Commander or policy at will. Some people would say that that meant the politicians interfering with the soldiers "and they may be right but I for one should never hold that opinion though naturally in one's present position one would insist on the right of resigning if one thought that the advice given was the correct one and the persons in power were most fitted to carry it out."[a]

Lord Derby's letter shattered Lloyd George's plan. His resignation over Haig and Robertson would bring strong, and indeed decisive, support from many Conservative members of the House, and all of the Liberals. Derby's voice could not be silenced or ignored. Lloyd George might indeed insist, with the support of his Cabinet, on removing Haig and Robertson. But the order of dismissal would at that time bring down in ruins the Prime Minister's own Government. Lloyd George and his two Generals would all three fall together.

Thus Lloyd George was saddled with a Secretary of State for War who professed his first allegiance to the High Command and not to the Prime Minister. While Derby remained at the War Office, Lloyd George could not rid himself of his Military Chiefs.

The very next day Derby made an amazing concession evidently intended to placate the irritated and angry Prime Minister. While continuing to defend Robertson and Haig he wrote a long letter to the Commander-in-Chief in France demanding the dismissal of many principal members of his staff at the Front. Brigadier-General Charteris, Haig's Chief Intelligence Officer, whose dismissal had been demanded by Lloyd George; Major-General Maxwell, the Quartermaster General; Lieutenant-General Sir George Fowke, Adjutant General to the Armies in France; and General Gough, Commander of the Fifth Army, were all to come under the axe.

Lord Derby gave detailed reasons for his insistence, including an account of Canadian opposition to Gough. "Canadians are especially bitter."[b] *

The Prime Minister, on receiving a copy of this extraordinary document, wrote a warm and even enthusiastic letter of approval. I reproduce it here.

Dec. 13th, 1917.

My dear S. of S.

Just read your letter. A fine straight letter that does you credit. It will do no end of good. The morale of the Army must be restored at all costs.

Ever sincerely,
D. LLOYD GEORGE.[c]

But the slaughter† of the innocent or guilty Generals of lesser degree did not deflect Lloyd George from his purpose. A second movement, really directed against Robertson and Haig, was launched in mid January. Lloyd George decided that the prop supporting the Generals must be removed. Another and more amenable Secretary of State must be substituted for Lord Derby.

Accordingly the Prime Minister offered to Lord Derby the post of Ambassador in Paris.

But Derby was too clever to fall into that ditch. He asked for terms sweeping in character and certainly extraordinary in practice. "Would the Ambassador in Paris be more or less of a colleague of members of the War Cabinet or would he be simply the mouthpiece of that

* The text of the letter is reproduced in *Appendix IV*, No. 9.
† Derby proposed to send four men to the guillotine; he succeeded only in beheading two, Charteris and Maxwell. Sir George Fowke escaped and remained Adjutant General till the war was over. Gough lived on as Commander of the Fifth Army until the German offensive of March, 1918.

body?"[d] he demanded in a letter to Lloyd George.*
It was apparent that the factor that would influence
his decision in accepting the Ambassadorship
would be the question of his own authority in
public concerns. Derby declared that if disagreement arose between the Military Chiefs and the
War Cabinet, he must be assured of the right to
take an independent line. He reserved, in particular, the right to resign if Robertson and Haig
should be dismissed. And Derby with such
powers could be just as dangerous to Lloyd
George in Paris as in London.

It was a skilful and cunning letter though
written in obscure terms with the evident intention
of maintaining secrecy even against his own staff.

Again Lloyd George had been frustrated in
his second plan—a plan to rid himself of the
impediment standing in the way of the dismissal
of the generals.

He tried once more, and for the third time.
He attempted the knock-out, with no question of
consolation prizes.

He made a frontal attack on Robertson and his
General Staff, charging them with communicating
to the Press, and particularly to the *Morning Post*
through Colonel Repington, a series of official
secrets.

He wrote to Derby complaining of a "grave
breach of discipline", and a "gross breach of Army
regulations". He proposed, he said, to appeal to
the House of Commons, and to take stern action.

Four days later, Lloyd George wrote again

* The letter is reproduced in full in *Appendix IV*, No. 10.

claiming that the Turks, who had been about to sue for peace,* had been bolstered up by the publication of the Repington dispatch.

Lord Derby answered. His reply was a strong defence of the Chief of the Imperial General Staff and his colleagues. The statements Repington had made, said Derby, were in the main inaccurate or were such as his long experience and profound study throughout the war, would supply. And Repington had himself affirmed that no Cabinet paper had been given to him by any soldier. He had seen the Man Power Report. But "it would lead us nowhere to threaten all recipients of the latter with dire pains and penalties." "I can see no ground", concluded Derby, "for singling out the officers of the General Staff for exclusive treatment on these lines."*†

The knock-out blow failed. The Prime Minister was checked by the overwhelming devotion of the Secretary for War to the cause of his military advisers. Besides, it was well known in Lloyd George's circles that Derby was consulting with willing helpers of high estate who honestly feared that the dismissal of Robertson would be a real national calamity. Draft copies of his letters were submitted to revision by able hands.

What now? There could be no question of Lloyd George and Robertson working together any more. Lloyd George had launched charges against Robertson that made any accommodation impossible. Indeed it is amazing that the Prime

* Negotiations for the surrender of Turkey were being conducted by Sir Basil Zaharoff.

† The full letter appears in *Appendix IV*, No. 11.

Minister, if he really believed these accusations, delayed so long in dismissing his Chief of the Imperial General Staff.

He was, of course, most unwilling to face a House of Commons uncertain in its loyalties. Just as Lord Derby had given his faith to the generals, so would many of the Back Bench members. Then what? Another Prime Minister and another set of Ministers! But Lloyd George believed he was the only man who could win the war. Therefore he must temporize.

Other methods must be adopted. Other plans must be matured. He would rely upon the wisdom and common sense of the old legend "If at first you don't succeed, try, try, try again".

His strength rested on the knowledge that he was sustained by Bonar Law, Leader of the Conservative Party, whose high character and good name carried conviction in the House of Commons and also in the country: and over everything on the sure and certain response which he could depend upon if a General Election could be snatched from the crisis.

He was now compelled to find some other way of dislodging his opponent at the War Office.

A programme had been prepared the previous November when the Allied Conference met at Rapallo. There, Lloyd George, pursuing a course he had long entertained, won approval for a scheme setting up a supreme directorate of the war. It was decided that a Supreme War Council should meet at Versailles with a permanent military representative from each of the participating powers.

Sir Henry Wilson was nominated to serve Great Britain in this capacity.

Loud were the outcries that this decision wrung from the generals and their political supporters. General Robertson signified his most bitter opposition. The hostile Press sprang to his defence. Lloyd George, stopping over in Paris to address a meeting and to describe the purpose of the new Supreme Council, returned to London to meet a determined outburst against him.* Even then his critics believed that this was a plan to equip himself with machinery which would enable him to receive and act on advice independent of General Robertson and the General Staff.

There were to be two sets of military advisers, said the Prime Minister's critics in his own Government.

Lord Robert Cecil, foremost amongst the opponents of the Prime Minister on this issue, expressed his grave dissatisfaction in a letter to Balfour, the Foreign Secretary.

> 100 Grosvenor Road,
> Pimlico.
> 18 November 1917

My dear Arthur,
    Further reflection (in bed) has made me more distrustful than ever of the Supreme War Council. Taken with the Paris speech there can be very little

---

* Speaking in Paris on 12th November, 1917, Lloyd George, Tom Jones records, "cast such aspersions on British generals that when it was published, the immediate fall of the Government was not only desired but expected in some quarters."/

doubt that one of the purposes which the P.M. had in view was to enable him to over-rule the C.I.G.S. and other advocates of the Western Front.

Churchill's presence at the luncheon confirms this and so does the article in this morning's "Observer". In other words, he wants to create machinery which will enable him to receive and act on military advice independent of the General Staff. That is to say there are to be two supreme advisers to the Government on the general conduct of the war. That cannot work. It must mean division and confusion. Until therefore it can be made absolutely clear that Wilson is really and not nominally subordinate to Robertson I do not see how I can make myself responsible for the plan. I shall await the Debate on Monday without great anxiety.

Yours ever,
ROBERT CECIL

If you think right, please show this letter to the P.M. or tell him of it.⁵

Lloyd George triumphed in the parliamentary encounter. The Debate in the House of Commons on 19th November, 1917, he turned to his advantage. The Council, he repeatedly assured his anxious audience, would have no executive authority. He had also committed himself to his critics. It would be impossible, in the face of his pledge, to make use of the Supreme War Council as an alternative to the General Staff. "No executive authority" was the charter of the soldiers.

But in February, 1918, there was something more for the generals to complain of. Lloyd George saw his advantage, and took it. In the mounting conflict, he devised a scheme for achieving his desire to put an end to the Military Junta at the War Office that he feared and detested.

At the Supreme War Council meeting on the first day of the month of February, with Lloyd George present, it was determined that a General Reserve should be set up. The control would be entrusted to an Executive Committee of the permanent military representatives at Versailles.

That was that. Thus real power would now pass to the Supreme War Council.

General Robertson made another effort to hold on to his authority over the Army Reserves in France. He demanded that the British Military Representative at Versailles should come under himself as Chief of the Imperial General Staff.

Not at all. At last Lloyd George had tracked down and cornered his enemy. He refused any accommodation. In reply, he offered General Robertson the alternative of remaining on as Chief of the Imperial General Staff under the reduced dispensation, or of taking up the post of Military Representative at Versailles.

What a dilemma for Robertson! What a desperate confusion of all his hopes and aspirations. Either way he was done.

For it was apparent that if he stayed on at the War Office, military power would be vested with Sir Henry Wilson at Versailles by reason of his authority over the Reserve. If he accepted the Versailles appointment, London would become the centre of military authority where Sir Henry Wilson would fill the role of Military Adviser to the Cabinet. The Prime Minister would, of course, throw his support behind whichever post Robertson rejected.

It was an ironic and a dismal end for the old soldier. Even though he had hurled defiance at his Prime Minister denying civilian control, demanding autocratic and unquestioning authority, his enemies may well have pitied him. He could not escape extinction.

Since Robertson absolutely declined to budge from the War Office and refused to relinquish his powers, Lloyd George decided to dismiss him.

He had made up his mind. He would face the resignations and he would meet the House of Commons. He understood that Derby would resign in support of Robertson. He fully expected Haig to take the same course. And he knew that some of his colleagues would support Robertson and the Military Junta.

Would he put these grave issues to the test? Would he stand or fall by the decision of the Members of Parliament?

It would be a brave decision, for the atmosphere of the House of Commons was already prepared for an insurrection with the rumoured news of Robertson's impending dismissal.

The Debate took place on 12th February. Asquith, who was of course fully informed of Lloyd George's plan, took the opportunity to make a considered and effective attack on the Prime

HIS MAJESTY KING GEORGE V AND EARL HAIG. Lloyd George wanted to put him out; the King wanted to keep him in.

Minister. He demanded on behalf of the House an assurance that no change was contemplated in the authority and power of either Haig or Robertson. "There have been many criticisms," he said, "some of them just, some of them unjust—upon the conduct of our naval and military operations during the past year, but there is nothing that has been done—I am speaking now more particularly of the military field—or left undone which has in the least shaken the confidence of the nation and of the Empire in the two great soldiers, Sir Douglas Haig, our Commander-in-Chief, and Sir William Robertson, the head of our General Staff at home."[b]

Lloyd George answered. He did not meet Asquith's challenge. Instead he intimidated the Members with an implicit threat of a dissolution and a general election. "If the House of Commons and the country," he said, "are not satisfied with the conduct of the War, and if they think there is any Government which can conduct it better, then it is their business, in God's name, to put that other Government in!"[i]

The following day, 13th February 1918, the Prime Minister sent for Sir Reginald Brade, the Permanent Under-Secretary at the War Office. Brade wrote "A Few Notes on the Recent Controversy between Sir W. R. (Robertson) and the Government." I quote an extract:

> During most of this crisis I was laid up with a poisoned foot, but Bonar and the P.M. [Prime Minister] sent for me about an hour before the latter was to see the King. . . .

P.M. told me that he was going to tell the King and his colleagues firmly that he refused to go on as he had done during the last year. He or W.R. [Sir William Robertson] was to be P.M., he did not care which.

Again I quote from Sir Reginald Brade's Notes:

On the Friday [15th February, 1918] I went with Max* to the P.M. [Prime Minister] to help in the discussion as to the P.M.'s statement to the House and as to Derby's resignation.† Hankey wrote out a long statement which Bonar was to give on the Monday, reserving for Tuesday the full statement to be made by P.M. (on Army Estimates) when his cold would probably be better. Max and I agreed it was rotten and I tried to get a shorter and more precise statement, omitting all reference to the A.C. [Army Council].

The Prime Minister had come to a solid resolution. He must announce forthwith the retirement of Robertson and the appointment of another C.I.G.S. True, the approval of the King was essential, but Lloyd George was the constitutional adviser of His Majesty and the advice would have to be accepted. The only alternative was dismissal of the Prime Minister and a change of government. Such a bold course would be dangerous indeed to the Royal master if another Government were set up and failed to find public approval.

Thus it was that Lloyd George on Friday night made a balance sheet of assets and liabilities, taking stock at the same time. None could deny that the surplus of goodwill was small. There were dissatisfied and discontented directors of the

* Lord Beaverbrook, then Minister of Information.
† Derby had intimated his intention to resign.

company, in the form of colleagues in the Government. Great were the forces drawn up on either side.

On the debit side of Lloyd George's balance-sheet the picture was far from encouraging, for against him there was a formidable array.

A spearhead of opposition was to be found among his colleagues and members of his Government. Lord Derby, the Secretary of State for War, was the civilian captive of the military faction, committed to supporting to the utmost his service advisers at the War Office. There was no escape for him. He was often called "Genial Judas". He would not be guilty now of betraying his two friends. He was frequently accused of changing his mind, and rightly. But in his support of Haig and Robertson he was unswerving in his devotion to his beliefs. Many efforts were made to disengage him from the generals' party. He maintained a firm front. Some observers declared that his hands were being held on high by Buckingham Palace. Certainly Derby's intimacy with the King was remarkable. They were in frequent correspondence. No doubt His Majesty influenced Derby greatly. In any event, Derby was in a position to inform His Majesty and offer advice.

Walter Long, Secretary of State for the Colonies and leader in Parliament of the country gentlemen, survival of the Tory aristocrats, was another adherent of the military caste. He wrote to Bonar Law that he was horrified over the proposal to abandon Robertson.[*] He was convinced that it

* See *Addendum*.

would give the Government a very severe shake. It was a tremendous step, to be taken only after great consideration. It was evident that Long felt he should have been directly consulted.

Lord Robert Cecil, too, belonged to the camp of the military section. Cecil was Under-Secretary at the Foreign Office and Minister of Blockade; but in this line-up of the civilian against the military authorities, he gave his allegiance and sympathy wholly to Sir William Robertson. So strongly did he support the cause of Robertson that he wrote to Bonar Law disclaiming all share in the Cabinet's responsibility, and making a spirited justification of the generals. "I confess it seems to me more just," his letter concluded, "to say that their [the soldiers'] civilian chief ought not to have tried to force such a scheme upon them."[k]

Derby, Cecil and Long were important members of the Government, but more to be taken into account because of the positions of influence and authority they held in the Conservative Party. They could dislodge a considerable following from the Tory Benches. There was also a powerful and numerous section of members who accepted absolutely the simple formula "The Army, right or wrong."

Then there was Carson, willing at any moment to lead an attack upon the Government in the House of Commons.

Austen Chamberlain, who was at this time a private Conservative member waiting the call to office, was another whose loyalty lay outside the administration on this grave issue. In an interview with Lord Curzon, Chamberlain had given the impression that Lloyd George would lose his political friendship if there was criticism of the generals.[1]

There was, of course, a large assembly of Liberals who were arrayed in close formation behind the leading generals of the day. Asquith and his Liberal ex-Ministers and all the following of Liberal Members who looked for the return of an Asquith Government were now aligned in readiness for the final clash. Here was the famous "Brass Hat Alliance", expectant of a victory in arms.

And in advance, and behind, and in all conceivable directions, the persistent and hostile voices of the newspapers joined the attack upon Lloyd George. The *Globe*, the *Morning Post*, the *Westminster Gazette*, the *Daily News*, the *Daily Chronicle*, all were the vehicles of an opinion damaging to the Government and directly supporting military control of the War machine.

But more important than any of these individual influences, the positive support of the King for the Military Advisers was a factor of the utmost weight in this critical division and distribution of loyalties.*

The generals were esteemed by His Majesty. He gave them confidence and trust. Sir Douglas Haig enjoyed his unswerving support and always

* The Memoranda of Lord Stamfordham are set out in full in *Stamfordham Memoranda*, page 408. Readers are recommended to pay close attention to these documents revealing at once the King's attitude to the dispute, and also indicating Royal proceedings in public concerns.

sheltered under Royal protection.'" Robertson
too had the tremendous reinforcement of the
backing and endorsement of his titular Commander-in-Chief, the monarch himself.

Lloyd George, from the outset of his Premiership and for the duration of the war, never won
the confidence of His Majesty. When Asquith fell
the King noted in his diary: "I fear that it will
cause a panic in the City & in America & do
harm to the Allies. It is a great blow to me &
will I fear buck up the Germans.'"

Bonar Law told His Majesty that both he and
Lloyd George had for long been convinced that
the war was being mismanaged.

"To this," writes Lord Stamfordham, "the
King demurred and said that the politicians should
leave the conduct of the war to experts. Mr.
Bonar Law said that Robertson and the soldiers
were all wrong, with the result that we have lost
Serbia, Rumania and very likely Greece. The
King expressed his entire disagreement with these
views."°

Nor did the King reserve these sentiments
reflecting a distrust of his Prime Minister for his
intimate advisers. He confided them to Colonel
House. In turn they reached the ears of the
American President. Thus we find House record-
ing in his diary following an interview with the
King at Buckingham Palace in October 1917:
"He (the King) touched, with a tinge of bitterness, upon the assumption of autocratic powers
by some of his Prime Ministers. He plainly

referred to Lloyd George, and I could see there was considerable feeling lurking under the surface. He spoke of Grey and Asquith in the highest terms, but was guarded in what he said of his present Prime Minister."[3]

It was said of the King that "politics and the politicians of the time worried him to distraction". He was aware of "quarrels and intrigue within the Cabinet and in the Army which outraged his loyal spirit."[4]

Yet, even as the King withheld his faith in Lloyd George's judgement, he gave his trust and confidence in abounding measure to the generals.

On the side of Lloyd George a tally of good sound assets could be made. Possibly they seemed less weighty and substantial than those of his opponents on that dark winter's evening. Their true worth, however, had yet to be measured.

The Prime Minister had the solid backing of his War Cabinet. He had the allegiance of Bonar Law, the Leader of the Conservative Party, as already stated. Bonar Law's sympathies were wholly on the side of asserting civilian responsibility for the direction of the war. Smuts was squarely behind the Prime Minister. Curzon had given his encouragement to Lloyd George over the High Command ever since his excursion with the Prime Minister to the Admiralty the previous April, when they had met and beaten the resistance of the admirals.*

* It is necessary to record, however, that Curzon was in secret communication with Derby and was leading the War Minister to believe that if Derby's decision was in favour of resignation, then Curzon would go with him. Curzon really meant that he would go with the winning side.

Lord Milner was most active on the Prime Minister's behalf. His attitude, indeed, had undergone a striking metamorphosis for, in the previous autumn, Milner's efforts had been turned largely towards carrying the generals with the Government. Where Lloyd George had preached drastic action Milner had striven for co-operation between the rival factions. This mood had now passed. In February, 1918, Lord Milner was the outspoken advocate of a Supreme War Council, and the principal critic of Sir William Robertson.

His counsel was of the most specific kind; he advised Lloyd George that it would be better to lose Haig and Robertson than to continue at the mercy of either of them. The one vital thing, he told the Prime Minister, was "that we should be able once for all to get free to do what we know to be right".

To Bonar Law he wrote in these terms:

Confidential   18.2.18*
                     17 Great College Street, S.W.
My dear Bonar,
    . . . I have often been told, though I don't know of my own knowledge, that Percy is the man who has been working the Press & Army opinion for Robertson.

        . . . .

    If R. is going to fight us, it is surely madness to let him do so from inside. As long as he retains his position, he will look the stronger party, & the large

---

* As Milner must have known of Robertson's dismissal before 18th February, it is evident that the date of writing was wrongly recorded.

number of people, who do not like the change, but would accept a *fait accompli* will rally to him. This is especially true of the Army.

The course we are pursuing, thanks to Derby, is the very course most likely to produce a considerable military combination against us.

Yours ever,

M.[5]

Balfour, the Foreign Secretary, had also given his loyalty. Lloyd George had sought a way of capturing Balfour's full support for his cause by using him as an emissary in the negotiations with Robertson. This was a favourite plan with Lloyd George. Often he would select an intermediary with the real intention of persuading him to swallow the case he was to present. If doubt had once clouded Balfour's mind in this issue with the soldiers, it was dispelled by his contact with Robertson. He failed to persuade the soldier, but he convinced himself.

Such then was the standing of the parties on that critical Friday evening. But there were more pressing speculations. Would the triumvirate— the two generals, Haig and Robertson, with Derby as their civilian delegate—act together? Would Sir Douglas Haig resign? If he took with him, not only Derby, but Cecil and Walter Long also, and if they were followed by eminent Conservatives outside the Government, with Austen Chamberlain and Carson at their head, would the House of Commons desert the Prime Minister? Lloyd George had good reason to worry.

What would the King do and say ? There was

no certainty. His attitude was in doubt. Lloyd George had seen Lord Stamfordham, the King's Private Secretary, on Wednesday, 13th February. The Prime Minister had been told that "the King strongly deprecated the idea of Robertson being removed from the office of C.I.G.S.'" The King considered that Robertson was the indispensable general and also the country had confidence in him, and so had the Army.

Lloyd George was aware that if the crisis resulted in the resignation of Derby, the withdrawal of Haig and the departure from his administration of Lord Robert Cecil and Walter Long, His Majesty might not wait upon a vote in the House of Commons. He might decide to refuse a dissolution, and dismiss his Prime Minister, setting up a new administration. Thus Lloyd George would be deprived of the opportunity of presenting his statement from the Government Bench. Instead he would have to make his case from the front Opposition Bench.

But all these speculations and questions were soon to be answered. On Saturday morning, 16th February, Lloyd George motored to Buckingham Palace from the country. It was a cold grey day. Lloyd George was resolute and forceful. In an interview with Lord Stamfordham he pointed out that if His Majesty insisted on retaining Sir William Robertson in his power and place, he would lay down his task. The King must choose other Ministers. Lloyd George declared that the Government must govern. He would not submit to military dictation on any account or in any direction. Lord Stamfordham hastened to assure Lloyd George that His Majesty had no idea of making such insistence (see *Stamfordham Memoranda*, page 408).

The King then saw his Prime Minister. His confidence in his Chief of the Imperial General Staff was absolute. There is nothing in Lloyd George's records to show that the King assented to Robertson's removal.

The news, nonetheless, of Sir William Robertson's retirement from his post at the War Office was announced by the Prime Minister late on Saturday afternoon.

Lord Derby also called upon His Majesty. Derby said that there was nothing left to him but to resign, though he appealed to the King to advise him of the proper course to follow. The King assured him there was no alternative but his resignation.

Derby then went off to consult and seek advice on resignation from several politicians and some soldiers in and about the War Office.

Lloyd George returned to his little Walton Heath home. He told his circle there: "I had one of the most anxious days I have ever had. I was with the King for an hour." In the evening he sang his favourite songs, with particular emphasis on that Calvinistic hymn, dear to orthodox Presbyterians, "And the changes that are sure to come I do not fear to see".

Haig had been summoned to London, and on

Sunday at noon, accompanied by Lord Derby, he called on Lloyd George. Now was the hour. This vital meeting might lead to anything; to a new Government, to a General Election with political strife in the constituencies, or, alternatively, to peaceful occupation of Downing Street.

The outcome was unexpected and surprising in an astonishing measure. Haig gave his allegiance to Lloyd George; Lord Derby gave his resignation. The triumvirate of Robertson, Haig and Derby was shattered in a moment. Haig's defection took Derby completely by surprise. Both he and Robertson had thought that the triumvirate was firm and strong.

What a relief for the Prime Minister! And yet what bitter disappointment! Relief because by retaining Haig, the measure of his peril in the House of Commons was lessened; disappointment because, in his heart, Lloyd George had hoped to make a clean sweep of his military advisers. To him, therefore, the outcome was a mixed blessing.

What was the reason for Haig's unexpected submission?

He must have known of Lloyd George's visit to Buckingham Palace on Saturday. Surely he had been instructed in the political realities of the situation. Possibly Lord Stamfordham may have spoken with him. He may have been told of Lloyd George's warning to the King that if Robertson's services were to be retained then His Majesty must find other Ministers.

It may have been explained that the King must

give way to his Prime Minister, for where could he turn to find another Prime Minister capable of commanding the support of the House of Commons? Bonar Law, the Conservative Leader, was fixed in his loyalty to Lloyd George. Who else could win the support of Parliament? Some advisers would say "not Asquith", because it was widely stated that he had no House of Commons following outside of the Liberal Rump. Austen Chamberlain could not secure Conservative support. He was severely damaged by a war muddle in Mesopotamia, though he had no responsibility for the tragedy. Carson was an impossibility. His Premiership would result in uniting the severed wings of the Liberal Party. He would be confronted by Lloyd George and Asquith joined together in opposition. The Irish members of Redmond's group, the O'Brien lot and the two Healys (factions among the Irish Nationalists), would all unite in assailing their old enemy. There was no possibility of a majority in the House of Commons for Carson. And if there was an election, Lloyd George would win it.*

But whatever may have been the influences prompting Haig, it is sufficient to record that he bowed at once to the civilian authority. He deserted his friends without an excuse or apology. He refused Lloyd George's suggestion that Robertson should be given command of an army in France. Lord Derby he left stranded like a whale on a sandbank.

* The Liberal leaders believed in their own fortunes and freely predicted the defeat of Lloyd George in a General Election.

Poor Derby! He had been destroyed by his zeal and fidelity. Derided by Haig, and accused of crooked dealing by Robertson," he was indeed a whale on a sandbank. His threats of resignation henceforth would no longer be political dynamite, just Chinese firecrackers. The supreme importance he enjoyed had rested in his membership of that dangerous triumvirate which had imperilled the Government. Derby had been faithful to his friends.

My home in the country was quite near to Lloyd George's house at Walton Heath, and Lloyd George would frequently call me to him, especially when he was in gloom or high spirits. On this day I was summoned and arrived at Walton Heath shortly after Haig and Derby had departed. I expected to see Lloyd George in low health and possibly in a depressed mood. Instead I found him in a state of jubilation. He was relieved of anxiety and reaction had set in after many days of doubt and uncertainty.

He telephoned Bonar Law to tell him of the outcome of the visit and to instruct him to offer the vacant Secretaryship of State for War to Austen Chamberlain.

But in the course of the afternoon Bonar Law rang up Lloyd George with the information that Derby wished to withdraw his resignation. I answered the telephone and carried the message to the Prime Minister. Lloyd George agreed that Derby could stay on provided he promised not to resign again.

It was really of no interest to Lloyd George whether Derby went or stayed; his staying would make it somewhat easier for the Prime Minister in Parliament. But Lloyd George intended to dismiss him shortly anyway. Indeed, within a month he had left the Government, with the consolation prize of the British Embassy in Paris.

Sir Reginald Brade gives an account of events in his paper "A Few Notes on the Controversy between Sir. W. R. and the Government".

> Prime Minister and Bonar Law thought Derby had resigned and had wired for Austin, (I had urged P.M. previously not to appoint Milner) but at 5 [p.m.] a telephone message came from Bonar Law to say that the active MacPherson* had intimated that Derby had not resigned, so Bonar Law was told to tell Austin if he turned up that there was nothing doing for the moment but that perhaps in a month's time! [Lloyd George made no concealment of his intention to send Derby to Paris.]

The next day, Lord Derby took the precaution of nailing down his dis-resignation in a letter to Bonar Law.

18.2.18.

My dear Bonar,

I thought very carefully over what you said to me, & discussed the question of my resignation with Weir and MacPherson—and then went to see Haig. As the result of these conversations I did not put the notice in the papers, and am prepared, if you and my colleagues wish, to withdraw my resignation. You may rest assured I should loyally work and defend the scheme, but I shall quite understand it, if you think that it had better be run by somebody else.

* Under-Secretary of State for War.

I shall await your answer here and shall carry on till I do so.

I know you told MacPherson last night that you could speak in the name of the cabinet in asking me to remain—or rather in allowing me to withdraw my resignation, but I think I had better have that from you in writing after consultation with the P.M. as he may not agree.

Yours sincerely,
DERBY."*

To return to Mr. Chamberlain. He motored up to town from his country place. He had been out of the Government for eight months when this high offer of the War Office was dangled before him. He had been critical of the civilian direction of the war. Now he would return to the inner councils of wartime administration. He believed firmly that he could make a considerable contribution to the successful conduct of the war.

But when Chamberlain arrived at Downing Street, the door of office had after all been closed to him.

Chamberlain's re-entry into the Government was postponed. But he held what the Canadians call a "rain check". In April he was to become a member of the War Cabinet.

True, the developments of the Sabbath day of excitement had not finally settled the conflict. But Lloyd George was in a far, far stronger and sounder position than he had imagined likely on the Friday evening. Yet he was not too con-

---

* Derby spoke in the House of Lords on 19th February, 1918. He had the benefit of Curzon's help in preparing his statement. He said he had been asked to continue in office. He did not mention that he had himself asked permission to withdraw his resignation.

fident. He said at his house on Sunday night after Haig had made his submission: "We have to face a very serious crisis, and the Government may fall." He was not, even then, sure of the House of Commons. The issue had still to be put to the test in Parliament. And on Tuesday, 19th February, 1918, the House assembled to pronounce its verdict.

But the fire had been taken from the attack. Mr. Asquith was mild and ineffective; he found nothing to dispute in the Prime Minister's statement. Lord Robert Cecil had been won over to acquiescence. Walter Long had been persuaded to withdraw from opposition by Bonar Law. He wrote:

19.ii.18.

My dear Bonar,

Thank you for your frank and most helpful talk: I also had some talk with Derby and Hankey. My difficulties on the question are removed.

From all I hear from our most reliable men the P.M. will be well advised if he makes a very short simple statement, avoiding detail.

Yours Ev.

WALTER H. LONG.

Chamberlain had been fully informed of the details of the conflict between Lloyd George and Robertson on Sunday evening. He decided to sustain the Prime Minister. Thus he remained silent on the military issue but addressed himself to civilian disputes, with considerable impact upon his colleagues and others. He attacked the association of the Government with the Press Lords (Northcliffe, Rothermere and me).

Lloyd George had escaped once again.

Haig, writing in his diary on Tuesday, 19th February—the day of the debate in Parliament—declared:

> I think I can fairly claim, as the result of my visit to London, that generally a saner view is now taken of the so-called military crisis, and the risk of a quarrel between "civilian and soldier" (which last Saturday seemed imminent) has been avoided.[2']

And at considerable pain to his two associates Robertson and Derby who had been faithful to Haig. Robertson, who had believed all along that Asquith would save him, was given the Eastern Command, a post of little importance. Derby was destined for dismissal before the spring tide of April.

But the quarrel between "civilian and soldier" had not been avoided. It had only been postponed.

Lloyd George had triumphed in this encounter. Walter Page, American Ambassador, who was a spectator with a seat in the front row, told the President of the United States: "His [Lloyd George's] dismissal of Robertson has been accepted in the interest of greater unity of military control, but that was a dangerous rapid he shot . . ."[2]

Indeed, his enemies were gathering for another assault. A pause that followed gave time for a remobilization of forces, before the final bid for domination was launched with all its fury.

CHAPTER VII

THE BIRTH OF THE ROYAL AIR FORCE

LORD JELLICOE had been dismissed. Sir William Robertson had been driven from the War Office. But their supporters were neither stifled nor acquiescent. Indeed, the adherents of the military clique were girding themselves for new and maybe decisive action. Their organs in the Press were sounding the challenge in words which were easily understood. Events presaged a showdown with the Prime Minister. They were a prelude to the final struggle which was fought out in the House of Commons in the Maurice Debate.

It was at this stage in the closely contested political struggle that a skirmish took place which centred upon the Air Force and involved Lord Rothermere, the Secretary of State for Air, and General Trenchard,* the Chief of the Air Staff. It was a clash of outposts yet it had some importance in relation to the main battle.

Lord Rothermere was a newcomer to the Government. His appointment to the Secretaryship of State for Air as recently as November

---

* Later Lord Trenchard.

1917 had followed the astounding public rejection of that office by his elder brother, Lord Northcliffe.

Rothermere was summoned to the Ministry from his post in charge of clothing supplies for the Army, a task which he carried out with brilliant results.

In the general estimation, Lord Rothermere was a lesser figure than his illustrious brother. He was certainly a less dramatic and a less contentious one. His relations with Northcliffe were not intimate, although in private he admired his brother's courage and industry. Yet he declined to follow all of the political campaigns of that brilliant and exciting leader of Fleet Street.

I always had a very high regard for Lord Rothermere. He was a generous and devoted friend, a man of warm affections. In journalism he had achieved considerable distinction. He was the proprietor of five important newspapers, the *Daily Mirror*, the *Sunday Pictorial*, the *Leeds Mercury*, the *Glasgow Daily Record* and the *Glasgow Evening News*.

In politics, he had no party affiliations. He was on friendly terms with Bonar Law and Lloyd George. He was a good friend of Winston Churchill, whose war articles were printed in his papers. But he never gained a following in Parliament. Thus, when his own administration at the Air Ministry was breaking down under criticism, there were no friends or associates in the Houses of Parliament who could be relied upon to give him substantial aid.

General Trenchard had joined the Air Council as Chief of Air Staff at the beginning of January, 1918. The office of Chief of Air Staff was an appointment of the King* made on the advice of the Prime Minister. It was thus constitutionally the responsibility of the Prime Minister rather than, as might be supposed, the prerogative of the Secretary of State for Air. This fact was later to have considerable bearing in the conflict that involved the Government over the Ministry.

In fact, however, Rothermere had asked for Trenchard, and Lloyd George had concurred in the appointment.

Now the task of the Secretary of State was to merge the two separate services, the Royal Flying Corps which was part of the Army, and the Royal Naval Air Service which was a Naval unit.

But Trenchard, the new Chief of Staff, was strongly and even violently opposed to this reorganization, according to the records of Sir Douglas Haig.

Haig's entry in his Diary for 28th August, 1917, reads:

> The War Cabinet has evidently decided on creating a new Department to deal with Air operations, on the lines of the War Office and Admiralty. Trenchard is much perturbed as to the result of this new departure just at a time when the Flying Corps was beginning to feel that it had become an important part of the Army.[a]

* The Order in Council defining the composition of the Air Council says that, of the Members of the Air Council, the Chief of the Air Staff shall be appointed by the King (*Daily Express*, 22nd December, 1917).

Trenchard was, of course, an Army man. He did not want the divorce of the Royal Flying Corps from the Army organization. Nor, it appears, did he want the job of Chief of Air Staff under the new dispensation. On 16th December, 1917, Haig was writing in his Diary:

> General Trenchard also came to see me on his way to his H.Q. from London. Lord Rothermere (head of the Air Board) insists on him (T) going as Chief of Staff. T. stated that the Air Board are quite off their heads as to the future possibility of Aeronautics for ending the war. I told T. that it was evidently necessary that he should become C. of S. of Air, much as I regretted parting with him.[b]

Thus it was that when Trenchard came to the Air Council, he had no sympathy at all with the plans for setting up an Air Ministry. He was opposed to the policy of his own civilian chief and also the War Cabinet. He was in fact hostile to his Minister's programme, and not in accord with the task he had been called on to implement.

Trenchard had already won a high reputation when he joined the Air Ministry in January, 1918. He had served for two years in the Army as commander of the Royal Flying Corps in France and was considered, as he is to this day, the Father of the Air Arm. But he can hardly be regarded as the founder of the Royal Air Force, for, of course, he opposed the merger of the Flying Services. He was a father who tried to strangle the infant at birth though he got credit for the grown man.

From the day he took office, he was a dis-affected and critical member of the newly formed Air Council. Within a few weeks of his appoint-ment he was communicating his disloyal com-plaints to the Commander-in-Chief in France.

> General Trenchard (now C. of Staff to Air Minister) who is on a visit to France came to report how things are developing at home [Haig recorded in his Diary on 26 January, 1918]. Lord Rothermere . . . who is Air Minister is quite ignorant of the needs or working of the Air Service, and is in great terror of newspaper criticism. Money is being squandered and officers and men wasted by being employed in creating units for performing work hitherto done by the Army (or Navy) for the Air Service. For example, Hospitals, Detention Barracks etc. All this is very sad at a time when officers and men are so badly needed. Trenchard thinks that the Air Service cannot last as an independent Ministry, and that Air Units must again return to Army and Navy. . . .
> He [Trenchard] could think and talk nothing else but the rascally ways of politicians and the news-paper men.[c]

Rothermere borrowed trouble when he asked for Trenchard who disbelieved in the programme and the man. He was also lending trouble to Lloyd George.

From the outset, Trenchard exercised a strong influence upon the Air Council. This developed rapidly into a demand for a consolidation of authority in the hands of the Chief of the Air Staff at the expense of the civil head of the Department. Since Trenchard did not believe in detaching the Air Arm from the Army and did not have confidence in his own Minister, Rothermere was annoyed and frustrated by his Chief of Staff. He could not carry out his own projects.

To bring a new Ministry into working order is a difficult and trying task for men acting in harmony. But discord and dispute within swiftly bring antagonisms and hostility.

The position, as it developed, is best summed up in the words of the Parliamentary Under-Secretary to the Air Ministry, Major Baird.[*] "General Trenchard," he stated, "took a view as to the powers and duties of the Chief of the Air Staff which the Secretary of State for the Royal Air Force could not accept."[d]

In this conflict of authority between the civilian and the military elements, Trenchard handed in his resignation on 19th March, 1918. It may be surmised that he intended to coerce Lord Rothermere. Rothermere at once applied to the Prime Minister, who gladly came to the support of his Minister.

Lloyd George had been hearing rumours of conspiracies directed by Asquith, leader of the Liberal Opposition, and supported by Trenchard, Robertson, Jellicoe and possibly Haig. It was said that these soldiers were meeting with Asquith and considering plans for driving Lloyd George out of office. Lloyd George believed these stories.[†] Certainly his position was being challenged by the military faction with growing force and strength. He had no doubt on that score.

[*] Later Lord Stonehaven.
[†] Lord Milner was aware of the conspiracy and held that the Squiffites (followers of Asquith) were making use of Robertson.

The removal, therefore, of Trenchard must have been regarded favourably for no other reason than for the benefits and advantages he would gain in his struggle to hold his own place against the assaults of the political and military alliance against him.

Here was a bird Lloyd George could kill with a stone, the stone being Lord Rothermere. He threw it gladly.

Lloyd George was reinforced in his determination by the War Cabinet which met in the middle of April to discuss the question of General Trenchard. General Smuts gave the Prime Minister every encouragement; he had been commissioned by the Cabinet to investigate the situation at the Air Ministry and to advise on a successor to Lord Trenchard. He wrote to Lloyd George:

13th April, 1918.

My dear Prime Minister,

Macready has been consulted about Sykes. His position as A.G. to French at the time when the Sykes-Henderson trouble occurred gives him authority in the matter. He has no doubt whatever that Sykes is the best man to appoint, and I have accordingly told Rothermere to have him appointed without further delay.

My deepest sympathy is with you in these days of supreme peril.* If your strength continues under the load you are carrying I have no doubt you will succeed.

* The great Smuts was not quite right about the "supreme peril" that confronted the country in April, 1918. True the threat to the Channel ports was so serious as to involve us in decisions of momentous portent as to whether, in the event of success attending the German breach in the Allied front at Amiens, our Army would retreat to the north or follow the French forces to the south.

But such a calamity, though menacing our safety, did not mean defeat and destruction, whereas the submarine menace of 1917 threatened us with absolute and irremediable disaster.

Now is the time for quietness and strength when everybody is becoming nervous. I have no doubt whatever we shall pull through this crisis both in a military and political sense. Whatever strength or resource I have is entirely at your command.

Ever yours,
J. C. SMUTS.[e]

Lord Rothermere was given permission to accept the resignation of General Trenchard, and the announcement of the Air Ministry changes, with General Sykes as the new Chief of Air Staff, was made in the Press on 15th April.*

By an unlucky circumstance, the first intimation of the reconstruction reached Buckingham Palace through the columns of the newspapers. Very soon afterwards Lloyd George received a letter of criticism from the King's Secretary, Lord Stamfordham:

Windsor Castle.
16th April, 1918.

Dear Prime Minister,

It was only last night that the King received the Secret War Cabinet Minute of Friday, 12th instant, approving the changes on the Staff of the Air Ministry and the scheme of development of the Royal Air Force formulated by Lord Rothermere in his Memorandum of the 9th instant.

Had His Majesty seen this document or been aware of the changes advocated in it by Lord Rothermere, he would not have been surprised when, on Saturday afternoon, Lord Rothermere announced General

* The public turmoil over the Air Ministry was intensified by the publication on the same day of Haig's famous message: "With our backs to the wall . . . each one of us must fight to the end."

Trenchard's resignation and the appointment of General Sykes as his successor; also the King's apprehension at the consequences which he subsequently learnt might ensue by these changes, would have been considerably relieved.

His Majesty entirely appreciates how necessary and, indeed, right it is for a Secretary of State, after due consideration, to make whatever changes in both personnel and organisation he may think are required for the efficiency of his Department; it is only necessary that confident relations should exist between the Ministers and the King to avert misunderstandings such as those which occurred in this instance.

As I endeavoured to explain to you, His Majesty's one desire is that the new Air Force should be as perfect as can be, and he regrets that it should lose any of those Officers who have, since the beginning of the War, helped to build up the Royal Flying Corps and the Royal Naval Air Service respectively.

The King fully recognises and agrees with what you say as to the selection of appointments being vested in the civilian head of the Department, and that any dictation on the part of subordinates is unjustifiable. At the same time His Majesty feels sure you would be the first to realise the importance of the personal factor in dealing with the administration of Departments under the Crown, and especially those of a new creation.

Believe me,

Yours very truly,

STAMFORDHAM. *f*

No sooner had Trenchard's resignation been accepted, than conflict broke out in public. The *Daily News*ᵍ opened the attack on the Government. "The list is steadily growing," it declared, "of acknowledged masters of their craft for whose services in the crisis of our fate the Government has no serious use. It is the same story on every element. Thus:

The Sea, Lord Jellicoe,
The Land, Sir W. Robertson,
The Air, Sir Hugh Trenchard."

The impact of the resignation upon the Air Ministry itself was devastating. Lieutenant-General Sir David Henderson, Vice-President of the Air Council, sent in his resignation within a matter of days. In a letter to Bonar Law on 26th April, he set out the reasons for his actions. He was anxious, he said, to escape from the atmosphere of "intrigue and falsehood which has enveloped the Air Ministry for the last few months". He was unwilling, moreover, to become "a focus of discontent and opposition".[b]* Although, in fact, Henderson's task was largely completed with the fusion of the Royal Flying Corps and the Royal Naval Air Service, his decision to retire was evidently directly prompted by the appointment of General Sykes.

The departure of the Vice-President of the Air Council gave strength to the widely held belief that Trenchard's resignation must entail the dislocation of the whole Air Service.

A more serious matter was an intimation from the Parliamentary Under-Secretary to the Air Ministry, Major Baird, that he felt unable to represent Rothermere's views in the House of Commons. His letter to the Prime Minister dated

* Sir David Henderson's letter, with its enclosure, is given in full in *Appendix IV*, No. 12.

22nd April requested that his own opinions should be heard before the War Cabinet.

> I regret that I am unable to agree with some of the views expressed by Lord Rothermere and, consequently, could not support them in the House of Commons. In view of the Debates which are certain to take place in Parliament on this subject in the near future I thought it advisable to write to you in this sense at the earliest moment, and I most respectfully beg that I may be given an opportunity of laying my views before the War Cabinet. This course is all the more necessary because the opinions which I have formed are largely based on figures and facts which it would be impossible to make public.[*]

His demand was tantamount to a threat of resignation and a matter of obvious concern to the Administration. By his letter Baird, in effect, declared himself a supporter of General Trenchard.

But there were other and more formidable allies of the General in the House of Commons—Sir John Simon and Lord Hugh Cecil.

Both were Flying Corps subalterns on Trenchard's staff, but they evidently had a humorous conception of the discipline demanded of non-combatant and combatant officers. For both were combining their positions on the Air Staff with violent attacks, as members of the House of Commons, on the political head of their own Service.

Both men were able Parliamentarians, exceptionally well-informed when it came to making

[*] The full text of the letter appears in *Appendix IV*, No. 13.

out a case against the Government. Sir John Simon was a leading member of the Bar, experienced in court, a redoubtable and practised advocate. There was no doubt that he and Cecil would force the issue of Trenchard's resignation to a debate in Parliament.

In the midst of this outbreak, and faced by a mounting opposition from Parliament and the Press, Lord Rothermere decided that he could not sustain the demands which the developing crisis was likely to exact from him. He went off to the country, sending in his resignation to the Prime Minister.

On the 24th April therefore I received a telephone call informing me that Rothermere had resigned, and summoning me to the Cabinet room. There I found the Prime Minister, Bonar Law and General Smuts with Lord Rothermere's resignation in front of them. The document was handed to me for my opinion. I was required to give my views without being told what was the reaction of the other three.

I had no difficulty in forming an opinion. The resignation was a devastating criticism of both Cecil and Simon, condemning them in outspoken terms for flouting disciplinary codes and for abusing their dual roles as Staff Officers and Members of Parliament.

Of his own position Rothermere declared that his work of blending the Royal Naval Service and the Royal Flying Corps was accomplished. There was hence no question of swapping horses. "The stream has been crossed."[*] The letter ended in eulogistic praise of Trenchard's successor in office, Major-General Sykes.

Lord Rothermere's letter of resignation at once struck me as being unsuitable, unsatisfactory and damaging to the Government.

From Lord Rothermere's point of view, it was sure to involve him in a difficult debate which he was in no condition to undertake. Rothermere had been in failing health, and he was weighed down by the heavy blows that fate had dealt him in his family. His two elder sons had been killed in action, one at Ancre at the close of 1916, and the eldest at Cambrai in February, 1918, less than two months before his letter was written. It was a burden almost greater than man could bear. He was suffering too from prolonged overwork.

Although the letter would relieve him of a task which was clearly beyond his power at that time, it would leave him to continue the controversy over the dismissal of General Trenchard even after he had left office. Indeed, it would lay him open to fierce attacks which would be based on his own communications.

Both Lord Hugh Cecil and Sir John Simon were capable of looking after themselves in the hurly-burly of Parliamentary debate. Moreover they longed to attack the Government on any and every count. The demand by Rothermere for "an enquiry by superior officers" into the conduct of these two serving soldiers in the Ministry might well become the overriding issue, thus

* The full text of the letter is reproduced in *Appendix IV*, No. 14.

raising constitutional discussion about the liberties and privileges of members of the House of Commons serving in the Armed Forces. There was no doubt also that the Prime Minister would be drawn into a heated defence of his approval of and responsibility for Trenchard's dismissal, in which the full battery of the militarists would be brought to bear against him.

Accordingly, I was opposed to accepting Lord Rothermere's letter without making energetic efforts to amend it. Bonar Law observed that if only I could be as wise in deciding my own issues as I proved myself in discussing the affairs of others, I would make a brilliant Minister.

Eventually, it was decided that a new letter of resignation should be secured from Lord Rothermere, and I was chosen as the Government's emissary charged with this task. I telephoned to Rothermere in the country, asking him to come to London to discuss the resignation with me. I met him on arrival at the Savoy Hotel. Almost immediately we were joined by Churchill, whom Rothermere had invited to take part in the discussion.

My dominating object was to help Rothermere to produce an entirely non-controversial letter which would leave him free from damaging attack and, at the same time, relieve the Government of the necessity of entering into a debate on the liberties of members of the House of Commons and also into a public defence of the dismissal of General Trenchard. My case was that unless he withdrew his present letter the whole conflict would go on more furiously than ever.

Churchill, however, gave quite different advice. He took his stand on the constitutional position that the appointment of the Chief of Air Staff rested with the Prime Minister and that it was his task to defend the removal of Trenchard and the appointment of Sykes. He said, in effect, to Rothermere, "Let the Government clear themselves." Lloyd George, he argued, had himself decided on the dismissal of Trenchard. It would not be right to throw the whole responsibility for it on Rothermere. There was something to be said for this position.

But there was another constitutional aspect which I pointed out. Lloyd George had acted on the advice and guidance of his Secretary of State and could therefore not be charged with responsibility by Lord Rothermere himself.

Churchill drafted a letter for Rothermere to sign. I advised a different approach and an entirely non-controversial letter.

Our discussion continued into the early hours of the morning. Rothermere was unable to come to any decision and we parted finally with no course of action settled. Very early next day, Lord Rothermere appeared at my rooms at the Hyde Park Hotel. He wakened me up, saying that he had decided to take my advice. He was a man worn down by anxiety and distress; the strain of the last days had greatly affected him. He was in fact quite ill. I got out of bed at once and after much discussion a letter was drafted with the promise that I should deliver it myself to the Prime Minister and bring back his reply.

Thereafter I set out for Downing Street. A meeting of the War Cabinet was in progress but I insisted on sending in a message to Lloyd George. This the secretary agreed to, provided I took full responsibility for interrupting the Cabinet. If my news pleased the Prime Minister and he wished to hear it—all would be well; if not, I was risking a snub by presenting myself in this way.

As I fully expected, however, the Prime Minister came out at once. He was delighted to see me. Together we drafted a reply to Lord Rothermere's letter.* Both Rothermere's resignation and Lloyd George's answer bear interpolations in Lloyd George's hand and mine.† Lloyd George's sole alteration in Rothermere's letter was to strike out a reference it bore to "April 1st" which he considered a necessary precaution.

I asked the Prime Minister for a recommendation of a Viscountcy for Lord Rothermere. To this Lloyd George agreed.

I reproduce both Rothermere's letter of resignation dated 25th April, 1918, and the Prime Minister's reply.

Hemsted,
Benenden, Kent.
25th April, 1918.

My dear Prime Minister,
I desire to relinquish my office as Secretary of State of the Air Force at the earliest possible date.

---

* Lloyd George's *War Memoirs*, Vol. IV, p. 1877, says the reply was sent "after it had been shown to and approved by my colleagues in the War Cabinet".
† The original letter and the original draft of Lloyd George's reply are preserved in the *Lloyd George Papers*.

The Royal Air Force is now one of the three established fighting services of the Crown. The fusion of the Royal Naval Air Service and the Royal Flying Corps has been successfully accomplished.

At times I have thought I would not be able to accompany the new Force so far. My second tragic loss in the war ten weeks since caused and causes me great distress of mind and body. Every day the burden of work and responsibility seemed crushing and I was suffering much from ill health and insomnia.

I felt as I told you my urgent primary duty to the Government and the nation required me to remain if at all physically possible until the date of the fusion and such time after as would suffice to establish the success of the amalgamation. My departure before might have gravely deranged what is now one of the nation's arms of war and have jeopardised the success of the whole scheme.

Lately I thought I might be able to remain but a recurrence of bronchial trouble with insomnia effectually prevents this.

I have entered into these particulars because I wish you to know the difficulties under which I have been working.

I cannot close this letter without an expression of my great regard and respect.

Yours very faithfully,
ROTHERMERE.[k]

The Prime Minister replied:

My dear Rothermere,

I have received your letter tendering your resignation as Secretary of State for the Air Force with the deepest regret. Your work there has been of inestimable service to the nation, and time will bring with it a full recognition of your achievement. It is no small thing to have taken over the conduct of an entirely new arm of the service in the middle of a great war, to have extricated it from the difficulties which surrounded it, co-ordinated the two services which made it up, and bestowed on its administration an initiative which has given the new force a real supremacy at the front. And all this has been done in such a brief period of time.

It is the more to be lamented that, having set the Ministry on its legs, you cannot remain to enjoy the fruition of your own brilliant work. But I feel on reading your letter that I cannot press you to stay, much as the Government must suffer from your retirement.

Your sacrifices to the National cause have been so heavy, and the strain imposed on you so cruel that it would be impossible to deny you the right to some repose. Sympathy in these matters is generally best given by silence, but I am sure that you know without my telling you how much I sympathise with you in your losses and in the way in which you have continued your public duties in spite of everything.

No Minister ever had greater difficulties to contend with than you had in effecting the fusion of the two services, and the Air Force has every right to be proud of its First Secretary of State.

I am authorised by my colleagues to state that they share fully the views I have expressed in this letter.

Yours very faithfully,
D. Lloyd George.[l]

A curious anomaly attaches to the resignation letters. When Lloyd George came to tell the story of Rothermere's resignation in his *War Memoirs* some years later, and before the death of Lord Rothermere, it was not Lord Rothermere's letter of 25th April, 1918, which he published but the earlier letter with all its implications.[m]

The explanation may be a simple one. Lloyd George was dealing with a tremendous range of documents.

To continue with my narrative. Having secured the Prime Minister's reply, I returned to Lord Rothermere. I left my office and my duties and took him to my house at Leatherhead.

Rothermere, despite his judgement and ability, was not the man to grapple with a political crisis. Instead, he invariably wished to pull down the blinds. He would never take part in any debate. He would never defend himself in the House of Lords. Yet he would have made a brilliant controversialist, and a good speaker.

I had made a practice of calling to see him in his rooms regularly. He was worrying acutely over his work. His nervous concentration was too tremendous to last. He was seeking forgetfulness from his personal grief, in labour—and not succeeding in finding it. His mind was invariably running either on his task or his tragedy. He seemed quite unable to distract himself with any other set of ideas and it became obvious that such a state of affairs could not continue indefinitely. Something was bound to give way.

Lord Rothermere's letter, and the Prime Minister's reply, were published in the afternoon newspapers of 25th April.

Following the announcement, *The Times*, Lord Northcliffe's newspaper, observed Lord Rothermere's retirement "follows so close on a much-debated change in the *personnel* of the Air Staff—

a change which has been joyfully hailed by the politicians as a counter in their game—that it would have been a real advantage from every point of view to have *Lord Rothermere's* own account of his action in Debate".*

Lord Rothermere's own account, though brief, is set out in a letter to Bonar Law, written to the Conservative leader after the storm had blown over. Here is the letter:

Hemsted,
Benenden, Kent.
3rd May, 1918.

My dear Bonar,

I am writing to thank you for your kindness last week. The H. of C. does not like newspapers much less newspaper Ministers. Their time is not yet.

In getting rid of Trenchard I flatter myself I did a great thing for the Air Force. With his dull unimaginative mind and his attitude of "Je sais tout" he would within twelve months have brought death and damnation to the Air Force. As it was he was insisting on the ordering of large numbers of machines for out-of-date purposes.

I am very grateful to you for the message from the P.M. brought me by Max that I am, on relinquishing office, to become a Viscount.

Yours always sincerely,
ROTHERMERE.*

With the publication of the letter of resignation, the lobbies buzzed with interest and speculation. In the House of Commons on the same afternoon, that formidable critic of the Government, Sir Edward Carson, questioned the Leader of the

House. Bonar Law replied: "It is true, I regret to say, that Lord Rothermere has resigned. His successor has not yet been appointed."[p]

Four days later the changes at the Air Ministry became the subject of acrimonious parliamentary debate. The language of the opposing elements was violent and excited. Lord Hugh Cecil launched a vituperative attack. "I cannot . . . speak very respectfully," he announced, "of the Prime Minister's letter accepting that [Rothermere's] resignation, and perhaps the kindest thing to say of it is that it is the effort of a strong Celtic imagination."[q]

The accusation that service members were using information gained in the course of their official tasks did not daunt or deflect him. "If you have a man like Sir Hugh Trenchard at the head of your Air Force," he persisted, "perhaps you may find he will not always listen to the ideas of every amateur strategist in the Cabinet quite as sympathetically as that strategist might desire."[r]

This brought the Prime Minister to his feet.

"I do not think he need show himself so very sensitive" Cecil retorted. "The right hon. Gentleman really seems to care about nothing except his own retention in office—himself, personally."[s]

Sir Edward Carson made a hostile attack on the Government. He gave outspoken support to General Trenchard. Indeed he went further. He contested in the House of Commons the principle of civil authority. "When a dispute arises," Carson declared, "between the Civil head of a great Department of the State and its great expert, in that dispute the Civil head is the judge. If a man goes to the Admiralty as First Lord, and has been there only a week or a fortnight, he can dismiss at his own will his expert advisers, and let the public know that when it comes to be a question whether an indispensable expert adviser, or an ignorant civilian who has only been there a fortnight, is to go, the decision rests with the civilian. That is the constitutional position. It is a very serious one, and I think that when these things happen it is at least the duty of the Government thoroughly to investigate on a case of this kind what has been the real cause of the State in its throes, as it is at the present moment, losing a great and an efficient soldier."' (Carson was returning to the contemplation of his King Charles's head, which was the dismissal of Lord Jellicoe.)

Carson had then been out of the administration for three months; his attack was of a most serious and damaging character. It was an outright advocacy of military domination.

At the same time, there was a concerted demand from the Opposition bench for the return of General Trenchard to his post. The attempt failed.*

For Lloyd George the storm of the morning became the sunshine of the afternoon. He avoided acrimonious exchanges.

Basing his defence on the letters which were

* The House of Commons was informed on 13th May, 1918, that Trenchard had accepted the command of "a very important part of the British Air Force in France."

composed in the Hyde Park Hotel and in the outer Cabinet office on that April morning, "General Trenchard," he said, "put in his resignation for reasons into which I do not wish to enter, because it involves a dispute which the Noble Lord himself has not thought fit to enter into, as I think wisely."[u]

He rode off, with consummate skill and ease, on Rothermere's resignation. It was a triumph of evasive action in debate.

In the House of Lords, Lord Curzon, the President of the Council, showed himself no less adroit in avoiding difficulty for the Government. Indeed, he managed to escape a debate on the question altogether. A motion tabled by Lord Sydenham, asking the Air Minister to state the reasons for the dismissal of General Trenchard, was abruptly abandoned.

Lord Curzon told the House, "an announcement has been made in the Press this afternoon as to the resignation of the Secretary of State for the Royal Air Force which puts a somewhat different complexion upon affairs. In these circumstances I feel that I have no right myself to ask the House to meet on Monday next for this debate. . . ."[v] Again Lord Rothermere's letter had served its purpose.

In carrying to the Prime Minister the request for a Viscountcy for Lord Rothermere, I was conscious that his work at the Air Ministry had produced outstanding results and the honour would please and hearten him.

But there was an immediate reaction in Royal circles against any further preferment for Lord Rothermere. On the day of his resignation Lord Stamfordham wrote to the Prime Minister.

Windsor Castle,
25th April, 1918.

Dear Prime Minister,

I have reported to the King the substance of what you told me this afternoon.

His Majesty will be prepared to approve the possible appointments you mentioned, if you finally decide to make them, but the King hopes you will not raise the question of Lord Rothermere's promotion in the Peerage. The newly constituted Air Force, of which he was Minister, has only been in existence twenty-four days when he resigns. Rightly or wrongly, his administration has been sharply criticised and is to be discussed in both Houses of Parliament. He has only just been made a Privy Councillor which, in itself, is high distinction. . . .

STAMFORDHAM.[w]

A year passed by. The Palace still maintained its resistance to the Rothermere peerage. On 11th April, 1919, Lord Stamfordham wrote to Frederick Guest, the Coalition Chief Whip, objecting once more to Lord Rothermere's name in the list of honours.

Buckingham Palace.
Confidential   11th April, 1919.

My dear Guest,

I have submitted to the King the list of honours which we discussed this morning.

As I anticipated, His Majesty takes exception to the proposed promotion of Lord Rothermere to be

STAMFORDHAM

ROTHERMERE. A firm friend and
a good companion.

a Viscount, and the King would like to remind the Prime Minister that in less than nine years, Mr. Harold Harmsworth has became a Baronet—1910, a Peer—1914, and a Privy Counsellor, which latter His Majesty regards as a very high honour, in 1917, only two years ago.

. . . . . .

I pointed out to His Majesty that I gathered from you that the Viscountcy had been promised to Lord Rothermere, but the King says he certainly has no recollection of this suggested promotion having been submitted to him . . .

> Yours very truly
> STAMFORDHAM.[x]

On 12th April, Lord Stamfordham wrote again[y] to inform Guest that he now recollected that the King had raised objections the previous year, and Stamfordham quoted his letter to the Prime Minister of 25th April, 1918.

Bonar Law then took part in the fray. He wrote pressing for the fulfilment of the pledge to Lord Rothermere, given to him just a year before.

17th April 1919

Dear Lord Stamfordham,

In the absence of the Prime Minister, I am writing to you with reference to some remarks in your letter to Guest about the promotion of Lord Rothermere.

I earnestly hope that this recommendation may be allowed to go through. I must point out to you that, while I fully realise the difficulties raised in your letter, the Prime Minister undertook, at the time of Lord Rothermere's resignation, that he would support this recommendation to the King, and the Prime Minister,

I think, would personally be placed in a very unpleasant position if His Majesty could not see his way to accept the recommendation.

Although some criticisms may be passed upon the success, or otherwise, of his short administration at the Air Ministry, his intense loyalty and assistance to the Government during the later and critical days of the war, and also at the General Election, have considerably increased the obligations due to him.

Yours sincerely,

A. BONAR LAW.ₓ

Lord Stamfordham replied:

Windsor Castle.

17th April, 1919.

Dear Bonar Law,

The King has read your letter of the 17th instant, urging the promotion of Lord Rothermere to a Viscountcy.

His Majesty gives his approval, but with much reluctance. He cannot help thinking that it would have been better if the Prime Minister had not given an undertaking to Lord Rothermere at the time of his resignation that he would be recommended to the King for promotion. This is another case of a quasi promise, and what is worse, a quasi committal of His Majesty!

Yours very truly,

STAMFORDHAM.[aa]

There had always been trouble over the recommendation of honours for the Press lords. Beginning with Lord Northcliffe in 1905, there was difficulty, although on that occasion the situation was in reverse.

Then two peerages were being contested, Sir

Herbert Stern's (later Baron Michelham) and Northcliffe's. The Conservatives had put forward Stern, the Palace was responsible for Northcliffe's nomination. But the Conservative Whip, Sir Alexander Acland Hood, objected to Northcliffe because he was not a reliable supporter of the Conservatives, and the Palace was not enthusiastic about an honour for Stern. In the end there was what is known in Canadian politics as a "saw-off", and King Edward VII agreed to approve a barony for Sir Herbert Stern while Hood acquiesced in the recommendation, in the name of Balfour, of the Northcliffe honour.

Then there was my own peerage. This provoked a tremendous storm. Indeed, my only regret is that the storm was not strong enough to carry me away!

On the fall of the Asquith Government, Lloyd George wanted the seat I held at Ashton-under-Lyne for Sir Albert Stanley, the new President of the Board of Trade. It is true that he also wanted a Government spokesman in the House of Lords. So he sought to promote me to the Peerage. But King George V did not see his way to approve the honour. This placed Lloyd George in a position of some delicacy as arrangements for a by-election at Ashton had already been set in motion. The King was obliged to give way; but not without a severe reproof addressed to Lloyd George.

I cannot conceal from you [wrote Lord Stamford-ham to Mr. Lloyd George] that His Majesty was surprised and hurt that this honour should have been offered without first obtaining his consent. . . . The King recognises (in view of the promises made and information given) that it is impossible for him now to withhold his approval. But, in thus signifying his acquiescence, His Majesty commands me to say that he feels that the Sovereign's Prerogative should not be disregarded; and he trusts that in future no honours whatever will be offered by any Minister until his approval has been informally obtained. His Majesty further asks that this be made clear to your Colleagues.[ab] *

There was more trouble over Lord Northcliffe in 1917. Lloyd George recommended him for a step in the varying and confusing hierarchy of nobility. He would be a Viscount. Colonel House wrote in his diary: "Wiseman tells me that the King talked to him of Northcliffe in a denunciatory way. However, he was compelled to make Northcliffe a Viscount the next day. He must have done it with a wry face."[ac]

The proposal that Sir Edward Russell, editor of the *Liverpool Daily Post*, should be given a peerage was opposed by the Palace in 1919:

I must tell you frankly [wrote Lord Stamfordham from Windsor Castle to Frederick Guest] that His Majesty is sorry that this proposal has been revived, as you will see from my letter of the 25th February last to Davies, that the King then questioned the advisability of granting a Peerage to a person who was only a Knight Bachelor at the age of eighty-five.

* Sir Harold Nicolson referred to His Majesty's objections without mentioning me. When Robert Blake wrote his life of Bonar Law (*The Unknown Prime Minister*) I informed him of this incident and authorized him to use my name. It has always been my habit to print everything about my own career, good and bad, pleasing and disagreeable.

Still more does His Majesty now deprecate bestowing a further honour on the Press when the list already contains—Lord Burnham, Lord Rothermere, Mr. Hulton, Mr. David Duncan, Mr. Madge and Coode-Adams.*

The King would not even consent to the case being brought up again for the Birthday Gazette.[ad]

A month later, on Lloyd George's insistence, the King reluctantly consented.

The peerage of Sir Henry Dalziel, proprietor of *Reynold's News*, was delayed.

> Forgive me putting it strongly, [wrote Guest to Lloyd George on 17th May, 1920] but I feel sure that you will be sorry if you further postpone the fulfilment of this definite promise. The old warrior has faithfully and patiently played the game and has helped me in very many ways since our connection. The moment is ripe. The Court will approve.[ae]

On Sir Edward Hulton, though promised a Peerage, the Palace would not go beyond accepting a recommendation for a baronetcy.

But the greatest row of all attended Lord Riddell's elevation to the House of Lords. When his name was submitted in 1920, the King had a further ground for complaint. Riddell had been the guilty party in a divorce action. He was then the chief proprietor of the *News of the World*. King George rejected the nomination on the grounds of Riddell's divorce. But Lloyd George

* Lord Burnham, *Daily Telegraph*; Lord Rothermere, *Daily Mirror*; Mr. Hulton, *Manchester Daily Despatch*, and others; Mr. David Duncan, *South Wales Daily News*; Mr. Madge, *The People*, and Sir John Coode-Adams, the *Pall Mall Gazette*. It was strange that my name should have been omitted. I hope it was in compliment.

was anxious to reward this friend of long standing and of great loyalty to himself, and so he undertook the task of collecting a number of letters from the Press lords of Fleet Street testifying in praise of Riddell's admirable work on behalf of the Newspaper Proprietors' Association.[af]

Thus Riddell had the distinction of becoming the first divorced Peer to enter the House of Lords.

Lloyd George put an end to the barrier against divorced men in the House of Lords. And the Constituencies would shortly make matchwood of the barriers against divorced men in the House of Commons. The honour of destroying the ban on divorced Ministers belongs to Ramsay MacDonald, leader of the Socialist Party. The practice now extends to all parties—the Judiciary, Parliament and Governments too. The Royal Household is the last stronghold.

No divorced persons had become Peers, or Ministers either, in May, 1918. Not even a divorced member of Parliament.

And it was on May Day of the last year of war that a hurricane was blowing up about the Prime Minister. The Government had steered safely through to harbour during the Rothermere tempest. Yet the serious nature of the situation was not for a moment in doubt. It had been demonstrated in the violence of the gale in the House of Commons and in the dangerous assaults of the Opposition members against the Administration.

Within ten days, the last and worst weather would come upon Lloyd George without any warning. The Daring Pilot who had survived so many perils in a journey that had lasted for nearly a year and a half, would be tried and tested. He would need all of his courage and plenty of luck.

CHAPTER VIII

THE LOST BOX

THE whole nation was in a stormy and troubled condition. For now the crisis of the battle of the Western Front rushed across the horizon. The military reverses in France gave anxious cause for alarm; there were disputes about manpower and the responsibilities for the disasters at the Front.

At this time Lloyd George was actually contemplating a General Election. He wrote to Bonar Law:

> It looks as if the Asquithians meant to challenge an issue on Irish conscription. If they succeed in defeating that part of the Bill, we ought to consider very carefully our next step. It should be resignation or dissolution. They are relying on the 40-50 call up.[a]

But a General Election did not appeal to Bonar Law. And indeed the Asquith party had no intention of dividing the House on any question likely to precipitate a General Election without first discrediting and even destroying Lloyd George.

Thus it was that the Opposition forces came to regard the quarrel between Lloyd George and the

Generals as a vital issue. Here they might find the weapon that could sufficiently damage the Prime Minister in the judgment of the electors.

Military leaders at the War Office and in France gave out statements to their newspaper friends and others to the effect that Lloyd George had deliberately withheld troops in Great Britain instead of reinforcing the Army in France. According to his critics, his conduct was entirely responsible for the disasters of March when the Germans crashed through the British lines.

The newspapers made insistent demands that the question of war direction must come under review.

Lloyd George recorded of the time: "The militarist Press took up the cue. There was a propagandist campaign organised in the Press, in social circles, in the clubs and in the Lobbies of the House, and it ultimately culminated in the cabal which, after working assiduously but in vain to overthrow the Government for attempting to organise a General Reserve behind our threatened Army, thought that, after repeated failures, their opportunity had at last arrived."[b]

In the final clash, Sir Frederick Maurice, a devoted admirer and confidant of Sir William Robertson, and just at that time transferred from Director of Military Operations to other employment, became the standard-bearer of the soldiers and their political allies against the Government.

On 7th May, 1918, a letter from Maurice was published in several morning newspapers accusing the Government of a series of misstatements on

the military situation. It was his intention to reinforce the claims of the Government critics that the
Army in France had been starved of manpower.

Maurice arraigned the Government on three
separate counts. In the first place he challenged
the statement made by the Prime Minister in the
House of Commons on 9th April, 1918, in which
Lloyd George had declared that the Army in
France was considerably stronger in January 1918
than in January of the year before. Such a statement, Maurice claimed, was entirely erroneous.
It implied that Sir Douglas Haig's fighting strength
on the eve of the German attack in March had
not been reduced. This, he said, was not correct.

He further denied an assertion made by the
Prime Minister regarding the number of white
troops in Palestine and Egypt.

His last allegation concerned Bonar Law. The
question of the extension of the British line in
France had been recently taken up in the House.
It was a matter in which there was much interest.
Bonar Law had stated in Parliament that the
extension had not been decided by the hated
Versailles War Council. Maurice gave him the
lie direct—a bold decision considering Bonar
Law's reputation for truth and honesty.

Such was the stern nature of Maurice's charges.
Each bore on a vital matter in the disputes that
raged with increasing public attention between
the civilian and the military factions.

Yet Maurice was at pains to make clear his
motives for his attack. The letter, he affirmed,

formed no part of a military conspiracy; he was, he professed, as sincere a democrat as the Prime Minister and had no wish to see the Government of the country in the hands of the soldiers. He had written because of the widespread distrust of the Government which was impairing the morale of the troops.

Lloyd George did not credit General Maurice's protestations of devotion to democracy. He naturally supposed, in the highly charged atmosphere of the moment, that the letter was the outcome of a deliberate and organised attack upon the Government.

Indeed, a few days after the letter's publication, Sir William Robertson himself felt bound to write to Lord Milner in the following terms:

> During the past week a story has been persistently circulated in a certain section of the London Press*— the same section which suddenly and simultaneously attacked me early in the year—insinuating that Mr. Asquith, Lord Jellicoe, General Trenchard and myself met recently at a special dinner or in conference— before the Maurice letter—and conspired together to upset or cause trouble to the Government. I wish to say that so far as I am personally concerned this story is an absolute fabrication.[c]

In sending Robertson's letter on to the Prime Minister, Lord Milner commented:

> There is no doubt in my mind that he himself was not the principal intriguer, but that he got into bad company, Repington and the "Morning Post" crowd

* Lord Northcliffe's *Daily Mail*

being really the devils of the piece, while no doubt the "Squiffites"* saw their chance of making use of him.[d]

This denial of Robertson's did not influence events. In fact it was received by Lloyd George after the struggle was all over. But in any case Lloyd George would not accept any denial of a conspiracy. He was convinced that the charges and counter-charges must be fought out in debate in Parliament.

For the real meaning of the Maurice charges was well known and fully understood. The intention was to reinforce the argument to which I have already referred that Lloyd George was deliberately starving the army in France of necessary reinforcements. Several reasons were offered for such conduct, most of them discreditable to Lloyd George and his Government.

Thus Maurice's imputations questioned more than ministerial veracity. They also condemned the Government* on their military direction of the war. If the case were proved, the Government must inevitably fall.

The hostile Press, which had been making charges against Lloyd George holding him responsible for the weakness of the British Forces in France and for the reduction in the number of battalions, was now quick to point out that the Maurice letter put an official seal upon all the newspaper denunciations.

Here then was the crucial test.

On the day the letter appeared, Asquith gave

* Followers of Asquith.

further strength to the Opposition by putting down a private notice of his intention to ask for a Select Committee of the House of Commons.

At the same time, at a meeting of Ministers on 7th May, the whole content of Maurice's allegations was reviewed.

Bonar Law was greatly perturbed by the charges. He was directly involved; the veracity of the Prime Minister and himself had been held up to public attack. He believed that the Maurice letter reflected on his personal honour, and he was convinced that a judicial enquiry should be instituted at once to examine the accusation.

The Cabinet was moved by wider considerations. There was evident difficulty about submitting documents of a highly secret nature to a Court of Enquiry. In the same way the proposal to set up a Committee of the House of Commons had to be rejected. It was decided that the Government should invite two judges to act as a Court of Honour to enquire into the charge that misstatements had been made.

Later that day Bonar Law communicated the Government's intention to the House of Commons. The decision failed to satisfy Asquith. He intended to have the matter opened to discussion on the floor of the House; he invited the Government to name a day for a debate.

Churchill was sitting beside Bonar Law on the Front Bench. He heard the proposal for a Judicial Committee for the first time. He urged Bonar

Law to withdraw the offer. Bonar Law made no answer. Later Churchill joined Lloyd George and Bonar Law in conference. He convinced them that a Minister should never ask a Judicial Committee to enquire into his own integrity.*

Churchill's intervention was decisive. The offer of a Judicial Committee was never renewed. Asquith had blundered by failing to accept it. He had saved the Government from an embarrassing error. Churchill's wise advice had strengthened the Government's hand.

The situation, however, was now plainly exposed. It was apparent that the Maurice letter was to be treated as a vote of censure on the Administration. The *Westminster Gazette*, the mouthpiece of the Asquith Alliance, loudly proclaimed that there was an alternative government and it was time it took the reins.[e] The *Manchester Guardian*, usually friendly to the Government, assured its readers that General Maurice's statements "went to the heart of the responsibility for our recent reverses".[f] The *Morning Post* took up the cry with bitter criticism of the Prime Minister.

"It is only the seriousness of the war position, the presumed difficulty of finding a successor, and, perhaps, a shrewd suspicion of the sort of 'support' any successor would be likely to have at his hands," it proclaimed, "which has kept him at the head of the Government ever since the demission of Sir William Robertson."[g] The

* See *Appendix IV*, No. 15.

Government must come out and face the challenge.

On the evening of 7th May, therefore, the lobbies were plunged into a crisis of immense proportions. The country was even more excited than the Members of Parliament. The political sensation was the subject of discussion in every meeting place; in pubs and bank parlours, in bars and board rooms.

There were three important considerations that had to be taken into account in estimating the danger to the Government. (1) The charge of deliberately deceiving the House, if sustained, is never forgiven, and must wreck a Ministry. (2) Some of Lloyd George's colleagues believed that there was a great deal of substance in the charges. (3) The Ministry was at that period suffering from the consequences of reverses in the field, and under those conditions a serious political assault might bring the Government down.

Ministerial Whips despatched telegrams demanding the attendance of their supporters on the day of the debate. There was just as much activity in opposition circles. Sir Edward Carson entertained the hope of playing an important role. Without doubt he expected that a new government would be formed and that greater power would be accorded to the military leaders. Possibly Jellicoe would be brought back again.

Lady Carson notes in her diary for 8th May, 1918: "Heard from Edward that General Maurice's letter had made a great stir. Edward always knew that Ll.G.'s and B.L.'s statements were lies, but only knowing so from being in the Cabinet he could not say so."[h]

The Unionist War Committee was called together. L. S. Amery gives this account of the meeting: "Went to the Unionist War Committee, a very large gathering, which was discussing today's vote in the House. Salisbury opened, very hostile to the Government, and then Carson suggested that the Unionist War Committee should as a body take an independent attitude by moving the previous question, thus neither endorsing Asquith nor approving of Lloyd George."

Such a decision would, as Carson well knew, be a death-blow to the Administration. If he had succeeded the Government would have fallen there and then. The War Committee rejected the proposal.

After the meeting, Carson met Colonel Repington at Lady Londonderry's luncheon table and told him that "he had been for three hours with the Unionists today, that their hate of Asquith overrides all other considerations, and that they will not back him tomorrow in the Maurice debate."[j] Carson added that it would be no use for him to speak as he would have no following.

Yet even though the Unionist War Committee refused to accept Carson's wrecking proposal, there was grave doubt of the outcome of the crisis. On the eve of the debate, the verdict could not be predicted.

The Liberal War Committee had also assembled

to discuss its course of action. There were unknown areas of weakness in the House from which a formidable opposition could be gathered. It was not possible to assess the strength of the Asquith Alliance.

As the storm grew in violence, Lloyd George displayed considerable force and determination. He had gone over the matter thoroughly with his colleagues in the Cabinet; he believed that the Government had a complete answer to its critics. He was eager to make a case in Parliament. He felt confident he could convince the House.

On 9th May, therefore, a resolute Prime Minister entered a tense and crowded House of Commons to present the case for the Government.

Asquith opened the Debate on the Motion for a Select Committee. His speech was suave and highly polished. It cannot be held to have been free from guile. Asquith concluded: ". . . I hold no brief of any sort or kind for military as distinguished from civilian and, what is called, politicians' opinion."[k]

In reply, Lloyd George dealt with the charges one by one. He referred to his own speech on 9th April, which General Maurice had challenged. He told the House that General Maurice had been at his post in the War Office some weeks after that speech had been delivered. Maurice had attended a meeting of the Cabinet, in the absence of the Chief of Staff, the very day after Lloyd George had made the speech. But, until the charges appeared in the Press, he did not say a word about the allegation that the Prime Minister's statements were inaccurate.

The most telling section of Lloyd George's defence depended on General Maurice's own figures.

"The figures that I gave," Lloyd George stated, "were taken from the official records of the War Office, for which I sent before I made the statement. If they were incorrect, General Maurice was as responsible as anyone else. But they were not inaccurate. . . . There is absolutely no doubt that there was a very considerable addition to the man-power of the Army in France at the beginning of 1918 as compared with the man-power at the beginning of 1917."[1]

Lloyd George went on to say he was not including in his estimate of the fighting strength in France the labour battalions and other non-combatant units. The combatant strength of the British Army was greater at the beginning of 1918 than at the beginning of the previous year. This information also came from General Maurice's Department at the War Office.

On a less important point, Lloyd George assured the House that his statement about the strength of British troops in the Middle East was based on official War Office information presented to the Cabinet when Sir Frederick Maurice was present, and later sent to the General for checking. Maurice had telephoned his answer, "No remarks."

It now remained for the Prime Minister to dispose of the charge concerning the veracity of

Bonar Law's statement on the extension of the British Line. He dealt with it swiftly. Not a yard, he pronounced, had been taken over by the British Army as a result of the Versailles Council. In fact, the extension agreed to between Haig and Pétain was an accomplished fact before the Council met, and Haig had reported it himself to the Versailles meeting.*

It was a triumphant reply. It was a complete vindication of Lloyd George and Bonar Law. No further attack was launched from the Opposition Front Bench.

Sir Edward Carson spoke only briefly and in a sense very different from his earlier intentions. He poured scorn on the idea that judges should be asked to decide whether the Prime Minister was, or was not, an honourable man. And he said that Asquith, his old enemy (whom he had once called a traitor), had always acted as a patriot.

He secured no backing to push home an assault. The dismal outcome of Carson's attempt to mobilize the Unionist [Conservative] War Committee was his last bid for power and his final defeat.

The House, dividing on the Motion for a Select Committee, returned an astonishing total of 293 votes for the Government. One hundred and six members registered their votes with the Opposition.

Thus Lloyd George's position was endorsed by

* Haig in his diary, published years after, denied that he agreed to take over any part of the French Front. He declared that this speech of Lloyd George's was "clap-trap", that the House of Commons was losing its reputation and that Maurice was not yet done with Lloyd George.[m]

an overwhelming majority. He was confirmed in the Premiership by a decisive backing in the House of Commons.

For the opposing one hundred it was a costly defeat. Indeed, for many of them it was to foreshadow their political extinction.

The importance of the Maurice Debate as an incident in political history cannot be forgotten. In the first place, it marked a turning point in Lloyd George's career. It left him in a position of considerable authority and it proved to be his conclusive victory in the struggle with the military alliance. For the first time since he had assumed the Premiership eighteen months before, it became possible to assess the strength of his support in Parliament.

But its implications went much deeper than this. For Lloyd George, the debate marked the final cleavage between his Liberal followers and those of Asquith. At the General Election that followed some months later, few of those who had voted against the Prime Minister on the Maurice question escaped exclusion from Parliament.

In the Maurice Debate were thus the seeds of the disintegration that soon overtook the Liberal Party. The party was really broken on 9th May when the division bells were ringing through the Palace of Westminster for the fateful vote. It has never since regained its political eminence. "The reverberations of the quarrel," Mr. Churchill has written of the Maurice issue, "continue to this day."[11]

General Maurice was scarcely more fortunate than the Liberal Party. He was retired from the Army on half-pay. Robert Donald offered him the position of military correspondent of the *Daily Chronicle* and from this fortress he was able to deliver an occasional glancing blow at the Administration.

But for all practical purposes, the heat of the controversy had been exhausted.

And now we come to the particular irony that surrounds an issue holding such vital consequences for English Liberalism.

In 1922, four years after the famous Maurice Debate, Sir Frederick wrote a letter to the Prime Minister.⁰ He was eager to bring forward complete evidence of what he claimed to be the facts. He said that the document from the War Office relating to the available troops in France on which Mr. Lloyd George had based his answer was prepared in a hurry. He declared that a mistake had been made and the whole strength of the Army in Italy was included in the strength of the Armies in France. With the addition of all these troops, a slight increase of the fighting strength in January, 1918, as compared with January, 1917, was shown.

Maurice affirmed that this mistake was discovered shortly afterwards, and reported to Philip Kerr, one of Lloyd George's Private Secretaries.

Therefore he declared that Lloyd George, on May 9th, 1918, had used an accidentally incorrect return to endorse his case, though he had in his possession another return showing the corrected figures.*

Where then was this document that corroborated General Maurice's claim? It would have given substance to his accusations against Lloyd George though not to the charge against Bonar Law. It was the hinge upon which the whole question hung. It invalidated the detailed defence Lloyd George had built up. But what became of it?

I now quote in full an extract taken from the Diary of Countess Lloyd George, which is included in the Lloyd George collection. It is dated 5th October, 1934.

Have been reading up the events connected with the Maurice Debate in order to help Ll.G. with this Chapter in Vol. V,† and am uneasy in my mind about an incident which occurred at the time and which is known only to J. T. Davies‡ and myself. Ll.G. obtained from the W.O. the figures which he used in his statement on April 9th in the House of Commons on the subject of man-power. These figures were afterwards stated by Gen. Maurice to be inaccurate.

I was in J. T. Davies' room a few days after the statement, and J. T. was sorting out red dispatch boxes to be returned to the Departments. As was his wont, he looked in them before locking them up and sending them out to the Messengers. Pulling out a W.O. box, he found in it, to his great astonishment, a paper from

* Lloyd George in his speech in Parliament on May 9th, 1918, declared that Sir Frederick Maurice had never made any correction of the statement of Army strength in France.

† Of the *War Memoirs*.

‡ Sir J. T. Davies, throughout the Premiership of Lloyd George, and after, his secretary and confidant; a treasurer of the Lloyd George Fund; a director of the Suez Canal.

the D.M.O.* containing modifications and corrections of the first figures they had sent, and by some mischance this box had remained unopened. J.T. and I examined it in dismay, and then J.T. put it in the fire, remarking, "Only you and I, Frances, know of the existence of this paper".

There is no doubt that this is what Maurice had in mind when he accused L.G. of mis-statement. But the amazing thing was that *the document was never fixed upon*. How was it that the matter was never clinched, and Maurice or someone never actually said: "The figures supplied by us were so and so"? They argued round and over the point, but never did one of them put any finger on it. I was waiting for the matter to be raised, and for the question to be asked: Why did L.G. not receive these supplementary figures? Or did he? But the questions never came and I could not voluntarily break faith with J.T., perhaps put L.G. in a fix, and who knows, have brought down the Government!

The only explanation is that Maurice and Co. were relying on getting their Judicial Committee, where every point would have been thrashed out in detail. When the judicial committee was turned down, it was by that time too late to bring up details again, and by that time also Maurice was beaten.

I suppose it is too late now for the matter to be cleared up and I had better keep silent. But I will talk it over with J.T. In any event, no good could come of any revelation made now, but the amazing thing to me still, is that in all these years no one has fastened on this particular point. There is a slight allusion in Colonel Repington's book about a discrepancy in figures, but this also seems to have escaped attention. And as the Official Statistics since compiled seem to justify L.G.'s statement at the time, it were better perhaps to let sleeping dogs lie.

* Director of Military Operations.

So it seems that the upward spiral of cause and effect, moving from one event to another and greater one, found its origin in a trivial event in a secretary's room at 10 Downing Street. If the amending figures sent by Maurice's department in the War Office had not been overlooked by the Prime Minister's secretary, Lloyd George would not have given misleading information to Parliament. Maurice would not have been able to make the charge which the newspapers published. There would have been no Maurice Debate. And maybe there would have been no exclusion of Asquithian Liberals at the General Election. The disruption of the Liberal Party might have been postponed or even averted.

The student of history may ponder these thoughts with humility, mingled with a sense of human comedy. Through the oversight of a secretary, Lloyd George's Government—for months the target of a military junta and the butt of powerful and contentious forces determined to drag down and utterly destroy the Prime Minister—was saved and indeed strengthened immeasurably. Never again, for the duration of the war, was Lloyd George in danger from the assaults of enemies of the right and left. The direction of the war remained unaltered. The Liberal Party was destroyed, while enemies were scattered far and wide.

Behold, how great a fire
a little matter kindleth!

CHAPTER IX

"DON'T RESIGN:
WAIT UNTIL YOU'RE SACKED"

ANOTHER crisis! February, 1918. And I was the crisis. The reason was simple. I had tumbled into office, and into trouble. Sailors had no part in the tempest that tossed my frail bark. Soldiers were not concerned with wrecking me in my stormy campaign. Politicians were my enemies, strengthened by high-born voices.

For long, public opinion in Britain had been pressing for an improvement in British war propaganda. It was felt that in this field the enemy was beating us. The demand grew and spread to the Ministers and to the brass-hats, as a consequence of the military and diplomatic reverses. There had been a mutiny in the French Army and a rebellion in Ireland. In the United States the British war effort was criticised; while in South America the conviction prevailed that the German military domination over Europe was complete and permanent. In the Far East, Japan, willing at the outbreak of war to join the allied armies in France, had come to the conclusion that Germany was the military master of the West. And in

265

Britain, in the factories and the shipyards discontent prevailed. Each of these conditions was in turn attributed to a well-organised system of German propaganda.

So far as Britain was concerned, this branch of the nation's effort was still in a rudimentary state. Each of the service Ministries had its propaganda section. So had the Foreign Office. A war-aims committee, set up under John Buchan* and others, was possessed of uncertain authority. While Sir Edward Carson remained a member of the War Cabinet he was charged with the duty of co-ordinating and directing these various projects. But he was hostile to the Prime Minister, critical of the Government, and nursing a grievance. His enthusiasm for the cause of propaganda was not apparent. And soon he resigned and went into opposition.

The public clamoured for a British Ministry devoted to the development of propaganda instruments able to raise morale at home, convince the Allies and the Dominions of the vast strength of the British effort, and persuade the neutrals to believe that the victorious armies of the Empire would bring peace to a war-weary world.

On 23rd January, 1918, Frederick Guest, Lloyd George's Chief Whip, wrote as follows:

12 Downing Street, S.W.

Dear Prime Minister,

I do hope you will consider *Max*† for Controller of Propaganda.

* Later Lord Tweedsmuir.
† William Maxwell Aitken, now known as Lord Beaverbrook.

He is bitten with it, knows it, and I want him anchored.

Yours sincerely,

FREDERICK GUEST.[a]

On 10th February, 1918, Lloyd George appointed me Minister of Information and Chancellor of the Duchy of Lancaster. I should be founding the first Ministry of Propaganda set up by a British government.

There was no blueprint to work on. No experience to guide the new department. There was no office, no staff. There was nothing but a decision of the War Cabinet decreeing that such a Ministry should be created and that I should be the Minister. Yet, although I had many misgivings about the appointment, these did not spring from any lack of confidence in what I was to do.

In explaining his choice of a Minister to the House of Commons the Prime Minister said:

Lord Beaverbrook had, at the request . . . of the Canadian Government, organised a Canadian propaganda, which is acknowledged to be amongst the most successful, perhaps the most successful, piece of work of its kind on the Allied side.[b]

I had been for some time the Canadian Government representative to the Army overseas. I was the channel of communication between Sir Robert Borden, the Canadian Prime Minister, Sir Sam Hughes, the Canadian Minister of Militia and Defence at Ottawa, and the British Ministers engaged in war activities as well as the military commanders in Britain and at the front.

In addition, propaganda relating to the Canadian war effort was in my charge and—according to my critics—had given the impression in the United States that Canada was bearing the brunt of the fighting in France.

This misunderstanding was fostered by Lord Northcliffe, who telegraphed from New York[c] that the Canadian Army was given undue prominence in the American Press and that in consequence it was asked, "When are the British going to begin to fight?" English regiments, said Northcliffe, were never mentioned, yet the papers were full of the brave deeds of the Manitobas. Northcliffe was convinced, so he said, that the Canadian propaganda damaged the prestige of Britain and interfered with British applications to Washington for financial assistance. He had supreme confidence in The Power of the Press.

Northcliffe's criticism was, of course, unjustified, but I had no doubt at all that the methods I had applied to Canadian propaganda could be used with equal success for Britain's propaganda generally.

My task would be to satisfy the body of Britons living in the United Kingdom, while convincing those who lived overseas that Britain was playing her full and effective part. How could it be done? By bringing to Britain groups of newspaper proprietors from abroad—the working owners of newspapers—who would do the work of propaganda for me when they returned home again. By pictorial publications of one kind and another. And especially by the cinema, which, by this time, was just emerging from the Nickelodeon Age. By exhibitions of paintings of war scenes by the artists of quality. By assuming control of Reuters, and other news agencies, so that good news was disseminated abroad instead of gloom and apprehension. By making the acquaintance of foreign news agencies with offices in London.

Then it was necessary that the troops should be convinced that the propaganda department was working effectively. Artists and cameramen must be seen at the front and a newspaper for the soldiers must be launched.

Munition workers in Britain must be persuaded to take an interest in the soldiers on the various fighting fronts. Production in the factories could be stimulated by exciting records in the form of pictures, and particularly cinema pictures showing action in battle. And, more particularly, deeds of bravery and sacrifice.

There would be an intense enemy propaganda. Lord Northcliffe might be given charge. He would provide the necessary drive and energy.

At that time the neutral countries were giving little or no attention to Britain's immense war effort. It would be difficult to make any strong or lasting impression on these non-belligerents. The best propaganda for their edification would depend upon British victories in arms.

The programme was simple. It was easy to set in motion. Its success was assured. But if I thought on that account that my path would be smooth I was swiftly disillusioned.

A powerful complaint came from Buckingham Palace. This concerned my position as Chancellor of the Duchy. It was reported that the King was disturbed by the idea of a Presbyterian administering the ecclesiastic preferments of the Crown. I did not believe it. But of a certainty he was animated by no great personal liking for me.

I was told that he was really hostile and that his dislike flowed in part from the old story when Balfour lost the leadership of the Tory Party that behind the scenes was the "little Canadian adventurer".* Then again when Asquith tumbled down there was the charge of "intrigue" which the fallen Liberal Ministers had spread.

There were, too, real reasons for complaint. These sprang from the early days of war when I was acting as Canadian Government Representative.

I had to deal with questions relating to the Canadian forces—often difficult and tiresome issues, which exposed me to the displeasure of official circles.

For instance, there was the issue between Lord Kitchener and General Hughes over Canadian casualties. Hughes objected to the system whereby the news of casualties was transmitted to London, and thence to next-of-kin in Canada, in the name of Lord Kitchener and often days after the information had reached Canada unofficially. He asked me to demand on his behalf

* On 10th November, 1911, J. C. Sandars, writing to Balfour, attacked Bonar Law's methods in seizing the leadership of the Tory Party, declaring that he was run by Max Aitken, the little Canadian adventurer who sits for Ashton-under-Lyne, introduced into that seat by him.

the right to direct notification from the Battle Front and through the Canadian Minister of Militia. It was an obvious necessity but it proved to be a tough assignment.

My application to Kitchener met with refusal. Prime Minister Asquith was my next approach, but he could not help me. He advised me to go to Army Headquarters in France and see if matters could be arranged there. I set out for St. Omer and called on General Macready.*

"It's a damn cheek," said Macready when I explained Sam Hughes's request to him.[d] Then I approached General Maxwell.† The entry in my diary for that day reads: "Maxwell said, 'Sam Hughes is never satisfied with anybody or anything.' "[e]

In such circumstances I had to work and work hard to get consent. Perhaps I worked too hard. My insistence did not endear me to anyone. The whole military hierarchy took a most unfriendly view of my activities. They did not understand that Canada had grown up. I tried to explain with patience that all Canadians would support the Minister. Still they abused me, as though I had personal responsibility. Thus on occasions when I expected words of praise and commendation, I got vigorous and outspoken condemnation.

Hughes had no friends in British military circles. He was altogether too critical not only of equipment but also of strategy. In Royal circles

*General Sir Nevil Macready, G.C.M.G., K.C.B., was Adjutant-General to the British Expeditionary Forces, 1914–1916.
† Major-General Sir Ronald Maxwell, K.C.B., K.C.M.G., was Quartermaster-General to the Armies in France, 1915–1917.

he was regarded with anxiety. The Duke of Connaught, the Governor-General of Canada and uncle of the King, was his bitter enemy. The measure of his bitterness was deep indeed. A letter from the Duke to Bennett, now in the Archives of Lord Bennett at the University of New Brunswick, condemned Hughes in the most outspoken terms.*

A Minute on the reasons for the anger of the Duke will be found in an Appendix† from Mr. John Bassett, the distinguished proprietor of the *Montreal Gazette*. This gives an explanation of the origins of the quarrel.

There was an occasion when His Royal Highness, the Duke of Connaught, threatened to resign. He wrote to the Prime Minister of Canada saying:

> I must however make it quite clear to you that I must have a written apology from Sir Sam Hughes or otherwise I shall be compelled to place my resignation in the hands of the King with a full statement of my reasons for doing so.^{g}

Hughes, of course, dodged the issue. He sent a memorandum to the Prime Minister. It did not serve to appease the hostility of the Governor-General.

A full account of the conflict appears in the papers of Sir Robert Borden in the Archives of

---

* The Duke of Connaught returned to England. His Governorship had been brought to an end. But his hostility to Hughes lived on. Writing to Bennett in Canada he declared that chaos reigned in all Canadian military matters and that there was ill-feeling between Imperial and Canadian military authorities. "However, it was only due to one person and now that that person is gone, let us hope forever, all will I know be right again."^{f}

† *Appendix II.*

Standing: Prime Minister, Borden. Seated: Canadian Government
Representative, Beaverbrook; Canadian Minister of Trade, Foster;
Canadian Minister of Defence, Kemp.

Ottawa, with a microfilm copy at the Library of the University of Toronto.

It was in such an atmosphere of friction and hostility towards the Canadian Minister that Sir Robert Borden authorized me during 1915 to ask for a Knighthood for General Hughes. The honour might bring Hughes into harmony with the British Service leaders. It might make rough places smooth. The Colonial Office agreed to put forward a recommendation to the King.

The Duke of Connaught made vigorous objection to the Knighthood. He joined the military hierarchy in determined opposition.

But the King rejected the protest of the Duke of Connaught and reluctantly consented to accept the recommendation of the Colonial Secretary. He expressed annoyance with me.

Now Hughes was entitled to the rank of Major-General in the British Army. In the autumn, I received the necessary authority to telegraph him as follows:

General Sir Sam Hughes, Ottawa.
16th October, 1915.
Do you wish to be gazetted Major General here stop If so Brade* will support

AITKEN[h]

Hughes asked for higher rank. I replied:

General Sir Sam Hughes, Ottawa.
Have dropped Major General and asked for Lieut. General and have assurance from very strong member

* Sir Reginald Brade, Permanent Under-Secretary at the War Office.

273   S

of Government* that he will secure consent in due course.

AITKENi

Thus it was that the Secretary of State for War (Lloyd George) and the Secretary of State for the Colonies (Bonar Law) joined in recommending Hughes for the rank of Lieutenant-General.

Then the storm broke. Field-Marshal, His Royal Highness, the Duke of Connaught joined the fray. After a year of struggle the Royal Gazette heralded the Hon. Sir Sam Hughes, K.C.B., M.P., in the list of Lieutenant-Generals and quietness prevailed for a time.

But His Majesty's Secretary wrote to Sir Maurice Bonham-Carter† that the promotion had been planted on the King by Lloyd George and Bonar Law.<i>j</i>

These unfortunate but unavoidable incidents did not commend me to His Majesty and perhaps explain resistance to my being given Cabinet rank in the form of the sinecure appointment of the Duchy of Lancaster.

The objections to my appointment were set out in a letter from Lord Stamfordham to Frederick Guest, the Chief Whip, dated 8th February, 1918, saying that His Majesty

> expressed much surprise that, considering past circumstances, he should now be asked to agree to Lord Beaverbrook's presiding over the Duchy, which, as it were, is the personal property of the Sovereign and

---

* Lloyd George.　　† Secretary to the Prime Minister.

entailing closer relations between the King and its
Chancellor than with many of his Ministers. . . .

I must again assure you that the Prime Minister
in saying to me that he was thinking of employing Lord
Beaverbrook in the Propaganda Department, never
referred in merely any way to the Duchy of Lancaster. . . .[k]

Lloyd George sent a firm answer back:

I am confident [he wrote to Stamfordham] that . . . I
shall receive a great accession of strength in Lord
Beaverbrook's appointment. His organisation of the
Canadian Propaganda Department entrusted to him by
Sir Robert Borden has been a conspicuous success. On
the other hand, our propaganda has been a conspicuous
failure. I have sought in vain for months for a man to
put it right. So far I have not succeeded. Propaganda at home and abroad is becoming increasingly
important. I consulted the members of the Propaganda
Committee and they thought Beaverbrook would be
the best available man. I cannot get him without
offering him Ministerial rank. He is a first-rate business
man and will administer the Duchy well.

In these circumstances I trust the King will be
graciously pleased to approve the recommendation
which I have thought fit to make to him. I wish you to
assure His Majesty that I attach great importance to the
appointment of Lord Beaverbrook to this post.[l]

That insistence by the Prime Minister confirmed me in my dual appointment. But I had
not reached the end of my troubles. Far from it!

At this time Lloyd George's government was
not looked on as a stable structure. The office-
seekers and those who dwell in the favour of
the powerful could not determine their future

allegiance. Where did the best advantage lie? Unable to make up their minds on this important issue, these unreliable followers of Lloyd George resembled a boatload of pleasure-seekers who rush from port to starboard endangering the safety of their own craft.

I became a victim of this lack of fixed and dependable allegiance to Lloyd George and his government. For in many quarters enemies of the Administration were waiting to spring out on me in the belief that I was the weakest link in the chain.

There was, of course, the group who accepted the leadership of Asquith. Their bitterness over the so-called "intrigue against Asquith", which had destroyed his Government, was directed against me.

In the Conservative Party, too, many looked on me with coldness. They were enthusiasts for the maintenance of the Parliamentary Union with Ireland, they knew that I had Irish sympathies.

The powerful Cecil family, wielding immense influence on Church and State, were angry with me for my persistent pursuit of food taxes. They held firmly to the belief that food taxes would shatter the Tory Party, thus destroying their hope of defending the establishment of the Church in Wales.

Balfour was my enemy. No doubt he too recalled the story of the little Canadian adventurer who had "intrigued" him out of the Tory leadership. Lord Milner attacked me. I don't know why he disapproved, perhaps on account of

LORD ROBERT CECIL. A sombre figure and a stalwart supporter of the Church.

DERBY. Excessive amiability.

my self-confidence. Possibly he disagreed with my public performance. Certainly he did not think well of me.

There were Army chiefs who feared that the real purpose was to set up a propaganda machine, not for Britain but for Lloyd George. This thought disturbed many honest and over-anxious Members of Parliament.

Then, again, the service ministries wished to be left unmolested in possession of their own propaganda departments; they resented being deprived of officials who were in effect their P.R.O.s. And outside Whitehall some newspapers, disliking the competition of the *Daily Express*, took an unfavourable view of my appointment. So when the *Globe* spoke of "a sense of profound misgiving which we have no hesitation in believing will be shared by the nation at large",[m] the newspaper was certainly speaking for many interests and personalities.

Then, immediately after my appointment was announced, I took the step which was certain to add to my difficulties in Parliament. I told Lloyd George of my desire to appoint Northcliffe in charge of propaganda in enemy territories. Lloyd George received the recommendation with enthusiasm. He said it was an excellent appointment, and would carry public approval.

He declared that no man had qualifications surpassing Northcliffe for this post. He also mentioned that Lord Northcliffe would be likely to show a restraint in the criticism of ministerial departments if he got to know something of the trials and difficulties of conducting them. Thus possibly Lord Northcliffe's circulation of newspapers, representing one-half of all newspaper sales in London, was being loosely hitched to the Government chariot.*

Northcliffe gladly accepted the offer I made him. He showed real enthusiasm. When Bonar Law heard of my great catch he said to me: "One of you newspaper barons was too much. Now there are two. Well, you'll hear of this. I hope you have not misunderstood the Prime Minister's approval."

Bonar Law's prophecy proved to be only too accurate. By appointing Northcliffe I had made a serious blunder in political tactics; Northcliffe was feared and detested in many quarters, and particularly in the House of Commons.

Trouble came upon me swiftly. It came from a quarter damaging indeed. It was Austen Chamberlain, the most important leader in the Conservative Party outside of the Government, who opened an attack from the Government benches against Lord Northcliffe and me. His language was strong, his attitude unbending and his support on the benches very considerable indeed. He said:

Three great newspaper owners are members of, or are intimately associated with, the Administration. . . . My right hon. Friend and his Government have

* Lloyd George displayed his usual political prescience. Northcliffe's appointment as Director of Enemy Propaganda was published on the same day as the announcement of Robertson's dismissal. His newspapers did not criticise the Government.

surrounded themselves quite unnecessarily with an
atmosphere of suspicion and distrust because they have
allowed themselves to become so intimately associated
with these great newspaper proprietors. I tell my right
hon. Friend what everyone is saying in the Lobbies,
outside the House, where men meet, but what I think
it is now time for someone to say publicly and as a
responsible man in this House. . . . As long as you have
the owner of a newspaper as a member of your Administration you will be held responsible for what he writes
in the newspaper. . . . My right hon. Friend and his
Government will never stand clear in the estimation of
the public, and will never have the authority which
they ought to have, . . . until they make things quite
clear, open, and plain to all the world and sever this
connection with the newspapers."

On the same day the Unionist [Conservative]
War Committee passed a strongly worded resolution, reading:

> That in the opinion of the Unionist War Committee
> no member of the Government or officer holding a
> post under the Government should be allowed to act
> as the correspondent of a newspaper in respect of the
> conduct of the war or the fitness of any naval or
> military officer for the post he holds and that no one
> who controls a newspaper should be allowed to be a
> member of the Government or to hold a responsible
> post under it so long as he retains control of that
> newspaper.[o]

In forwarding the Resolution to Bonar Law,
Lord Salisbury, Chairman of the Committee, put
himself in a somewhat complex position. He
apologised for a disagreeable letter but said that,
as he had been requested by the Committee to

send the Resolution, he had no choice. "I write of course as Chairman without reference to my own opinion," Lord Salisbury assured him, "though on the subject of this connection with the Press I entirely agree with the Committee."[p]

The resolution of the Unionist War Committee was in fact a long step further than Austen Chamberlain was prepared to go. Some days later, I received a letter from him dissociating himself from any connection with it.

2.3.18.

Dear Beaverbrook,

I am not in any way responsible for the terms of the resolution passed by the Unionist War Committee, nor had I seen their resolution or any part of it till I received this morning the memo enclosed in your letter.

The Committee have evidently gone far beyond my position and I am not concerned to defend theirs which is obviously open to criticism.

My publicly stated objection was to such a connection between the Government and the Press as destroys the independence of the Press and involves the Government, in responsibility for all the opinions expressed by the Press . . .

The organisation of the Bureau or Ministry of Information and its propaganda raise distinct questions into which I will not now enter. I only regret that they have been confused and prejudiced by the character of the general connection established between the Government and the Press.

You are good enough to recognise my sincerity. I spoke as a public duty—not a pleasant one—and as a well-wisher on public grounds to the present administration. Their friends may under existing conditions endure, but they will not forgive, persistence in a

course of action which independent public opinion so
unanimously condemns. I hope that in my speech
and by my silence and inaction since, I have avoided
anything in word or deed which would make it more
difficult for the Prime Minister or his friends to meet
public opinion and satisfy the public conscience.

Yours sincerely,

AUSTEN CHAMBERLAIN.[7]

This was a tough letter. The implication was
clear. The Prime Minister would be given an
opportunity to rid himself of his Minister of
Information! Otherwise Chamberlain would return to the subject. He would be a formidable
opponent.

The War Committee's Resolution, however,
was too preposterous to be dangerous. It was
directed against the Ministry of Information as a
body. If acted upon, it would have made impossible any propaganda organisation whatsoever.

But the speech of Chamberlain and the action
of the War Committee certainly put the Government in a position of much difficulty. Who could
assess the voting strength the Committee might
muster in the lobbies of the House of Commons
should they decide to put the issue to the test?

Some of the Ministers thought that immediate
concession should be made. But by most of his
colleagues Lloyd George was stoutly urged to
stand by his Press appointments. Not to do so,
they argued, would only involve him in deeper
difficulties; thus F. E. Smith and Winston Churchill both thought Lloyd George should not

budge. As for Frederick Guest, the Chief Liberal Whip, his opinions were put before the Prime Minister in a closely argued memorandum.*

The gist of Guest's Memorandum was that if Lloyd George followed the resolution of the War Committee, then he must dismiss Northcliffe, Rothermere and me as none of us would resign. Guest declared his belief that I would continue to support Lloyd George and his Government up to and through the next General Election. Rothermere would feel inclined to do the same. "Northcliffe may do anything."

Guest's advice was that Lloyd George should stand by his friends and his appointments. He had sounded the following Ministers on the general situation and reported as follows.

"*Talbot*† is anxious to find a way out. He thinks the movement serious, but does not think it will be forced to extreme.

"*Hewart*‡ and *Illingworth*§ entirely agree with the advice which I submit.

"*F. E. Smith and W. S. C.* think that you should stand by your guns."

Guest added a note embodying his suggestions for dealing with the Unionists' objections. It is an interesting document. I reproduce it here in full.

---

* The full text of the memorandum, entitled "Notes on the Resolution Forwarded by the Unionist War Committee to the Prime Minister", is reproduced in *Appendix IV*, No. 16.

† Lord Edmund Talbot was Chief Conservative Whip and Senior Coalition Whip.

‡ Sir Gordon Hewart was the Solicitor-General.

§ A. H. Illingworth was Postmaster-General.

SUGGESTION RE UNIONIST WAR COMMITTEE'S RESOLUTION ON NEWSPAPER PROPRIETORS HOLDING OFFICE

Could it not be stated that it would be clearly pre-judicial to the National interests to disturb Ministers concerned?

The Air Force is now in its most critical period of reconstruction and co-ordination.

The Department of Information, which has been so long needed, is now in process of being established.

In view however of the strong Parliamentary feeling expressed the Government think it advisable that some form of Commission should be set up to consider this and many other similar cases which have arised [*sic*] in connection with Ministerial appointments during the war, e.g.

1. Newspaper Proprietors holding office. Director-ships, etc.*
2. Shipowner acting as Shipping Controller or President of the Board of Trade.†
3. Men with wide commercial interests placed in important positions in relation to contracts, etc.

This Commission might be judicial and non-party and its recommendations might prove of great constitutional value.

FREDERICK GUEST.'

There was without doubt a strong feeling, not confined to the detractors of the Government or to those supporting a military regime, against the participation of Press Lords in the war-time administration.

Austen Chamberlain, who was canvassing for

* The paper is typewritten and signed by Guest. The words "Directorships, etc." are added in Guest's handwriting.
† The words "or President of the Board of Trade" are added in Lloyd George's handwriting.

283

support, appears to have made a convert of Walter Long, the Colonial Secretary, even to the point of Long's offering to resign if urged to do so.[s]

Lord Milner wrote to the Prime Minister a long letter of advice, in which I was singled out for special attack:

> There really is more stir about this than I have yet known in any of these purely domestic rows. The important point is, that so many of our real friends are disgruntled. Of course the "Squiffites"* make the most of it. I don't mind that. But the number of people, who are your friends, and hate the notion of a return of Squiff† and Co., but are nevertheless seriously upset about the relations of Government and Press, is not negligible.
>
> I have no doubt, as I have pointed out to lots of them, that there is no motion, which can be brought forward on the subject, which cannot be riddled with criticism. The fact remains that a strong feeling exists, with which we have got to reckon.
>
> At bottom it is much more connected with the newspaper campaign than it is with the ownership of certain newspapers by members of the Government. Obviously the attacks which appeared in the Press on Jellicoe, Robertson, Derby and others, were by no means confined to papers owned by members of the Government, and Government inspiration of the Press is as easy or indeed easier, if newspaper proprietors are not Ministers. It is the *inspiration itself* or rather the clumsy and extreme nature of some of it which is objected to.
>
> Sutherland‡ is the man whom everybody has got his

---

* Asquithites.
† Asquith.
‡ William Sutherland, originally a civil servant, was Lloyd George's private secretary and dealt with the newspapers on behalf of the Prime Minister. He wielded immense power and authority, especially over patronage. He was exceedingly talkative, often revealing secrets, cunning and never disloyal to his master. Like every court favourite he suffered derision, scorn and hatred.

knife into just now, rightly or wrongly. About this there is, I think, nothing to be done except to lie low till the storm blows over, and *to keep the friendly Press off the war path* as far as possible. The less people hear or see of Northcliffe, Beaverbrook (certainly the most unpopular name of all) etc. for the next few weeks the better.

Please don't think I exaggerate. I have been fighting this case with all sorts of people and argumentatively we have quite a good case. But it is no use arguing with a really strong tide of feeling especially when it has some justification. And there is no doubt that the feeling is strong just now *in* quarters essentially friendly.'

Yet while hostility to the newspapermen in the Government, and possibly particularly to me, moved men in many groups, there was no liaison between them. Chamberlain did not seek support from the Liberals or the Labour members. When he renewed his enquiry into the Government's relations with the newspapermen in the Commons on 11th March, he got plenty of support from the Opposition Liberal benches. Their encouragement did not please him.

"They and I," he stated, "do not act from the same motives or pursue the same objects. I have tried from the first since this War broke out, whether under the Premiership of my right hon. Friend opposite (Mr. Asquith) or under the present Prime Minister, to support the Government of the day in carrying the War to a successful conclusion. When these hon. Gentlemen can say the same, and not before, shall I desire their cheers or their approval."*u*

285

Thus there was hope that I might escape the fury of my enemies so long as they pursued me in opposite directions.

Lord Hugh Cecil took the opportunity to criticize me. He said:

"I listened with great attention to the Prime Minister. I think he has a very strong case in respect of propaganda. The case he makes, that these gentlemen whom he has appointed to be Ministers of Propaganda are indeed experts in that function, is a case that strongly appeals to the whole House.

"The only criticism that occurred to me about that matter is that the appointment of Lord Beaverbrook as Minister of Propaganda is only one of the honours which the Government has bestowed upon him.

"It sounds to me quite reasonable to say that Lord Beaverbrook is a great expert in propaganda, and should be entrusted, therefore, with the work he so well understands. But is he also so ideally well fitted to be a Peer of the Realm? Is he also so ideally well fitted to be Chancellor of the Duchy of Lancaster? The Chancellorship of the Duchy of Lancaster is an office of very considerable distinction. I believe it brings the Minister in close contact with the Sovereign, and it has a certain amount of ecclesiastical patronage.

"It is, of course, possible that Lord Beaverbrook is equally well fitted for that function as for propaganda, but I am a little suspicious, when I find that these various distinctions have been bestowed upon him, that there is probably some other motive at work leading the Government to honour him besides his fitness for the work of propaganda."ᵛ

My old friend and former Parliamentary colleague, the Irish Nationalist M.P., Tim Healy, came to my defence. He was one of the ablest parliamentarians; his sling was full of sharp and witty verbal stones. He now cast one at Lord Hugh.

"I do not know what religious duties there are attaching to the post of the Duchy of Lancaster," he observed, "and no doubt the Noble Lord (Lord Hugh Cecil), whose High Churchism is one of his most distinguished attributes, has some suspicion of Lord Beaverbrook in that respect.* But I can only say for myself that an abler man or a man of clearer mind and better judgement I have never met."ʷ

After this second debate, Bonar Law came to see me at my office. He told me that the temper of the House was entirely hostile to my appointment. He said it was doubtful if I could survive, and he advised me in the interests of the Administration to hand in my resignation.

I asked him to frame such a document in writing. After several attempts he handed me a draft which he thought might meet the situation.

Now, I was never given to retreat in the face of attack. And when Bonar Law informed me that the House of Lords was shortly to take up

---

* The Chancellor of the Duchy has much Church patronage. Tim Healy therefore referred to my Presbyterian allegiance.

the issue I knew that I could go there and make a very considerable defence, not only for myself but for my newspaper colleagues too. The prospect opened up possibilities.

Tim Healy responded at once to my call for advice. When he had examined the whole position and considered the proposed resignation as prepared by Bonar Law, he said to me: "Don't resign; wait until you're sacked."

That was counsel which was congenial to me. If I was to be wrecked along with the office which I had only that moment taken on, then I would sink to the bottom with my flag at the top of the mast.

It was said that Lord Salisbury and Lord Beresford would raise the issue in the House of Lords. I attended quite often while expecting a motion on the Order Paper.

I was determined to show myself to my foes, and to give them a chance to join battle at the earliest moment. But the hullabaloo died down. Members of the House of Commons became involved in other issues. Chamberlain by this time was carrying on conversations which resulted in his rejoining the Government. He had no difficulty at an early date in entering the War Cabinet and accepting these objectionable newspaper men as his colleagues.

Apart from the troubles that I ran into on political grounds, I had also difficulties springing from the jealousies of other departments. I was no sooner established as Minister of Information than I encountered organised, vigorous and determined opposition from within the Ministries. The War Office, Admiralty and the Foreign Office all joined together in determined resistance. There is always resistance when a new Ministry is created. There is always an outcry when the ribs are removed from the old Adam and set up in the new Eve. Here, however, three Ministries were involved. And three surgical operations were necessary to set up the new organisation. All these old-established Ministries must be persuaded or compelled to hand over their propaganda functions to the new Ministry.

What a hubbub! What a hullabaloo!

These service departments and the Foreign Office sought to hold on to their authority. With what skill and letter-writing activities they tried to defeat the prospects of the little Ministry struggling to draw a breath of life! These Ministries would not yield any measure of their powers or of their work to a new department. They resolutely held on to their own propaganda machines. The Foreign Office went so far as to make a successful raid upon the staff being built up by the new Ministry of Information.

Balfour, the Foreign Secretary, was convinced that the work contemplated by my propaganda department would dislocate entirely the intelligence branch, not only of the Foreign Office, but of the Admiralty and the War Office also.

Lord Robert Cecil, the Foreign Under Secretary, shared his opinion.

T

At the Admiralty the disposition of the First Lord (Sir Eric Geddes) was no more favourable to me.

Thus, at a time when I was seeking by new techniques to present Britain at war to her allies and neutrals, I found myself engaged in a remorseless battle with the departments. It was a battle without compensations.

It now appeared that I must abandon the contest, accept the rebuffs of the departments, and, in a word, allow my office to suffer the same fate as befell Neville Chamberlain at the Ministry of National Service or I must carry on the fight for independent authority. I was resolved that something must be achieved.

My efforts to interest Lloyd George in my Ministry's struggle had up till then met with no positive success. Now I determined to write a letter to the Prime Minister, offering my resignation and explaining my difficulties. I set out my case in some detail.

I explained that, since the appeal of the new Ministry must be to public opinion abroad and not to diplomatic representatives, its methods must be different. But the Foreign Office, refusing to recognise this, had obstructed almost every mission which the Ministry of Information proposed to despatch abroad. And from the War Cabinet no support was forthcoming. In these circumstances, I argued, either the Ministry of Information should be abolished or given an equal status with the Foreign Office in its propaganda operations abroad.

The outcome of this offer of resignation was that Lloyd George promised to intervene to establish a working arrangement between the Ministry of Information and other departments. But his efforts were of little avail. The obstinate resistance of the Foreign Office exceeded all expectations. Yet, at this time an incident occurred which illustrated the need for a clear and official delineation of authority.

It was in relation to the Jewish National Home in Palestine.

Lloyd George directed me to make much of the fall of Palestine and the Capture of Jerusalem. The event had little or no influence on the course of war on the Western Front. But "victory" was a blessed word and the deed gave the right to widespread use of the word.

In preparing propaganda material, particularly for distribution in America, I made full use of Balfour's declaration in support of a Jewish National Home, which he had issued in November 1917.

There arose at once a fierce outcry from one section of Jewry, objecting to this conception of a National Home for the Jewish people.

Edwin Montagu, Secretary of State for India, became the passionate exponent of this viewpoint in the Government. He regarded the Jews as a religious community and himself as a Jewish Englishman. To commit the Jews to the expression of a National Home was, he argued, to prejudice their civil rights in the country of their birth. How could he, Montagu asked, as Secretary of State for India, negotiate with the peoples of India on behalf of His Majesty's Government if the world understood that His Majesty's Government regarded his National Home as being in Turkish territory?

Montagu was one of my personal friends and I had respect for his judgement. He was settled in his political philosophy and tenacious in his advocacy of his faith.

Shortly I was called upon by Sir Charles Henry, an intimate friend of Lloyd George of long standing, and Mr. Lionel de Rothschild, both Members of Parliament and prominent figures in British Jewry, both anti-Zionist. They urged me to do nothing to encourage the idea of a Jewish National Home. Sir Charles Henry reported that in an interview the Prime Minister had given his assent to the anti-Zionist view. This was an important statement, since, if it were well founded, it would have involved me in a reorientation of official propaganda on Palestine.

I asked the Prime Minister for a clear ruling. He would not answer Yes or No.

A curt letter from the Foreign Secretary dismissed the claims of the anti-Zionists and disposed of their conversations with the Prime Minister.

Dear Beaverbrook,

The policy of His Majesty's Government in Palestine is that laid down by the Foreign Secretary in his last speech. Until it is altered officially, it is in no way affected by conversations between Sir Charles Henry and the Prime Minister.

Yours sincerely,
ARTHUR JAMES BALFOUR.*

Another curt letter addressed to the Prime Minister himself made complaint of my conduct in severe terms.

August 22nd, 1918.

My dear Prime Minister,

I am sorry to have to bother you when you are on holiday, but the question of the relationship between the Foreign Office and the Ministry of Information is becoming too difficult to allow the present position to continue.

As you know on November 2nd last year after prolonged discussion at Cabinet I wrote a letter setting out the policy of His Majesty's Government in regard to Zionism. The formula contained in the letter had been approved by the Cabinet.

I now find that Beaverbrook has written to you on the subject asking for a clear direction on Jewish policy. He states that he has done so because Sir Charles Henry told him that he had laid certain arguments before you which had impressed you and which you were taking into consideration; and meanwhile Zionist propaganda is being suspended. I need not go into the Zionist and anti-Zionist arguments. They were discussed at considerable length in Cabinet last year; but I think you will agree that an incident of this kind necessitates an immediate decision as to the distribution of functions of the Foreign Office and the Ministry of Information.

Yours sincerely,
ARTHUR JAMES BALFOUR.*

Lloyd George wrote a soft answer which gives the impression Sir Charles Henry was not entirely wrong in his interpretation of the conversation with the Prime Minister.

Brynawelon, Criccieth.
27th August, 1918.

My dear Foreign Secretary,

Your letter on Propaganda followed me down here. I quite agree that the position must be regularised, otherwise friction and misunderstanding are inevitable. I hope to be back on Friday. We can discuss the question either that day or some early day next week.

As to the Jewish policy, Henry has, I am afraid, misinterpreted the statement I made to him and his fellow anti-Zionists. I am not quite sure what he said, but I gather from your letter that he must have given a false impression of my conversation with him and Lord Swaythling when I met them some weeks ago, at their request, to hear their views.

I have always been a strong supporter of your policy on the question of Zionism and nothing that was said by Henry, Swaythling, or Philip Magnus in the least affected my opinions.

Ever sincerely,
D.Ll.G.[3]

At the beginning of August my Ministry again encountered stormy weather. I was told that a violent attack was going to be launched against me in the House of Commons, on the motion of Leif Jones. Many others were to join in the assault on 5th August, and I was to be "wrecked".

Having been attacked twice before in a brief period of office, I resented the injustice. The post was difficult enough in any case.

The assault was apparently to be based on some charges made in the *Westminster Gazette* that I was "a capitalist", and that my heads of departments were "capitalists".

Bonar Law would not take up the task of replying for me on the ground that our friendship was so close that his remarks might not seem impartial. He deputed the business to Stanley Baldwin, in whose parliamentary experience I had no confidence. As it turned out, I was wrong there, for Baldwin made a very good speech in my defence.

Feeling, therefore, thoroughly worried about the whole business, I wired to Tim Healy in Dublin to come over and help me. He reached my country house on Sunday, 4th August, having kept me in suspense by wiring that he would arrive "shortly after Mass"—a phrase which left me in doubt as to the time of his appearance.

When at last he came, he gave me small comfort. I wanted to show him all the documents I had accumulated for my defence. Healy put me off, talking about everything else as we wandered about the garden.

I pressed him hard to discuss the matter seriously, and asked what line he intended to take. He put me off until after lunch, when he had taken some claret. I reopened my case. He brushed my defence aside.

"Whatever line I take tomorrow," he said, "will have nothing to do with a prepared case. I shall watch the House and decide."

I tried again after dinner and champagne. He would not listen.

He laughed at my anxiety. He refused to look at the documents which I had gathered together for the purpose of supporting my defence.

"Leif Jones," he said, "is a teetotaller and can't hurt a fly. He's one of those who tried to stop the tot of rum to the soldiers in the trenches. I killed that move, and I'll checkmate him to-morrow."

"But how?" I enquired.

"Well," he said, "Neil Primrose once was angry with Lord Loreburn, the Lord Chancellor, and felt sure he would force him to resign over the non-appointment of Liberal magistrates, as Lloyd George was behind Neil. Loreburn telegraphed for me as you have done, and laid all his cards on the table at breakfast before the debate came on, and though Neil had a good case, and many Liberals were strongly with him, I beat them, for Loreburn had stood by Ireland in the old days."

I got little satisfaction out of this, and early in the morning of the next day I called on Bonar Law and told him that Tim Healy would fail me. He would not listen to my case. Bonar Law said he would stand by. This promise comforted me.

Leif Jones made his attack on the expected lines, describing me as a "menace to national freedom and Free Trade"; he spoke of a film for which my Ministry had some responsibility, *The Man Who Saved the Empire*. "Who is he?" asked Leif Jones. "It is in Lord Beaverbrook's power to decide that.

TIM HEALY AND BEAVERBROOK. Arnold Bennett is at the extreme left.

He can put the Prime Minister . . . or Admiral Beatty . . . or Lord Beaverbrook.

"Is it true," he asked, "that Lord Beaverbrook wishes to take over the control of the war correspondents at the front? . . . He wants to control . . . the news to be flashed all over the world. . . . A power like that . . . is most dangerous to this country. There is talk of a daily newspaper being provided [by the Government] for soldiers. It that is to be like the films . . . it will be used for propaganda purposes. . . . A General Election is coming along. Is this newspaper to contain propaganda for the electors at the front?"[aa]

After Leif Jones came some pretty wild accusations from Mr. Pringle, the Scottish Radical.

As a matter of fact, most of what they tried to lay at my door had happened when Lord Carson from the War Cabinet had general control of propaganda.

Tim Healy would occasionally interject, "That was done in Carson's time."

Mr. Baldwin rose in my defence. "We have proof," he said, "that the work being done by the Ministry of Information is being well appreciated now, because, during the summer, there have been articles in some of the German papers to the effect that admirable work is being done now by English propaganda and suggesting that the Germans should organise themselves as efficiently."[ab]

He displayed a keen appreciation of the mood of the House in making his defence of me personally. I quote his summing up: "The Minister of

Information is a man of very strong personality. Men with strong personalities have this in common, that the magnetism which comes with that personality either attracts or repels. . . . I want to say this in all seriousness. Lord Beaverbrook has taken on a most difficult, delicate and thankless task. Do not let his pitch be queered. Give him a fair chance and judge him by results."[ac]

But as the debate was going, it was likely that I would be judged on the trend of the discussion rather than on results, and this was not likely to be satisfactory. For if a whole discussion turns on one man, more charges are made than can possibly be answered—and a bad atmosphere is created.

Then Healy spoke.

He wanted to know what all this nonsense was about. It was a waste of time in war. Anyhow, what had Carson done when he was in charge of Propaganda? And if that was all Carson had done it would not have mattered much.

But Carson had made his department an organ for anti-Irish propaganda and filled it with his nominees from Trinity College, Dublin. The result had been the absolute ruin of Irish recruiting. He spoke passionately in exposition of the whole Irish case.

On this, the vials of inter-Irish wrath were poured forth. Mr. Ronald McNeill intervened to defend Carson. Mr. Shortt, Chief Secretary for Ireland, was brought up to make a lengthy statement on behalf of the Government.

The debate was abruptly switched off from the discussion of my supposed iniquities, and a regular Irish squabble ensued. By the time Mr. Devlin had summed up for the Nationalists, the speeches of Leif Jones and Pringle had been completely forgotten, and the question of the Ministry of Information and its chief had faded out of the picture.

Healy's performance was a perfect exhibition of Parliamentary tactics.

Later Healy joined me at the Hyde Park Hotel. He said, "Get me some pea-soup and a steak and a bottle of beer, and I will tell you the fun."

After this debate my life as Minister ran a more even course. One of my most dangerous critics in Parliament, Austen Chamberlain, now a member of the administration, made no more trouble for me. Northcliffe gave me his newspaper support when criticism broke out in public.

There was an interlude when I got into difficulties over the publication in the *Daily Express* of the dismissal of Lord Derby, who, as I have told, was banished to the Embassy in Paris.

It was easy to understand the complaint of Lord Stamfordham on behalf of the King. But I was in a position to answer that I had nothing to do with the disclosure.

At the end of August the *Daily Express* printed a leading article about a proposal for a General Election in terms which irritated the Prime Minister.

"We do not want a new Khaki Election. We

cannot vote in the dark. If the Prime Minister seeks re-election as head of a Coalition Government which is to endure, he must satisfy those who are to vote for him that his views and theirs are the same. . . .

"What, for instance, is the Prime Minister's programme on Tariff Reform and Imperial Preference? . . . What would be the Irish policy of the Government which hopes to be returned? Is the Welsh Church to be sacrificed simply because the Party of Spoilers just tottering to its fall over the Irish Crisis of 1914 was saved for a moment by the outbreak of the Great War?"[ad]

From Lloyd George's point of view, the offence of the article was that it referred to his political dilemma: he had to cling to his Free Trade principles on account of his Liberal following, but the Conservative element in his Coalition wished to have tariffs included in the election platform. Lloyd George wrote indignantly to Bonar Law:

> Have you seen the leader in to-day's *Daily Express*? That is Max. Having regard to the risks I ran for him and the way I stood up for him when he was attacked by his own Party, I regard this as a mean piece of treachery. It explains why no man in any Party trusts Max.
>
> The reference to the Welsh Church is deliberately introduced to make it impossible for me to arrange matters with the Unionist [Conservative] leaders.
>
> I am sorry, for I have sincerely tried to work with him.[ae]

Winston Churchill came to see me. He asked if I took responsibility for the substance of the

Private   *seen by C / 8*   Verchocq

8. 9. 18

My dear Bonar,

Please see enclosed. A Nitrate negotiator is not without honour save in his own country & from his own Treasury.

Look after Max or he will make a gt mistake wh all of us & he most of all will have cause to regret.

Ever yours,

Winston S. Churchill

THE CHURCHILL LETTER TO BONAR LAW. "Look after Max."

leader. I judged his enquiry came from the Prime Minister. And I felt compelled to reply in defence of the editor, who had been encouraged by me on all occasions to promote and expound the doctrine of tariff reform and imperial preference.

On 8th September Churchill wrote to Bonar Law:

> Look after Max, or he will make a great mistake which all of us and he most of all will have cause to regret.[af]

Churchill was, of course, the real leader of the Liberal free-trade element in the Government. They all feared greatly that the policy of imperial preference would be promoted by me into an election issue, thus cutting across the Coalition structure. Hence his letter to Bonar Law.

I surely needed looking after. But not by Bonar Law. At the end of October I was stricken by an unusual and serious infection known as actinomycosis. I resigned. And I felt like the prisoner of old who was freed from the chains and the ball of servitude, even though I was compelled for more than six months to devote every hour and all of my physical resources to conquering an affliction which seldom spares its victims.

Twenty-two years after and in the Second War I had another term of duty. But that calls for another volume, on another day.

The final debate on the Ministry of Information occupied the time and attention of the House of Commons on 7th November, 1918.

The occasion was of little importance. Criticism or praise counted for nothing. The labour was over. The work was done. The blinds were pulled down; the doors were closed. Sir Edward Carson, however, took the opportunity to intervene in the debate. He had nothing to say about the Ministry.

Just as Healy had made an attack on Carson on my appearance in Parliament at the last debate, so now Carson made a bitter and vituperative assault on Northcliffe.

Baldwin answered for the Government. He made no defence of Northcliffe. For me he had words of warm praise.

"I should like to say, what I am sure the Committee will endorse, that the combination of rare vision he has shown, with ability to master details, has enabled that Department, in spite of much criticism it has received, to form itself in the short time it has had, and to become an engine this year that has really done most valuable work for the Allied cause and done it at a reasonable expense."[ag]

Sir Hamar Greenwood, a Liberal Member, who had been a critic of my appointment, told the House:

"When Lord Beaverbrook was appointed Minister of Information many people expected that things would not go right. I am, myself, only an acquaintance of Lord Beaverbrook, but I am bound to confess this, that his career at the Ministry of Information has been one of the most successful careers of any Minister in this

Coalition Government. He actually rescued from the Germans the neutral countries and America by launching out on a system of propaganda the success of which can be vouched for by everybody who has been in those countries both before the Ministry was established and since its work has commenced."[ab]

A final tribute came from a strange source. In *My War Memories* General Erich von Ludendorff said:

"We were hypnotised by the enemy propaganda as a rabbit is by a snake. It was exceptionally clever, and conceived on a great scale. It worked by strong mass-suggestion, kept in the closest touch with the military situation, and was unscrupulous as to the means it used.

". . . While Entente propaganda was doing ever more harm to the German people and the army and navy, it succeeded in maintaining the determination to fight in its own countries and armies, and in working against us in neutral countries. . . . In the neutral countries we were subject to a sort of moral blockade. . . .

"In England the whole propaganda service was placed under Lord Beaverbrook, with three directors, of whom Lord Northcliffe attended to the enemy countries, Kipling to home and colonial propaganda, and Lord Rothermere* to the work in neutral countries. . . ."[ai]

* Rothermere joined the Ministry of Information after his retirement from the office of Secretary of State for Air. His support was of immense value.

CHAPTER X

HIS ROYAL POMP*

THE last political crisis of the war, and this time a crisis of which no whisper reached the outer world. The crisis which may be called: Lord Curzon and "Hang the Kaiser!"

The public outcry for Hanging the Kaiser resounded throughout the land. It was a favourite subject for speeches and much attention was given to the Emperor and the Rope in the political meetings up and down the country.

Now that all the dust of those ancient struggles has settled, it is difficult to realize how important the issue of "Hang the Kaiser" became. But the truth is that Lloyd George's Government won the 1918 general election on two slogans—one, "Hang the Kaiser"; the other "Make Germany Pay". Both had a powerful appeal to a public which was sick of the war and unable to tolerate the notion that the victory would yield no material spoil.†

It is easy now to see that "Hang the Kaiser" was an emotional outcry. At the end of 1918 and in the

---

* His Royal Pomp was the title given to His Excellency the Marquess Curzon of Kedleston, K.G., G.C.S.I., M.A., P.C., F.R.S., D.C.L., L.L.D., J.P., D.L., by the American Ambassador in writing to President Wilson.

† An official statement from Downing Street set forth five election pledges. The first was Punish the Kaiser and the second, Make Germany Pay.

months immediately following, it was a serious factor in British politics. Business men might be impressed by the notion of an indemnity. The vast public were more concerned with putting the Kaiser's neck in a noose.

At the December election, candidates made ample use of this vote-catching issue. Lloyd George's huge majority was to a large extent founded on the popularity of the Hanging Craze. On that account any suspicion that Lloyd George's Government was weakening on the issue roused the whole House and threatened the Prime Minister's position. The issue became, in time, a real crisis—a crisis flowing from the war although breaking out after it was ended.

Lloyd George himself gave encouragement to the slogan. He was strengthened in his enthusiasm for this sound election plank by the vigorous denunciations of the German Emperor which flowed from the Curzon chamber.

Two days after the Armistice, Curzon wrote of it to the Prime Minister.

Public opinion will not willingly consent to let this arch-criminal escape by a final act of cowardice. The supreme and colossal nature of the crime seems to call for some supreme and unprecedented condemnation. Execution, imprisonment, these are not, or may not be, necessary. But continued life, an inglorious and ignoble exile under the weight of such a sentence as has never before been given in the history of mankind, would be a penance worse than death.[a] *

* For the full text of the letter, see *Appendix IV* No. 17.

On 20th November, 1918, Curzon, after consulting Clemenceau, demanded that the Kaiser and the German Crown Prince should both be brought to trial. The proposal fell in admirably with the Prime Minister's own inclinations. He agreed with Curzon, while Churchill, supported by Milner, was against it. Churchill would never give his support to anything that savoured of regicide. So far as he was concerned, monarchs were safe from the gallows.

The decision to try the Emperor was accepted by the Allies and embodied in the Peace Treaty. As the Kaiser had taken refuge in the Netherlands, that country was now invited to extradite him.

Thus Lloyd George was supported by the terms of the Peace Treaty. He would not deviate from his harsh and stern purpose. Churchill and Milner might absent themselves on the Day of Judgment. But, after all, there was Curzon. But not for long.

For Curzon listened to the King, and the King had received a memorial from three German princes, the King of Saxony, the Duke of Württemberg and the Grand-Duke of Baden, calling upon him in the name of "all unanimously thinking German Princes" with an urgent appeal, and more serious, with a warning, that should His Majesty, by tolerating the Kaiser's trial, lay hands "on the Royal Dignity of a great and at one time friendly and related Ruler, then every official authority, every throne (including the English throne) will be threatened".[b]

The King referred the memorial to the Foreign

Secretary and the Prime Minister. Lord Curzon considered it "impertinent" in tone and substance and held that no reply should be returned. The King did not share this firm view. He felt himself bound to send an answer back to his fellow monarchs. And, in due course, a change came over Curzon's attitude. A remarkable change!

For when Lloyd George announced in the House of Commons in July 1919[c] that the trial of the Kaiser would take place in London, Curzon at once began to raise every conceivable objection to the plan.

He wrote to Lloyd George an elaborate and what can only be described as hysterical composition, conjuring up the embarrassment of the Royal Family at finding their cousin up for trial within their precincts, where he had often stayed; depicting with vivid strokes the English crowd, either incommoded by the Kaiser's occupation of Hampton Court Palace or, alternatively, depressed by the shadow of despondency and gloom that would be caused by his presence in Westminster; and picturing finally the permanent and far-reaching resentment of Germany against Great Britain for this act of vengeance.

> Never mind that the Court is International [he warned], the verdict will be regarded as having been inspired, just as in all probability it will have to be executed, by ourselves. Would it be possible ever again to make friends with Germany after that? Would not it be a root of bitterness which would last till the end of time?[d] *

*The full text is reproduced in *Appendix IV*, No. 18.

Finally Curzon turned his indignation upon Holland. With the Kaiser already within her boundaries, was she not shelving her responsibilities in refusing to hold the trial there?

This passionate document failed to inspire Lloyd George. Indeed it moved him to very considerable anger, and he replied to Curzon, rebuking him in the strongest terms for his reversal of opinion.

July 8, 1919.

My dear Lord President,

The arguments you advance in your letter against trying the Kaiser in England I had already heard from the King—every one of them. I therefore assume it was the result of a conversation which you had with H.M. I can hardly, however, believe that it was his suggestion that the Cabinet should be invited to throw over its principal delegate at the Peace Conference in an important decision which he had taken on their behalf and which he had already announced to the House of Commons. If it is raised in the Cabinet I hope, at any rate, it will be after my return ...

All the reasons which you assign are really arguments against trying the Kaiser at all. You tell me that Churchill and Milner agreed with you. Of course they did; they were firmly opposed to a trial. They are, therefore, quite consistent in their attitude. You, on the other hand, took the initiative in proposing his trial. The proposal you made was ultimately adopted by the Cabinet, pressed on their behalf on our Allies, and ultimately adopted by them after a full investigation by a very able Commission* representing the leading Allies, including Belgium. To go back on it now would indeed be not only to make the representatives of this country at the Paris Conference look

* Commission on the Responsibility of the Authors of the War.

silly, but to make Britain, France, Belgium and all the other Allies look extremely foolish. . . .

. . . . .

I took the action which was the natural sequence of decisions arrived at deliberately after long reflection and discussion by the Cabinet, and I do not like the idea of running away from them at the first difficulties that present themselves. . . .

Ever sincerely,
D. LLOYD GEORGE.*

It was a stinging rebuke, an insulting reply which would have driven most Ministers to hand in their resignation forthwith. Not so Lord Curzon. He remained in office unabashed. And his will, in due course, prevailed. For the Kaiser was never brought to trial. The Dutch refused to give him up. And the Allies, with varying degrees of relief and annoyance, accepted this refusal and dropped the matter.

The incident is of interest now mainly because of the light it throws on the character of Lord Curzon. What a strange man he was! And how much the reality of the man was at variance with his public reputation. For he gave the impression that his views were rigid and inflexible. Yet he had a talent for being on both sides of every controversy.

Before the outcry over "Hang the Kaiser", there had been many striking examples of Lord Curzon's capacity to carry out an agile if undignified and belated *volte face*.

The worst of all Curzon's contradictions in public life relates to the fall of Asquith.

From the outset of the first Coalition Curzon became Asquith's most active supporter in the Tory ranks. He was out-and-out an Asquith man. This was the impression in political circles and was held by Asquith himself. In the political crisis of December, 1916, it was assumed by Conservatives and Liberals alike that Lord Curzon gave his support to the Prime Minister, Asquith.

There is, however, evidence produced after the event, and now at our disposal, which reveals how Curzon, in the critical days before the fall of Asquith's Government, played an increasingly ambiguous part.

On the one hand we find him writing to his Tory colleague Lord Lansdowne on Sunday, 3rd December, describing the happenings of the Unionist meeting that afternoon.

It had been decided, he said, that Bonar Law should tell the Prime Minister that internal reconstruction of the Government was no longer possible and that Asquith should hand his resignation to the King. Should he not be willing to take that step, the Unionists would place the whole of their resignations in his hands.

"Had one felt," Curzon confided, "that reconstitution by and under the present Prime Minister was possible, we should all have preferred to try it. But we know that with him as Chairman, either of the Cabinet or the War Committee, it is absolutely impossible to win the War, and it will be for himself and Lloyd George to determine whether he goes out altogether or becomes Lord Chancellor or Chancellor of the Exchequer in a new Government, a nominal Premiership being a protean compromise which, in our view, could have no endurance."*

Yet at the same time he appeared to be working openly and actively for Asquith. Indeed, only a few hours later, on the Monday morning, Curzon despatched a friendly note of reassurance to the Prime Minister. I reproduce it here.

> 1 Carlton House Terrace,
> December 4th, 1916.

My dear Henry,
Lansdowne has, I think, explained to you that my resignation yesterday was far from having the sinister purport which I believe you were inclined to attribute to it. However, I have not written to emphasize that but to strike a note of gaiety in a world of gloom. Just now I recalled these lines of Matthew Arnold—I cannot remember in what poem:

> *We in some unknown Power's employ*
> *Move in a rigorous line;*
> *Can neither when we will enjoy*
> *Nor when we will resign.*

We are hourly expecting you to facilitate the process by asking for our seals.

> Yours ever,
> CURZON.[8]

In other words, Curzon was inviting Asquith to ask for the Seals of his Ministers just as he

* The full text of the letter is reproduced in *Appendix IV*, No. 19.

had required their Seals in 1915. Thus Asquith was to remain Prime Minister, selecting a new slate of Ministers.

Was not this, Curzon's critics ask, the limit of political cynicism? Asquith's biographers judge it so. "If the two letters were not in evidence," they write, "it would scarcely seem possible that they were written by the same hand."[b]

Asquith therefore continued to be lulled into a false sense of security. Not surprisingly. For on that critical Monday the Three C's—Cecil, Chamberlain * and Curzon—making Lord Curzon their spokesman, called on the Prime Minister at Downing Street. Lord Crewe, in his Memorandum on the crisis, has confirmed that these powerful Conservatives came, not to disclaim their fealty to Asquith but rather to explain that their consent to the Unionist resolution calling on him to resign "in no way indicated a wish that he should retire. On the contrary, they did not believe that anybody else could form a Government, certainly not Mr. Lloyd George; so that the result would be the return of the Prime Minister with a stronger Government and a greatly enhanced position."[i]

It was this apparent reinforcement that led Asquith to count noses among his supporters and to believe that his position was impregnable. Curzon's firm assurance that neither he nor the Tory Ministers for whom he was acting would take office under Lloyd George or Bonar Law[j] confirmed him in his confidence.

* Austen Chamberlain denies that he saw Asquith on the Monday.

Yet so swift and dramatic were the events of those few days, that when the Lloyd George Government was successfully formed on 7th December, Lord Curzon's participation in that administration had already been secured. He had accepted office as Lord President of the Council and as a member of the small War Cabinet.

His pledge to Asquith was ignored; nor did he delay to consult with his faithful Tory colleagues. An appeal to his patriotism from Lloyd George's envoy had clinched the matter.*

It is clearly difficult to understand a move of such startling swiftness. What is certain is that Curzon emerged elevated by the crisis, and that few men could have executed a feat of such political duality and daring.

Although Lord Curzon proved a valuable addition to the War Cabinet, from time to time he reverted to his habit of steering two opposing courses. Therefore, at the height of the military controversy, we find him at one moment defending the soldiers' cause, advising Lloyd George to seek co-operation with General Robertson and urging moderation on military issues in the House;[j] yet three months later, Curzon was supporting the Prime Minister in his dismissal of the same General Robertson, though at that moment encouraging Lord Derby in resistance.

* Lord Crewe, Asquith's foremost colleague and supporter, whose account of the December crisis has been accepted by Asquith and published in his *Memories and Reflections*,[k] wrote to me in October, 1928: "The prompt agreement of Curzon and one or two others to take part in the Government at the end of 1916 has always stood in need of some explanation after what they had previously said to Asquith. And it is quite true that Curzon gave the reason which you mention, that he was told it would be unpatriotic to decline at that moment of crisis.'

Such was the extraordinary nature of this man that no decision of his on a point of policy could be regarded as irrevocable. Again and again he would throw over a cause with which he had been long and publicly identified without sign or warning—leaving his supporters stunned and dishevelled in the sudden gust of his departure.

Curzon's acts of desertion plainly expose him to the charge of political expediency. But there were also times when in his reversal of thought he himself exhibited no outward recognition of the change. His feelings on the question of the Coalition fell into this category.

In February, 1918, Lord Curzon addressed a letter to Bonar Law on the problem of continuing the Lloyd George Coalition Government after the end of hostilities. He flatly rejected the suggestion.

> I should like to say at once that the movement is one which not only can I not support, but which I think to be entirely mistaken. As matters stand, I agree that if there were to be a General Election in the near future, it would be the duty of our party to give the fullest support to the Prime Minister for the prosecution of the war to the end—the object, indeed the sole object, for which the Coalition was formed and still exists. But, from the idea that our party should merge its identity in some new party, or should pledge its allegiance after peace has returned, I entirely dissent and I hope that you as our Leader will give no encouragement to it.[m]

But in November, a different view had replaced his earlier misgivings. He wrote to Bonar Law:

AUSTEN CHAMBERLAIN AND CURZON. Both stumbled on the threshold of 10 Downing Street. Disappointment was their portion.

One thing is certain, viz., That the old party pro-grammes are obsolete. Asquith's attempt to serve up the stale dishes of his—and the reception it has met with—are sufficient proof of this."

Curzon had changed his mind again. If not his mind, then his allegiance. He changed it because Lloyd George asked. A letter of 12th November, 1918, written to the Prime Minister from Paris, where Curzon was staying at the British Embassy, closes with this message:

I wrote to Bonar [Law] as you suggested about General Election.°

Lloyd George often dragged the portly Curzon, the President of the Council, round and round the political arena at the tail of his chariot.

Perhaps the most amazing decision was taken by Curzon during the dispute over Turkey. Throughout the discussion in Office and among his colleagues, the Foreign Secretary (Curzon) opposed with powerful and consistent argument the pro-Greek, anti-Turkish policy of His Majesty's Ministers.

The moment he was overborne, he changed his attitude and took part to the fullest extent in the very course which he had rejected and denounced.

Could a man of such political contradictions be taken seriously? The answer is that he could be, and was.

The Unionist Peers may have resented Cur-zon's abandonment of them over the Parliament Bill in 1911; the Carlton Club may have been

disconcerted and estranged by his sudden surrender over the suffrage cause, but in the event
both proved to be matters where Curzon's decision
put him on the right side of majority opinion of
the day. He was a political jumping-jack, but a
weary acrobat who was still called upon to
take part in the circus performance.

There was also about Lord Curzon a suspicion of
humbug, which sometimes amused but more often
annoyed his colleagues. This showed itself in
several ways.

In March, 1917, Bonar Law was asked in the
House how many state-owned cars were at the
disposal of Lord Curzon; he replied that a certain
number of cars were at the disposal of Government officials engaged in the discharge of their
duties: "Any member of the War Cabinet is at
liberty to indent upon this reserve for the use of
a car when required for official purposes only."*

Thus Lord Curzon was cleared of the implicit
charge that he was using official cars for private
purposes. But not all of his colleagues were
persuaded of the righteousness of his conduct.
On the very day that Bonar Law gave his answer
in the House, Lord Derby, Secretary of State for
War, political head of the department controlling
the pool of motor-cars, wrote to Bonar Law:

> War Office,
> Whitehall, S.W.
> *Personal & Confidential.*   5th March, 1917.
> Dear Bonar Law,
>   I am sorry for going away, but I really could not
> stand hearing George Curzon talk, and I did not want

to enter into incriminations. As a matter of fact he has behaved disgracefully about the car, and it is undoubtedly his own fault that there is any trouble. There was a car placed at the disposal of the Air Board, but when I was Chairman I never once used it. When Curzon came to the Air Board he calmly took it for himself. He talks about it being for general use, but I should doubt a single soul having been in it except himself and his guests. He motors them down to Hackwood and uses the car for sending to the Station for his Saturday-to-Monday parties, and I should like to have asked him whether it is not true on the occasion of his Dance the other night the car came backwards and forwards to London three times. I am sure he would never deny that Lady Curzon invariably uses it, and he himself admitted to me that although he was ill in bed he had sent for the car in order to send a note down to Mrs. Harry Cust. Now this is a scandalous abuse of a Government car and needless to say makes everybody talk. He was to say the least of it incorrect as to what happened about the car in the beginning. I am going to try and find his letter, but he wrote to me, if I remember rightly, to say that the Prime Minister had authorised him to have a car. It now turns out that he telephoned to the Prime Minister to know whether he could have one and got no answer. He then told me that he meant to keep the Air Board car. I told him that was entirely a matter of agreement between him and the Air Board, but a second car would have to be supplied and it did not make the least difference which it went to, upon which he telephoned to Cowdray* (Cowdray told me this himself) to say that I had agreed, with the Prime Minister's consent, to his keeping his present car. It is very amusing his saying that his health can only be kept going by being able to go to Trent every Satur-

---

* Lord Cowdray was President of the Air Board from January to November, 1917.

day or Monday. He has only had Trent since he married.

I am going to try and get out for you the amount of petrol that he has consumed in that car since he has had it, and I think it will be surprising. Of course he kept on quoting me, and it is quite true that both in peace time as well as in war, there is a car which is supposed to be the Secretary of State's, and I do have the same car, but if that is wanted for any other military duty I should go without, and it probably will be wanted as we have to supply cars for all our Colonial Conference visitors. The real truth is he is just what he *says* he is not. He is one of the meanest men that I know. He was a tenant of mine at one time and I have good reason for knowing it.

Yours v. sincerely,

DERBY.[q]

These were bitter words, with personal resentment behind them. They were tough. Yet they illustrate how Curzon was disliked by his colleagues.

Allowance must be made for Derby's hostility to Lord Curzon. Indeed, more than a year after the motor-car dispute there was discord between them. The Lord President of the Council (Curzon) wrote to the Prime Minister while staying at the British Embassy in Paris in November 1918:

I received your orders on Sunday to stay on here in case any War Cabinet questions required to be decided. Derby was very much irritated at this. He is a sensitive person and has not shown much pleasure at my presence even though I am a guest in his house.[o]

The next day, however, Curzon's feudal spirit was uppermost. The Prime Minister was informed that Curzon's presence was required by the Belgian King when he re-entered his kingdom. On 13th November, 1918, Curzon wrote to Lloyd George:

> I have just heard from the King of the Belgians that the Queen and he re-enter Brussels on Saturday. Lady Curzon and I have always promised to be with them on that day and accordingly we are returning to Belgium by motor tomorrow for this ceremony and shall be back in England on Monday.'

The journey to the Belgians was interrupted. Lloyd George summoned the traveller to return to his own native land.

Now Curzon was to win laurels for himself. Wilson, the American President, who was journeying to Paris, refused to come to England. It was intimated to him that the King and Queen would invite him and his wife to Buckingham Palace. Wilson, however, would not have any political entanglements with Britain. Then it was that Lord Curzon concocted a plan which he rightly thought was certain to bring the American President to "this sceptred isle, set in a silver sea". And what a plan. He wrote to Lloyd George on 12th November, 1918:

> I think I helped to solve the problem of getting Wilson to come to England on his way to Paris. For, a little before leaving London I had got my University of Oxford to vote him an honorary degree and to ask him to deliver the Romanes Lecture. As soon as I told

House this he said it was the one thing the President would love and that it would bring him to England without fail—giving him an academic rather than a political excuse for his visit. He accordingly wired at once to Wilson and has no doubt of his acceptance.

Curzon captured his man, and "my" University gave Wilson his degree.

Unjust claims have been put forward on behalf of Lord Northcliffe. An American life of Wilson recounts that Northcliffe was entitled to a share of the glory. But Curzon cannot be deprived of his credit. He worked the racket all by himself.

Curzon's patronage indeed extended far behind "his Oxford". He embraced in his arms Eton and the Order of the Garter. A letter written to Lloyd George in 1918 gave a clear indication of the extent of his protectorate.

P.M.

I see in the papers that Dr. Warre is about to resign the Provostship of Eton. As an old Etonian I hope I may be consulted before you fill it. On the hypothesis that the vacancy would occur in his time Asquith often spoke to me about it.

It is an important appt. & difficult to fill & will require a good deal of consideration.

Perhaps also later on when the time comes you will speak to me about the Garter vacant by the death of the Duke of Northumberland.

The Leader of the House of Lords is rather closely interested in these matters.

C.'

Curzon was capable of malice, though often dressed up in satire or ridicule. His characteristic disposition is revealed in a letter to Lady Curzon written on 5th November, 1923, the day of the funeral of his friend and colleague Andrew Bonar Law.

My darling girl,

I have just come back from the Abbey funeral of Bonar. It was rather a sombre performance; and one could not help thinking that many of the congregation were wondering how poor old Bonar ever got there. I met Burnham afterwards and asked him what the general sentiment on the subject was. He said that everyone knew it to be absurd; but that the Press had been stampeded by Beaverbrook who as soon as the breath was out of poor Bonar's body, turned on the full blast of the Rothermere cum Beaverbrook furnace and practically forced the entire Press into line. He concurred in thinking that in a month or two Bonar would be completely forgotten, and that in days to come people would ask who he was and how he ever got there. When we marched down from the Choir to the Nave—where a little casket containing his ashes (for he had been cremated) was let down into a small hole in the pavement, shaped like this— I found myself near the Prince of Wales. He fidgeted and looked about; never once turned a glance to the grave or the coffin, and showed himself profoundly bored with the whole performance. Of course cremation has the advantage of saving a great deal of space and thereby admitting of many future interments. But it has its ridiculous side. For a sham coffin was carried under a great white pall and deposited on a catafalque before the Sanctuary in the earlier part of the service and subsequently borne to the grave, where it was put on one side and disappeared, everyone knowing that there was no body in it at all."

This was one side of Curzon's nature. There was another. Lord Curzon was a hard-working and devoted public servant providing his own interests did not clash with the public concern. He was equipped with good understanding, a certain measure of native cunning, and an immense capacity for believing what suited his own interests.

His years in India as Viceroy had increased his endowment of pomposity, and also his measure of knowledge of conditions in the Far East. He was a real authority on native politics there.

In foreign affairs Curzon's standing was held on high by his sure grasp of the subject. Unfortunately, in his contacts with foreign potentates his manner did not correspond with his matter. In Cabinet councils he was a powerful and vigorous force.

Lord Curzon was endowed with immense social gifts. He was an entrancing conversationalist, bringing to the dinner table humour, wit, satire and plenty of malice. As an orator he was a good performer, and the painted chamber was just about the size to retain his pompous diction and his rolling periods. But to find yourself in a room with Lord Curzon was to suffer the feeling that you were being jostled mentally or physically or both. The outward sweep of the hands reminded the onlooker, like other aspects of his life, that his crest was "a popinjay rising with wings extended".

He was disliked by his colleagues, yet admired by them. He was a ceaseless intriguer. His ambition was to be leader of the Tory Party. He wished to share the crown of joint party leadership with Bonar Law, as Lord Lansdowne had done. He was always furious because he could not succeed. Only one position would have satisfied Curzon's sense of what was due to his talents and industry —the Premiership. And for four and a half hours in 1923, during the journey from Yeovil to London, Lord Curzon believed himself Prime Minister of Britain. But after he arrived at Paddington he discovered that the King had chosen as successor to Bonar Law—Stanley Baldwin.

CHAPTER XI

THE HERO

THE war was over. Lloyd George was now the most powerful man in Europe. His fame would endure for ever. He was admired and praised in all countries. His prestige in the United States was so high that men said he would be elected as their President if he could run for office there.

He had beaten his German enemies in the war. He had scattered and destroyed his British enemies at the polls in the course of a General Election which disclosed an overwhelming popular judgement in his favour. Hardly any political opponent escaped. They had fallen like autumn leaves.

It is not now possible to realise the immense position of this man Lloyd George. He had risen to such heights that only his contemporaries can understand the pre-eminence he enjoyed. Winston Churchill, whose fame has endured, never reached such a position. And the electors in 1945 showed it clearly.

When Lloyd George arrived in Paris for the Peace Conference he at once took control. He really dominated the French Prime Minister

Clemenceau. He had immense authority with President Wilson. He was giving the law to Europe, fixing the boundaries of all the nations, giving out encouragement to some countries and severely reprimanding others. He was the arbiter of all Europe.

Bonar Law said of him, "He can be Prime Minister for life if he likes." And Bonar Law's judgement was firmly and rightly based on the facts of the situation.

In June, 1919, after the signing of the Peace Treaty, on Lloyd George's return to London he was received by the King, who drove with him through the streets to Buckingham Palace. The public reception was a delirious event.

Churchill, Secretary of State for War, recommended that the Prime Minister should be awarded the Distinguished Service Order. The recommendation was rejected. Churchill was never easily put off. In October he wrote to the King that the Army Council wished Lloyd George to have the war medals.

The Palace resisted. The King thought that Asquith should be on the same footing as Lloyd George. He objected that it would be difficult to give the medals to Lloyd George and ignore the other ministers.[a] Nor, it appeared, was he entirely persuaded that the inspiration had come from the Army Council. But he was awkwardly placed for it was probable that Lloyd George had already been told.

And, in fact, Churchill wrote again[b] on 7th

December, 1919, acknowledging that Lloyd George had been consulted and had expressed great pleasure, saying "I would rather have them than an Earldom".* On 8th January, 1920, the newspapers announced:

> At 10 Downing Street, last night, Mr. Winston Churchill and the members of the Army Council waited upon the Prime Minister to present him with the special award of the 1914–15 Star, the British War Medal, and the Victory Medal, approved by the King.
>
> The proceedings, which were private, lasted only a few minutes. The speeches of Mr. Churchill, who presented the medals, and of the Prime Minister were quite informal.
>
> We understand that the King has also approved the special award of the three war medals to Mr. Asquith.[c]

But in politics nothing is permanent, and often what seems to be made of marble and bronze turns out, after a little, to be composed of lath and plaster. So was it with the reputation of Lloyd George.

By the end of the first year of peace, the prestige and authority of His Majesty's Chief Minister had softened. There were signs and portents.

It was always thus. In the moment of supreme triumph decline begins to do its work, undermining, weakening and finally destroying not only the reputation but also the power and the authority of our heroes.

---

* After many years the Earldom came to both in time, the Earl of Oxford and Asquith in 1925 and Earl Lloyd George in 1945. Recommendations for honours flow from the Prime Ministers. Baldwin was responsible for recommending the Earl of Oxford and Asquith. Winston Churchill put forward the name of Lloyd George. But some Prime Ministers are not backward in recommending themselves. Almost every Prime Minister from Asquith to Eden has been honoured with one or other Order, excepting only Chamberlain and Bonar Law. Law disapproved of the system.

It is hard to explain to a new generation the full measure of dislike, distrust, even loathing, with which the public came to regard his government. It is easy, on the other hand, to enumerate the causes which, insufficient as they may now appear, brought about the extraordinary turn from public favour to popular animosity. Here are some of them:

(1) Lloyd George's series of foreign conferences which produced nothing and ended in futility and ridicule.

(2) His hostility to France and his preoccupation with Germany.

(3) The failure of his German policy, which finally resulted in driving Germany into the arms of Russia.

(4) The grave risk he ran when he threatened war in the Near East. At that time war was sure to involve other nations and likely to end up in another European conflict.

All the while, unemployment was widespread through the land.

Agriculture declined. The Government had given a subsidy for the production of wheat and then repealed the Act. The farmers believed themselves to have been betrayed. These domestic miseries sharpened the impatience with which the public regarded Lloyd George's busy and impulsive foreign policy.

Certain personal factors played their part. Scandal after scandal broke out over the collection of a Lloyd George Party Fund. The Prime Minister agreed to sell his memoirs to the *Daily Telegraph* for £90,000. When the public took offence over this transaction, Lloyd George was compelled to declare that the proceeds of the book would go to war charities.*

But the immediate cause of his fall may have been his arrogance coupled with the decline of the trust and confidence which he had inspired during the war. A Prime Minister without a party cannot dispense with the trust and confidence of his supporters in the House of Commons. At the very height of his popularity he became impatient, critical and dictatorial in manner.

He quarrelled with Lord Milner, who had joined his Government in 1916 as a member of the War Cabinet without departmental duties. Milner was much discussed and widely praised. He was sought after in political circles. Lord Esher, who was constantly urging a change at the Paris Embassy, frequently nominated Milner for the post. †

In 1918, when Lord Derby was moved from the War Office to the Paris Embassy, Milner succeeded him. He had discussed with Lloyd George whether Sir Maurice Hankey or himself should have the post. Milner in a letter thought he "would be more generally acceptable to the Army", but had "absolutely no feeling one way or the other. I only want the best thing done".[d]

---

* In fact, ten years passed before he returned to the book. Its earnings did not go to charity.

† In January, 1917, leading a British mission to Russia, Milner formed the impression that a revolution was not immediately likely. In January, 1919, when Germany was in revolution, he advised an easy peace for the Hohenzollerns.

Milner's friendly relations with the Prime Minister did not long survive his appointment to the War Office.

At the time of the 1918 General Election he was responsible for a scheme for newspaper propaganda among the troops in France which was a fiasco. Soon he was complaining that Lloyd George rebuked him publicly before outsiders and subordinates. On 7th December, 1918, he wrote to the Prime Minister asking for his discharge.

> 7.12.18
> 17, Great College Street, S.W.

My Dear Prime Minister,

. . . .

To be quite frank, and I know how you love frankness, my desire to withdraw from the arena has been quickened by the impatience, which you have of late frequently manifested, of my conduct of affairs at the War Office. Whether or not you are justified in that impatience, the fact remains that I am unable to do any better. I work myself as hard as I can. I press those working under me as much as I think right or wise. If the result is not satisfactory, the obvious remedy is to put some one else in my place, and I am most willing that that course should be adopted.

What I am not willing to accept is a position, in which I am exposed to such vehement charges of dilatoriness and neglect as you made yesterday in the presence of a large number of people, many of them not Ministers, in connection with the discharge of miners from the Army.

To submit to that sort of public rebuke without a protest, or to expose myself to a chance of its repetition, is, I feel, not consistent with self-respect.

The last thing I wish to do is to add to your burdens and embarrassments at the present time, and I am quite ready to carry on at the War Office till the Election is over, when there will no doubt in any case be a reconstruction of the Ministry, and my retirement can be effected with the minimum of fuss.

At the same time I should like you to feel that, if you found it convenient to make a change even before then, I am prepared at any moment to fall in with your wishes.

Believe me, my dear Prime Minister,

Yours very sincerely,

MILNER.*

Milner's resignation was accepted on an understanding that it should be held over until the Cabinet was reconstructed. Meanwhile rumours about Milner's position appeared in the newspapers which, he alleged, were inspired by Lloyd George's office.* In the end, the differences were patched up and Milner went to the Colonial Office. In this post he was concerned with the peace negotiations, especially those which related to the disposal of the German Colonies. This brought down on him a new outburst from Lloyd George.

British Delegation,
Paris.

14.5.1919.

My dear Colonial Secretary,

I earnestly hope that you will not find it necessary a second time to leave Paris without achieving a decision on the important questions entrusted to your charge. There are at least five matters essential to the peace settlement which you alone can pilot to a conclusion—Togoland, Kameroons, German East Africa, Nauru & Somaliland.

You will forgive me for saying quite emphatically that there can be no colonial business which more urgently presses for treatment than these affairs.

I could see you today at any time between 2 and 4 if
that suits your convenience. Later on I am leaving to
say farewell to a division with which I have been
closely associated. I return Friday evening.

Ever sincerely,
D. LLOYD GEORGE.[5]

On 27th November, 1920, Milner informed
the Prime Minister that he wished to resign, for
private reasons, but would be willing to assist the
Government in a private capacity.

At the New Year Milner refused to preside over
a committee to work out the details of the
proposed transfer of Palestine and Mesopotamia
to the Colonial Office. He said he did not agree
with the scheme and that he would not take any
hand in the work. At the same time he pressed
for the acceptance of his resignation.[4]

In the following month he resigned. Lloyd
George's quarrel with him was indeed a stupid one.
It is extraordinary that Milner was so patient and
accepted so many rebukes with such good temper.

If Milner was reprimanded for leaving Paris,
Lord Birkenhead (as F. E. Smith had by then
become) was rebuked for the opposite reason.

Birkenhead, after being appointed Lord Chancellor, went to Paris when Lloyd George was
attending the Peace Conference. Birkenhead's
purpose was to interest his Prime Minister in
questions concerning his office.

Lloyd George refused to see him, wrote him an
angry letter telling him he had no right to leave
the Kingdom, and ordered him to go back at once.

On 15th March, 1919, Lloyd George wrote a sharp letter to Birkenhead rejecting a report of the Lord Chancellor's Committee on the Land Acquisition Bill. "It has been transformed," said the Prime Minister, "into a Bill which will be represented as making sure that the landlord gets a good price, that the lawyers * get their pickings, and that there should be no undue hurry in the completion of the transaction."[i] †

Birkenhead, as Lloyd George should have remembered, was a formidable figure. He had a considerable capacity for friendship but was also capable of resenting and avenging any insult.

Lord Curzon was the real butt of Lloyd George's criticisms which were delivered on occasion in hectoring and bullying terms. It was, of course, the language his Lordship understood, though he did not like it when he was on the receiving end.

Even in the dark days of war Lloyd George was impatient and even intolerant of Lord Curzon's long and tedious harangues on public issues. There was at one time a proposal to take over the British Museum for the use of the Air Ministry. The plan found favour. Curzon then demanded a reconsideration and led off the discussion by reading a long statement setting forth his objections.

The Prime Minister checked him. Unhappily for his Lordship's pride, the Archbishop of Canterbury and Sir Frederic Kenyon, the Director of the Museum, were present to give evidence.

---

* Lord Birkenhead was a former Leader of the Bar.
† For full text of letter see *Appendix IV*, No. 20.

When asked if he had any alternative suggestion, Kenyon replied, "The Bethlehem Hospital—more commonly known as the Bedlam Lunatic Asylum." The Ministers felt that this would hardly be suitable accommodation.

No doubt Kenyon's good-humoured comment helped the Ministers to the revocation of the decision, thus saving the Museum for the public. But even though Curzon won the struggle his vanity was not appeased. In a weighty and dignified letter he protested that the Prime Minister had treated him roughly.

I reproduce a shortened version of his letter.*

Dear Prime Minister,

Although I hope I am not quick or resentful of temper, I do not like to let the incident of this morning pass without a word from me.

·　　·　　·　　·　　·

Before you came into the room Bonar Law in the Chair had asked me to open the discussion and in order to shorten the proceedings I had commenced to read my brief memo instead of recapitulating its substance. It was there that you cut me short in a manner which I venture to say left a painful impression on all who heard it.

I certainly felt it acutely myself and that others felt it too was shown by the Archbishop of Canterbury, who came up to me in the H. of Lords this afternoon and said he had been astonished at the manner in which a member of the Cabinet could be treated by his Chief and at the good temper with which the latter had borne it.*j*

* The full text appears in *Appendix IV*, No. 21

333

Long after the war was over, Curzon still
suffered from the barbs of Lloyd George's criticism. He appealed to nearly every member of the
Cabinet and at last drew a response from Austen
Chamberlain, a good-natured and sympathetic
listener. Chamberlain wrote to Bonar Law on 6th
January, 1921, inviting him to intercede, "because
I know that you have an influence with him
(Lloyd George) to which the rest of us cannot
pretend. You will therefore be our best interpreter & you are the man most likely to put things
right."ᵏ *

His letter was a most detailed defence of Lord
Curzon, whose resignation, said Chamberlain,
would be fatal to the Government and the Coalition. Churchill, he declared, had suffered a similar
treatment at the hands of the Prime Minister.

But in spite of Chamberlain's appeal, there was
no improvement in the relations of Lloyd George
and Curzon.

The Chamberlain protest against the Prime
Minister's treatment of Churchill, who was at
that time Secretary of State for War,† was certainly justified. Correspondence in the Lloyd
George Archives extending over these years
reflects the impatience of the Prime Minister.

On unemployment Lloyd George wrote to Churchill a most intemperate letter,ˡ actually charging
him with attempting "to lay the blame on your
colleagues for present unemployment conditions".

* The full text of the letter is reproduced in *Appendix IV*, No. 22.
† Churchill was transferred to the Colonial Office on February 12, 1921.

Then Lloyd George attacked Churchill on his support of "this fatuous policy" of giving out contracts for new houses in advance of the capacity of the Building Industry.

He was charged with waste in Mesopotamia where "forces far beyond the need were being kept". Churchill, as Colonial Secretary, had been given special responsibility for Mesopotamia and the Near East.

On the question of unemployment, Lloyd George concluded, "I entreat you to judge more charitably the efforts put forth by your colleagues during the last two years."

Even when Lloyd George agreed with Churchill's Irish negotiations, there were complaints that the Colonial Secretary was giving battle "on the very worst grounds" which could possibly be chosen.

In this day it is strange to read of Churchill having been bullied by Lloyd George.

But the Lloyd George letters certainly confirm the charge.

Churchill's letters preserved in the Lloyd George Archives, on the other hand, are nearly always of a conciliatory nature. When he was assailed over his views on unemployment, he replied:

The first & greatest mistake in my opinion was leaving the profiteers in possession of their ill-gotten war wealth. Had prompt action been taken at the beginning of 1919, several thousand millions of paper wealth cd have been transferred to the State, & the internal debt reduced accordingly. The question was however deliberately held over & delayed until the moment was lost.[m]*

* See *Appendix IV*, Nos. 23 and 24, for the text of correspondence between Lloyd George and Churchill, October, 1921.

The Prime Minister even quarrelled with Lord Riddell, his most intimate friend, a man who had supported and sustained him in his darkest hours. At the Paris Peace Conference the French made a great fuss of Riddell, persuading him to support their claims in opposition to Lloyd George. Then at Lucerne in 1920, when there was a dispute with the French over Turkey, Riddell warmly espoused the French cause at dinner. Lloyd George suggested that he was a traitor to his country. Riddell left for London next morning. From that moment their friendship dwindled and fell into decay. It was, in effect, the end.

When, in 1921, the partnership between Lloyd George and Bonar Law came to an end, after many strains and stresses, the Prime Minister was dealt a mortal blow.

Lloyd George, on the retirement of Bonar Law, appeared to me to be relieved. I was under the impression that he was weary of hearing that Bonar Law kept him straight. He seemed to welcome the opportunity of ruling his Government and ruling it alone. He would show that his power was supreme and his will absolute.

I was wrong.

Correspondence in the Lloyd George files shows that the Prime Minister recognised the difficulties confronting him. I quote a letter from Lord Stamfordham written to the Prime Minister on 19th March, 1921.

My dear Prime Minister,

The following are extracts from a letter just received from the King at Knowsley in reply to what I wrote after seeing you yesterday morning.

"I am sorry the Prime Minister is low on account of B.L.'s resignation: but he must not be despondent as I firmly believe *he* is now more necessary to this country than he ever was & that the vast majority of the people are behind him. He wants my views on the points he put to you this morning. They are not very easy to give from a distance. If I were talking to him it would help me to do so. I should agree to anything that would help him most. If the Cabinet resigned & there was a 'general post' & he dropped out Illingworth, Addison or any others: or if he formed (as has been advocated) a National Party: but the latter I agree would take time, as it is a big change. His difficulty will be finding a successor to B.L. Could he get the same advice and support from Chamberlain? or Horne. But the Unionists [Conservatives] will of course elect the former as their leader. You can tell the P.M. that I have complete confidence in him & will do everything in my power to help him. I will be in London on Monday & could see him that evening at any time that suits him. What a pity Balfour is away as he could give most useful advice!

I am very strong in maintaining a Coalition Govt. I am sure it is the best plan at the present moment & until these many very difficult questions have been settled. Anyhow I am against a general election which would upset everything. There really ought to be two P.M.'s! No man can do the work he L.G. has to do now. I quite understand his feeling lonely & almost lost without B.L. who did so much for him.

I fear these views will not be of much use to the P.M. What a pity I am out of London. I fear it would be almost impossible to return before Monday at 3 p.m. unless I travelled Sunday which I dislike doing—

but I am ready to do so if he wishes. I was talking to
2 Labour M.P.'s here today & they were loud in
singing the P.M.'s praises & both said he is the strongest man we have had since Pitt."

Yours very truly,

STAMFORDHAM."

Now this letter is the first occasion on record
when the King shows sympathetic consideration
for his Prime Minister, Lloyd George. The King
not only tells him of his complete confidence in
him, but that he will do everything in his power
to help him. He assures him that the Coalition
Government must be sustained.

And all this just at the moment when Lloyd
George's Ministry was showing signs of change
and decay and the shadows were gathering over
the Prime Minister himself.

But it could not be expected that the King would
know of the many reasons why the power and glory
of his great and splendid Prime Minister, triumphant in the day of battle, was now passing away.

Lloyd George had become something of a
dictator without having a dictator's apparatus of
power and terror. Instead his strength depended
on his personal ascendancy with the public which
a shift in the wind of popularity could dissolve,
and upon the Conservative political machine
which was only used effectively for Lloyd George's
benefit so long as Bonar Law was its custodian.

After Bonar Law left the Government, Lloyd
George interfered increasingly with Departmental
Chiefs. He sometimes appealed to subordinates to
act against and independently of the Ministers.

He often gave directions to Under-Secretaries without regard to the Ministers concerned.

A letter to Hilton-Young, who was Financial Secretary to Sir Robert Horne, Chancellor of the Exchequer, directed him to provide a plan for £250,000,000 of inflationary expenditure. Lloyd George wrote:

> Pray do not be too easily frightened by city pundits who are as stuffed with stale orthodoxies as old McKinnon, the Wee Free Minister who afflicted me yesterday with theological banking principles.[o]

To Sir Philip Lloyd Graeme, Under-Secretary to Stanley Baldwin, President of the Board of Trade, a letter from Gairloch, where the Prime Minister was holidaying, informed him:

> I am relying upon you to go into this matter very thoroughly . . . and see what can be done, and if you can wake up the Board of Trade you will, incidentally, render a great service to the community.[p]

Again, on 30th April, 1922, he wrote from Genoa a letter of remonstrance rejecting recommendations from his Cabinet.

> The strain of the Conference is great enough without further complications of that sort, and you will recognise that I cannot be expected to accept any variation of my instructions, however desirable they may seem to some of my colleagues in London, while I am doing my utmost to give effect to the agreed policy of the Cabinet under circumstances of exceptional difficulty out here in Genoa.[q]

With the exception of Lord Riddell, Press Peers, * however, did not suffer from Lloyd George's dictatorial habits. He always envied newspaper proprietors and sincerely tried to keep on good terms with them. After I retired from his Government my social relations with him were either pleasant or in abeyance. My political position might be described as much the same as the entrance to a well-known club which gives rise to the title "The In and Out Club".

We had several disputes but always I was called back to collaboration when Lloyd George would discuss with me the prospects of a General Election on the Empire issue. Nothing ever came of these discussions, but each time my hopes were again aroused.

The last occasion on which I had formed great expectation was at the Villa Valetta in Cannes.

That great event was in January, 1922. Lloyd George was of course Prime Minister. He was contemplating a General Election. And he might have been persuaded to go to the country on an Empire Commercial Union platform.

On the sunny shores of the Mediterranean he held court. Several Cabinet Ministers were in attendance, Churchill among them. Of course I was present. I always managed to be present when Empire was at issue. So was a parrot in a cage. An English parrot. A parrot endowed with a gift of prophecy.

---

* Lord Northcliffe had been excommunicated in 1918. He died in August, 1922.

Should Lloyd George, the Prime Minister, call for an immediate General Election? And on what issue would he seek the support of the public?

Sir Laming Worthington-Evans, the Secretary for War, spoke brilliantly in favour of an election. He had a splendid voice.

It seemed that he was carrying everything before him. When he concluded his argument, a hush fell on the company. The opponents of the election were silenced. Then suddenly, from that cage, the shriek of the English-speaking parrot cried: "You bloody fool. You bloody fool."

Evans' argument was lost in laughter. The parrot had decided the issue. There was no election.

Churchill gave me a lift back to my hotel ten miles away. As we drove through the night what do you think we talked about? The parrot.

The parrot had stood in the way of Empire policy. The parrot had put an end to the prospect of an election. The parrot had put an end to Lloyd George! Within a year he was driven from office, never to enjoy power again.

After Cannes, one more Foreign Conference and another disaster for the Prime Minister.

It was the Genoa Conference from mid April to May, 1922.

Lloyd George returned to the House of Commons high in spirits, but low in political prospects. His official life was surely ebbing to its close. For some of the representatives of Foreign Powers who sat with him at Genoa, more than power and office was ebbing to its close.

Dr. Rathenau, the German Foreign Minister, was dead within a month. Driving from his villa in the suburbs of Berlin on 24th June, to attend a Cabinet meeting in the Wilhelmstrasse, he was shot by two former Army officers.

Six months later, the Greek Prime Minister at the Conference, M. Gounaris, was put to death in circumstances of brutality and horror. Deposed by the Revolutionary Government, he was dying in hospital from typhus when his executioners seized him. He was given a heart stimulant and with four members of his Cabinet and the Commander-in-Chief of Asia Minor, he was executed before a firing squad.

M. Stambolisky, the Bulgarian Premier, too, was murdered in the following year. He had been driven out of his office by revolutionary forces. He fled to a wood, concealing himself beneath a covering of leaves. He was discovered and executed by troops who pursued him.

In the same year, violent death had claimed M. Vorovsky, a Soviet representative at Genoa. He was assassinated while dining at the Hotel Cecil in Lausanne. The accused was acquitted.

The last Foreign Conference and Failure! The last of many Foreign Conferences! And where were the triumphs? All turned to dust.

The glory departed from Lloyd George after sixteen years of power. His defeat at the General Election of 1922 was humiliating to him, and devastating to his followers. Few of his friends were returned to Parliament. In the shadows of Opposition, many of his old colleagues fell away and new political friends were hard to find. His imperious temper did not improve and his criticisms of his former Ministers increased in force and frequency.

What manner of a man was this mighty champion in the critical period of British History? How did I measure him in the last two years of the Great War?

As a witty and genial companion the Prime Minister had few equals. He was gay and generous in sharing conversation. He did not monopolize the company with monologues. He was neither egotistical nor vain, save only of some physical characteristics—his big head, long hair and small feet.

No man rallied more generously to meet any chaff which might be on the wind. "You know, George" (as Bonar Law always addressed him), "Winston * means to seize your Liberal leadership." "Maybe," said Lloyd George, "but he will get your leadership of the Conservative Party first." Lloyd George showed foresight.

His colleagues, in his glorious hours, looked upon him as a dazzling and triumphant figure. Is it possible to pierce to the heart of his real character?

Easy to detect and explain individual actions, failures and successes, his motives high and low, the caution of the man with his ear to the ground, the quality of physical weakness, joined to stark moral courage, the cool cynicism of the man of affairs, the magic of the orator, the glowing range of Celtic imagination so profound as to pass here

* At this time a Liberal Minister.

and there into the far country of idealism, the kingdom of romance.

But even so, the question reverberates, what manner of man was this wizard of Wales, as he was dubbed by some of his colleagues; "the Goat" by others?

What thread of consistency bound those dull or glistening beads together? What was the secret spring of character from which all these diverse qualities flowed?

Perhaps we are too near the masterpiece to see the real worth of the picture. We can say, however, that in the day of our dire need, when the blast of the terrible one was against the wall, a strange figure sprang into the arena to do battle.

It was clad in a jewelled breastplate set in a vesture of rags and tatters. It faltered in its walk, and yet leapt with a wonderful swiftness. The sword looked as fragile as a rapier and yet smote with the impact of a battle-axe. As it was held on high, so was the hope of Britain. And when the swordsman stumbled, anxiety filled the breasts of the multitude.

The last stumble was the worst. When the Allied line was pierced by the enemy in early 1918, hope stood still. Then the final stroke, and Britain was ablaze with glory. An Empire as broad as the earth was bathed everywhere in the sunlight of victory. Liberty was secured. The dream of a living Empire appeared to be a reality.

And in the midst of that brilliant sunlight stood

the central figure, young as Prime Ministers go, sharing the glory of Chatham and Pitt.

Then the mists gathered, other banners were unfurled, night fell.

It was my duty to deliver the speech on behalf of the Government in the House of Lords on 28th March, 1945, mourning the death of the great War Leader. I reminded the House that there were several members who served under Lloyd George, but of those of his colleagues who knew and felt the full force of his genius, those who served with him in his War Cabinet, nearly all have gone out in front of him. Many will say that Lloyd George's greatest days, his most splendid efforts were in times of peace when he put upon the Statute Book more social legislation than any single statesman in our history; but I do not hold that view. To me his greatest hour came as late as the spring of 1918, when our line of defence had been broken, our troops were in retreat, the Russian Armies were out of the war, and the American Armies had not yet come into it.

The Cabinet at that moment was concerned above all else with the dominant question, "Shall we retreat north and west to protect the Channel ports, or shall we retire south to Paris to sustain contact with the French Armies?" The history books will tell the truth. A Cabinet of strong men had been diverted for the time by the sheer gravity of the situation from the bigger issue—the issue of defeat or victory. It was at that moment that Lloyd George penetrated the gloom of doubt and indecision. It was in the hour of our peril that he refused to contemplate any plan for retreat. He would talk only of counter-attacks. It was then his leadership showed itself supreme, his courage undiminished.*

What new assessments will tomorrow bring forth, and what judgement will posterity accord to David Lloyd George, born in a cottage, brought up in a shoemaker's shop, strayed from the fields of Llanystumdwy to that narrow street so many desire to tread, yet so few deserve to enter, the path that leads to No. 10?

* For the speech in full, *see* APPENDIX VII.

APPENDIX I

MEMBERS OF THE GOVERNMENT
1917–1918

The War Cabinet

Prime Minister and First Lord of the Treasury. David Lloyd George.

Lord President of the Council. Lord Curzon.

Chancellor of the Exchequer. Andrew Bonar Law.

Lord Milner (December, 1916 to April, 1918).

General Smuts (June, 1917 to December, 1918).

Sir Edward Carson (July, 1917 to January, 1918).

Austen Chamberlain (April, 1918 to December, 1918).

Arthur Henderson (December, 1916 to August, 1917).

George Barnes (August, 1917 to January, 1918).

Ministers of Cabinet Rank.

Lord Chancellor. Lord Finlay.

Secretary of State for Foreign Affairs. A. J. Balfour.

Secretary of State for War. Lord Derby (December, 1916 to April, 1918). Succeeded by Lord Milner.

Secretary of State for the Colonies. Walter Long.

Secretary of State for India. Austen Chamberlain (December, 1916 to July, 1917). Succeeded by Edwin Montagu.

First Lord of the Admiralty. Sir Edward Carson (December, 1916 to July, 1917). Succeeded by Sir Eric Geddes.

President of the Air Board and Secretary of State for Air. Lord Cowdray (December, 1916 to November, 1917). Lord Rothermere (November, 1917 to April, 1918). Succeeded by Sir William Weir.

Secretary of State for Home Affairs. Sir George Cave.

President of the Board of Trade. Sir Albert Stanley.

President of the Board of Agriculture and Fisheries. Rowland Prothero.

President of the Board of Education. H. A. L. Fisher.

Minister of Munitions. Dr. C. Addison (December, 1916 to July, 1917). Succeeded by Winston Churchill.

Minister of Labour. John Hodge (December, 1916 to August, 1917). Succeeded by George Roberts.

Chancellor of the Duchy of Lancaster. Sir Frederick Cawley (December, 1916 to February, 1918). Succeeded by Lord Beaverbrook, who held also the office of Minister of Information.

Other Ministers Mentioned in this Narrative.

Attorney-General. Sir F. E. Smith.

Solicitor-General. Sir Gordon Hewart.

Postmaster-General. A. H. Illingworth.

Minister of Blockade and Assistant Foreign Secretary. Lord Robert Cecil.

Shipping Controller. Sir Joseph Maclay.

Minister of Reconstruction. Dr. C. Addison (July, 1917).

Joint Financial Secretaries to the Treasury. Sir Hardman Lever, Stanley Baldwin.

Parliamentary Secretaries to the Treasury. Lord Edmund Talbot, Hon. Neil Primrose (December, 1916 to May, 1917). Succeeded by Capt. Frederick Guest.

APPENDIX II

MEMORANDUM
By John Bassett

John Bassett, President and Chairman of the *Montreal Gazette*, the oldest and one of the best edited of all the morning newspapers in Canada, and President of the *Sherbrooke Daily Record*, was for long a Press Gallery Correspondent in the House of Commons at Ottawa.

When war broke out in 1914 he became Staff Officer and served throughout the war years. He was attached to General Sir Sam Hughes, accompanying him to France on all the journeys to the Front made by the Minister of Militia and Defence, which was the title in those days of the War Minister.

Mr. Bassett is Chancellor of Bishop's University and his association with that University has done much to develop and extend its influence.

THE friction between the Duke of Connaught as Governor-General of Canada and Colonel the Hon. Sir Sam Hughes, Minister of Militia and Defence, began prior to 1914. Hughes was wrongly obsessed with the idea, indeed the conviction, that there was a pro-German atmosphere at Government House, because the Governor-General was the son of Prince Albert, a German Prince, and Queen Victoria's consort, and his wife was the daughter of another German prince, and spoke English with an accent.

As everybody knows, Hughes prophesied a war with Germany from the time he became Minister of Militia in

1911 and before, until the war broke out. He expanded the Canadian forces; he built drill halls all over Canada to encourage the training of troops. So firm was his conviction that he bought surreptitiously, months before the war broke out, a huge tract of land at Valcartier. It was close to Quebec, so that the troops could embark at Gaspe. Then when the war broke out, troops assembled at Valcartier for training and mobilisation before setting sail for England.

As the troops became welded into some sort of organisation, the Duke of Connaught with his staff proceeded to interfere, and he took advantage of his position as Governor-General and Commander-in-Chief to do so.

The Minister of Militia and Defence resented his interference, and it came to a boiling point when the Duke of Connaught wished to review the troops at Valcartier on several occasions. Hughes refused, stating that he, the Duke of Connaught, was simply the titular head of the Canadian Army and that he, Hughes, was the civilian head, and therefore entitled to review, as he called them, "his boys".

The Duke of Connaught in his attitude towards Hughes was aided and abetted by one called Colonel Stanton, who was his military secretary. He had been a Governor in the Near East, and upon one occasion Hughes told him in a letter in reply to one from Stanton to mind his manners, and remember he was in Canada, and not driving a lot of "buck niggers up the Nile".

The Duke of Connaught was badly served by Stanton.

The relationship between Prime Minister Borden and Connaught was strained, due mainly to the attitude taken by the Duke of Connaught and his staff towards the Canadian military machine. Borden usually supported Hughes, although he differed with him on other matters.

It must be remembered that in the First World War one saw the deep stirrings of Canadian nationhood, and that Borden himself was responsible for insisting that Canadian Ministers should sign the Treaty of Versailles.

APPENDIX II

When the Duke of Connaught left Canada as Governor-General, a dinner was given to him by the members of the Rideau Club. Sir Robert Borden was present as a matter of courtesy as Prime Minister. Sir Wilfrid Laurier, the Leader of the Opposition, was also there.

In the speeches made Sir Robert was very non-committal about the Duke. Sir Wilfrid made one of his charming and eloquent utterances, which touched the Duke very deeply. On his return to England he sent Sir Wilfrid and Lady Laurier a loving-cup of remembrance, but gave no recognition whatever to Borden or his wife.

A study of the communications in those days between the Colonial Office and Sir Robert Borden would be interesting and illuminating. But much is to be found in the Memoirs of Sir Robert. The papers tell more than Sir Robert disclosed in his Memoirs, because Borden was very cautious in all his actions and writings.

CATALOGUE OF LETTERS PUBLISHED
FOR THE FIRST TIME

The Royal Archives, Windsor.

Stamfordham Memoranda, February, 1918.

W. S. Churchill to Lord Stamfordham, 7th December, 1919.

Bonar Law to Lord Stamfordham, 17th April, 1919.

Lord Stamfordham to Frederick Guest, 11th April, 1919.

Lord Stamfordham to His Majesty, King George V. Memorandum, 5th July, 1917.

Lloyd George Papers.

John Baird to Lloyd George, 22nd April, 1918.

A. J. Balfour to Lloyd George, 22nd August, 1918.

Sir Edward Carson to Lloyd George, 31st December, 1917.

Lord Robert Cecil to Lloyd George, June 1917.

W. S. Churchill to Lloyd George, 17th May, 1917.

W. S. Churchill to Lloyd George, 19th May, 1917.

W. S. Churchill to Lloyd George, 29th December, 1918.

W. S. Churchill to Lloyd George, 8th October, 1921.

Lord Curzon to Lloyd George, 30th April, 1917.

Lord Curzon to Lloyd George, 8th January, 1918.

Lord Curzon to Lloyd George, 12th November, 1918.

Lord Curzon to Lloyd George, 13th November, 1918.

Lord Curzon to Lloyd George, Undated (1918).

Lord Derby to Lloyd George, 19th February, 1917.

Lord Derby to Lloyd George, 20th February, 1917.

Lord Derby to Lloyd George, 8th June, 1917

Lord Derby to Lloyd George, 11th December, 1917.

Lord Derby to Lloyd George, 18th January, 1918.

Lord Derby to Lloyd George, 29th January, 1918.

Frederick Guest to Lloyd George, 10th May, 1917.

Frederick Guest to Lloyd George, 18th June, 1917.

Frederick Guest to Lloyd George, 23rd January, 1918.

Frederick Guest to Lloyd George, 17th May, 1920.

Lloyd George to A. J. Balfour, 27th August, 1918.

Lloyd George to Lord Birkenhead, 15th March, 1919.

Lloyd George to W. S. Churchill, 1st October, 1921.

Lloyd George to Lord Curzon, 8th July, 1919.

Lloyd George to Lord Curzon, 30th April, 1922.

Lloyd George to Lord Derby, 13th December, 1917.

Lloyd George to E. Hilton Young, 26th September, 1921.

Lloyd George to Sir P. Lloyd Graeme, 26th September, 1921.

Lloyd George to Lord Milner, 14th May, 1919.

Lord Milner to Lloyd George, 26th June, 1917.

Lord Milner to Lloyd George, 16th July, 1917.

Lord Milner to Lloyd George, 27th February, 1918.

Lord Milner to Lloyd George, 19th May, 1918.

Lord Milner to Lloyd George, 7th December, 1918.

Lord Reading to Lloyd George, 22nd July, 1917.

Sir William Robertson to Lloyd George, 26th May, 1917.

Sir William Robertson to Lord Milner, 17th May, 1918.

General Smuts to Lloyd George, 13th April, 1918.

Lord Stamfordham to Lloyd George, 16th April, 1918.

Lord Stamfordham to Lloyd George, 25th April, 1918.

Lord Stamfordham to Lloyd George, 19th March, 1921.

Lord Stamfordham to Frederick Guest, 25th April, 1919.

Sir George Younger to Lloyd George, 8th June, 1917.

Countess Lloyd George, Diary Extract, 5th October, 1934.

Bonar Law Papers.

Sir Edward Carson to Bonar Law, 20th December, 1916.

Austen Chamberlain to Bonar Law, 6th January, 1921.

W. S. Churchill to Bonar Law, 8th September, 1918.

Lord Curzon to Bonar Law, 4th June, 1917.

Lord Derby to Bonar Law, 5th March, 1917.

Lord Derby to Bonar Law, 18th February, 1918.

Sir David Henderson to Bonar Law, and enclosure, 26th April, 1918.

Bonar Law to Lloyd George, 19th September, 1918.

Lloyd George to Bonar Law, 10th April, 1918.

Lloyd George to Bonar Law, 29th August, 1918.

Walter Long to Bonar Law, 19th February, 1918.

Sir Joseph Maclay to Bonar Law, 28th June, 1917.

Lord Milner to Bonar Law, 28th June, 1917.

Lord Milner to Bonar Law, 18th February, 1918.

Lord Rothermere to Bonar Law, 3rd May, 1918.

Lord Salisbury to Bonar Law, 22nd February, 1918.

Lord Stamfordham to Bonar Law, 17th April, 1919.

Sir Henry Wilson to Bonar Law, 16th May, 1915.

Beaverbrook Papers.

Lord Beaverbrook to Sir Sam Hughes, Cable, 16th October, 1915.

Lord Beaverbrook to Sir Sam Hughes, Cable, October, 1915.

Lord Beaverbrook Diary Extract, 9th March, 1915.

Sir Reginald Brade to Lord Beaverbrook, 6th January, 1917.

Sir Reginald Brade Diary, Extracts of 13th, 10th and 21st June, 1916.

Sir Reginald Brade, "A few Notes on the Recent Controversy between Sir W. R. (Robertson) and the Government."

Austen Chamberlain to Lord Beaverbrook, 2nd March, 1918.

Lord Crewe to Lord Beaverbrook, October, 1918.

E. M. House Collection, Yale University Library.

The Diary of E. M. House. Extracts of 18th and 29th October, 1917.

Walter Hines Page Papers, Houghton Library, Harvard University.

Walter Page to President Wilson, 16th January, 1918.

Walter Page to President Wilson, 7th March, 1918.

Papers of Sir Robert Borden, Toronto University.

Bonar Law to Sir Robert Borden, 1st May, 1916.

H.R.H. the Duke of Connaught to Sir Robert Borden, 18th April, 1916.

Archives of Lord Bennett, University of New Brunswick.

H.R.H. the Duke of Connaught to R. B. Bennett, 14th December, 1916.

Other Manuscript Collections.

Lord Robert Cecil to A. J. Balfour, 18th November, 1917. *Balfour Papers*, British Museum.

W. S. Churchill to R. D. Blumenfeld, 6th September, 1914. *Blumenfeld Papers.*

F. E. Smith to J. C. Sandars. *Margaret, Countess of Birkenhead.*

LETTERS PREVIOUSLY PUBLISHED IN PART; PUBLISHED IN FULL FOR THE FIRST TIME

Lloyd George Papers.

Lord Curzon to Lloyd George, 8th June, 1917.

Frederick Guest to Lloyd George, 26th February, 1917.

Lloyd George to Sir Edward Carson, 6th July, 1917.

Lloyd George to Sir Edward Carson, 7th July, 1917.

Lord Milner to Lloyd George, 7th December, 1917.

Sir Joseph Maclay to Lloyd George, 28th June, 1917.

General Smuts to Lloyd George, 6th June, 1917.

FULL TEXT OF LETTERS
AND DOCUMENTS

1

Record of Correspondence that passed between Mr. Balfour's Secretary, Mr. J. S. Sandars, and Mr. F. E. Smith (Lord Birkenhead).

Rt. Hon. J. S. Sandars, P.C., Private Secretary to Mr. Balfour, wrote:

"Your little boy will be proud of his father in the years to come for such a great act of self-sacrifice."

To which Mr. F. E. Smith replied:

"My little boy is only four, but if I thought he was such a bloody little fool as to be proud of his father for committing such an assinine act, I should indeed despair of him."

2

Correspondence between Lord Beaverbrook and Lord Horder.

21st April, 1952.

My dear Tommy,

On the 14th May, on Television, I propose to say of Northcliffe, if you have no objection, "he died with a pistol concealed under his pillow. He had just used it to threaten Lord Horder, his physician, who was struggling to save him from death that was inevitable."

Yours ever,

MAX.

LORD HORDER,
32 Devonshire Place,
London, W.1.

25.4.52.

Dear Max,

Not quite correct. When I entered the bedroom N. put his hand under the pillow and brought out a revolver. "One of G's bl— knights," he said, & was about to fire when the male nurse struck his hand up. . . .

. . . .

Yours ever,

TOMMY.

3

HOUSE OF COMMONS

Monday night
June 18, 1917.

Dear Prime Minister,

I made a tentative proposal to Winston on the grounds of the Chancellorship of the Duchy with elaborated uses and functions but without success.

He wished me to say that he regarded the offer as completely friendly.

He feels however that he could neither serve a *national purpose* nor *your purpose* by being included in this manner.

He is prepared to forego & forget all political considerations in order to help to beat the "Hun" in either of the following capacities.

1. To assist you in council in the War Cabinet, if necessary without salary.

2. To accept charge & responsibility for any War Department, as long as he has powers to actively assist in the defeat of the enemy.

I have used my utmost powers of persuasion but can do no more in this direction.

My only comment on the situation is that your will & influence with your Tory Colleagues is greater than you have credited yourself with and that sooner or later you will have to test it—why not now?

I have the strongest reasons to believe that the Tories mean to support your leadership even at the expense of their personal feelings.

Yours sincerely,

FREDERICK GUEST.

4

Derby House,
Stratford Place, W.
8 June 1917.

Confidential

Dear Prime Minister,

I much appreciated my talk with you this afternoon and I know you do not resent one saying exactly what one thinks. As to whether Winston Churchill will strengthen your Government or the reverse we must agree to differ as I do not think either could convince the other. I am really anxious to serve you and your Government and therefore feel that you will forgive me if I put before you somewhat bluntly the position as it concerns me as head of the War Office.

If Winston Churchill is only to be a second Lord Cowdray I do not mind if he will only do his work half as well. Lord Cowdray has done a real amount of good for the Air Service and has worked most cordially with the War Office without in any way attempting to interfere with the administration of that office.

While I regret Winston Churchill's inclusion in the Government—if he be included—as being a source of weakness I feel that it would not affect the War Office if it was clearly understood:—

(1) that he was not a member of the War Cabinet and did not attend any meetings unless specially summoned for business connected with the Board;

(2) that his duties as Chairman of the Board were the same as those of Lord Cowdray and that he had nothing to do with either personnel, tactics, or the nomination of the War Office representatives on the Board; and

(3) that he received no War Office telegrams other than those which were in any way connected with his particular department.

I gathered from you this afternoon that the conditions I have named were certainly those on which you would understand that he should enter the Government and that being so as far as my own office is concerned I personally can offer no objection, though I am bound to say I think there is a big 'if' in the question and that is *if* Winston Churchill will ever consent to occupy a comparatively minor position and do his own work without interfering with other people's. Perhaps you would let me know on Monday when I see you if I am right in my statement as to what your views on the position are.

I had an interesting talk with Henry Wilson this afternoon and I have a suggestion to make to you with regard to him which if you will give me 5 minutes on Monday afternoon I could easily explain. He is a great friend of mine and has in my opinion very great ability which I think might be made use of. As a Corps Commander not only is he not very good but his particular abilities would be lost to the Country.

I sent you over Ramsay Macdonald's views as to terms of peace and I am bound to say if he would stick to them I do not think his visit could do the slightest harm. I think however we are going to have great trouble with the seamen about conveying him there.

You might let me know if you could give me a few minutes on Monday afternoon any time most convenient to yourself.

Yours sincerely,

DERBY.

The Rt. Hon. D. Lloyd George, M.P.

5

My dear Prime Minister,   29. xii. 18.

I realise that you ought to have a speedy answer to the question you put to me this morning about going to the War Office or the Admiralty.

My heart is in the Admiralty. There I have long experience, & any claim I may be granted in public goodwill rests on the fact that 'the Fleet was ready'. In all the circumstances of the present situation I believe I shd add more weight to yr Administration at the Admiralty than at the War Office.

There wd be good reasons for connecting the air with the Admiralty; for aeroplanes will never be a substitute for armies & can only be a valuable accessory whereas they will almost certainly be an economical substitute for many classes of warships. The technical development of the air falls naturally into the same sphere as the mechanical developments of the Navy— & this becomes increasingly true the larger the aeroplanes grow.

Therefore I have no doubt what my choice shd be.

Yours always,

W.*

* Winston Churchill.

6

19th February 1917.

Dear Prime Minister,

I am sorry to say Lytton has so far not arrived, and therefore I am as completely in the dark as to the circumstances under which Haig's interview was given as I was at Luncheon time. Any suggestions therefore for an answer that I could put forward to you now would be of little use. Robertson is coming back tonight and I am arranging to meet him, and we will try and draft something that will be satisfactory to you before the meeting of the War Cabinet tomorrow morning.

May I impress one thing upon you, and that is, that while definite statements appear in all the accounts of the interview, there are widely divergent accounts as to the operations proposed; in fact I do not think any two accounts agree. Nor, I suggest, should the statement that we are short of big guns be read from the light of the intimate knowledge that the War Cabinet possesses on this point. It was only an expression of opinion that has found vent in many other ways, viz., that nobody can have too many big guns. The ideal of enough big guns can probably never be reached.

Candidly also, I do not see what military information is given to the Germans by saying we have 225 miles of new railways behind the line. In the first place they know pretty well through their aeroplanes what we are doing and can estimate accordingly, and, secondly, the fact that we have got these increased railway facilities will put them more than ever in doubt as where attacks are likely to be made.

I do hope that you will check Curzon's desire to send a telegram to Haig forbidding him to have any further interviews. I am trying to find out the truth of the origin of this interview, but if, as I believe it **No. I now hear it was** was, at the instance of the propaganda department **not.** of the Foreign Office, his answer to the telegram will be obvious. Of course, if you like to say in a telegram that you think it would be advisable in any future interviews not to give any forecast of future operations and to confine himself entirely to past matters, I do not think the same objection would arise. I do think that to reprimand him—as this practically is—for having an interview which one of your own Departments has asked him to have, and at the same time to accept as gospel the account of that interview (an account which he denies) can only have one effect and that is to drive him into resignation: a state of affairs which I know you would deplore, and which I do not think the country would consider justified by this indiscretion.

Yours sincerely,

DERBY.

7

20th February 1917

Dear Prime Minister,

I was very glad to get the solution which you arrived at with regard to Haig today. It is perfectly obvious that he has been badly let down by Charteris, and I am sending an official Army Council letter to him on the subject, saying that we deplore the position which has arisen, and that we think it is indefensible that a subordinate should behave as Charteris has done, and to ask him whether he considers it is not advisable to remove the latter. I deplore the whole thing. As you know, I am a strong adherent of Haig, but I cannot help feeling that his action has undoubtedly lowered him in the eyes of others, entirely owing to the fact that words were put into his mouth which he never used, & which we could not repudiate because it would give away the French & show the incapacity of our Censors office.

Yours sincerely,

DERBY.

The Right Hon. D. Lloyd George, M.P.

8

Derby House,
Stratford Place,
W.

Strictly Confidential. 11 December, 1917.

My dear Prime Minister,

Our talk this afternoon has considerably disturbed
me and while I would not ask you to look upon this
as a very carefully thought out letter I want to put
down what on the spur of the moment occurs to me
with regard to what you said.

In the first place if you are really thinking of making
a complete change in the Supreme Command both at
home and abroad, it is not the least use my going out
and having a very unpleasant interview with Sir
Douglas Haig with regard to the dismissal of what
is after all only a subordinate officer.* As it at present
stands I must go out on Thursday but if you are
really determined to make the big change I would not
go if you would invent the excuse for me that you
particularly wanted me at meetings on Thursday and
Friday mornings. I leave this entirely to you but
unless I hear from you to the contrary I shall go.

This
requires
an
immediate
answer

Now as regards the change of Haig and Robertson.
I will deal with the former first. I do not think that
the Cambrai affair is one on which you ought to hang
so momentous a decision as the removal of a Commander in Chief. You may remember that the day
before you went to Paris you told me that you had
more confidence in Haig than you ever had before
and if you had that confidence, and I believe you had,
it would not be fair to remove him simply because a
part of his line broke when the main attack for which
he was chiefly prepared was successfully repulsed.

---

* It was the intention to dismiss Brigadier-General John Charteris, C.M.G.,
D.S.O., Haig's Chief Intelligence Officer.

APPENDIX IV

I agree with you that it somewhat shakes ones confidence in anybody when you see the complete change of view that takes place between his letter of October 29th and those which he wrote subsequently but I ascribe, as I know you do, the first letter to the influence of Charteris whom it would be my mission to dismiss if I went out on Thursday. Therefore to dismiss Haig simply because of the Cambrai affair would to my mind be extremely unjust and I feel that I could not be a party to it.

Let us take however the other suggestion that it should not be a case of dismissal but rather a promotion and that he should be made Generalissimo of all the British Forces. There are certain difficulties in doing that which would have to be overcome, the principal one being the finding of a suitable Commander in Chief for the Western Front. Plumer is sound but certainly I think does not have that imagination for which you are looking. Birdwood to my mind would be absolutely out of the question. Munro would be the best man you could get and personally I look upon Rawlinson as a first class soldier. I think Haig's successor, if the change is made, should lie between Munro and Rawlinson.

Now as to Haig's position if he is made Generalissimo. I am going into the question as to what the duties and powers of the Commander in Chief of old days was but things have changed very much and I doubt whether the rules applicable then would apply now. The first question I would ask is what would be his relationship to the War Cabinet? Would he be the Chief Military Advisor to the War Cabinet? If so it is a most important post and one which anybody should hesitate before refusing. If on the other hand the advice to the War Cabinet is to be given by some other individual than the Generalissimo he is nothing more than an Inspector General, an inferior post which I do not think you could possibly ask Haig to accept.

365

It would be much better to dismiss him altogether rather than to ask him to take a sinecure post.

With regard to Robertson the position is equally difficult and I do not see what post you could put him in and again it would be much better to dismiss him rather than degrade him.

To return to Haig. If his position is Generalissimo and Chief Advisor to the War Cabinet it is as I have said a most important post, but supposing you do not agree to that who is to be the Chief Military Advisor of the Government? You mention Maurice as the Chief of the Staff who would come daily to the Cabinet to give the usual War information, but I did not gather from you that he would be anything more than an exponent of what had happened and you did not contemplate him as an advisor. I hope you are not thinking of making Henry Wilson in Paris the Chief Advisor. That I could not possibly support. I hope and believe he will do well in his present position but I am sure that if you put him in London as your Chief Military Advisor you would defeat the very object you have in view, namely the promotion of confidence in our Military Chiefs.

Now as to my own position. I am deeply grateful to you for what you were good enough to say with regard to your confidence in me. You know that I am not a seeker after office and that I supported you, not in any way to get official position, but I thought, as I still think, that you are the only possible Prime Minister for the country during the present crisis, and whether I remain in office or went out would make no difference in the support that I gave you. If Haig was promoted in the way that I have suggested and Robertson given suitable employment, and that they both accepted the positions voluntarily and not under compulsion, I should feel that I had nothing to reproach myself with but if on the other hand they are practically compelled to resign then I have to consider my own position and I hope not from an egotistical point of view. In the first place I do not think that my going would have the least effect on the stability of your Government. If you are right in thinking that the confidence of the Army in Haig and Robertson has gone then in going with them I should simply be looked upon as a person who supported a policy in which the Country had no confidence and you know perfectly well that no word or deed of mine would ever be used against you or your Government. Where I differ from you, and perhaps from the public, is that I have confidence in Haig and Robertson. I think Haig is very misguided in the Staff he keeps about him. He is one of those men who is so thoroughly loyal to his subordinates that he will not recognise that his own position is threatened by that loyalty but that he is the best man we have got for Command in the Field, I have no doubt whatsoever. I see nobody who can compare with him and to see him ousted from his present position, unless it is to promote him would to my mind be most prejudicial to our Military position.

With regard to Robertson. I confess that what you told me with regard to your suspicions today has shaken my confidence but I cannot believe that he would deliberately ask Allenby to send in a false telegram in order to deceive the Government. I agree with you that read in the light of subsequent events Allenby's telegram asking for the enormous increase of force in order to do what he has done with the existing forces seems very ridiculous but that his former proposal should be put forward with a deliberate attempt to deceive the Government and that at the instance of Robertson, is almost beyond belief. I want to be perfectly frank with you and confess that I was not very desirous of seeing the Jerusalem attack. I was afraid of being committed in a way which would require either a retirement or a reinforcement which we could not give. I was entirely wrong but I think you know me well enough to realise nothing would have induced me to be a Party to a deliberate attempt to deceive the Government and that is what you think Robertson did. If he did it and it can be proved, I could have no further faith in him but I cannot believe it and assuming therefore it is not the case I take Robertson as I have found him and that is a very honest man endeavouring to give the Government the best advice that it is in his power to give. I know that he is what you call sticky and at times a very difficult man to deal with. I feel sometimes, and I think you do, that there is more at the back of his mind than he will tell one, but still I think you might go much further and fare much worse than to accept his advice.

I am putting down my thoughts just as they occur to me and therefore they are rather disconnected which please forgive.

To turn to the position of the War Cabinet. I hold that the War Cabinet has got an absolute right to change any Commander that they may think fit and to change any policy if they think it is right to do so. They naturally have to take the responsibility if they go against their military advisors but on the other hand as they have finally to bear all responsibility they must be allowed to insist on their policy being carried out and get people they think best fitted to carry it out. Some people would say that that meant the politicians interfering with the soldiers and they may be right but I for one should never hold that opinion though naturally in one's present position one would insist on the right of resigning if one thought that the advice given was the correct one and the persons in power were the most fitted to carry it out. I mention this and it brings me to the end of what I am afraid is rather a long letter. Put yourself into my position. I have had confidence, and still have it, in Haig and Robertson. I have told them that I have this confidence in them time after time and if they were suddenly superseded altogether what confidence would the new Commander in Chief have in me? He would say and with perfect justice—"You told my predecessor up to the very last moment that you had confidence in him and yet when it came to the point of showing that confidence in a practical way you deserted him". That is the position that I am sure you yourself would never take up and I know you would never ask me to.

I shall come and see you tomorrow so of course there is no need to answer this letter except on the two points (1) as to whether I should go to France on Thursday, and that requires an immediate reply; and (2) as to what position Haig as Generalissimo would occupy as regards the War Cabinet. The latter question I only want answered in view of your desire that I should discuss with a certain person the powers and position of a Commander in Chief and Generalissimo.

Yours sincerely,
DERBY

The Prime Minister.

9

Lord Derby to Sir Douglas Haig.

Strictly Personal and Confidential
12th December, 1917.

I had hoped to come over and see you tomorrow, though it was only for a flying visit, but the Prime Minister has insisted on my remaining for the discussion on Man-Power, and I agree with him it is important that I should do so as on this, in my opinion, must stand our possible success in the war. I am, therefore, obliged to deal by letter with matters which I would infinitely have preferred discussing with you.

APPENDIX IV

I want to preface my remarks with a repetition of what I think you know already, namely, that I have and always shall have implicit confidence in you, and anything I may write is written from the point of view of a friend and not of an adverse critic. There are two kinds of friends. There is a friend who always tells you everything which he thinks you would like to hear, and there is a friend who tells you things which he thinks you should hear, even if they are not always pleasant. I look upon the latter as being the true friend, and it is from that point of view that I mean to write to you today.

First of all I will deal with the Charteris question. In the note I sent you yesterday I told you that I did not think that you could look upon me as wishing to make Charteris a whipping boy for the Cambrai affair. I have mentioned to you on more than one occasion that he was doing you an infinity of harm by his optimism and by what I consider his inaccurate information, and I have begged you to make a change. You tell me that you invariably make an allowance for the optimism of Charteris. That may be so, but I cannot think that you make sufficient allowance, and the best proof I have of that is your letter of October 8th. That letter is clearly based on wrong information, and for that, although signed by you, I cannot hold you responsible. In view, not only of subsequent events, but of subsequent letters to you, I am sure you would never have put it forward if you had had proper information as to the enemy's reserves and possible reinforcements from the Russian Front.

It appears to me that too often the opinions, not only of the public but even of your subordinates and of the Army as a whole are not put before you. If they had been you would have realised that my view of Charteris as a public danger is shared by practically the whole of the Army, and I feel that if they do not put forward disagreeable facts to you, it is my duty to do so, however unpleasant it may be. I am afraid it is quite impossible for me to allow Charteris to remain as your Intelligence Officer, and much as I dislike giving you any instruction which I know is repugnant to you, I look upon you as a National asset and I cannot allow your loyalty to a subordinate to affect your position. I must, therefore, ask you to make a change within the next month, and shall be glad to hear either of your suggestions as to who should take his place or, failing that, that I should make suggestions to you. So much for Charteris. Now there are other members of your Staff who I think in your interest it would be as well to make a change. The two first are Maxwell and Fowke.

First of all Maxwell. Of him I have nothing to say except that he is undoubtedly a very tired man. He has done you splendid service, but I think that he requires a rest. I do not know at the present that I have any post that I could offer him, but I can assure you that I recognise his good qualities and his excellent work, and it will be my desire as soon as he is rested to find him some further employment. Fowke is a different case. I do not think Fowke is a strong enough man to maintain the discipline of your Army; especially under the present circumstances when everybody is feeling the strain of war. Equally I should be ready, if possible, to find him some other employment if you replace him.

The next case is a still more difficult one to bring to your notice, and that is the question of the retention of Gough in a high command. I believe him to be a most gallant soldier, but that does not affect the question that he has created a feeling of hatred against himself both on the part of officers and men that it is almost impossible to describe to you. Canadians are especially bitter. Sir George Perley has been to see me on the subject and he would have wished to have made a formal protest against his having Canadians under his command in future, but I persuaded him to leave it in my hands, promising to represent his views to you. The feeling in the Canadians is perhaps more intense than in other Units in the Army, but I can assure you that at the present moment there is not a wounded officer or man who comes back, and they naturally talk, who does not express an equally bitter opinion of him. There is nothing I dislike more than to think that the question of an officer in high command should be in any way decided by public opinion; but you must remember this fact, we are going through a very difficult time in this country. Everybody is war weary. The glamour and enthusiasm of the first two years have worn away, and you must take into consideration the views of this country which reflect to a very large extent the views of your own Army. It is not only the letters that come back, but still more the talk of men of all ranks when home on leave which shows that there is a disgruntled feeling in the Army which is impossible to ignore.

Now I come to the Cambrai affair. There is no doubt it has created a great feeling in this country which, personally, I do not share. There must be ups and downs in a war like this, and you cannot always have matters your own way. But there is an unfortunate feeling that somebody is to blame. Who it is naturally nobody knows; but I would ask you to have the most thorough enquiry into the affair, as, indeed, Bonar Law has promised in the House of Commons that you will, and if anybody has been guilty of neglect that that man should be punished. Please don't think that I am asking you to find a scapegoat. Nothing of the kind. I am asking you to find out who let you down—who failed you—and having found him out, send him home because you have no confidence in him. Once you do that the public, and I am one of them, would be absolutely satisfied. But the public will not be satisfied if the whole affair is passed over without a full explanation.

Yet another matter. The public are asking this—

What lines have you got in the rear of our present one to which you can fall back. They have heard of this wonderful Hindenburg line with its extraordinary dugouts, etc. All this information has been used, and rightly used, to show what extraordinary courage it required on the part of our troops to take it. All people are asking if we have got any thing of the same kind behind our line, and if not, why not. We hear of concrete pillboxes—huge dugouts immune from artillery fire, etc., and they feel we ought to have the same, and I should be glad of your assurance that such lines exist.

All these are extremely disagreeable things for me to have to say to you, but I repeat in conclusion what I began with, that they are matters which a true friend must bring to your notice. Your position is unassailable, but only so long as the Country thinks that it is being told the whole truth and that nobody is screened from the punishment he deserves.

I shall back you through thick and thin, and because I am prepared to do so I feel I equally have the right to ask you to take in good part any remarks I may make, to consider them dispassionately, and to as far as possible act on my suggestions. You and I have got to stand or fall together, and that must be my excuse if as a civilian I bring to your notice matters that are continually being brought before me, and ask you to take action which will prevent either of us being the subject of reproach.

10

Derby House,
Stratford Place, W.

Confidential & Personal.   18 January 1918

My dear P.M.,
   With reference to the question of a new Ambassador for Paris which you and I discussed at luncheon the

APPENDIX IV

other day and whom you wished to appoint with special powers, I think before the man we had in mind would take it his powers would have to be clearly defined.

I do not know what powers have been given to Lord Reading* but I presume that they are largely in excess of those which are given to the ordinary Ambassador. Would they equally apply in the case of Paris? Your answer will probably be No because there is a great difference between Washington and Paris and to that I agree. But the real question is this. Would the Ambassador in Paris be more or less of a colleague of members of the War Cabinet or would he be simply the mouthpiece of that body?

I am sure that what the person in question would first of all consider would be whether or not his acceptance of the post was in the National interest and I am quite sure that he would subordinate all questions of a personal character, which might make him inclined to refuse, if he thought he could be of any real use and assistance: but there is one thing I am convinced of and that is that he would never give up, except to a limited extent, his independence and it is on that question that the difficulty might arise.

A man in office is not only entitled, but it is his duty, to resign if he thinks that the Government to which he belongs is doing something which he dis-approves of and which in his opinion is detrimental to the best interests of the Nation. I am naturally only referring to big questions, but would the same liberty be given to him as an Ambassador as would be given to anybody who was in a Government Department at home?

It is always best if possible to take a concrete case. I presume the new Ambassador would be in close touch with Versailles and would be kept fully informed

* Lord Reading's appointment as Ambassador to the United States, to replace Sir Cecil Spring-Rice, had been announced at the beginning of January 1918.

of all that was going on there. The man in question*
as you know supports the Versailles arrangement
and has told both you and me that he thinks great
advantage can be gained from it but suppose Versailles
put forward a proposal to which the War Cabinet
agreed but to which the other Military advisers,
Sir Douglas Haig and Sir William Robertson, or anybody who might be in their place, were in strong
disagreement. Would he be expected to support the
Government view even if he was convinced it was
wrong? Personally I do not think that such questions
will arise with this particular individual but still he
would have the right to have his position made
perfectly clear, in order that if he did take an independent line, which if he remained in England he would
undoubtedly be entitled to take, he should not be
accused of acting disloyally to the Government.

On the other hand I do see that great advantage
will be gained by having somebody in Paris who would
be in close touch with you and your War Cabinet
and who knows what I may call the train of thought
there and knowing this would be able to transact
business with the French Government which now you
have to get done either yourself or by a member of
your Government going personally to Paris.

I think also that he probably would be more able to
get in personal touch with all political sections in
Paris than Bertie has been able to do and by entertaining
be able to bring the British Embassy in Paris more,
what I may call, 'into the picture' than it is at the
present moment.

I only put down these heads because I should like
to have another talk with you on the subject because
I think the man in question is likely to accept provided
he is able to keep his independence—at all events to
a limited extent, and is not called upon to be simply

* Lord Derby himself.

a mouthpiece of the Government and gagged on all these questions on which I know he holds a very strong opinion.

Yours v. sincerely,
DERBY

The Right Hon.
D. Lloyd George M.P.

11

29th January, 1918.

Dear Prime Minister,

I have had the article by Colonel Repington in the *Morning Post* of the 24th examined in conjunction with the Man Power Committee's Report—G.185—and some other papers on the subject circulated to the Cabinet, i.e. the Memorandum by the Military Members of the Army Council (G.T.3265), a note by Sir D. Haig dated 8th January, 1918 (W.C.317), a memorandum by myself, dated 14th January (M.P.C.29), another by General Smuts, dated 17th January (M.P.C.30), a note by the Chief of the Imperial General Staff, dated 23rd January, 1918 (M.P.C.31), the Weekly General Staff Summaries, and Sir A. Geddes' speech on Man Power in the House of Commons on 14th January 1918. A schedule showing the results of this comparison is enclosed.

Before I had time to send you this, and answer your letter of the 24th, I received yours of the 28th. Later, I heard from the Cable Censors that Repington had written a reply to the charge that he had been supplied improperly with official information, and that the *Morning Post* was to publish it today. I have now seen this article, and in the face of his statements that many official persons, civil as well as military, have communicated with him from time to time on the subject of man power, and that no Cabinet paper has been given to him by any soldier, I don't see how we can single out the General Staff as the source of his information. With one or two exceptions, Repington's figures and statements are wrong, or are such as his long experience, wide knowledge, and profound study throughout the war would readily furnish him with, or they are such as would naturally come to him in the course of his well-known constant communication with Clemenceau and other French authorities.

I must point out that the Man Power Report was circulated more widely than may be usual with such papers. I enclose the list supplied to me from 2, Whitehall Gardens. I cannot see what other documents than those I have enumerated above Repington could be charged with having been shown, and the principal one is undoubtedly the Man Power Report. It would lead us nowhere to threaten all recipients of the latter with dire pains and penalties, and, as I have said, I can see no ground for singling out the officers of the General Staff for exclusive treatment on these lines.

In reply to your second letter, you should see Lovat Fraser's attack in the *Daily Mail* of yesterday. It is much more "encouraging" to the Enemy than Repington's statements. However, I have sent both to the Director of Public Prosecutions for advice, and I will in due course, when I receive that, submit to the Cabinet whether proceeding shall be taken against either or both. A Prosecution would give really the best opportunity of finding out all that there is to know as to the sources of inspiration of these writers.

Yours sincerely,
DERBY.

12

22 Hans Crescent,
S.W.1.

26th April, 1918.

My dear Bonar,

I have been rather worried about the announcement which you made in the House of Commons, to the effect that I had resigned my appointment on the Air Council on the ground that I could not work with the new Chief of the Air Staff. That is not the reason which I gave to Lord Rothermere as you will see by the enclosed copy of my letter to him.

The fact is that my previous relations with Sykes, and my opinion of him, were not secrets, and had I remained in the Air Force, there was grave danger that I might become, however unwillingly, a focus of discontent and opposition.

Further, there was very little question of my "working" with Sykes. I had no executive duties left. The organisation of the Air Force in which I had been engaged since my transfer from the Army Council for the purpose, was complete, and I had clearly told Lord Rothermere, when he asked me to be Vice-President, that I could only hold the position while there was work for me to do.

I am ready to admit that I earnestly desired to escape from the atmosphere of intrigue and falsehood which has enveloped the Air Ministry for the last few months. On the other hand, I quite understand that my action has probably cut me off from any prospect of useful employment, either in the Army or in the Air Force. But I did not allow either of these considerations to influence me. I left, as I said, in the interests of the Service.

I spoke to Baird about this matter and he advised

me to write to you, as there would shortly be an opportunity of correcting the mistake.

Yours very sincerely,
DAVID HENDERSON.

(*Enclosure*)

Dear Lord Rothermere,

After our conversation on Friday last, when I expressed to you and to General Smuts a very unfavourable opinion of Major-General Sykes, and considering my previous relations with that officer, his appointment as Chief of the Air Staff makes it most undesirable, in the interests of the Service, that I should remain in the Air Force.

I am not aware whether the acceptance of a temporary commission in the Royal Air Force, for reasons of administrative convenience, affects my right to refuse attachment to the Royal Air Force given by the Air Force Constitution Act. If this be so, I beg that the point may be waived in my favour, and that this letter may be taken as giving notice that I do not desire to be attached and that my attachment may be annulled.

Yours sincerely,
(Copy initialled) D.H.

13

April 22, 1918.

My dear Prime Minister,

I have recently had an opportunity of seeing the Memorandum which Lord Rothermere addressed to you on the 9th instant in which he reviews the general situation in the Royal Air Force with a view to deciding what reorganisation, if any, is necessary or desirable.

I regret that I am unable to agree with some of the views expressed by Lord Rothermere and, consequently, could not support them in the House of Commons. In view of the Debates which are certain to take place in Parliament on this subject in the near future I thought it advisable to write to you in this sense at the earliest moment, and I most respectfully beg that I may be given an opportunity of laying my views before the War Cabinet. This course is all the more necessary because the opinions which I have formed are largely based on figures and facts which it would be impossible to make public.

Lord Rothermere is unfortunately away in the country ill, and I have to-day sent him the letter of which the enclosed is a copy. There are some other points connected with the Ministry with regard to which I regret that I do not see eye to eye with my Secretary of State and I think it my duty to bring these points before the War Cabinet also.

Yours sincerely,
JOHN BAIRD.

14

Hemsted,
Benenden, Kent.
Tuesday, April 23rd, 1918.

My dear Prime Minister,

I desire to relinquish my office as Secretary of State of the Air Force at the earliest possible moment.

There are three reasons actuating me in reaching this decision. One is that my stock of health is hardly adequate for such an anxious and harassing post.

Another and more decisive reason is that this young Force after all the publicity it has received during the last few weeks requires a rest from comment and criticism. So far no harm has been done. I feel, however, that a continuance during the next few months might impair discipline and prejudice efficiency.

With myself as Secretary of State there is every reason to suppose that comment and criticism will continue. With the office in the hands of someone else there is a fair chance of a moratorium as far as newspaper and parliamentary publicity are concerned.

The danger to discipline through constant publicity is well illustrated in the report of this morning's newspapers of yesterday's proceedings in the House of Commons. Two of the three Members of Parliament pressing Mr. Bonar Law to give an early day for a debate on Air Ministry affairs are officers of the Royal Air Force holding junior Staff appointments under me in the Hotel Cecil. These two officers, viz. Major Rt. Hon. Sir John Simon and Lieut. Rt. Hon. Lord Hugh Cecil, are not privileged persons. Why in the House of Commons should they flout disciplinary codes where elsewhere similar conduct by any other Staff Officer would form the subject of enquiry by his superior officers?

Sequestered in the Hotel Cecil, Major Sir John Simon has acted as an assistant secretary or clerk to Major-General Sir H. Trenchard, late Chief of the Air Staff. Two months ago I mentioned to you the extreme unsuitability of this arrangement with its possible dangers. As events have proved, I was not wrong.

A new Force like the Royal Air Force in which the number of senior officers is extraordinarily small requires iron discipline. Unless this is stamped upon it at its birth it is most improbable it will reach the full measure of its possible achievements in this war.

The third reason for my resignation is that the immediate work I set out to accomplish is finished. The blending of the Royal Naval Air Service and the Royal Flying Corps is complete; their fusion into the Royal Air Force went through on the 1st April without a hitch. So there is no question of "swapping horses". The stream has been crossed.

The recommendations set out in my secret memorandum which received the sanction of the War Cabinet are being carried out. The Strategic Council has been formed and has already held meetings. In a few days Major-General Sykes has impressed his personality on all with whom he has come in contact.

In my opinion this brilliant officer with his singularly luminous mind, great knowledge of Staff work, and grasp of service organisation, is an ideal Chief of Staff of the Royal Air Force. He has the sovereign gifts, particularly necessary now, of elasticity of outlook and receptivity of mind combined with youth and energy.

Aided by the able coadjutors he has found on the Air Council and at the Air Ministry the future of the Air Force can safely be left in his hands.

I cannot close this letter of resignation without an expression of my great respect and regard for yourself.

Yours very faithfully,

ROTHERMERE.

15

Extract of a letter from Winston Churchill to Lord Beaverbrook, 27th November, 1926.

... *The Maurice Debate.* This seems to have made no impression upon me. I may have been in Paris. All I recollect is being horrified to hear Bonar offer Asquith a judicial enquiry. I was with him on the bench and implored that this offer should be withdrawn. I think I was the one who convinced both him and L.G. that same afternoon. It would have been a frightful trap, and no Government ought to put up a set of judges to say whether they are liars or not. Asquith saved the situation by boggling about the enquiry, most foolishly from his point of view; and the Government were able to withdraw their offer in good style. ...

16

26th February, 1918.

NOTES ON THE RESOLUTION FORWARDED BY THE UNIONIST WAR COMMITTEE TO THE PRIME MINISTER

Dear Prime Minister,

The first half of the Resolution is rather cryptic and may be directed against anyone.

The second half explains itself.

If you intend to act in the spirit of the above Resolution it will be necessary for you to dismiss Rothermere, Beaverbrook and Northcliffe, as none of them will resign. Beaverbrook would continue to support you and your Government up to, and through, the next General Election. I think Rothermere would feel inclined to do the same. Northcliffe may do anything.

My advice is to stand to your guns, for the following reasons:—

1. It is essential that you should stand by your friends and your appointments.
2. That out of the eighty members of the Unionist War Group I do not think more than thirty-five would vote against the Government on this question.
3. The other Conservatives will stand by their leaders.
4. I am almost sure that within two or three months at the latest both Rothermere and Beaverbrook will resign; Rothermere on account of ill-health, and Beaverbrook because he will, by that time, have set up for you a perfectly organised Propaganda Department and will want to regain his liberty.

No pledge is obtainable or reasonable and might even end in deeper difficulty.

I, however, believe that the agitators have very inconvenient proofs of Sutherland's activities, and that, at times, our Press opponents have got the better of him and have given him away. There is also some evidence available to the effect that he has subordinated the interest of your colleagues in his intense loyalty to yourself.

An atmosphere has thereby been created which, I fear, cannot fail to accumulate to your disadvantage.

I do not recommend that so loyal a friend should be thrown to the wolves, but I do recommend that he should be instructed to curtail his activities.

When I first took over, last May, I agreed to leave all connection with the London Press entirely in his hands and have, therefore, no responsibility for any of the so-called "inspirations", but I believe it would be wise that the Whips' Office should resume its traditional function of being the chief repository of information suitable for the Press. Of course I exclude the issue of Government announcements, appointments, etc., which bear the official stamp of No. 10.

I have sounded the following Ministers on the General situation and report as follows:—

Talbot is anxious to find a way out. He thinks the movement serious, but does not think it will be forced to extreme.

Hewart and Illingworth entirely agree with the advice which I submit.

F. E. Smith and W.S.C. think that you should stand by your guns.

Yours sincerely,
FREDERICK GUEST.

The Rt. Hon. David Lloyd George, M.P.

17

1 Carlton House Terrace,
S.W.1.

PRIVATE November 13, 1918.

My dear Prime Minister,

I received just now your telephone message confirming my departure tomorrow. I have just heard from the King of the Belgians that the Queen and he re-enter Brussels on Saturday. Lady Curzon and I have always promised to be with them on that day and accordingly we are returning to Belgium by motor tomorrow for this ceremony and shall be back in England on Monday.

Meanwhile I should like to report to you the result of my conversation this morning with M. Clemenceau. He treated me as he has done throughout with the greatest confidence and cordiality.

(1) He does not at all want Wilson at the Conference or Conferences. As the Head of a State Wilson ought not to attend the Conference. If he did attend he would probably expect to preside and this Clemenceau thought would be unacceptable to all.

(2) Clemenceau showed me some further messages from Germany appealing to Wilson for compassion. He thinks, and I agree, that this constant communication behind the back of the Allies with Wilson ought to be stopped at once and that all such appeals should be addressed to or communicated, before reply —to the principal Allies.

(3) I do not see how you are to wait till mid-December for Wilson. My own impression is that the Allied representatives should start work at once. I hear that the Italian is coming. Problems are arising every day that call for instant examination, and solution. House's plea that, if the President is coming, he (House) will be without interim authority, is not I

think valid. Postpone big decisions if you like. But go ahead with the preparation of all the cases and the settling of all the minor ones.

(4) Clemenceau is very angry with the Italian about their tricks with the Austrian fleet.

(5) I asked him his view about a possible trial of the Kaiser and the Arch-Criminals, and told him we had a Committee investigating the matter and reporting on a possible Tribunal. He said he had not seriously considered the point, but would like my ideas.

Speaking for myself alone, I suggested the possibility of creating—as the first step to a League of Nations—an international tribunal of jurists of the highest eminence (they might or might not include neutrals, probably Yes) for the express purpose of trying the Kaiser, his son and the other offenders. They might be cited before it. I do not know enough of international law to be sure whether Holland having interned them, if she has, could or would give them up for trial. But would that matter in the case of the Kaiser and his son? The charges could be sent to them and their replies invited. Either these would be just and considered, or they would be refused.

In either case the Tribunal could consider the evidence and eventually pronounce its verdict. If the sentence was that of outlawry from the principal countries of the world, it would be a punishment signal, crushing, unheard of in history.

Clemenceau thought that such a proposition had in it immense possibilities. He was greatly taken with the idea. He thought that as an act of international justice, of world retribution, it would be one of the most imposing events in history and that the conception was well worthy of being pursued.

He prayed me to communicate with my Government on the matter and to let him have any papers or reports on the subject that we might prepare.

I pass this on to you at once since you may be talking the matter over with Balfour before you all come here. I pray you to consider it seriously. Public opinion will not willingly consent to let this arch-criminal escape by a final act of cowardice. The supreme and colossal nature of his crime seems to call for some supreme and unprecedented condemnation. Execution, imprisonment, these are not, or may not be, necessary. But continued life, an inglorious and ignoble exile, under the weight of such a sentence as has never before been given in the history of mankind, would be a penance worse than death.

Yours sincerely,
CURZON.

This afternoon in the absence of the Ambassador I was called upon to address a shouting and enthusiastic crowd of English and Dominion soldiers who made their way into the courtyard of this building, and was there and then publicly kissed by Miss Decima Moore!

18

Monday, 7 July 1919

My dear Prime Minister,

I venture, for what they are worth, to put before you some views about the contemplated trial of the Kaiser in England.

I have always been in favour of his trial. Indeed, I was the first to raise the subject in the Imperial War Cabinet last year. On the whole, I adhere to the views which I then expressed, though perhaps less strongly than at the time when the subject was first raised. But I confess that I had never contemplated, and am a good deal staggered at, the idea of the trial taking place in England; and, the more I reflect upon it, the more I am inclined to think that we may be on the verge of committing a great mistake. The considerations which appeal to me are the following:—

In the first place, we cannot get away from the fact that he will have been brought to the country of those whom he regards as his chief enemies, and who have really compassed his downfall. In practice, I fully believe that he would get a fairer trial from us than from any other people; but outside this country it will be said and thought that those whom the German Emperor hated most and did his best to injure have insisted on seizing him and executing the final act of vengeance. There will thus spring up an idea, if he is brought here, that he will not receive fair play; and, if he is condemned and sentenced here, that he has not had it. It will be said that we insisted on getting him, in order to be sure of his fate. Unquestionably there will be this amount of truth in the charge, that, while the feelings towards him in France and Belgium may be even more passionate than they are here, the sentiment of this country as a whole will be one of violent hostility and prejudice, affecting, not, it may be, the minds of the judges, but the temper of the people.

Secondly, does not there seem to be a certain refinement of severity in bringing the Kaiser here, to the country the most famous Sovereign of which was his Grandmother; where his Mother was born; and from which she was married; where he has constantly stayed as a Royal Guest; and where his Cousin is at the present moment on the Throne? I do not suppose that the King was consulted on the matter. I doubt if he knew anything more about it than the rest of us. But surely it is putting him in a very delicate and invidious position if his near relative, however great his crimes, is to be tried almost within sight of the Palace where the King lives and where the culprit has so often stayed? This, it seems to me, is a question of taste rather than of anything else; but a good many people, looking at it from that point of view, will, I

think, be disposed to hold that such a proceeding
ought to be avoided.

Thirdly, if the Kaiser is brought here, we have to
choose the place where he and his associates are to be
tried. It is really almost inconceivable that he should be
placed in a spot where day after day, through a period
extending very likely over many months, he will have
to be brought backwards and forwards to the Court of
Justice amid the jeers and insults of the crowd. Such an
arrangement would begin by being disgraceful and,
after it had lasted a long time and the public had become indifferent, would end by being ridiculous. The
only alternative would be to fix the Court in some
place where the Kaiser could be accommodated in close
proximity to the building, if not inside it. But such
places are not easily available. If he were to be tried
in the Royal Gallery of the House of Lords, he might,
I suppose, be lodged in the apartments which the Lord
Chancellor has been prevented by the Commons from
occupying because he insisted on a bath. But surely
we do not want him in Westminster, in close proximity
to our every day proceedings. Again, it is suggested,
I am told, that he might be taken to Hampton Court.
But a place of holiday resort, where thousands of
people would be hanging about every day is hardly a
suitable "mise en scène" for such a trial. Similar
objections apply to almost every place that can be
suggested. Even if the difficulty can be overcome in
the case of the Kaiser, how are we to meet it in the case
of his associates? I assume that, if he comes or is
brought here, he will make a sustained and prolonged
defence. He will summon to his side his sons, his
ex-Ministers, his Generals, his friends. He will try to
overwhelm the Court with evidence as to his innocence
and irresponsibility. He will endeavour to break down
the proceedings by every form of delay. We shall run
the risk of a trial that may extend over many months,
perhaps longer. If Bethmann-Hollweg, Hindenburg,

Ludendorff, and a crowd of other witnesses appear upon the scene, they also will have to be accommodated, and will there not, in their daily procession to the scene of the trial, be an opportunity for the same sort of displays of which I have already spoken?

Fourthly, is it desirable that we should distract the attention of the country from all the difficulties with which we are confronted by providing them with a sensation of this description? They might welcome it, and we might welcome it, to start with. But I cannot help feeling that before long a feeling would grow up that we had made a desperate mistake, and, if it were so, that we should be the sufferers.

Fifthly, let me take the three contingencies which may conceivably occur. The first is that the Dutch Government may decline to surrender the Kaiser, or that he may refuse to come, and the trial will have to take place in his absence. If no one comes to speak on his behalf, would it really do for us to put up some learned British or foreign jurisconsult to plead his case? If, on the other hand, a stream of witnesses comes, unaccompanied by the Kaiser, is it not conceivable that a case may be made which, in the absence of the principal defendant, would result in an inconclusive verdict, if not in an acquittal?

But, however this may be, and whether he comes or not, shall not we be in all probability the main sufferers by any verdict that may be given? If he be pronounced guilty, and sentence be passed upon him, and it is left to us to carry it out, shall not we in the eyes both of Germany and the rest of the world have to bear the entire responsibility, now and in History? Never mind that the Court is international, the verdict will be regarded as having been inspired, just as in all probability it will have to be executed, by ourselves. Would it be possible ever again to make friends with Germany after that? Would not it be a root of bitterness which would last till the end of time?

If, on the other hand, he is acquitted or an inconclusive verdict is reached, upon us will fall the blame and ridicule of the fiasco; and the effects of our military triumph will be largely dissipated by this bathos.

The question therefore arises whether it is possible to extricate ourselves from the position of bringing the Kaiser here, and whether he could be tried anywhere else. I do not, of course, know the arguments which prevailed upon the Council of Four to decide in favour of England. I expect that the other countries represented were only too anxious not to shoulder the responsibility themselves. France and Belgium, I can well imagine, might be considered unsuitable places. Italy is too remote, and the Italians are not to be trusted. But why should Holland be debarred? Is it altogether impossible that the Kaiser should be tried at The Hague? The trial and verdict will surely be independent of the particular locality in which the former will be held, and the judges are as likely to deliver a fair and reasonable finding in one country as they are in another. On the other hand, we would escape all the difficulties, or some at any rate of them, in respect of the contemplated demand of surrender to be addressed to the Dutch Government, and their possible refusal. The Kaiser is already in Holland. It might be easier for them to transfer him from one part of the country to another without raising the question of his leaving Holland. This would also lessen the difficulty as to his witnesses, if he summoned them, reaching the place of trial. It would be much simpler for them to cross a land frontier into Holland than to be brought across the sea to our own shore.

I assume that Holland must have been considered and ruled out for some reason that I do not know, but at least the point seems worthy of consideration.

I have rather hastily dictated this letter, in order to let you know what is in my own mind. I have had a brief talk with both Milner and Winston on the

matter, and I find that their views coincide with mine.
Insofar as I have spoken to other people, of whatever
shade of thought, I find that the same opinions prevail.
Indeed I have not come across any one who, whatever
he thinks about the wisdom of the trial—and about
this there are a good many doubts—, is in favour of the
particular suggestion that is made. I did not like to
bring the matter before the Cabinet in your absence,
and therefore I have written this to you, feeling sure
that you will seriously consider the matter and will
give the Cabinet the opportunity at an early date of
discussing it with fuller knowledge than they now
possess.

I believe that the view of the Foreign Office is well-
nigh unanimous in the direction which I have described.

I am,

Yours sincerely,

CURZON.

19

Lord Curzon to Lord Lansdowne
(Published by Lord Newton in *Lord Lansdowne: A
Biography*, pp. 452-3)

Confidential.   December 3rd, 1916.

I am sorry that you could not be present at the
meeting at Bonar Law's which is just over.

It is a long story. For a fortnight *pourparlers* have
been going on between Lloyd George and the Prime
Minister, in which Bonar Law (without telling us) has
taken a prominent part.

The letters were read to us just now. Practically
Lloyd George issued an ultimatum to the Prime
Minister, putting the latter in the complete background, and constituting a War Committee of three,
under himself.

The Prime Minister refused, and stuck to the
arrangement (of two Committees) mentioned at the

last Cabinet and agreed to at our last meeting in Bonar
Law's room, with himself as Chairman. Lloyd George,
as the papers of yesterday and today will have shown
you, has attempted to force the situation by announc-
ing his own resignation, which is apparently to appear
in the Press tomorrow. Derby is to resign with him,
and Bonar Law has been so far implicated that his
name appears with theirs in the papers, and he told us
he meant to resign this afternoon.

We felt three things: (a) that this was unfair to the
Prime Minister; (b) that it placed Lloyd George in a
position where he could dictate his terms; (c) that
Bonar Law ought not to act independently, but that
we ought both to think and act unitedly. Accordingly,
it was unanimously decided that Bonar Law should
see the Prime Minister early this afternoon (he has
been summoned back from Walmer, whither, with
characteristic nonchalance, he had slipped away
yesterday evening); that Bonar Law should tell him
that in our opinion the events to which I have referred
had rendered internal reconstruction no longer possible; that he (Asquith) should this afternoon place his
resignation in the hands of the King (including, of
course, ours); and that if he was not able to take that
step we placed the whole of our resignations in his
hands.

All our colleagues were at the meeting except
A.J.B., who is in bed, and yourself.

The object of these tactics, which are, in my opinion,
fundamentally sound and essential, is this:

When the Prime Minister resigns, the King will
send for Lloyd George. The latter will then, for the
first time, be confronted with the difficulties of the
situation. He will cease to be a merely destructive
and disloyal force. He will have to make terms with
the Prime Minister and with all the rest of us. He will
soon find out what is the attitude of the Irishmen, the
Labour men, and so on. His Government will be

dictated to him by others, not shaped exclusively by himself.

For instance, no one of us would accept a dictatorship of Carson and himself. The following, both in the House of Commons and country, of the Prime Minister will become apparent, and Lloyd George will have to make terms with them. In other words, he will for the first time have the responsibilities of his action in breaking up the Government.

In passing, I may say that he does not mean to have Balfour at any cost, and I suppose the majority of the present Government are doomed to disappearance.

Had one felt that reconstitution by and under the present Prime Minister was possible, we should all have preferred to try it. But we know that with him as Chairman, either of the Cabinet or War Committee, it is absolutely impossible to win the War, and it will be for himself and Lloyd George to determine whether he goes out altogether or becomes Lord Chancellor or Chancellor of the Exchequer in a new Government, a nominal Premiership being a protean compromise, which, in our view, could have no endurance.

20

15th March 1919.

My dear Lord Chancellor,

I have received the Report of your Committee on the Land Acquisition Bill with profound disappointment. The Bill was supposed to be one to facilitate acquisition of land for most urgent public purposes, speedily and at a fair price. It has been transformed into a Bill which will be represented as making sure that the landlord gets a good price, that the lawyers get their pickings, and that there should be no undue hurry in the completion of the transaction.

To entrust the valuation of land to a man whose future prosperity and even livelihood depends on the goodwill of owners of land, is to guarantee an interest and bias in favour of the landlord against the State. And as for employing lawyers to argue out the value of the land, would you or any other member of the Committee ever dream of buying an estate assessed by means of a wrangle between rival lawyers on the merits or demerits of the particular fields? Of course you would not. Why then should schemes for housing be condemned to failure by the handicap of such grotesque methods of valuation? This is apart altogether from the piling up of fees and bills of costs, which would be the inevitable result of this unbusinesslike procedure.

It is these methods in the past that have rendered all housing schemes barren. It is owing to these that land producing only a few shillings an acre fetches hundreds of pounds per acre the moment it is requisitioned to build houses for the workmen whose labour has created the adjoining wealth.

I could not accept these alterations and I should be glad if your Committee would reconsider the question before submitting its proposals to the Cabinet.

I trust that the result of the West Leyton election will suffice as a warning to those who have drawn wrong deductions from the overwhelming majority of the last election. Mason's record spread broadcast through the Constituency marked him down as a reactionary. I beg you to assist in making these Bills a reality.

Why was Howard Frank invited to give evidence? He is an out and out landowners man. Surely there ought to have been a witness on the other side brought in to balance his testimony. The country is in no mood to tolerate reactionaries, high or low.

Yours sincerely,
D. LLOYD GEORGE.

21

(*Undated*—8th January 1918)
1 Carlton House Terrace,
S.W.

Private

Dear Prime Minister,

Although I hope I am not quick or resentful of temper, I do not like to let the incident of this morning pass without a word from me.

It was a very trying, and, I think, unmerited experience for a Member of the War Cabinet, who was exercising his legitimate functions, to be pulled up by his Chief, as I was by you this morning, in the presence not merely of his colleagues, but of outsiders. It is quite a new idea that a Cabinet Minister is not to be allowed to express whatever opinions he may choose in Cabinet, until persons other than Cabinet Ministers have spoken. It has certainly not been the rule observed in this Cabinet, where, on scores of occasions Ministers have been asked by yourself to summarise the views which they have placed on paper before their colleagues. This is indeed the ordinary procedure.

It was I, and not Mond or Rothermere or anyone else, who had asked & obtained leave to reopen the question (with what good reasons the result has shown). I had circulated last night a note explaining my reasons, which many of my colleagues, including yourself, had not had time to read. Before you came into the room Bonar Law in the Chair had asked me to open the discussion and in order to shorten the proceedings I had commenced to read my brief memo instead of recapitulating its substance. It was then that you cut me short in a manner which I venture to say left a painful impression on all who heard it.

I certainly felt it acutely myself & that others felt it too was shown by the Archbishop of Canterbury, who came up to me in the H. of Lords this afternoon and said he had been equally astonished at the manner in which a member of the Cabinet could be treated by his Chief and at the good temper with which the latter had borne it.

I do not want to magnify what I am quite content to regard as a trifling incident, & which I should not have noticed had it not occurred before.

I hope that I have always shown in Cabinet courtesy to my colleagues & deference to my chief and I should be sorry if I had done anything this morning to provoke the treatment that I received.

But it is much better to write frankly than to nurse a silent resentment, all the more that our personal relations have always been so pleasant that I, at any rate, could not contemplate a shadow being cast upon them without very sincere regret.

I am,
Yours sincerely,
CURZON.

22

9 Egerton Place,
S.W.3
Jan. 6, 1921.

Confidential
My dear Bonar,

Curzon asked me to dine with him alone two nights ago to talk over what he described as some rather serious matters.

I found him very depressed & very disturbed in mind, uneasy about his position, doubtful of his usefulness & influence—in short very unsettled and wondering whether he could or ought to continue in the Government. I have never before seen him in at all the same mood.

Something of this was due to the impending retirement of Milner with whom he has been on terms of friendship older & more intimate than with any other of his colleagues, but more was due to the course of discussions in Cabinet, to the feeling that the Prime Minister had more than once treated him with scant courtesy—almost with contumely—in the presence of his colleagues & attached little weight to his opinion on matters directly within the sphere of his departmental responsibility. How, he asked, must his colleagues regard him & what use was he under such circumstances? Surely no previous Prime Minister had ever addressed one of his Secretaries of State in such a way or appealed to the votes of minor members of the Cabinet to overrule the advice of two Secretaries of State in the common affairs of their two offices.

I need not tell you that I did all that I could to combat his depression. I assured him of the respect of his colleagues, of his influence & importance in the Government. I told him what I believe is the truth that his resignation would be fatal to the Government & to the Coalition as it now exists & that it must gravely affect my own course of action. Indeed in present conditions I think that the resignation of any one of us three, you, Curzon & myself, would be the end of the combination on whose continuance the Government itself depends, and I put before him as strongly as I could the grounds of public policy on which I hold that it is our duty to maintain that combination if we can.

Lastly—& here I come to the more personal & delicate aspect of the case—I told him that of course I had observed the attacks on himself & his department of which he complained & similar attacks on Winston, that I deeply regretted them, that I, & I was certain all his colleagues, far from misinterpreting his silence as weakness, had admired his self control (which under incomparably less provocation I had myself recently failed to imitate) & been grateful to him for it. I urged that the P.M. did not premeditate these attacks, did not exactly weigh his words or realise the effect of his tone & language, & I suggested that a personal explanation between himself & the P.M. might clear the air & prevent the recurrence of any cause for complaint. Unfortunately, he said, he had already tried this. He had once—or twice—written to the P.M. after one of these scenes & had received a very friendly letter in reply, but then sooner or later the offence was renewed.

It is always dangerous for a third party to meddle in such affairs, but I feel bound to write to you & through you to George. Frankly I have been shocked by the P.M.'s attacks on Curzon on more than one occasion, thinly disguised sometimes as criticisms not of himself but of his department. It has been painful to me to listen to them as I am sure that it has been to you & others. I have wondered at Curzon's reticence under such provocation, & though I do not think that I am generally rash or hot-tempered, I cannot conceive of myself as remaining in the room if I were subject to similar invective.

And I write as one who has no similar cause for complaint. The P.M. has treated me always with great courtesy, & is giving me generous support. It is therefore only as an onlooker, the friend and colleague of both parties, that I write. I am certain that if such attacks are repeated, there will be a smash. I am confident that whatever differences of opinion there may be among us, they are not, at present at any rate, of the insoluble kind. I don't believe that the P.M. wishes to part with Curzon or to quarrel with him or is conscious that on more than one occasion he has spoken to him in a tone & manner which are almost personally insulting. I feel sure that, if the P.M. realised the effect produced not only upon Curzon but upon his other hearers, he has both the good feeling & the good sense to refrain. Finally I suggest—& for this suggestion I appeal to what I believe to be an unbroken Cabinet tradition—that if the Prime Minister & yourself should ever again find yourselves as you did the other day in the question of the administrative arrangements of the Middle East, differing from two important colleagues & those two the ones most immediately concerned, you should not then & there swamp them by a poll of the Cabinet but should defer the question for further conference with them.

I address myself directly to you because you & I have been longer & more intimately associated than the Prime Minister & I, & because I know that you have an influence with him to which the rest of us cannot pretend. You will therefore be our best interpreter & you are the man most likely to put things right. But this letter is written for Lloyd George to see, & I hope that you will hand it to him. It is of so personal a character that I do not like to give it even to my very confidential secretary to copy, & I should not like to say so much even to you behind the back, so to speak, of the Prime Minister.

Yrs. ever,
Austen Chamberlain.

I am leaving early tomorrow so do not trouble to send an answer.

23

Flowerdale House,
Gairloch,
Ross-shire
October 1st, 1921

My dear Winston,

Your memorandum perplexes me. The latter part consists of an incomplete summary of suggestions which were put forward by various members at the Gairloch discussions, and which are the subject of very thorough investigation at the present moment by the

Departments concerned. But the first part consists of an attempt to lay the blame on your colleagues for present unemployment conditions. Although in the first paragraph you attribute the responsibility to the Cabinet as a whole you are careful to point out later on that the Finance Committee of the Cabinet were completely responsible for the policy. This is not in the least accurate inasmuch as all first-class decisions received full Cabinet discussion, and you, amongst others, expressed your views very freely from time to time on all these questions when definite conclusions were being arrived at.

What is it you complain of?—fluctuations. You instance housing. You could not choose a more unfortunate illustration from your point of view. There has been no change in our policy from the start. We assumed a shortage of hundreds of thousands of houses. We urged all those who were concerned in supplying the deficiency—Ministry of Health, Local Authorities, building contractors, landowners etc.—to use the whole of their resources to supply this deficiency without flagging or delay. We have not departed in the least from that policy. The resources of the building industry are necessarily limited. The skilled artizans being the bottle-neck, and by using the whole of our building resources in material and labour we could only turn out so many houses per annum. What did Addison do? He let contracts far in advance of the capacity of the trade to assimilate. The market was glutted with offers. What is the result? Any business man could have told him, in fact every business man did tell him, what the effect would be; prices soared higher and higher. He was urged to halt, but he continued flogging prices up hill in spite of all warnings. You supported him in this very fatuous policy with considerable vehemence and passion, and all those who in future will read your memorandum, are entitled to distil for you such credit as they can out of that fact.

We insisted however, on the advice of the Finance Committee, and compelled Addison to cry a halt. The number of houses being built, so far from being reduced, increased, but contracts were circumscribed. The result was that prices tumbled down. Even then the contracts were still beyond the capacity of the market, and were still being let out. We decided therefore on a further restriction of contracts until those already undertaken had been liquidated. Result, a further fall in prices. But no local authority or builder, who has either the material or the labour for building houses, is prevented from doing so. The Anti-waste campaign was only dangerous where it was justified. It was justified in Mesopotamia, where forces far beyond the need were being kept. That you are putting right. It was justified in the fighting services; it was justified in the excessive staffing of departments; it was certainly justified in the unbusinesslike way in which Addison was forcing up prices over housing. To that extent the Anti-waste campaign has been very useful. It brought the necessary pressure to bear upon Ministers. That is not a change of policy. I had urged all these considerations upon my colleagues for two years. As a matter of fact, I pressed some of these considerations upon you at Deauville two years ago. I consider that Mond is placing our housing programme on a thoroughly businesslike footing, and the only blame I attach to myself is, that out of personal consideration for Addison, I kept him at the Ministry of Health much longer than I ought to have.

You plead for a consistent policy about unemployment. You lay down the principles of that policy in language which I cordially approve. Men who are willing to labour but cannot find it must not be left to starve. I expressed the same sentiments to the Labour Mayors when I said to them that no man who was willing to work ought to be allowed to starve as long as there was a crust in the national cupboard. But you

APPENDIX IV

do less than justice to the Cabinet when you suggest
that this is a new policy which you are inculcating now
for the first time. As you pointed out at Dundee,
no Government has ever taken as great risks in carrying
out this policy as the present Government. £106,000,000
spent on unemployment allowances. That is without
precedent in the history of this or any other country.
Relief work found for something under 100,000. In
the Cabinet of which you and I were members £200,000
was the maximum spent on unemployment in 1908. The
question now is not whether we ought to change our
policy but whether we are not bound to take a step
forward. All the anticipations of business men as to
trade revival have been falsified. Many expected it last
spring, both here and in America. They were wrong.
Many more expected it in the autumn. It has not yet
arrived. I am afraid therefore that we cannot depend
upon these hopeful anticipations any longer, and that
we must look forward to a further prolonged period of
considerable unemployment. Had it been possible to
trust to a return to what is known in America as
"normalcy", it would have been better in the general
interest to do so rather than resort to artificial stimu-
lants; that is true in every disease; but we cannot do
so, and therefore, as I very emphatically pointed out at
Gairloch, I was of opinion that we must resort to
expedients which can only be justified by the continuance of abnormal conditions.

Hilton Young has done his work uncommonly well.
His investigations have been very thorough and most
helpful. I have not yet had the result of Mond's
enquiries. Those will take another week or fortnight,
but when we meet next week we shall be in a position
at any rate to take big decisions along the lines of the
Gairloch discussions.

As to inflation, there is no question here of a
fluctuating policy. As long as trade was good and
there were plenty of orders and great profits were

403

being made Chamberlain was perfectly right in pursuing his policy of deflation, but now that trade is depressed and our industries are barely able to keep going we must adapt our financial policy to those conditions. This is a fluctuation not in policy but in conditions, and the fact that we deflated so steadily and courage-ously in 1919 and 1920 makes it easier for us, without detriment to the national position, to do a little in-flation now.

I entreat you to judge more charitably the efforts put forth by your colleagues during the last two years. Abroad this policy has won a good deal of admiration and respect for this country. You will forgive me for writing in this strain, but I know that recrimination will not help in the solution of any problem, and I am anxious to get the full benefit of your resourceful brain without embarking upon discussions which will be not only fruitless but exasperating, and will divert our energies into channels which are neither fertilising nor navigable.

(Unsigned copy).

24

8 October 1921

My dear Prime Minister,

I very much appreciate the trouble you have taken to write to me about my recent memorandum on Unemployment and Finance, though I regret to have been the cause of adding to your personal labours at such a busy time.

I am sorry that you think my judgment of the record of the Government in these matters is unduly critical. I do the best I can to defend the Administration in

Parliament & on the platform, but it would be useless for me to pretend that I admire our post-war policy in several important aspects.

The first & greatest mistake in my opinion was leaving the profiteers in possession of their ill-gotten war wealth. Had prompt action been taken at the beginning of 1919, several thousand millions of paper wealth cd have been transferred to the State, & the internal debt reduced accordingly. The question was however deliberately held over & delayed until the moment was lost. Most of this war-made capital has faded as fast as it was created, but the internal debt, wh it might so largely have cancelled, & which was incurred in similar abnormal conditions, towers up over us like a precipice. The assets of taxation to wh the State might have looked have vanished: the war debits of the State are consolidated & will even grow heavier as trade revives & money regains its purchasing power. If I had not pressed this by every means open to me while there was still time to deal with the matter, & more than a year before the House of Commons Committee was appointed wh reported in favour of the principle, I shd not feel entitled to refer to it now. In looking back on this lost opportunity, I feel that it constituted a very great & irreparable disaster to the country.

With regard to the fluctuations in housing policy & in regard to agriculture, it is extraordinary to me that you have not been struck by them. So far as Dundee is concerned, I know from my own personal investigations that up till April the Town Council, in response to the strong pressure of the Ministry of Health, were pressing on with lay-outs & development work for building; that when the new declarations were made on the dismissal of Addison they protested violently against the arrest & curtailment of their work; & I had a bad time with them. Now, almost as soon as this development work has been brought to a standstill, all sorts of new schemes are being considered for increasing employment by starting relief works. I am sure if you make enquiries you will find that many other local bodies have been conscious of similar violent fluctuations—no doubt each explained by a reason very good in itself—in the directions they have received from the Government.

So far as the last part of my memorandum is concerned, it certainly did not originate out of discussions wh we had at Gairloch, altho' these matters were refreshed in my mind by many of yr very illuminating & suggestive comments. But I remember two long discussions wh we had together—the first nearly a year ago in the Hyde Park Hotel after a dinner at wh Max & Rothermere were present, & the second at Lympne at the beginning of this year. In each case I had the feeling that we made great progress in cutting our way into the heart of the post-war monetary & financial mystery, & the contributions of yr own thought, so far as they went, seemed to me of incomparable value & far more searching than I have heard on this subject from anyone else. But it seemed to me that all this process stopped short of reaching any conclusion of a definite character on which a policy or even a provisional policy cd be based; & the fact is undoubtedly as I have stated in my memorandum, that we have not at the present time got a clear view on the fundamental question to wh I have drawn attention. *I* certainly do not pretend to have a clear view upon them, tho' I have a feeling that if we went on hammering away for say a week or two, we shd get to the bottom of it & frame a definite policy wh cd be announced, explained, & defended, & wh wd carry us through the temporary & baffling fluctuations wh are affecting us so violently at the present time. It is quite true that owing to yr vy great skill in navigation we have avoided many dangerous rocks & shoals, & in the Coal Strike have come through one of the greatest industrial hurricanes that have ever blown. But for all that we are drifting about in a fog without a compass.

It was certainly not with any intention of making recriminations about the past, but solely with a view to an amelioration in the future, that I embodied my thoughts in the memorandum wh I have circulated. Still less do I flatter myself with superiority of judgment. But I always try to give the best advice I can sincerely to you & to the Cabinet on the great general questions of our affairs as they come up. If I did not do so, I shd be no use whatever to you or to the Administration.

Let me say in conclusion how glad I am you are reconsidering your decision about going to Washington for the opening of the Conference. I do not think there wd be any necessity for you to exhaust yrself in making speeches to the American multitudes. But I feel you ought to establish friendly personal relations with Harding & Hughes, that you ought to make them conscious of the loyalty & friendliness of our motives, & at the same time of our strong determination not to be ousted from our world-position; & generally to get the Conference started as far as possible on sound lines & to arrive at some informal understandings on its great underlying issues with the Statesmen of America & Japan. This I believe you cd do in a fortnight, with a week at each end for the voyage. Meanwhile I have no doubt that all parties in the country wd respect yr absence & the reasons for it, & that the political position wd be consolidated & not weakened on account of the all-important work on wh you wd be engaged.

Yours sincerely,
WINSTON S. CHURCHILL.

P.S. I was so glad to see you so much restored in health.

W.

APPENDIX V

STAMFORDHAM MEMORANDA
(Published for the first time

Buckingham Palace
3.15 p.m., 13 February 1918

I expressed the King's surprise to learn from the Minutes of the Cabinet that Sir William Robertson was no longer Chief of the Imperial General Staff, but that he was to be succeeded by Sir Henry Wilson, and it was suggested that Sir William Robertson should go to Paris as a Member of the Executive Committee of the Supreme War Council.

The Prime Minister when he saw the King on the 4th February never mentioned any idea of this change, indeed he told His Majesty that everything had gone smoothly in Paris the previous week, and that the agreements come to by the Supreme War Council were unanimous, and it was only on the 12th inst. that the King chanced to send for Lord Derby, who then told him of the contemplated new arrangement.

The Prime Minister replied that as Lord Derby told him that he was going to see the King on the 12th he (the Prime Minister) asked him to tell the King everything, and to show him a copy of the conditions which Lord Derby had agreed to and signed, governing the two appointments of C.I.G.S. and Member of the Executive Committee respectively. I said that I had not heard of this document, but the Prime Minister said that he

knew Lord Derby had it in his pocket and more than
once Mr. Lloyd George said 'Are you sure the King
did not see it?' I could only answer that of course I
could not be sure as I was not present at the interview,
but that His Majesty had not mentioned anything about
the document in question. The Prime Minister sent
for the original and I brought away a copy. I told him
that the King strongly deprecated the idea of Robertson being removed from the office of C.I.G.S., that
his loss in that capacity would be an incalculable one
to the Army, would be resented in the country, re-
joiced in by the enemy, and I thought would damage
the Government, and the King considered that Sir
William Robertson had enjoyed the absolute confidence
of the Army—Officers and Men. The Prime Minister
said that he did not share the King's extremely favourable opinion of Sir William Robertson, who had never
fought at the Front, had hardly ever visited the
trenches, and was not known by the rank and file, and
their confidence in him could not be compared to that
which they reposed in Sir Herbert Plumer, and Mr.
Lloyd George said that the opinions I relied on must
be manufactured for the King. The previous week in
Paris Robertson never raised any objections to the
proposal, but just as on the occasion of Rapallo, he
waited until his return to London to make these known
far and wide.

The Prime Minister said that Robertson had been
offered either Paris or to remain as C.I.G.S., he declined either and wished to dictate to everyone,
whereas the Prime Minister repeated what he said on
the 22nd January, that Robertson had displayed no
capacity as a strategist, and asked where anyone could
put their finger on the map and say that this or that is
due to Robertson's advice. In fact his forecasts had
generally been wrong.

I pointed out that Robertson was only asking to be
in a position similar to that of General Foch, who is

both C.G.S. and Member of the Executive Committee in France. The Prime Minister replied that there was no analogy. For Foch is on the spot in Paris whereas Sir William Robertson would be in London, while it might be necessary to give orders to the Reserves at a moment's notice in cases of emergency.

Afterwards on returning to Buckingham Palace I rang up Lord Derby and told him of my conversation with the Prime Minister, the former said that Robertson was unreasonable in his demands, swollen headed, and that he (Lord Derby) was so tired of the whole question that he sometimes thought he would be better without Robertson, but himself felt ready to resign.

Later on Lord Derby and Sir William Robertson met in my room, and the whole question was threshed out and examined from all sides. Sir William Robertson gave me a copy of his written opinion as to the suggested plan, which to him had spelt disaster. Lord Derby did not agree, and reminded Sir William Robertson that Sir Douglas Haig had approved of the conditions and thought that they were workable. However, Lord Derby said that he should back up Sir William Robertson. But he knew that if the Prime Minister agreed to Sir W. R.'s terms namely, that he should be both C.I.G.S. in London, and Member of the Executive Committee, with a Deputy to act for him in his absence, Lord Milner and Mr. Barnes would resign: if on the other hand Sir William Robertson were to resign, Lord Curzon, and he (Lord Derby) would leave the Government, and if this resulted in the fall of the Government there was a serious danger of its fate being attributed to the work of the Army and might be a very disagreeable cry with which to go to the country.

I begged Sir William Robertson in the King's name not to relinquish his post as C.I.G.S., but to record his disapproval of the system, his belief that it was unworkable, and might even cost us the War, but for the sake of the King, the Army and the Country, to

410

remain on and do his best to carry out the new arrangement. He undertook to think it over, and said that he had to go with Lord Derby to breakfast with the Prime Minister in the morning. During this discussion Sir W. R. said with considerable warmth that the truth was the Prime Minister hated him.

I reported what had happened to the King at about 8.15 p.m.

14 February 1918

At 8.30 a.m. I sent a note to Sir William Robertson saying that I trusted that after sleeping over the matter he had decided to give effect to the King's wishes. Later on I heard that he had not breakfasted with the Prime Minister, but was to attend the Cabinet and lay before them his views.

Soon after 3.30 p.m. I called at 10 Downing Street, and found that the Cabinet had decided that Sir William Robertson must make up his mind to take either of the two appointments suggested, but he was to see Mr. Balfour about four o'clock.

I went to the War Office and saw Mr. Balfour and Lord Derby, immediately after the former had left Sir William Robertson, upon whom he said he had failed to make any impression, or to divert him from the attitude he had taken up.

I discussed Sir William Robertson's objections to the scheme, which Mr. Balfour thought were exaggerated, and would not hold water. He did not seem to recognize as much as I did the serious view which Sir W. R. took as to the results of the proposed arrangement, and indeed said that Sir William Robertson had not put the case as strongly as I had put it: I replied that I was merely repeating what Sir W. R. had said the previous evening, and I appealed to Lord Derby and asked him to show Mr. Balfour a copy of the paper which Sir William Robertson had given me, but Lord

Derby replied that Sir W. R. had modified his views
of the previous evening. I said that Sir William
Robertson maintained that one man only could give
orders to the Army, and that was the C.I.G.S., whereas
by this plan there would be *two* namely, the C.I.G.S.
and the member of the Executive Committee.

Later on I saw Lord Derby, who said I was mistaken
in thinking that he said Sir William Robertson had
changed his views. I told him that Sir William Robertson would not give way or continue to be C.I.G.S.
while disapproving of the scheme. Lord Derby said
'*He believed it would work* and so did Sir Douglas Haig'.
I said I thought there was nothing more to do. Lord
Derby asked me to tell Sir William Robertson of the
change in the opinion of Lord Curzon and Mr. Balfour,
who now no longer supported him, and also to say that
Sir H. Plumer would be telegraphed to and offered the
appointment of C.I.G.S.

I accordingly wrote to Sir William Robertson, from
whom in the meantime I had received a note confirming
what he had said in conversation.

16 February 1918

The King saw the Prime Minister. Before doing so
Mr. Lloyd George told me that the question of Sir
William Robertson had now reached a point that if His
Majesty insisted upon his (Sir W. R.) remaining in
office on the terms he laid down the Government could
not carry on, and the King would have to find other
Ministers. The Government *must* govern, whereas
this was practically military dictation.

I assured the Prime Minister that His Majesty had
no idea of making any such insistence. That since I saw
him (Mr. Lloyd George) on the 13th February, I had
by the King's instructions done all in my power to
induce Sir William Robertson to remain as C.I.G.S.

even though he might consider that the Government's scheme was so dangerous as even risking our loss of the War. But Sir William Robertson said he could not do so, therefore the King regarded the matter as settled, and considered that Sir William Robertson had practically ceased to be C.I.G.S.

The King then saw the Prime Minister, and in discussing the question, stated that in his opinion Sir William Robertson's resignation would be a serious loss to the Army for both Officers and Men had the fullest confidence in him. This however the Prime Minister would not admit. He reminded the King that the scheme was agreed to in Paris when Sir William Robertson never raised a word of objection. Sir Douglas Haig, who after all was the person most concerned, accepted it, and Lord Derby thought it workable; so that the opposition really only came from Sir William Robertson, and Mr. Lloyd George thought that the personal dislike of Sir William Robertson to Sir Henry Wilson was a powerful influence in the case.

The Prime Minister quoted General Smuts as having no opinion of Sir William Robertson as a strategist, and his (Gen. S.'s) last words before leaving for Egypt were to the effect that we should never get on with the War so long as Sir William Robertson remained C.I.G.S.

Mr. Lloyd George asked His Majesty's permission to repeat the offer to Sir William Robertson either to go to Paris as Representative of the Executive, or to remain C.I.G.S. If he refused both, to appoint Sir Henry Wilson C.I.G.S., but without the powers specially granted to Sir William Robertson when he took office. The Prime Minister also asked for permission to consult Sir Douglas Haig, who arrives this evening, as to who should go to Paris.

Later in the day the King saw Lord Derby, who said that he felt there was nothing left for him to do but to resign, though he several times appealed to His

Majesty to advise him as to the proper course he should follow. Lord Derby explained that although he personally thought that the Government's scheme was workable, on the other hand two high authorities—namely Sir William Robertson and Sir Herbert Plumer—both held opposite opinions, and in these circumstances he (Lord Derby) felt that he could not carry out the scheme, especially with Sir Henry Wilson as C.I.G.S.

The King told Lord Derby that after hearing his statement there seemed to be no alternative but his resignation.

Subsequently I saw Lord Derby who told me that he should resign, and that an announcement to that effect would be in Monday's morning newspapers, and that he would make his statement in the House of Lords on Tuesday.

Lord Derby admitted that his case was a weak one, for while supporting the Government's scheme he felt unable to carry it out. Lord Derby added that in his statement he should quote the opinion of Sir William Robertson and Sir Herbert Plumer, although Mr. Bonar Law said that he ought *not* to refer to the latter as the communication made to Sir Herbert Plumer was entirely confidential.

APPENDIX VI

ADDENDUM

Permission to publish the following letter was received after the book had gone into page proof.

Walter Long to Bonar Law, 15th February, 1918

My dear Bonar,

I have seen Robertson. I must say I am horrified at the idea of a change now of all moments & I feel very strongly that every effort should be made to avert it. I do not doubt that the Gov. can ride the storm but I am convinced that it will give the Gov. a very severe shake, what is much worse, may be held, if things go wrong, to have been the cause. Surely so tremendous a step should not be taken without much more deliberation? It is no business of mine as I am not on the War Cabinet, but I confess that having regard to the effect this must have on the Overseas Troops & upon the conduct of the War I think I ought to have been allowed to have a say : however for this it is too late—but not too late to pause before taking a decision which will be irrevocable.

Yours ever,

WALTER H. LONG.

15. ii. 18.

APPENDIX VII

HOUSE OF LORDS DEBATES
28th MARCH, 1945

The Late Earl Lloyd-George of Dwyfor

2 p.m.

The LORD PRIVY SEAL (Lord Beaverbrook): My Lords, in the unavoidable absence of the noble Viscount the Leader of the House, it falls to me to express the sorrow of your Lordships at the death of Earl Lloyd George. There are several members of this House who served under Lloyd George, but of those of his colleagues who knew and felt the full force of his genius, those who served with him in his War Cabinet, nearly all have gone out in front of him. Almost alone the survivor of his war administration is the present Prime Minister. Many will say that Lloyd George's greatest days, his most splendid efforts were in times of peace when he put upon the Statute Book more social legislation than any single statesman in our history; but I do not hold that view. To me his greatest hour came as late as the spring of 1918, when our line of defence had been broken, our troops were in retreat, the Russian Armies were out of the war, and the American Armies had not yet come into it.

The Cabinet at that moment was concerned above all else with the dominant question, "Shall we retreat north and west to protect the Channel ports, or shall we retire south to Paris to sustain contact with the

French Armies?" The history books will tell the truth. A Cabinet of strong men had been diverted for the time by the sheer gravity of the situation from the bigger issue—the issue of defeat or victory. It was at that moment that Lloyd George penetrated the gloom of doubt and indecision. It was in the hour of our peril that he refused to contemplate any plan for retreat. He would talk only of counter-attacks. It was then his leadership showed itself supreme, his courage untarnished. No other moment in Britain's recurring story of escape from disaster can surpass it, save only the decision of the summer nights after the defeat of France in 1940. It was then, I say, that Lloyd George's strength and fortitude, his judgment and courage, led and guided the nation during the weary pilgrimage that was to be so suddenly, so unexpectedly, so completely crowned with victory. If this were a single incident in the life of Lloyd George, it would make for a great name, but the story of Lloyd George as leader of the nation abounds in trials overcome, in temptations resisted, in opportunities for error withstood. On every occasion when men were contained in their conflicting counsels Lloyd George followed his own vision. It seems to me now, as it seemed to me then, he was seldom wrong. It was always the genius of this man that he knew the conditions on the other side of the hill.

It would be wrong of me to attempt any review of Lloyd George's life. This story has been told in part and will no doubt in history be told in full, but I believe it will throw into the shadow every other story, save only the narrative of these present days. In this House we have not seen him, for he was not spared to take his seat. Many present among your Lordships were his supporters. Others marching like Lloyd George himself straight across the political landscape in pursuit of the beliefs which they held, found themselves sometimes his allies and sometimes his opponents. To-day allies and opponents alike are oppressed by a feeling of irreparable personal loss. To his wife and family we will send our deep sympathy. Lloyd George was the idol of the nation, the Premier under whose aegis Germany was overthrown and the Empire saved. He attained an authority greater than that held by any British Prime Minister who had gone before him. He dictated to Europe; he flung out great dynasties with a gesture; he parcelled out the frontiers of races; everything was in his hands, and his hands showed that they had the power to use everything. Now all that is ended. Nothing remains but the picture of him in the days of glory. There on the walls of memory, outstanding in power and vitality, amid the faded pictures of his predecessors, is Lloyd George, Prime Minister of Great Britain.

NOTES

INTRODUCTION

aIntimate Papers of Colonel House, Vol. III, p. 233. *b*Page to Wilson, 7 March, 1918. *Walter Hines Page Papers*, Houghton Library, Harvard University.

Chapter I. THE CLEVEREST MAN IN THE KINGDOM

*a*Robert Blake: *The Unknown Prime Minister*, p. 294. - *bHistory of The Times*, Vol. IV, p. 274. - *c*F. E. Smith: *My American Visit*. - *d*Bonar Law to Borden, 1 May, 1916. *Borden Papers*. - *e*D. Lloyd George: *War Memoirs*, Vol. V, p. 2786. - *fThe Globe*, 18 April, 1918. - *gThe Globe*, 3 May, 1918. - *hThe Morning Post*, 22 April, 1918. - *i*Letter published in *Daily Chronicle, Morning Post* and *Times*, 7 May, 1918. - *j*W. S. Churchill: *The World Crisis, 1916–1918*, Part I, p. 244.

Chapter II. THE FALL OF A GIANT

*a*See Lord Beaverbrook, *Politicians and the War*, Vol. II, pp. 198–9 - *bIbid.*, p. 122. - *c*Lloyd George: *War Memoirs*, Vol. IV, p. 2228. - *d*See *Politicians and the War*, Vol. II, p. 324. - *eIbid.*, p. 342. - *f* See R. S. Baker: *Woodrow Wilson, Life and Letters*, Vol. VII, p. 96. - *g*Tom Clarke: *Northcliffe in History*, p. 120. - *h*Lloyd George: *War Memoirs*, Vol. III, pp. 1688–9. - *i*Baker: *Woodrow Wilson, Life and Letters*, Vol. VII, p. 96. - *j*Robert Cecil to Lloyd George, undated. *Lloyd George Papers*. - *k*Hankey to Lloyd George, 7 June, 1917. *Lloyd George Papers*. - *l*House of Commons Debates, Vol. 95, cols. 1105–6. - *mDaily News and Leader*, 21 June, 1917. - *nDaily Chronicle*, 21 June, 1917. - *oDaily News and Leader*, 21 June, 1917. - *pMorning Post*, 30 June, 1917. - *q*David Davies to Lloyd George, dated "Sunday night" (June, 1917). *Lloyd George Papers*. Quoted, Frank Owen: *Tempestuous Journey*, p. 381. - *rIntimate Papers of Colonel House*, Vol. III, p. 89. - *s*Frederick Dixon to Balfour, 22 June, 1917. *Lloyd George Papers*. - *t*Baker: *Woodrow Wilson, Life and Letters*, Vol. VII, p. 96. - *uIbid.*, p. 102, fn. Letter House to Wilson, 7 June, 1917. - *vIbid.*, p. 108. House to Wilson, 12 June, 1917. - *w*Northcliffe to Davies, 20 June, 1917. *Lloyd George Papers*. Quoted, Lloyd George: *War Memoirs*, Vol. III, pp. 1693–5. - *x*Spring-Rice to Balfour, 13 July, 1917. *Lloyd George Papers*. Quoted, *Ibid.*, pp. 1695–6. - *yWalter Hines Page Papers*, Houghton Library, Harvard University. - *z*Spring-Rice to Balfour, 5 July, 1917. *Lloyd George Papers*. Quoted, Lloyd George: *War Memoirs*, Vol. III, p. 1715. - *aaIntimate Papers of Colonel House*, Vol. III, p. 91. - *ab*Diary of E. M. House, Vol. XII, p. 317, 18 October, 1917. - *ac*Quoted, *Intimate Papers of Colonel House*, Vol. III, p. 90. - *adWiseman Papers*, Yale University Library. Quoted, Lloyd George: *War Memoirs*, Vol. III, p. 1697. - *ae*Lloyd George: *War Memoirs*, Vol. IV, p. 1871. - *af*Diary of E. M. House, Vol. XII, p. 359, 16 November, 1917. Quoted, Stanley Morison, "Personality and Diplomacy in Anglo-American relations, 1917": *Essays Presented to Sir Lewis Namier*, ed. R. Pares and A. J. P. Taylor, pp. 465–6, 468. - *agIbid.*, p. 367. 20 November, 1917. *ahIbid.* - *aiThe Times*, 21 November, 1917. - *ajHouse of Commons Debates*, Vol. 104, col. 77.

NOTES

Chapter III. NABOBS AND TYRANTS

[a]Stephen McKenna: *Reginald McKenna*, p. 236. - [b]Page to Wilson, 16 January, 1918. *Walter Hines Page Papers*, Houghton Library, Harvard University. - [c]McKenna: *Reginald McKenna*, p. 238. - [d]Cunliffe to the Prime Minister, 3 July, 1917. *Lloyd George Papers*. - [e]Letters from Cunliffe to Bonar Law, 3 and 6 July, 1917. *Bonar Law Papers*. - [f]Bonar Law to Lloyd George, 9 July, 1917. *Lloyd George Papers*. - [g]Bonar Law to Lloyd George, 9 July, 1917. *Lloyd George Papers*. - [h]The letter communicating this information to Bonar Law was dated 5 July, but it is not contained in the *Bonar Law* or *Lloyd George Papers*. Bonar Law, however, alludes to it in his letter to Lloyd George of 9 July, 1917. - [i]*Bonar Law Papers*. - [j]*Lloyd George Papers*. - [k]*Lloyd George Papers*. - [l]Cunliffe to Bonar Law, 16 July, 1917. *Bonar Law Papers*. - [m]Cunliffe to Bonar Law, 12 August, 1917. *Bonar Law Papers*. - [n]*The Times*, 9 November, 1917. - [o]*Daily Telegraph*, 26 March, 1918.

Chapter IV. "IF YOU CAN TRUST YOURSELF WHEN ALL MEN DOUBT YOU"

[a]Ian Colvin: *Life of Lord Carson*, Vol. III, p. 150. - [b]*Bonar Law Papers*. - [c]*Daily Telegraph*, 14 May, 1917. - [d]Ed. Robert Blake: *Private Papers of Douglas Haig, 1914-1919*, pp. 208-9. - [e]Churchill to Blumenfeld, 6 September, 1914. From the papers of R. D. Blumenfeld. - [f]Undated. *Bonar Law Papers*. - [g]*Lloyd George Papers*. - [h]Churchill: *The World Crisis, 1916-1918*, Part I, p. 255. - [i]*Lloyd George Papers*. - [j]*Lloyd George Papers*. - [k]Lloyd George: *War Memoirs*, Vol. III, p. 1068. - [l]Bonar Law to Joseph Larmor, 14 October, 1914. *Bonar Law Papers*. - [m]Wilson to Bonar Law, 16 May, 1915. *Bonar Law Papers*. - [n]Churchill to Lloyd George, 9 November, 1921. *Lloyd George Papers*. - [o]*Lloyd George Papers*. - [p]Dr. Addison to Prime Minister, 4 June, 1917. *Lloyd George Papers*. - [q]Guest to Lloyd George, 18 June, 1917. *Lloyd George Papers*. - [r]*Lloyd George Papers*. - [s]*Bonar Law Papers*. - [t]*Bonar Law Papers*. - [u]Derby to Prime Minister, 8 June, 1917. *Lloyd George Papers*. - [v]See *History of The Times, 1912-1921*, Appendix, p. 1006. - [w]Churchill: *The World Crisis, 1916-1918*, Part II, p. 293. - [x]Cable Northcliffe to Churchill, 27 July, 1917. *Wiseman Papers*, Yale University Library. See also Lord Riddell: *War Diary*, p. 259. - [y]*Lloyd George Papers*. - [z]Lloyd George: *War Memoirs*, Vol. III, p. 1072. - [aa]Long to Lloyd George, 18 July, 1917. *Lloyd George Papers*. - [ab]*Morning Post*, 4 August, 1917. - [ac]*Ibid.*, 3 August, 1917. - [ad]*Ibid.*, 18 July, 1917. - [ae]*Ibid.*, 19 July, 1917. - [af]*Ibid.*, 20 July, 1917. - [ag]Long to Bonar Law, 29 July, 1917. *Bonar Law Papers*. - [ah]Churchill: *The World Crisis, 1916-1918*, Part II, p. 335. - [ai]Churchill to Lloyd George, 29 December. 1918. *Lloyd George Papers*.

Chapter V. THE ULSTER PIRATE

[a]Lloyd George: *War Memoirs*, Vol. III, pp. 1175-6. - [b]*Politicians and the War*, Vol. II, p. 335. - [c]Cmd. 2870. *The Record of the Battle of Jutland*. - [d]Letter of 13 December, 1916. Quoted, Colvin: *Life of Lord Carson*, Vol. III, p. 217. - [e]*Daily Express*, 9 March, 1917. - [f]Lloyd George: *War Memoirs*, Vol. III, p. 1150. - [g]*Ibid*. - [h]Figures from *Statistical Review of the War against Merchant Shipping, Appendix A.* - [i]Quoted, Colvin: *Life of Lord Carson*, Vol. III, p. 257. - [j]*The*

NOTES

Globe, 7 May, 1917. – *k*30 April, 1917. *Lloyd George Papers*. – *l*Lloyd George: *War Memoirs*, Vol. III, p. 1164. – *m*Ibid., p. 1170. – *n*Walter Hines Page Papers, Houghton Library, Harvard University. – *o*Colvin: *Life of Lord Carson*, Vol. III, p. 268. – *p*Page to Wilson, 4 May, 1917. *Walter Hines Page Papers*. Quoted, Hendrick: *The Life and Letters of Walter H. Page*, Vol. II, pp. 259–60. – *q*Quoted, Colvin: *Life of Lord Carson*, Vol. III, p. 266. – *r*Lloyd George: *War Memoirs*, Vol. III, p. 1176. – *s*Colvin: *Life of Lord Carson*, Vol. III, p. 269. – *t*See *Private Papers of Douglas Haig, 1914–1919*, p. 242. – *u*Ibid., p. 255. – *v*Lloyd George Papers. – *w*Lloyd George Papers. – *x*Lloyd George Papers. – *y*Bonar Law Papers. – *z*Windsor Archives. – *aa*Lloyd George Papers. Quoted, Owen: *Tempestuous Journey*, p. 417. – *ab*Lloyd George Papers. Quoted Ibid. – *ac*Lloyd George Papers. Quoted, Owen: *Tempestuous Journey*, p. 418. – *ad*Lloyd George Papers. – *ae*Christopher Addison: *Four and a Half Years*, Vol. II, p. 411. – *af*Sir R. H. Bacon: *Life of John Rushworth, Earl Jellicoe*, p. 377. – *ag*Colvin: *Life of Lord Carson*, Vol. III, p. 287. – *ah*Private Papers of Douglas Haig, 1914–1919, p. 255. – *ai*Ibid., pp. 251–2. – *aj*Speech at the Constitutional Club Luncheon, 20 November, 1917. *The Times*, 21 November, 1917. – *ak*Morning Post, 17 November, 1917. – *al*Lloyd George Papers. – *am*House of Commons Debates, Vol. 103, col. 2024. – *an*Bonar Law Papers. Quoted, Blake: *The Unknown Prime Minister*, p. 378. – *ao*Bonar Law to Lloyd George, 19 September, 1918. *Bonar Law Papers*. – *ap*House of Commons Debates, Vol. 117, cols. 1233–4.

Chapter VI. ALL THE KING'S MEN

*a*Derby to Lloyd George, 11 December, 1917. *Lloyd George Papers*. – *b*Derby to Haig, 12 December, 1917. *Lloyd George Papers*. – *c*Lloyd George Papers. – *d*Derby to Lloyd George, 18 January, 1918. *Lloyd George Papers*. – *e*Derby to Lloyd George, 29 January, 1918. *Lloyd George Papers*. – *f*Tom Jones: *Lloyd George*, p. 134. – *g*Balfour Papers. – *h*House of Commons Debates, Vol. 103, col. 16. – *i*Ibid., col. 30. – *j*Long to Bonar Law, 15 February, 1918. *Bonar Law Papers*. – *k*Lord Robert Cecil to Bonar Law, 17 February, 1918. *Bonar Law Papers*. – *l*Letter from Curzon to Lloyd George, 18 November, 1917. *Lloyd George Papers*. – *m*See *Private Papers of Douglas Haig, 1914–1919*, p. 208. – *n*Harold Nicolson: *King George V*, p. 288. – *o*Ibid. – *p*Diary of E. M. House, Vol. XII, 29 October, 1917. – *q*John Gore: *George V. A Personal Memoir*, p. 304. – *r*Milner to Lloyd George, 8 February, 1918. *Lloyd George Papers*. Quoted, Lloyd George: *War Memoirs*, Vol. V, pp. 2790–2. – *s*Bonar Law Papers. – *t*Nicolson, *King George V*, pp. 321–2. – *u*See *Private Papers of Douglas Haig, 1914–1919*, p. 286. – *v*Bonar Law Papers. – *w*Bonar Law Papers. – *x*Private Papers of Douglas Haig, 1914–1919, p. 288. – *y*Page to Wilson, 7 March, 1918. *Walter Hines Page Papers*, Houghton Library, Harvard University.

Chapter VII. THE BIRTH OF THE ROYAL AIR FORCE

*a*The Private Papers of Douglas Haig, 1914–1919, p. 252. – *b*Ibid., p. 273. – *c*Ibid., p. 280. – *d*House of Commons Debates, Vol. 105, col. 43. – *e*Lloyd George Papers. – *f*Lloyd George Papers. – *g*Daily News, 16 April, 1918. – *h*Henderson to Bonar Law, 26 April, 1918. *Bonar Law Papers*. – *i*Baird to Lloyd George, 22 April, 1918. *Lloyd George Papers*. – *j*Rothermere to Lloyd George, 23 April,

NOTES

1918. *Lloyd George Papers.* - *kLloyd George Papers.* - *lLloyd George Papers.*
Quoted Lloyd George: *War Memoirs*, Vol. IV, p. 1877-8. *m*Lloyd George:
War Memoirs, Vol. IV, p. 1877. - *n*The Times, 26 April, 1918. - *o*Bonar Law
Papers. - *p*House of Commons Debates, Vol. 105, col. 1128. - *q*Ibid., col.
1316. - *r*Ibid., col. 1320. - *s*Ibid., col. 1321. - *t*Ibid., cols. 1342-3. - *u*Ibid.,
col. 1330. - *v*House of Lords Debates, Vol. 29, col. 870. - *w*Lloyd George
Papers. - *x*Windsor Archives. - *y*Windsor Archives. - *z*Windsor Archives. -
*aa*Bonar Law Papers. *ab*Nicolson: *King George V*, p. 512. - *ac*Diary of E. M.
House, Vol. XII, p. 381, 27 November, 1917. - *ad*Stamfordham to Guest,
25 April, 1919. *Lloyd George Papers.* - *ae*Guest to Lloyd George, 17 May,
1920. *Lloyd George Papers.* - *af* See Owen: *Tempestuous Journey*, p. 698.

Chapter VIII. THE LOST BOX

*a*Lloyd George to Bonar Law, 10 April, 1918. *Bonar Law Papers.* - *b*Lloyd
George: *War Memoirs*, Vol. V, p. 2973. - *c*Robertson to Milner, 17 May, 1918.
Lloyd George Papers. - *d*Milner to Lloyd George, 19 May, 1918. *Lloyd George
Papers.* - *e*Westminster Gazette, 8 May, 1918. - *f*Manchester Guardian, 8 May,
1918. - *g*Morning Post, 8 May, 1918. - *h*Colvin: *Life of Lord Carson*, Vol. III,
p. 351. - *i*L. S. Amery: *My Political Life*, Vol. II, p. 154. - *j*C. Repington: *The
First World War, 1914-1918*, Vol. II, p. 298. Quoted, Colvin: *Life of Lord
Carson*, Vol. III, pp. 351-2. - *k*House of Commons Debates, Vol. 105, col. 2353. -
*l*Ibid., col. 2359. *m*The Private Papers of Douglas Haig, 1914-1919, p. 309. -
*n*Churchill: *The World Crisis, 1916-1918*, Part II, p. 422. - *o*Maurice to Lloyd
George, 15 July, 1922. *Lloyd George Papers.*

Chapter IX. "DONT RESIGN: WAIT UNTIL YOU'RE SACKED"

*a*Lloyd George Papers. - *b*House of Commons Debates, Vol. 104, col. 41.
- *c*Cable, 26 August, 1917. *Wiseman Papers*, Yale University Library. - *d*Entry
in my diary dated 9 March, 1915. - *e*Ibid. - *f*H.R.H. the Duke of Connaught
to R. B. Bennett, 14 December, 1916. *Bennett Papers*, University of New Brunswick. - *g*H.R.H. the Duke of Connaught to Sir Robert Borden, 18 April,
1916. *Borden Papers*, University of Toronto. - *h*My files. - *i*Ibid. - *j*See Blake:
The Unknown Prime Minister, p. 346. - *k*Stamfordham to Guest, 8 February, 1918.
Lloyd George Papers. Quoted, Owen: *Tempestuous Journey*, p. 464. - *l*Lloyd
George to Stamfordham, 9 February, 1918. *Lloyd George Papers.* Quoted, Owen:
Tempestuous Journey, p. 464. - *m*The Globe, 8 February, 1918. - *n*House of
Commons Debates, Vol. 103, cols. 656-7. - *o*Enclosure Salisbury to Bonar Law,
22 February, 1918. *Bonar Law Papers.* - *p*Salisbury to Bonar Law, 22 February,
1918. *Bonar Law Papers.* - *q*My files. - *r*Lloyd George Papers. Quoted, *History
of The Times*, Vol. IV, pp. 351-2. - *s*See Charles Petrie: *Life and Letters of Austen
Chamberlain*, p. 107. - *t*Milner to Lloyd George, 27 February, 1918. *Lloyd
George Papers.* - *u*House of Commons Debates, Vol. 104, col. 77. - *v*Ibid., col. 130.
- *w*Ibid., col. 135. - *x*My files. - *y*Lloyd George Papers. - *z*Lloyd George Papers. -
*aa*House of Commons Debates, Vol. 109, col. 958. - *ab*Ibid., col. 1000. - *ac*Ibid.,
col. 1001. - *ad*Daily Express, 29 August, 1918. - *ae*Lloyd George to Bonar
Law, 29 August, 1917 (sic). *Bonar Law Papers.* - *af* Churchill to Bonar Law,
8 September, 1918. *Bonar Law Papers.* - *ag*House of Commons Debates, Vol. 110,
col. 2363. - *ah*Ibid., col. 2380. - *ai*Ludendorff: *My War Memories, 1914-1918*,
Vol. 1, pp. 361, 365 and 367.

NOTES

Chapter X. HIS ROYAL POMP

*a*Curzon to Lloyd George, 13 November, 1918. *Lloyd George Papers.* - *b*Quoted: Nicolson, *King George V*, pp. 336-8. - *c*1919, Lloyd George said that the tribunal would be an Inter-Allied one and it would sit in London. *House of Commons Debates*, Vol. 117, cols. 1216-17. - *d*Curzon to Lloyd George, 7 July, 1919. *Lloyd George Papers.* - *e*Lloyd George Papers. - *f* Quoted, Lord Newton: *Lord Lansdowne: A Biography*, pp. 452-3. - *g*Quoted, Stephen Spender and Cyril Asquith: *Life of Lord Oxford and Asquith*, Vol. II, p. 260. - *h*Ibid. - *i*H. H. Asquith: *Memories and Reflections*, Vol. II, p. 133. - *j*See *Politicians and the War*, Vol. II, p. 240. - *k*Asquith: *Memories and Reflections*, Vol. II, p. 128 et seq. - *l*Lloyd George Papers. - *m*Curzon to Bonar Law, 25 February, 1918. *Bonar Law Papers.* Quoted, Ronaldshay: *Life of Lord Curzon*, Vol. III, pp. 195-6. - *n*Quoted, *Ibid.*, p. 197. - *o*Curzon to Lloyd George, 12 November, 1918. *Lloyd George Papers.* - *p*House of Commons Debates*, Vol. 91, col. 26. - *q*Bonar Law Papers. - *r*Curzon to Lloyd George, 13 November, 1918. *Lloyd George Papers.* - *s*David Lawrence: *The True Story of Woodrow Wilson*, p. 249. - *t*Undated. Curzon to Lloyd George. *Lloyd George Papers.* - *u*Lady Curzon: *Reminiscences*, p. 180.

Chapter XI. THE HERO

*a*Minute Clive Wigram to Stamfordham, 18 November, 1919. *Windsor Archives.* - *b*Churchill to Stamfordham, 7 December, 1919. *Windsor Archives.* - *c*The Times, 8 January, 1920. - *d*Milner to Lloyd George, 13 April, 1918. *Lloyd George Papers.* - *e*Milner to Lloyd George, 7 December, 1918. *Lloyd George Papers.* - *f* Milner to Lloyd George, 4 January, 1919. *Lloyd George Papers.* - *g*Lloyd George Papers. - *h*Milner to Lloyd George, 3 January, 1921. *Lloyd George Papers.* - *i*Lloyd George to Birkenhead, 15 March, 1919. *Lloyd George Papers.* - *j*Undated (8 January, 1918). *Lloyd George Papers.* - *k*Chamberlain to Bonar Law, 6 January, 1921. *Bonar Law Papers.* - *l*Lloyd George to Churchill, 1 October, 1921. *Lloyd George Papers.* - *m*Churchill to Lloyd George, 8 October, 1921. *Lloyd George Papers.* - *n*Lloyd George Papers. - *o*Lloyd George to Hilton-Young, 26 September, 1921. *Lloyd George Papers.* - *p*Lloyd George to Lloyd Graeme, 26 September, 1921. *Lloyd George Papers.* - *q*Lloyd George to Curzon, 30 April, 1922. *Lloyd George Papers.*

INDEX

INDEX

Beaverbrook, Lord—contd.
Churchill's inclusion in Government, 136
his views of Carson, 146
helps Lloyd George in statement to the House, 200
finds Lloyd George in triumphant mood, 212
attacked by Chamberlain, 216
meets Cabinet to discuss Rothermere's resignation, 230
assists Rothermere to redraft resignation letter, 230–1; the letter, 232–3; interrupts Cabinet meeting and helps reply to Rothermere, 232
recommends viscountcy for Rothermere, 232; the King's objection, 240–2
storm over receiving peerage, 243, 244 f.
politicians his enemies, 265
appointed Minister of Information and Chancellor of Duchy of Lancaster, Feb. 1918, 267; King disturbed, 270, 274–5; his dismissal urged, 279–81, 383; attacked in the House, 286; defended by Tim Healy, 287; advised to resign, 287; Healy advises "wait until you're sacked, 288; organized opposition from War Ministries, 288–90; warmly praised on final debate, 301–3
impression Canadians bearing brunt of fighting in France, 268
accused of helping Balfour to lose leadership, 270
victim of allegiance to Lloyd George, 276–7
the King's annoyance, 273
disliked by Balfour, 276, 293
attacked by Milner, 276–7, 284–5
blunder in appointing Northcliffe as propaganda chief in enemy territories, 278 et seq.
fierce outcry at conception of National Home for the Jews propaganda, 291–2
relationship with Foreign Office questioned, 293–4

Beaverbrook, Lord—contd.
accused of being "a capitalist", 294–5
a menace to national freedom and Free Trade, 296–7
Chamberlain ceases to be a trouble, 299
resigned, 301; Churchill solicitous, 301
malice by Curzon, 321
social relations with Lloyd George, 340
consulted on Empire issues, 340–1
Lloyd George's characteristics, 343–5
pays tribute at Lloyd George's death, 345–6, 416–18
Northcliffe's threat to shoot Lord Horder, and correspondence thereon, 90, 357–8
Beaverbrook Newspapers on London newspaper market, 59
Belgians, King and Queen of the, 385
Belgium supports bringing Kaiser to trial, 308
Bennett, Lord, Prime Minister, Canada, disposal of records, xxvii–viii, 272
Bennett Room, University of New Brunswick, xxviii
Beresford, Lord, 288
Bernstorff, Count, 78
Bethlehem Hospital, London, 333
Bethmann-Hollweg, Theobald von, 389
Birdwood, Gen. Sir William, 365
Birkenhead, Lord (see also Smith, F. E.):
sham battles with Carson over Home Rule for Ireland, 184–5
interview with Lloyd George refused and ordered to return from Paris, 331
receives sharp letter rejecting Committee's report on Land Acquisition Bill, March 1919, 332
Birkenhead School, xxiv
Birmingham, ix, xiii
Bishop's University, Canada, 349

427

INDEX

Bismarck, xxi

Blake, Robert, xxxii

Blumenfeld, R. D., xxviii
  letter from Churchill concerning
    attacks in *Daily Express*, 119

Bonar Law (*see* Law, Rt. Hon.
  Andrew Bonar)

Bonar Law-Bennett Library, New
  Brunswick, xxviii

Bonham-Carter, Sir Maurice, visits
  G.H.Q. in France, 178–9; 274

Borden, Henry, Q.C., xxviii

Borden, Sir Robert, Canada's First
  World War Prime Minister,
  xxviii, 267, 275
  recommends knighthood for
    Gen. Hughes, 272–3
  strained relations with Duke of
    Connaught, 273, 350–1
  insists Canadian Ministers sign
    Treaty of Versailles, 350

Bowles, Gibson, 149

Bradbury, Sir John, 108

Brade, Sir Reginald Herbert, xii,
  xxviii, 44; writes on Asquith,
  45; quarrel between Lloyd
  George and Robertson, 55,
  199–200, 213; supports Gen.
  Hughes, 273

Brasenose College, Oxford, xviii

Brass Hats (*see* Asquith-Brass-Hats
  Alliance)

British Army (*see also* Cambrai,
  Battle of):
  stalemated in France, xxxv
  military reverses cause alarm,
    248 *et seq.*

British Government denounced by
  generals, xl, 46; threat to
  overthrow, 52–8

British Museum, proposal for use
  by Air Ministry, 332–3

British Navy (*see also* Submarines)
  naval weakness, xxxv
  Battle of Jutland disaster, 147–8
  survival of Britain depends on
    combating submarine peril,
    150
  Admiralty against use of con-
    voys, 152–8

Broadstairs, 61

Brooks Club, xxi

Brooks, Colin, xxxi

Buchan, John, 266

Burnham, Lord, 245

CAMBRAI, Battle of:
  Haig blamed for failure, 186–7
  Derby's faith in Haig, 188
  Rothermere's loss, 229
  dismissal of Haig projected,
    364–7
  Robertson's removal considered,
    367–8
  inquiry into disaster demanded,
    372

Canterbury, Archbishop of, 332,
  396

Carlton Club, disconcerted at Curzon's surrender over suffrage
  cause, 315–16

Carnarvon, xvii

Carnegie Steel Works, xvi

Carson, Rt. Hon. Sir Edward
  Henry, 169, 207, 347, 348
  biographical sketch, xii–xiii
  disgruntled with Lloyd George's
    Administration, 54, 120
  castigates Northcliffe, 86
  advises Churchill to leave front
    line and resume politics, 113
  opposes office for Churchill, 114;
    receives pledge, 127 f.
  his strength in the Commons,
    120–1, 156
  no trust in Lloyd George, 144,
    145
  helps to bring down Asquith's
    Government, 144
  as First Lord of the Admiralty,
    145, 148–76, 297
  excluded from inner Cabinet
    circle, 145
  'uncrowned King of Ulster', 149
  depends on advice of naval
    experts, 150–1
  denounces amateur strategists,
    151–2
  receives no support in favouring
    convoy system, 153 f.
  removal from office contemplated
    by Lloyd George, 156, 158–9
  tension with Lloyd George,
    159–60

428

INDEX

Churchill, W.—contd.
on disintegration of Liberal Party, 260
urges Lloyd George to adhere to Press appointments, 281–2
fears Beaverbrook's downfall, 300–1
opposes "Hang the Kaiser" outcry, 306; stated otherwise, 308
enduring fame, 324
recommends honours for Lloyd George, 325–6
blamed by Lloyd George for unemployment conditions, fatuous policy of house-building and waste in Mesopotamia, 334–51; full text of unsigned letter, 400–4; reply thereon, 404–7
Irish conciliatory negotiations, 335
at Cannes, Jan. 1922, 340–1
offers his services in any capacity, 358–9
conditions laid down by Derby if appointed to office, 359–60
prefers going to the Admiralty, 361
against Unionist War Committee Resolution, 384
City of London Division, xi
City of London School, x
Clemenceau, M., xi, 385
agrees to trial of Kaiser and Crown Prince, 306
dominated by Lloyd George, 324–5
angry with the Italians, 386
Clifton, xviii
Coal Strike an industrial hurricane, 406–7
Coalition Government, 1916, refusal to serve with Churchill, 113
Cokayne, Sir Brien (Lord Cullen of Ashbourne):
Deputy Governor of Bank of England, intercedes for Cunliffe, 109–10
becomes Governor of Bank of England, 111
Colvin, Ian, biographer, xxxiii; quoted, 163, 178

Commission on the Responsibility of the Authors of the War, 308
Connaught, H.R.H. the Duke of, Governor-General of Canada:
opposes knighthood to bitterest enemy, Gen. Sir Sam Hughes, 272–3, 274
declares chaos reigned in all Canadian military matters, 272 f.
friction with Hughes, 349–51
his interest in training of Canadian forces resented, 350
desire to review troops forbidden, 350
strained relations with Prime Minister Borden, 350
departure from Canada, 351
Conservative Ministers in Coalition Government refuse to serve with Churchill, 113
—— hatred of Churchill, 114, 121, 125–6, 130–9
Convoy system causes political storm, 152–8
Coode-Adams, Sir John, 245
Cornell University, xix
Cousins, Mrs. Ann, xxxiii
Cowdray, Lord, 317, 348, 360
humiliated by Northcliffe, 87
resigns from Government, 87
eulogized by Derby, 359
Crewe, Lord, on demand for Asquith's resignation, 312, 313 f.
Crewe, Marchioness of, xxxi
Cunliffe, 1st Baron of Headley (Walter Cunliffe):
biographical sketch, xv
dictator of finance and tyrant as Governor of Bank of England, 92–111
refuses Chancellor's invitation to meeting, 99
rules world's greatest banking centre, 100
opposes six per cent War Loan, 100–2
accusation of usurping Bank of England Exchange Committee, 103–4
demands dismissal of Chalmers, 103

431

INDEX

INDEX

INDEX

INDEX

INDEX

INDEX

438

INDEX

INDEX

INDEX

441

INDEX

Maclay, Sir J. P.—contd.
biographical sketch, xx
resignation as Shipping Controller feared, 161
letters to Lloyd George and Bonar Law urging Admiralty changes, 169–70
McNeill, Ronald, defends Carson against anti-Irish propaganda, 298
Macpherson, Rt. Hon. Sir Ian, 213
Macready, Gen. Sir Nevil, 223, 271
Madge, Mr., 245
Magnus, Philip, against National Home for the Jews, 294
Man Power Report, 193; considered in conjunction with Repington's article, 376–7
Manchester Daily Despatch, 245
Manchester Guardian alleges Government responsibility for reverses in France, 254
Marconi scandal, 140
Margaret, Countess of Birkenhead, xxxi
Marlborough College, xxvi
Mary, Queen, discusses Northcliffe, 84–5
Maurice, Major General Sir Frederick:
declares for democracy, 57
charged by Lloyd George as telling lies, 183 f.
accuses Government in newspaper articles of misstatements on military situation, 250
declared Lloyd George's figures of Army in France erroneous, 250
allegation against Bonar Law concerning British line extension in France, 250
hostile Press supports charges against Lloyd George, 252
letter treated as a vote of censure on the Government, 254, 255
the allegations refuted in the House by Lloyd George, 257–9
retired from the Army and on half-pay, 261
eager to forward evidence of the complete facts, 261

Maurice, Sir F.—contd.
informs Lloyd George he accidentally quoted wrong figures to the House, 261–2; the missing corroborated document burnt purposely, 262–3
Maxwell, Maj.-Gen. Sir Ronald, dismissal demanded, 190; 271; displaced, 371
Melchett, Lord (*see* Mond, Sir Alfred)
Melland, Helen, Asquith's first wife, x
Mellet, Lowell, American correspondent, 101
Memories and Reflections (Lord Crewe), 313 f.
Mercantile Marine: heavy losses, 150, 153; an improvement, 177; confidence in Admiralty frittered away, 170
Mesopotamia, transfer of, 331; Churchill charged with waste, 335
Meux, Admiral Sir Hedworth, defends Carson, 159
Michelham, Baron (*see* Stern, Sir Herbert)
Military control of war-time policy, struggle for, 46–7, 52–8, 62, 115–16, 151–2
Milner, 1st Viscount (Alfred Milner), 176, 347
biographical sketch, xx–xxi
opposes Churchill's introduction to office, 133–4
member of War Cabinet, 144
critic of Carson's administration, 166
advises bringing Carson into Cabinet, 168–9, 172
suggests Admiralty changes, 175
described as a "tired, dyspeptic old man" by Robertson, 179 f.
strives for co-operation between Lloyd George and the Generals, 206
advises dismissal of Haig and Robertson, 206
charges Squiffites with using Robertson, 222 f.
Robertson refutes charges, 251

442

Milner, Viscount—contd.
against "Hang the Kaiser" outcry, 306, 308
leads mission to Russia, 328 f.
quarrel with Lloyd George leads
to resignation, 328–31, 397
refuses to preside over committee, 331
impending resignation causes
Curzon concern, 397–400
supports Lloyd George in removing Robertson, 410
Milner, Lady, xxxi
Ministers of Cabinet rank, 1917–18,
347
Ministry of Information (*see under*
Beaverbrook)
—— of Munitions created, 60;
Churchill appointment causes
indignation, 136–9, 141–2
—— of Propaganda in a rudimentary state, 265–6
Mond, Sir Alfred (Lord Melchett),
396
succeeds in housing programme,
402
unemployment enquiries, 403
Montagu, Edward, exonerated from
suspected disclosures, 68–9
Montagu, Edwin, 347
resents National Home for the
Jews, 291–2
Montreal Gazette, 272, 349
Moore, Miss Decima, 387
Morgan & Co., New York bankers,
all gold of Bank of England
in Canada placed with them,
104–5
Morison, Stanley, historian, 47
Morning Post, 47, 71, 251; favours
military control of war-time
policy, 56, 203; frantic support
to the Generals, 180
hostile to Churchill's appointment to office, 138–9
Repington's articles cause alarm,
192–3, 376
bitter criticism of Lloyd George,
254
Morshead, Sir Owen, xxxi
Munro, General, suggested successor to Haig, 365

My Political Life (L. S. Amery),
xxxii, xxxiii
My War Memories, 1914–18 (Ludendorff), xxii, xxiii; quoted, 303

NATIONAL Archives of Canada,
xxviii
—— Party advocated, 337
Nauru, peace settlement sought,
330
New Brunswick University, xxxiii
News of the World, xxii, 245
Newspaper Proprietors' Association, 246
Newton, Lord, 392
Nicolson, Sir Harold, xxxii, 244
1900 Club, regret Churchill inclusion in Government, 138
Nivelle, General, his army smashed
in Battle of Aisne, 115
North-Eastern Railway, xvi
Northcliffe, 1st Viscount, xxxi,
145, 151, 172, 218, 242, 285,
299
biographical sketch, xxi–xxii
quarrels with Lloyd George, 46
favours Asquith's removal, 47,
61
attacked by Churchill, 57–9
supreme power over public
mind and war-time Govern-
ment, 60
an appreciation, 61
political views, 62
hated and feared by politicians,
62
favours military dictatorship, 62,
115–16
no close relationship with Lloyd
George, 62–3
rejected by political leaders, 63,
67
war-time mission to U.S.A.
causes political storm, 63–82;
mission unacceptable to U.S.A.,
73–4; cold reception in U.S.A.,
75–7; Lady Spring-Rice declines to receive him, 77; his
prestige serves him well, 79–
82; welcomed home, and con-
gratulated and receives viscountcy, 82

INDEX

Northcliffe, Viscount—contd.
  fuel shortage in British Navy remedied, 80
  offered post in Air Ministry, 83; refuses post of Air Minister in open letter, 84
  Government delays attacked, 83-4
  praises Haig and his generals, 83-4
  guilty of political etiquette, 84-5
  feared by Lloyd George, 86
  political career finished, 87-8
  man of destiny obsession, 88-9
  excluded from Peace delegation, 89
  humiliating defeat at General Election, 1918, 89
  brandishes revolver at Sir (Lord) Thomas Horder, 90; correspondence thereon, 357-8
  his death, 90
  hostility to Churchill ceases, 134
  campaigns to remove Balfour from office, 148
  attacked by Chamberlain, 216
  denunciatory remarks by the King concerning viscountcy, 244
  asserts Canadian propaganda damaged Britain's prestige, 268
  political storm as propaganda chief in enemy territories, 278, et seq.
  his propaganda work praised by Ludendorff, 303
  unjust claims on his behalf, 320
  unpredictable, 383
Northcliffe Press experience humiliating defeat, 89
Norway, merchant shipping losses, 158

O'Brien, William, 211
O'Connor, T. P., 75
Ohio, xvi
Owen, Frank, xxvii, xxxii
Oxford University confers honorary degree on President Wilson, 319

Paderewski, Ignace Jan, 75
Page Walter Hines, American Ambassador to Britain, Papers, xxix, xxxviii, 80, 355
  supports Northcliffe's mission to U.S.A., 65
  views concerning Lord Reading, 96-8
  illuminating letter to President Wilson on tonnage losses, 157-8
  endorses Robertson's dismissal, 216
Palestine, fall of, 291; transfer of, 331
Pall Mall Gazette, 245
Parrot decides fate of General Election, Jan. 1922, 340-1
Peace Conference, French make a fuss of Riddell, 336
——————, Lloyd George takes control, 324-5
—— Treaty, decision to try Kaiser embodied, 306
—— signed, June 1919, 325
People, The, 245 f.
Perley, Sir George, protests at Gough commanding Canadians, 371-2
Pétain, Marshal, 259
Plumer, General Sir Herbert, 365, 414
  rank and file confidence, 409
  offered appointment of C.I.G.S., 412
  accusation of dislike by Robertson, 413
Politicians and the War (Beaverbrook), xli
Portland, Duke of, xxiii
Primrose, Neil, angry at non-appointment of Liberal magistrates, 296; 348
Prince Albert, consort, 349
Pringle, Mr., wild accusations against Beaverbrook, 297
Private Papers of Douglas Haig, The, 1914-1919 (ed. R. Blake), xxxii, 164
Privy Councillorships, quarrel over Coronation honours, 49-50
Prothero, Rowland, 348

444

INDEX